Business as Usual

An Off the Subject Novel

Other books by Denise Grover Swank

Rose Gardner Mysteries
(Humorous southern mysteries)
TWENTY-EIGHT AND A HALF WISHES
TWENTY-NINE AND A HALF REASONS
THRITY AND A HALF EXCUSES
FALLING TO PIECES (novella)
THIRTY-ONE AND A HALF REGRETS

Chosen Series
(Paranormal thriller/Urban fantasy)
CHOSEN
HUNTED
SACRIFICE
REDEMPTION

On the Otherside Series
(Young adult science fiction/romance)
HER
THERE

The Curse Keepers
(Adult urban fantasy)
THE CURSE KEEPERS
THE CURSE BREAKERS

New Adult Contemporary Romance
AFTER MATH
REDESIGNED
BUSINESS AS USUAL

Business as Usual

An Off the Subject Novel

Denise Grover Swank

This book is a work of fiction. References to real people, events, establishments, organizations, or locations are intended only to provide a sense of authenticity, and are used factiously. All other characters, and all incidents and dialogue, are drawn from the author's imagination and are not to be construed as real.

To my friend and assistant Heather, who insisted I tell
Lexi's story

Prologue

Lexi

His hand glides up my bare stomach and my back stiffens.

"Relax, Lexi." His breath warms my neck as his lips skim along my jaw.

I take a breath and hold it for a moment, staring at my dress laying on the floor. A soft light glows from the bathroom. *Close your eyes, Lexi. Concentrate.*

His movements are slow, trying not to startle me, but the slowness only feeds my anxiety.

One of his hands slides behind my back while the other reaches around to unfasten my bra. His fingertips skim across my bare back as he lowers the straps over my shoulders and down my arms. He leans back and smiles at me, a soft, tender smile full of hope and worry. He lifts his hand to my cheek, his thumb rubbing my skin. "How are you doing? Okay?"

I nod, trying not to shake.

Brandon strips his shirt off in one fluid movement before he kisses me, keeping his hands on my arms. I think I can do this. We've made out countless times and I've enjoyed it. More than enjoyed it. I think about those times now, allowing myself to get lost in the moment, lost in his arms and his mouth and the sensation of our bare skin pressing together. I wrap my arms around his neck and cling to him, the familiar shot of electricity and need shooting through my abdomen to my core.

Sensing my new eagerness, he lowers me onto the bed and lies next to me on his side. His hand moves from my arm to my stomach again, his forearm resting on my hip. Lying on my back has me on edge, and the pressure he's putting on my hip fuels my anxiety. My breath comes in shallow pants.

I can do this. I have to do this.

His mouth is on mine again, his tongue running over my bottom lip then slipping into my mouth, exploring and coaxing my own tongue to join it. And then his hand is pushing under the lace of my panties, his fingers finding the spot that makes me ache for more. I try to focus on his mouth and his hand and ignore the panic. Surely both sensations—amazing on their own, incredible combined—can cancel out my fear. And for a few brief minutes, they do. I glory in the carnal need that races through my blood. Maybe I can do this. Maybe I can be normal.

His fingers withdraw from their pursuit, hooking on the edge of my waistband and tugging the scrap of lace over my hips and down my thighs.

I shimmy and help guide them down and he tosses the lingerie to the floor alongside my dress.

I'm completely naked and he's only in his boxers, and I want to cry with happiness. I'm comfortable with our nakedness and I want to see more of him. Feeling more confident and in control, I offer him a soft smile and reach for the waistband of his underwear. He helps me pull them down his legs and as he kicks them off, I'm reaching for him, taking the length of his erection in my hand.

Brandon moans and rolls on his back as I stroke him. I feel empowered by my lack of panic. We've never gotten this far before. I usually freak out before my panties come off, and then turn the focus onto his pleasure. I've gotten him off multiple times—so often that wrapping my hand around him is a familiar act. But the fact that both of us are unclothed and I'm not freaking out is encouraging.

It's apparently encouraging to him too. His hand covers mine. "Stop or I won't last much longer. I want to be inside you when I come." He wraps his fingers around my wrist and pulls my hand away, pushing it to the bed next to my shoulder. In the same movement, he rolls to his side, his mouth finding my breast as his other hand slides between my legs.

My elation washes away and I feel trapped.

No. No. No.

I refuse to give into my fear. Brandon is a better guy than I could ever hope for. He's been infinitely patient with me, but I know this has been difficult for him. How emasculating is it when your girlfriend freaks every time you try to have sex with her?

He's concentrating on his task and I can tell he's taking my breathlessness as sign of my mounting passion.

Focus, Lexi.

His pressure eases on my chest and when I open my eyes, he's moving to the end of the bed, positioning himself between my legs. His mouth replaces his hand and I gasp, suddenly feeling free again. I lean my head back against the pillow as his tongue does things to my intimate parts that I never dreamt possible. I've never had oral sex before and I'm caught off-guard—in a good way—at the intensity of the sensation.

Brandon reaches a hand up to my breast and the trapped feeling is back. I bat his hand away instinctively. He takes the hint and grabs my hips, lifting them for better access, and I release a low groan, surprised at the growing need for something more from him.

Unexpectedly, his mouth is gone and I gasp in shock, opening my eyes to see why he's stopped. He's on his knees, rolling on a condom. Seconds later, his mouth returns and I'm panting with need.

And when I'm close, so incredibly close, writhing at the mercy of his tongue, he quickly slides his chest up my abdomen and over my body. I'm still flushed with desire when he buries himself inside me, groaning my name as his mouth skims my neck.

His body presses mine to the bed and all desire flees, replaced by unadulterated panic.

No, Lexi. I plead with myself. *No. It's Brandon. He would never hurt you.*

And for a brief moment, I calm down even though nausea is brewing in my stomach. I try to participate, but I'm too busy focusing on not throwing up. Brandon's lost in the moment, his tempo increasing. I try to move with him as I bite my lip, tears stinging my eyes.

My chest feels tight and I struggle to take a breath. I have no idea how much longer I can keep it together. Based on all the times I've given him a hand-job, I know he should be done soon, within a minute.

He gives several more deep thrusts before a low groan erupts from his chest and he collapses on top of me. His mouth finds mine and it's the final nail in my casket of hysteria.

I give his shoulder a hard shove, gasping for breath as I burst into sobs, my panic overriding all my protests that I'm safe. He rolls to his side as I scramble off the bed, standing in the middle of his bedroom, trying to figure out what to do.

I have to get out of here. Now.

"*Lexi?*" Brandon has bolted upright, terror on his face. "Oh, my God. *Did I hurt you?*" His words are drenched in horror and self-loathing. It somehow makes things worse.

I shake my head as my sobs burst free and I pick up my dress, struggling to put it on.

"*Lexi?*"

He leaps from the bed and grabs my shoulders to get my attention, but his touch only intensifies my panic. I violently jerk away and collapse into a heap on the floor, close to hyperventilating.

Brandon falls to his knees next to me. "Did I hurt you?" He asks again, his voice insistent.

"No," I force out between sobs.

We sit like this for a while, me on my butt, my legs twisted awkwardly to one side, and Brandon on his knees in front of me, studying me with equal parts sympathy and horror.

He shifts uncomfortably and I notice that he still hasn't disposed of the condom.

I tilt my head toward the bathroom. "Go."

He looks uncertain, as though this is a test.

I close my eyes. "Please. Just go, Brandon. Give me a moment to pull myself together."

When I hear the bathroom door close, I slump to the floor.

Pull myself together. What a joke. Lexi Pendergraft, Southern University's campus freak-show.

But I know Brandon will keep my private humiliation to himself. He's too much of a gentleman, too much of a nice guy to hurt me or ruin my reputation, even if his complaints would be legitimate.

Frigid. Ice Queen. Freak.

But it's his kindness that is my undoing now. Brandon is the type of guy I've dreamed of since high school. Smart. Good looking. Ambitious. Kind. Attentive. Brandon McKenzie is the kind of guy girls line up to date. I know in my heart that this was my last chance to salvage this relationship, and I blew it.

When he finally emerges, worry and exhaustion knotting his brow, I'm sitting on the edge of the bed fully clothed. He squats to pick up his clothes and puts them on in a silence that threatens to impale me with my own humiliation. As soon as he's fully dressed, I stand and move to the door, picking up my purse from his dresser. We walk out to his car, and when he opens my car door for me— even after what I just put him through—fresh tears sting my eyes.

We drive in silence until he parks in the lot next to my apartment, the apartment I share with my brother Reed and his girlfriend Caroline.

I take a deep breath and blow it away. I must address this. I must try to right this in some way, even if the attempt is feeble. "I'm sorry," I whisper. "I wish…"

Brandon picks up my hand and presses it between both of his palms, the touch gentle and reassuring. "I know."

"I just… I…"

"Shhh." He lifts my hand to his mouth, his lips brushing my knuckles before he sets my hand back in my lap with a surprising gentleness. His hand withdraws and rests in his own lap. The significance of this action is not lost on me.

"Do you go back to Nashville tomorrow?" I ask, my voice cracking slightly. This is a nonsense question and we both know it. I already know the answer, but I'm desperate to fill the uncomfortable silence.

He clears his throat and shifts his legs, the leather on his seat creaking. "Yeah, after my last final."

The silence that follows hangs like a heavy veil, choking the air from my lungs. "Thank you," I finally say.

Those two words uncork his emotions. "*Thank you? Are you fucking kidding me?*"

I cringe even though his anger is directed toward himself, not me. And that upsets me more than anything else. "I'm sorry." Fat tears spill out, falling down my cheeks. "It's not your fault."

"Then whose fault is it, Lexi?"

Mine? But even while buried under a mountain of guilt, I know the source of this monumental disaster doesn't rest at my feet. It rests at *his*. That monster did this to me. I may not bear physical scars from his attack, but some days I wish I did. A physical sign would be tangible proof of the injuries I sustained last April. Instead, my trauma is locked inside my brain, where only I can sense it. He has forever ruined me. Tonight is proof enough of that.

But I can't tell Brandon any of that. I'm here at Southern University to escape my past, with my new last name and my brother as my guard dog. Brandon has no idea what happened to me last spring and I have no intention of him ever finding out. Especially now. "Not yours." I finally say, looking out the windshield into the parking lot.

"Not mine." He shakes his head with a bitter laugh, picking at a loose tear in the leather on his steering wheel. "Not. Mine."

I realize that Brandon will forever blame himself for this moment. His psyche might not ever recover from the stupid girl who freaked out when he fucked her. While the ultimate trigger for tonight's debacle lies at *his* feet, it's my responsibility to fix this mess I've made. Still, I'm not sure how. A tear falls down my cheek.

"Am I that revolting, Lexi?" Pain fills his words.

I shake my head, clamping down the anguish rising up inside. "No, Brandon. I swear to God—it's not you. It's me." I swallow and grab the end of the belt of my wool coat, twisting it in my hand. "I'm just broken."

"I don't understand. Please help me understand," he pleads.

How can I explain what I don't really understand myself? I turn toward at him, surprised I have the courage to look him in the eye. "Brandon, I really, really like you. In fact, I think I'm falling in love with you."

His eyes widen slightly.

"But I'm a mess. It's pretty apparent that I have issues. Bigger issues than you should be stuck dealing with."

He reaches for my hand and squeezes. "Lexi, I'm not the kind of guy to take off when there's the first sign of trouble."

"I know, and that's why this is even harder." I pause and take a breath. "I can't give you what you need. I'm not sure I can ever give anyone…that." I close my eyes as new tears fall. "I wish I could, but I'm just too…"

"Broken," he finishes, sounding devastated.

"Yeah," I whisper, dropping my gaze.

He gently tilts my chin up, and when I look into his eyes, they are determined. "I'm not breaking up with you over this."

"I know." I offer him a sad smile. "That's why I'm breaking up with you."

His mouth drops open.

Tears stream down my face. "That's why I'm letting *you* go." I open the car door and the cold air blasts my face. I suck in a breath of surprise and hurry across the parking lot, my heels clicking on the asphalt.

Brandon catches up to me in seconds, grabbing my elbow and trying to pull me to a halt. But I twist my arm out of his grasp and continue walking. I need to get away from him before I change my mind. I'm smart enough to know that Brandon McKenzie is probably as good as it gets. I'll never find anyone more patient, understanding, or attentive than him. I reach into my purse and pull out my keys, ready to punch in the security code to enter the building.

But Brandon grabs both of my elbows and turns me toward him. "Lexi, *please*. Don't do this. We can work through it."

I look up into his kind brown eyes and I want to tell him everything. I want him to know that I haven't always been this way. Contrary to what my brother Reed believes, I wasn't a virgin when I graduated from high school. I've had sex before last spring without incident. But to tell Brandon what changed everything, to tell him about that night, would mean reliving the horror of it. Worse, I would be forced to see the horror and pity in his eyes, just as I do whenever Reed and Caroline look at me. I'm tired of being *Poor Lexi*. Still, if anyone will understand and help me, it's Brandon. He could and would help me through this.

My lips part and the words are on the tip of my tongue:

I was raped.

But I can't do it. I've never spoken the words out loud, as preposterous as that seems. In my head and my heart, I know I didn't do anything wrong and that it wasn't my fault. It doesn't matter. I'm carrying this life sentence around anyway. As I look into Brandon's sweet eyes, which have become so dear to me, I realize again how unfair it would be to include him in my personal hell. He deserves better.

"Have a good life, Brandon." I turn and punch the code then open the door, slipping through the opening as soon as it's wide enough, leaving him stunned and silent on the sidewalk.

The door closes and he comes to his senses, banging on the glass door while I stand in front of the elevator, waiting for the doors to slide open.

"Lexi!" My name is muffled by the glass. His fist beats on it and I worry he'll break the glass and hurt himself.

Tears burn my eyes, but I refuse to look at him, grateful when the elevator doors slide open. I rush inside the empty car and spin around, pressing my back against the cool metal. And as the doors close, I feel as though my fate is sealed with them.

I will forever be alone.

Chapter One

Lexi

Two months later

"Ten minutes, Lexi," the stage manager calls out. My stomach jitters with nerves even though this is only a dress rehearsal for a play with a two-night run. But I have to admit part of my anxiety has to do with the image in the mirror that looks nothing like me.

"Lexi. You look so…"

"Slutty?" My naturally blonde hair is covered by a jet-black wig and Caroline has applied enough makeup on my face to make me look like a streetwalker. I'm wearing a silver sequined shell with a black leather skirt and silver strappy heels.

Caroline snorts. "I was going for *not like yourself*, which Reed will probably find comforting in this situation."

She has a point. If you look up the definition of overprotective big brother, you'll find a picture of Reed. "Tell me again why I'm wearing a wig instead of just fixing up my normal hair."

She looks at my hair piece and adjusts it slightly. "Because it's fun. You've been moping since your break up with Brandon. Maybe this will help shake things up a bit."

I bite the inside of my lower lip to keep from confessing what really happened with Brandon. Caroline would never understand. As far as she knows, he got back with his ex-girlfriend from high school, who decided being a lesbian wasn't for her after a brief affair with a girl from her chemistry class. It's entirely true, except it happened *after* I broke up with him…

Nevertheless, she's right. I've been miserable about it for two months, throwing myself into school and my work with the Middle Tennessee Children's Charity, which is headquartered here in Hillsdale. The charity is why I'm here tonight, backstage at the community theatre. There's a mutually beneficial partnership between my university, the charity, and the local community, and I'm the student liaison this semester. I helped set up this fundraiser—the production of a comedic play, with students and locals filling all the parts in the cast and crew. Caroline is a senior fashion design major, so she's helping with the costumes.

While my friends are already aware of my proposed expansion of the charity's summer camp program to include middle-school children, I haven't told anyone about my plans to transform it from a glorified babysitting service into something special. The university has given me an independent study course for my work with the charity and I've used my time to model a program that will not only engage and challenge the middle-school kids, but possibly change their futures.

I'm not looking forward to my small acting role in the play, but when I look in the mirror, I like what I see. Caroline is forever saying that clothes can change how you feel about yourself. Turns out a wig can do the same thing. I love the way I look, but I'm worried it'll be too much for my brother to take. "Which one of us is going to prepare Reed for my costume?"

Her lips twist as she tries to hide her conspiratorial grin. "Maybe it should be a surprise."

I tilt my head to the side. Caroline has even covered my dirty blonde eyebrows with black mascara. I don't look anything like a natural blonde. "Good idea. He might not even realize it's me."

She shakes her head with a laugh. "Trust me, he'll figure it out. I suppose I should warn him or he's liable to rush the stage when you walk out and throw his coat over you."

"The sad thing is, I wouldn't be at all shocked if he did." There's a hint of bitterness in my voice.

Caroline, who was packing up her makeup, pauses and meets my eyes in the mirror. "You know he loves you, Lexi."

Guilt pricks at me. I've never, ever doubted Reed's love for me. If not for his sacrifice, I would be stuck in Boston taking a year off to regroup from the "incident," as my parents call it. When I called Reed in tears, telling him about their plan for me, he was quiet for a long moment, so long I thought we had been disconnected. Then he asked in a soft voice, "What do *you* want to do, Lexi?"

"I want to go back to school—" my voice broke "—I need to go back to school."

"You will. I promise. I'll fix this."

He stormed into the house an hour later and got into a historic shouting match with our parents. He told them they needed to put what was good for their daughter before their worries about themselves. Reed's a stubborn guy and he refused to back down, even when our father threatened to disown him. Hours later, my brother found me in my room, where I'd retreated from all the hysterics. He sat on the edge of my bed and told that me he'd worked it all out with them. That I'd go back to school in the fall and live with him in an apartment. Then he kissed my forehead and made me promise to call if I needed anything in the meantime.

"I'm here for you, Lexi," he'd said. "I won't let anything else happen to you."

I didn't discover the extent of Reed's sacrifice until days later. He'd been accepted to Stanford University to do his Ph.D. under his idol Dr. Donald Knuth—his lifelong dream—and he gave it up for me. When I protested, he refused to listen. So instead of embarking on a sterling career, he became a grad student at Southern University, where he teaches beginning algebra and runs the math lab. When we moved, our parents made us use our maternal great-grandmother's maiden name—Pendergraft—to avoid any family embarrassment, which means Reed also lost much of the reputation and credibility he had accumulated over his academic career. Yet he has never once acted hurt or angry over the choices he made for me.

It's a debt I can never repay.

Caroline kisses my cheek. "I'll talk to him, okay?"

I smile at her, grateful she's in our lives. Caroline may be Reed's fiancée, but she's also a dear friend. I wouldn't love her any more if she were my own sister. She loves me too, which is why she always intervenes on my behalf. "I'm sorry, Caroline," I say. "I put you in this awkward situation. I know you and Reed fight over me."

She laughs. "Did I tell you that our first fight was over you?"

Reed and Caroline first met at a party, and sparks flew the second they laid eyes on each other. Only Caroline was intent on getting a date with another guy that night. "I thought your first fight was over Dylan Humphrey."

She smirks. "I mean our first fight as an actual couple. If you don't count Reed blowing his gasket over me walking across the campus by myself after midnight." She sobers a bit. "But after I found out why…" I sigh as worry wrinkles her brow. "Sorry. I shouldn't have mentioned—"

"Lexi, we're ready for you," the stage manager says. "We're about to start the party scene."

I hop out of my chair and pull Caroline into a hug. "You didn't do anything wrong. It's the elephant in the room we all ignore." I drop my arms and give her a sad smile. "But one of these days it's going to sit on me if we keep doing that."

I hear my cue and go onstage, staying to the background until it's time for me to say my single line. We're supposed to be at a party, so I pretend to talk to Sylvia, my friend and fellow business major, whom I roped into participating in my work with the charity. My role is simple. I'm supposed to be a vivacious, life-of-the-party girl, so my movements are all exaggerated. Rob, one of the Hillsdale actors, walks onstage with another girl and I spin toward him and deliver my one line.

"Why did I ever let him go?"

It's not a difficult line to remember. I ask myself that question about Brandon almost every day. Sometimes I see him walking across campus hand-in-hand with his old girlfriend and my heart fills with a crushing ache. Of course, it's not necessarily Brandon who makes me feel that way. It's the wish to be normal—to have a boyfriend and a chance at a family someday. I fear that that most simple of wishes has been stolen from me.

We finish the scene and I walk off with Sylvia. Caroline is right where I left her, her sketchbook open. She looks up and grins. "You were great."

"I was passable. But that's okay. It's for a good cause and it was nice of them to include me."

She shakes her head and grins. "Give yourself more credit. That wig makes you sassy." She winks. "I like it."

She spins her sketchpad around. "I've come up with designs for T-shirts for the summer program. See what you think."

She's drawn a shirt with the charity's logo for the girls and a toned-down version for the boys. "I know it would make things easier if they were unisex shirts, but I think the girls will be more inclined to wear them if they're different."

"Oh, Caroline! I love them!"

Sylvia wanders over. "Let me see." She leans over and voices her approval. "You are definitely lucky to have this woman on your team."

I release a nervous sigh. "Now, if we can just make enough money to fund the expansion of the program."

"That was our best rehearsal yet," Sylvia says as she hops onto the table in front of us and swings her legs, complete with her four-inch heels. "Maybe the play won't suck."

"Well, that's good to know since our pre-show ticket sales are much higher than expected." I have to admit the play wasn't coming together very well last week. "We're on track to fund almost a third of what I'm planning for the kids this summer."

Her eyes widen. "You say that like you're surprised."

"Well...we threw this together pretty fast."

Sylvia shakes her head. "Girl, no one can say no to you. You're like a force of nature. Once you have your sights on something, you make it happen."

Caroline spins her notebook around and laughs. "Don't I know it."

My mouth parts. "Why would you say that?"

Sylvia shakes her head in disbelief. "How about the way you got the Monroe Foundation to help sponsor the Southern Fall Fashion Show just so you could get Reed and Caroline to work together?" She tilts her head toward my future sister-in-law, whose mouth tips up in a smirk. "All that effort just to get them to see how perfect they were for each other."

"For the record," Caroline says, "I'd like to think Reed and I would have found our way together eventually anyway, but Lexi's intervention definitely played a key role."

"That's not the only reason I set it up," I add. "I did it to help a worthy cause."

Sylvia's eyes bug slightly as she gives me a skeptical look.

I laugh. "Okay, so I helped *two* worthy causes at the same time. But how could I not? I knew they were meant to be together." I turn my gaze on Caroline. "But we're talking about two very stubborn people here, and sometimes drastic times call for drastic measures."

Caroline's grin grows wider as she starts sketching again.

Sylvia slides off the table. "I'll be honest, when you first told me about your plan last fall, I thought you were crazy. But when it actually worked, I decided you were a mad genius."

I roll my eyes with a snort. "No need to kiss my ass. I already told you that I'd give you my notes from the ethics class you missed yesterday."

She grins and gives me a half-shrug. "I mean it. You're a natural, Lexi. You're a born problem solver. No hemming and hawing for you." She crosses her legs and leans forward. "Take the Middle Tennessee Children's Charity.

Sure, maybe you didn't get involved for purely altruistic reasons—"

"Hey!"

"—but you saw a great organization that could use some fresh blood and ideas. And now look at everything you're doing with them. And you're only a sophomore in college. Imagine what you'll accomplish when you graduate. Hell, I wouldn't be surprised if Monroe Industries gave you a job as soon as you get your degree."

Little does she know my family owns Monroe Industries, the international multi-million dollar corporation that funds the foundation and that my parents expect me to fulfill some role in the corporation one day.

"I'm just glad I sat next to you in statistics last August. Otherwise I probably wouldn't have gotten involved with the charity, which will look *great* on my resume."

"I didn't ask you because we're friends, Sylvia. I asked you because you're a great asset. The fact that we're friends is bonus."

She waves her hands up and down the length of her body. "No, I'll tell you what the real bonus is having a reason to look hot." She's wearing a short, tight grey dress that shows cleavage. Her brown hair is curly and teased and her makeup is just as dramatic as mine. She looks amazing. "I can't even remember the last time I got dressed up."

I sigh. "Neither can I."

She gives me a sad smile. "I still can't believe you and Brandon broke up. Why would he go back to his ex? You two were perfect for each other."

A heavy weight crushes my chest, just another reminder of my emotional scars. "Some things just aren't meant to be."

Caroline's attention is back on me. Both of them are clearly hoping for more details. But they're about to be disappointed.

"You already know what happened. He went home for Christmas break and got back together with his high-school girlfriend. There's not much else to tell."

"But things had been going so well with you two," Sylvia says, kicking one foot into the air.

"I was a rebound." I like to tell myself this late at night as I try to fall asleep. I tell myself it doesn't matter that I gave him up without a fight because I would have lost him anyway. Too bad I don't believe it.

"Ouch."

I shrug.

"You know what they say about getting thrown off a horse. You need to get back up there on it." She winks. "And by *get back up on*, I mean—"

"Yeah, I get it." I laugh, but it's forced—her joke comes a little too close to home. "I'm too busy. School and work take all my time and energy."

"You know that's just an excuse, don't you?" Caroline asks. "I was busy with the fashion show and I still found time for Reed."

"Excuse or not, this is my choice." I put enough force into my words to get them to drop the subject. "Working on the summer program for the kids is my focus right now. I'm still trying to find the right location."

"I thought you had a place."

"We do, and it'll work, but it's the local park. I'd like to have a variety of activities for the kids every day. I'm putting together a proposal to take to my advisor, and it's taking up all my spare time. The partnership between the university and the charity has gone well so far, but this will really take things up a notch."

Sylvia narrows her eyes suspiciously. "So, I know the basics, of course, but what's your plan for the expansion of the program?"

"Well, the charity's after-school program has done a great job with helping kids who are struggling in their academic work. Caroline found that out firsthand last fall when she met Desiree." My brother's girlfriend gives me a soft smile. Desiree was a girl Caroline discovered on her first visit to the tutoring center. The little girl reminded Caroline so much of herself at that age that she came up with her own line of children's clothing for the fashion show. "But we all know that kids lose a lot of information over the summer and lower-income kids are at a greater disadvantage than upper-socioeconomic income children." I pause, certain they'll think I'm crazy. I've never told them this much about my plan before. "So I'm proposing that we have a summer university for middle-schoolers."

Sylvia raises her eyebrows. "I thought the idea was to get them to do fun things. No one wants to go to summer school."

"They will if the right classes are offered." I give Caroline a pleading look. "Like how to design your own clothes from thrift store finds or a *fun* interactive chemistry class. Classes where they'll actually learn something and keep their minds active, but they'll have fun too. Plus, a lot of these kids don't plan to go to college. If they spend some time on the campus and in the classrooms, they might realize it's not such a scary place. Of course, this all depends on if the chancellor agrees."

Sylvia looks skeptical.

"I think it's a wonderful idea," Caroline says. "Why are you worried about that?"

"I'm asking for classroom space to augment the outdoor space we already have. And even if the university helps with that, there will be a million other things to do. We'll have to find the instructors, coordinate with them to come up with classes..."

"Okay, Lexi." Caroline holds up her hands. "Slow down. You're right. This is a huge undertaking. Why didn't you tell me more about it before now?"

"I wanted to sort out the details in my head first."

"I see what you mean about there not being much time. It's already the end of February. If you're going to implement the program this summer, you needed to have it in place, like yesterday."

"I know."

"So why not hold off a year?"

"Because what if there's one kid we can help *this year*, and he slips through the cracks just because I didn't want to work too hard?"

"Oh, Lexi." Caroline sets down her notebook and pulls me into a big hug. "You have such a big heart, but you need to remember that you can't save them all."

"*You* try to," I say.

She grins. "Fair enough. But this is a huge task that will take months to organize. There probably isn't enough time."

I stiffen.

She squeezes me again. "But you know that I of all people understand. Let me help."

"And me too," Sylvia says.

Tears sting my eyes. I'm blessed to have such amazing friends.

Chapter Two

Ben

My eyes sink closed and my cheek falls out of my open palm, jerking me awake. I look around to see if anyone notices, but I'm in the back row and the professor is looking at her notes. I sit up straighter, trying to shake off my drowsiness, but it hangs on like a whore to a rich john.

I glance down at my notes and up at the graph projected on the wall, wondering how much of the lecture I've missed. This might just be an intro course, but I hate history, which is part of the reason I put it off until the final semester of my senior year. The combination of the class's nine a.m. start time, my shift ending at two a.m. at the bar, and my strong dislike of the subject matter means I tend to nap in here a lot. But whether or not I like Intro to American History, at fourteen hundred dollars per fucking credit hour, I hate to miss a single minute. I estimate I just pissed away fifty bucks with that nap and I didn't even get a wet dream out of it.

Funny how I never gave much thought to how much classes cost when I was on a full-ride scholarship. Funny how I never thought about a lot of things.

But there was nothing funny about losing my scholarship right before the second semester of my senior year. Especially since I go to Southern University, "an Ivy-League-inspired school nestled in a Tennessee small town." Who falls for that bullshit? But every year, one thousand or so new students find their way to our "picturesque campus, to embark on their exciting new lives."

Embark on their exciting new lives, my ass.

The majority of students who attend Southern University are dripping in money. Their daddies have their future all figured out for them. I'm part of the one percent, the unlucky few who didn't come to school with trust funds and beemers and daddy's gold card. Those of us who were raised on PB&J and got old clunkers when we turned sixteen. We're here on a combination of scholarships and student loans. Although, at this moment, I can't figure out why we bother.

But that's a lie. I came here because I was given a full-ride scholarship based on academic merit and financial need. I was a local boy, so it made sense to live at home and let my scholarship money do the heavy lifting for my college education. The reputation of the mechanical engineering department helped. It was a no-brainer that ended up biting me in the ass.

No, Sabrina Richmond bit me in the ass.

The prof starts to change the graph and I've only written down half the information on the screen. Son of a bitch. I don't know a single person in this class other than a passing acquaintance with a cute red-headed freshman who has let me borrow her notes before, but she's not here today. I'm fucked. Again.

When class is almost over, Dr. Kensington reminds us that there will be an exam in our next class. I consider asking my boss for Sunday night off. But Uncle Tony's short-staffed after one of our bartenders quit, which means I work enough for two people some nights. It's exhausting, especially on a busy night, but the girls like me and they leave me good tips when I flirt. Christ knows I need all the cash I can get. But I'll be the first to admit that I can't wing this exam. I'm going to have to put in some solid hours of studying.

I can't afford to take off work and I can't afford not to.

I pack up my bag and head for the Higher Ground coffee shop. I can load up on caffeine and study before my next class, Topics in Stress Analysis. It's a tough course, but it's math intensive, which has always been easy for me. Using equations to evaluate thermal stress is something that's squarely in my comfort zone, much more so than Dr. Kensington's interminable lecture about the industrial revolution. I would so much rather study the geniuses who created the technology that simplified our lives than I would the slum lords who profited off lower income workers, but that's exactly why I'm behind in history.

The cold February wind blows across the *picturesque* campus. Girls clutch their coats and run toward the scattered buildings. I'm not surprised to see a line at the coffee shop, but I *am* surprised that the line isn't out the door. The Higher Ground is the only place on campus that serves decent coffee, and it's a cold Friday morning.

I order a cup of black coffee, exactly what I always order. A couple gets up from a two-person table and I snag a chair and plop my bag on the table. I can get in an hour of study time if I get right to work.

I've been at it for at least half an hour when someone sits in the chair across from me. Irritated by the interruption, I glance up at Tucker Price, campus ex-soccer star. We're no more than passing acquaintances, so I'm surprised he's decided to sit with me.

"How's it going, Masterson?" Tucker asks.

I wave my hand over my open book and notes. "History's kicking my ass. What about you?"

"Never better." His grin lights up his face. Everyone at Southern knows he quit the Chicago Fire to come back to Southern and his girlfriend. Most people think he's an idiot, but I've got to respect a guy who puts his relationship before money and a pro-soccer career. I doubt you'll find anyone else on this fucking campus who would do that. Still, he and his girlfriend are such opposites that you'd never imagine them together. Who knows, though, maybe that's what makes it work.

"That's awesome, dude. I couldn't be happier for you," I say. And I mean it.

"I'm surprised I haven't seen you on Saturday mornings."

My confusion must be obvious, because he jumps in with an explanation. "You always came to Kyle's soccer games last fall. I thought you'd come to his basketball games too. He's a hell of a player, and he's a great leader for the team too."

"Oh," I say as I make the connection. I can't help but smile. I love my kid brother, maybe because I spent so much time taking care of him growing up. Not many preteen boys learn about child care, but I was forced to when our mom split, leaving baby Kyle behind. "You're Kyle's basketball coach."

His brow lowers. "He didn't tell you he was on my team?"

"I haven't talked to him in a few weeks. I've been busy." Which is true. I knew he was playing basketball, but I've been working as a janitor at a local office building on Saturday mornings. The main reason I haven't been at his games, though, is that my father has decided I'm a bad influence on my eleven-year-old brother. How ironic that I was exactly the opposite just a few months ago. But Kyle has been caught in the middle of my fallout with my dad, and I miss the little guy more than I care to admit. I can thank fucking Sabrina for that one. "I've got a job on Saturdays. I can't make his games."

Tucker lowers his voice. "I heard about your arrest and how you lost your scholarship. All I can say is when I look back at everything I did in the years before I met Scarlett, I'm amazed it never happened to me." He sighs. "I'm sorry you're stuck in this mess."

"They dropped the charges, but code of fucking conduct and all that shit..." I shrug, pretending it's no big deal, but the bitterness still leaks out in my words. "Just one semester left in my mechanical engineering degree. I couldn't go anywhere else to finish up without practically starting over, so I sucked it up and got two part-time jobs."

He grimaces. "That's a bitch."

There's no denying it. "I'm looking for another one in the afternoons. Something on campus would be great, but we both know those jobs are next to impossible to get."

Tucker studies me for a second. "Actually, I know of one that just opened up. One of the tutors in the math lab quit a couple of days ago and Scarlett has been filling in for him. You're an engineering student, so you should be damn good at math, right? It could work. No one knows about it yet, either."

Math lab. I hadn't considered it as a possibility before now. "Do you know how many hours?"

"That's the problem, not many. Maybe ten? But it's something."

"No, it sounds good." Tucker's right. This could be a great job for me. "Thanks for the heads up. Who should I get in touch with?"

"Sure thing. Reed Pendergraft is the guy. Tell him I sent you."

"Thanks." I try to keep the disappointment out of my voice. Of course it was too good to be true. Reed Pendergraft has been on campus for less than two semesters, but he already has a reputation of being a total hard ass both inside the classroom and out. Austin, one of my roommates, had a run-in with him in the fall semester and almost lost his spot as a student liaison on the academic advisory committee. Still, I'm desperate.

"I know for a fact that he's at the math lab right now if you want to run over. I just saw him after walking Scarlett over there."

I'm torn. I need this job, but *Pendergraft?* I close my history book, hoping I'm not wasting precious study time on this. "Thanks, I'll do that. And thanks again for the heads-up."

"No problem."

When I arrive, the math lab is full of students waiting for help. The only tutors are a cute brunette, a curly-headed guy who looks like he stuck his finger in a light socket, and a guy who has to be Reed Pendergraft. He's seated at a table with a student, going over an equation. I stand by the door and wait.

Pendergraft looks up. "You can take a seat and we'll get to you as soon as possible."

I take a step toward him. "Actually, I'm here about the tutoring position.

His mouth parts as if he's about to say something, but instead he looks me over as if he's taking my measure.

While he's wearing dress pants and a button-down shirt, I'm dressed in faded jeans, a long-sleeved T-shirt, and a hoodie. The look on his face says he finds me lacking.

"I'm Ben Masterson. Tucker Price sent me."

The brunette girl smiles and shoots me a look of recognition. I haven't seen Scarlett in over a year. We had a couple of classes together freshman year, but we never interacted much. She was always extremely quiet and self-contained. She looks different now—happier and surer of herself.

"Your name sounds familiar," Reed says. "Have we had a class together?"

"No." I'd remember if I'd had anything to do with Reed Pendergraft. He probably recognizes my name from the news about my arrest, but there's no way in hell I'm going to mention that.

He watches me for a long moment. "What are your qualifications?"

"I'm a senior majoring in mechanical engineering. I've had over twenty-hours of math courses with a 3.8 GPA."

He gives a brisk nod. "I'll need a copy of your transcripts and a recommendation from one of your mathematics instructors. I'll also need a copy of your schedule."

While I don't necessarily like taking orders from a guy who's barely a year ahead of me in school, it's the way he poses his requests that irks me. The rumors are clearly true—the guy is a demanding dick. "Is that all?" The question blurts out of my mouth without any forethought. If I want this job, I'm going to have to rein in the attitude.

As expected, Pendergraft doesn't look amused. "I haven't posted the position, but I'll hold off if you can get me everything by this afternoon."

I give a quick nod. "Can do. When would I start?"

"If your information checks out, you can start today if you like. The sooner, the better." Then he tells me the hourly wage, which is higher than I'd expected. "We'll work around your schedule, of course."

"Thank you." I only hope I won't regret this, despite the pay. *It's only for three months*, I tell myself. I can do anything for three months. Can't I?

Chapter Three

Lexi

I knock on the door of Dr. Tyree's office promptly at four o'clock, my stomach a bundle of nerves.

He looks up from his desk, a bright smile on his face as he sets down his pen. "Lexi, come in. You've had me intrigued since our phone call this morning."

As I walk into the room, he motions to a chair beside his desk. I sit down and pull a folder out of my bag and place it on his desk. "As I mentioned, my independent study class this semester focuses on my liaison work with the children's charity and the expansion of their summer program to include middle-schoolers. But I want to take this beyond the basics of child care. I'd like to make it a fun experience that will excite the kids. Let's face it, it's hard to make a tween or early teen do anything they don't want to do."

"You're preaching to the choir." Dr. Tyree smiles and tips a picture frame in my direction. "I have a twelve-year-old daughter."

"So you understand the importance of making sure they're engaged." I open the folder and slide out one of the papers. "I'm proposing an interactive program. Although a park has been lined up to host the original proposed project, I'd like my expanded project to be held at the university, with the permission of the school, of course."

He watches me, his face expressionless.

"Each middle-school-aged child in the program would pick a schedule of courses that would last for a week or two." I then explain my concept, giving several ideas for courses and how the scheduling would work.

He looks over the document I gave him and removes his glasses. "This is a very ambitious project, Lexi."

I nod my agreement.

"Do you think you have enough time to pull this together and implement it this year? You're only a sophomore. Perhaps it would be better for your sanity if you plan on launching it next summer."

"While I understand your concerns, Dr. Tyree, I'm confident that I can pull this together."

A grin tugs the corners of his mouth. "One thing that I've learned since you transferred to Southern last fall is that you like a challenge. I suggested this independent study period after you did such a wonderful job coordinating the fundraiser for the charity last fall. If you're going to take on ambitious projects, you might as well get academic credit for it. If anyone can do this, it's you."

"Thank you for your confidence."

"It's well earned. How's the play coming along?"

I tell him about the strong early ticket sales and the support from local businesses. "And the play is actually pretty good too," I joke. "Despite my guest-star appearance."

"This work we're doing with the charity is good for the relationship between the university and Hillsdale. I've always found it ironic that such an elite university is located in a town as blue collar as Hillsdale. It's caused a lot of animosity between the citizens and the students. This joint project gives both sides the chance to work together and will hopefully ease tension."

"And help children in need." That's far more important to me than how the university gets along with the town, although I'm smart enough to know that I need both sides to be receptive to my ideas for the summer program in order to get the results I want.

"Yes, of course." Dr. Tyree says as an afterthought. "Help children in need. Good luck tonight. I'll be there in the audience."

I leave his office, planning to grab some food at home before heading to the theater for opening night. Everyone is bound to be jittery, but surprisingly enough, I'm not anxious about the opening now that everything has been set into motion.

As I head across campus, I decide to stop in the math building and say hi to Reed. Yet another student quit in the math lab, so he's been under a lot of stress lately. When I walk in, he's at a table talking to a guy whose back is to me. I figure he's tutoring the guy until I get close enough to overhear their conversation. Reed's giving him instructions on how the lab works.

My brother looks up and smiles when he sees me. "Lexi. This is a surprise."

"I thought I'd drop in and say hi. I know Fridays are late for you this semester, so I'll be gone when you get home."

Reed stands, looking down at the guy across from him. "Excuse me for a minute."

Now I feel guilty. It's obvious he's training this guy to take the recently vacated position. "You don't have to stop what you're doing."

"Don't be ridiculous. I could use a break, and I'm sure Ben won't mind waiting a minute."

I follow him into his office and he shuts the door. "I'm glad you stopped by," he says with a smile. "Both of us have been so busy for the last few weeks that I feel like I haven't seen you for days. How are you? Caroline says everything's ready for opening night."

"Well, as long as no one's expecting Broadway, I think it'll go well."

"That's not how Caroline put it."

"That's because she stays backstage." I tilt my head with a grin. "So she's missed a lot of the actual play. But it's a comedy, which helps cover most of our screw-ups."

"That's the spirit." There's no sarcasm in his voice. "I know what a perfectionist you can be. I'm proud of you for letting go a bit."

His words make me stop and think. I've always wanted things to be done right—we're both like that—but maybe I *do* need to let go. "If I've learned anything, it's that we can't control everything. If I don't let some things go, they'll eat me alive."

The recognition flickers in his eyes, quickly followed by anger.

We've never talked about what happened, not explicitly. Part of the reason is that Reed never brings it up. I know why, and it's not just that he doesn't want to upset me. It pains him that something so horrible happened to me and that he couldn't do anything about it. It's why he's so overprotective now. My therapist has pointed this out to me multiple times.

"Not to worry, big brother." I kiss him on the cheek. "It's called growing up."

He sits on the edge of his desk, at a loss for words.

I help him out by changing the subject. "Are you still coming tonight?"

A smile spreads across his face. "I wouldn't miss it. It's your stage debut, since I don't think we can count your riveting performance as Little Bo Peep in the third grade play."

I laugh. "I can't believe you remember that."

"How could I forget it? Mother made me wear a tie to the school program. Some of my friends were there, so I was teased mercilessly for weeks."

I release a contented sigh, happy to be here with him in this moment. We've gotten pretty close since we moved to Hillsdale together. "I miss you."

His brow wrinkles. "I miss you too. I'm sorry if school and Caroline are sucking up my time."

"No, don't be sorry. Both are worthy of your attention. Besides, I want you to be happy."

He stands and gently grabs my shoulders, turning me around so that he's looking into my eyes. "I want you to be happy too. Sometimes I wonder if I did the right thing by bringing you here... if you would have been better off in Boston."

My mouth drops open and I blink in confusion. "How can you say that?" Then it hits me. "Are *you* sorry?"

"*No*, Lexi. Southern's not Stanford, but if I hadn't come here I would never have met Caroline. And I can't even begin to imagine a life without her. I'm grateful for the choices I made."

I offer him a tight smile. I always worry that someday he'll decide I'm not worth the sacrifice.

"No, it's you I worry about." He pauses then adds. "You've been so unhappy since your break up with Brandon."

"I'm fine, Reed. I promise. I was sad, but I'm better and I thoroughly love what I'm doing with the children's charity. I've never felt more fulfilled."

He looks relieved.

"I want to concentrate on school and work. I don't need a boyfriend right now." I offer him a smug grin. "I thought you of all people would appreciate that."

"Trust me, I do. But Caroline disagrees. You're a college sophomore who lives with her brother and his fiancée. Caroline worries that I'm sheltering you too much and that you're not getting the most out of your college experience. And I have to wonder if she's right, as hard as that is to accept."

I gasp. "You're admitting that someone else is *right*? Is the world coming to an end?"

He looks out the windowed partition at the guy he left at the table and moves toward the door. "Very funny. I have no problem admitting if someone's right and I'm wrong. It's just a rarity."

"No wonder all your tutors are quitting."

He scowls. "No. It's a matter of rules. The tutors who left refused to follow them."

"Just go easy on them and they might stick around longer."

"Now you sound like Caroline." He gives me an amused look as he opens the door.

I stare into his eyes and say in mock sincerity, "Listen to the women in your life, Reed. We want what's best for you."

"So you keep *saying*..." I love it when my serious brother teases me. "Come on, I need to get back to work." He walks with me through the tutoring room and into the hall. "I probably won't see you before the play, so break a leg."

"Thanks. But I'll see you *after* the performance, right?" I want to ask him if Caroline has warned him about my costume, but another part of me doesn't want to start that potential argument.

He grins. "Of course."

I head to the parking lot and search for my car. It's not hard to spot. Reed and I shared a car last semester, but in Caroline's quest to convince him to give me more independence, Reed and I went car shopping shortly after the New Year. He insisted on something "safe," so we found a used Volvo. White, of course. The safest paint color for cars, according to him. A family-style sedan is hardly my dream car, but at least it's not a minivan. And it's all mine.

When I walk in the front door of the apartment, a delicious smell hits me in the face. "Oh, what is that?"

Caroline is in the kitchen standing in front of the stove with a spatula in her hand. "Some frozen meal I found at the grocery store. Want some?"

"Sure. I'm going to change first." While the business-casual ensemble I'm wearing would work for the speech I've prepared for the audience before the play, I want to look as polished and professional as possible. I'm hoping to get more pledges tonight. I settle on a blue dress that looks professional but is soft enough not to look cold and overbearing.

When I return, there are two plates with some pasta and chicken concoction on the bar with glasses of water.

"I thought we could ride together since I'm helping with the costumes and makeup." Caroline says, setting silverware down next to each plate. "Then I can ride home with Reed and you can have the car. Maybe go out and have some fun with the cast afterward."

"Caroline," I grumble as I sit down in front of my dinner. "You don't have to organize my social calendar. I'm doing just fine."

"You're not," Caroline says softly from the seat next to mine.

"Just because—"

She leans toward me, her eyes serious. "You're not, Lexi. I see it in your eyes. Something happened to you that night you went out with Brandon before Christmas. Something broke inside you. I keep hoping I'm wrong about that, that I'm seeing things that aren't there, but something's wrong. I know it." She takes my hand. "Lexi, I love you. Tell me what happened."

I'm tempted. But it's humiliating enough to talk about my issues with my therapist. I can't imagine discussing them with Caroline. "I'm just sad. Brandon was a great guy, but I always suspected he had feelings for his ex. Turns out I was right." My lies will surely land me in hell, yet I tell them anyway. "But now it's behind me and the work I'm doing has given me a purpose, which is making me a different kind of happy."

"But it's not fun. To get a full college experience you need to have fun."

I shake my head and chuckle. "Some days I swear Southern has hired you as a student ambassador."

"I care about you. When did that become a crime?"

"Caroline, you were throwing the full college experience line at me before you and Reed even started dating."

She laughs. "So I want you have fun. Humor me just this once."

"Okay," I give in with a grin. "If anyone goes out tonight, I'll go too."

Her face lights up. "Great. Promise?"

"Fine, I promise." She never specified how long I had to stay. I take a big bite of my pasta to put a stop to the conversation.

An hour later, things are progressing well behind stage at the theater. The director and the stage crew manager have everything under control. There are some opening-night jitters, but everyone seems upbeat and ready. Promptly at seven, I walk out in front of the curtain to address the audience. Even though ticket sales have been brisk, I'm surprised to see a mostly full theater. Granted, the Hillsdale Theater isn't huge, but there are at least three hundred seats. At ten dollars a ticket, we're bound to make even more money than expected. And we still have a performance tomorrow night.

"Hi, my name is Lexi Pendergraft and I'm a student at Southern University." I pause, flashing a smile. "I also work with the Middle Tennessee Children's Charity. As most of you know, the charity has provided a multitude of invaluable services to children in need in the Middle Tennessee area, from after-school tutoring and assistance with clothing and school supplies to the popular summer program for elementary-aged children. Middle-school-aged children tend to slip through the cracks—they're too old for daycare but too young to leave unsupervised for eight to ten hours a day. With that in mind, we've decided to enhance the summer program by adding activities for these children. After the play tonight, cast members will be in the lobby with buckets. We are so grateful that you've already contributed to our work by purchasing a ticket, but if you could be generous enough to make an additional donation, it would very much appreciated. Also, if you own a business or know of any business owners who might be willing to sponsor the program, please stop by and see me after tonight's production of *The Eternal Bachelor*."

The audience applauds and I walk offstage as the house lights fade and the show begins. Even though my short scene isn't until the second act, Caroline helps me with my makeup and stuffs the long black wig on my head.

I stare at my reflection, unnerved by the sight without being entirely sure why. It's me. I can see that, but there's something different in the face of the woman in the mirror, something I can't place. And then I realize what it is.

She doesn't look broken.

Caroline stands behind me, leaning over my shoulder. "You're stunning."

I don't say anything. I look exactly like I did last night, so I'm not sure why something about tonight is different.

"I'm going to find Reed. Break a leg, Lex."

"Thanks."

She leaves me sitting in front of the mirror, and I finally realize what has happened. Playing a part is all about trying on someone else's skin, and my character in the play is a woman who's confident in her sexuality. Maybe this is what I needed to do all along.

Only I'm not naïve enough to think it's that simple, that you can make something happen just by wishing it were so.

I give my head a sharp shake. How ridiculous. The woman in the mirror is me.

I feel narcissistic staring at my reflection so long, and I look around to see if anyone has caught me. Everyone is hanging out, waiting to perform their various roles. I push my chair back and get up. I need to make sure everything is still going well.

The cast and crew are psyched at intermission. Tonight's performance has gone even better than any of the rehearsals. The second act is shorter than the first and soon it's time for me to walk onstage and deliver my line. I'm surprised to find myself nervous. I've played a role in my mother's philanthropy projects for as long as I can remember, so I'm used to standing in front of large crowds and delivering speeches. One line should be nothing.

Thankfully, I deliver my line flawlessly. But as I wait for the play to wrap up, I realize there's a major downside to wearing a wig for my appearance in the play. My hair is pinned up and under the wig, so I won't be able to take it off before I meet and greet people.

Rob, the guy who struts on stage when I deliver my one line, takes one look at me and walks over. "What's wrong?"

I blink up at him in confusion.

"Your face is an open book, Lexi. You're worried about something." He puts his hands on my arms and rubs briskly. "Relax. It's our best run yet."

"It's my wig." I reach up to touch it, feeling stupid and superficial. "I need to meet people after the play. I can't take this off because my hair will be a disaster, but I suspect no one will know who I am if I have a different hair color. I'm liable to miss out on some networking opportunities."

He studies me for a moment then places his finger under my jaw and gently lifts it, a grin spreading across his face. "Chin up. Gotcha covered."

Rob is a seriously good-looking guy and I can see why so many girls fall all over themselves to go out with him. He looks like a surfer dude with his blond hair, unseasonal tan, and playful eyes. Still, I'm not his type at all. He seems interested in girls who have fluff for brains and Victoria Secret pushup bras. I'm barely a B-cup.

Before I can ask what he has planned, the curtain lowers and the cast begins to line up for their curtain call. Since I'm an extra with a line, I'm in the first group to take a bow. The crowd applauds and by the time Rob and the actress who plays his love interest take their bows, there's a standing ovation. Rob backs up and grabs my arm, pulling me to the front of the stage. He announces, "This wouldn't have been possible if it weren't for the amazing efforts of Lexi Pendergraft."

The cast and crew point to me as the cheers in the audience grow louder.

He grins. "Like I told you," he said in an undertone. "Gotcha covered."

Heat rise to my cheeks.

Rob leans into my ear and whispers, "You're adorable when you blush."

I cast a quizzical look in his direction, wondering if I've pegged him wrong. When the applause dies down, the curtain lowers and I follow the cast into the lobby. Dozens of people offer me their congratulations, and the cast members with buckets seem to be surrounded by people, particularly Rob, who's attracted the attention of quite a few younger women. His container seems to be fuller than any of the others.

I speak with several small business owners who seem genuinely interested in sponsoring the program, especially when I describe the expanded scope to them. Three businesses agree to set up meetings with me. None of them are solid agreements, but this is a huge step.

Once I have a breather, Reed and Caroline walk over. I can tell Reed is less than thrilled with my costume, but surprisingly enough, he doesn't say a word. Instead he hugs me. "I'm so proud of you, Lexi. What you did tonight is nothing short of amazing."

"My part was very, very small, Reed."

"Not the part. The coordination of this whole event. I know it was a huge undertaking that came together in a matter of weeks."

I squirm. "I didn't do it on my own."

"No, but it wouldn't have happened without you."

Caroline grabs my arm. "Lexi, will you just admit that you worked your ass off to make this happen and that it was a huge success?"

"Well, we still have a performance tomorrow night. Things might still go wrong."

"Lexi." Her voice takes on a threatening note.

"Okay. I worked hard and it turned out well." I tilt my head. "Happy now?"

Her grin lights up her face. "Yes."

I grin back. "Thank you."

"So what do you need to do before you head home?" Reed asks.

Sylvia sneaks up behind me and wraps her arm around my shoulders. "She's going out with the cast and crew to celebrate a successful opening night."

Reed's eyes dart to my costume. "You're going to change first, aren't you?"

"Reed!" Caroline protests.

"Yes," I say to keep the peace. "I'm going to change. This is my costume and I have to wear it for tomorrow night's performance."

"What do you plan on doing?" Reed asks.

"*Reed.*" Caroline glares at him.

"We're going to walk down to the bar down the street and have a drink," Sylvia says, dropping her hold on me.

I shake my head. "Don't worry, big brother. We won't be out late because we have another performance tomorrow night."

Reed doesn't look convinced, but he just frowns and says, "Just be careful, Lexi."

"You know that I will."

His struggle is obvious, and though a part of me bristles, his protectiveness makes me love him even more.

"Don't worry," Sylvia says. "I'll keep an eye on her."

Not surprisingly, Reed doesn't look reassured by this.

Caroline gives me a hug. "Have fun."

She drags my brother away and Sylvia releases a low whistle. "How in the world do you deal with him? He's a bigger hard-ass than my dad, and that's saying something."

"He means well."

"He's stifling."

I could argue with her, but it's pointless, especially when there's some truth to her statement.

The cast is already in the back changing while the crew counts the buckets of money. When we're ready to leave, they've finished tallying it up. "Four thousand, three hundred and fifty six dollars in addition to the two thousand in preshow ticket sales," Leo, the guy in charge of the light crew, announces. "And that's just for the first night."

We all cheer our success and someone shouts, "To the bar!"

Sylvia links her arm through mine. "Let's go have some   fun."

Chapter
Four

Lexi

The cool air hits us in the face. Februaries in middle Tennessee are typically mild, and tonight is no exception, but the sun is down and there's a wind from the north. I may still be wearing my wig, but I've changed out of my sequined shirt and leather skirt. I'm wearing the dress I wore to address the audience before the play, and the breeze chills my bare legs. Despite my freezing limbs, I'm happy with my appearance. I'd intended to look professional while addressing the audience, and the collar helped with that, but the V-neck and flouncy skirt of the soft blue fabric will help me look less boardroom and more up for a night of fun.

"Oh, shit it's cold." Sylvia grabs my wrist and tugs me along as she tries to run in her stilettos past a group in front of us.

"You're going to break both of our necks." While I'm used to walking in heels, I've never tried sprinting in them.

As we approach the bar, I'm surprised to hear live music, and even more surprised that it's not three decades old. I've passed this place several times while going to and from rehearsals. The outside isn't exactly flashy, so I expected it to cater to an older clientele.

One of the crew members has reached the door and he holds it open as Sylvia and I arrive at the entrance, gesturing for us to go in first. The bar is only half full and couples are dancing in an open space in front of the band. We spot several empty tables against the wall and head in that direction. The room is warm and I slip off my coat and sling it over the back of the chair. The rest of the group, about fifteen in all, settles in around a few of the tables.

I haven't been in a bar since I was dating Brandon. Strangely enough, Reed has never had a problem letting me go to bars with my fake ID. The ID is good enough to get me through TSA at the airport under my alias—the benefits of money—so there's no concern of getting caught. Last fall, Reed was usually with me when I went out, even if he stuck to the background, making sure nothing happened. But mostly, he knows that I'm not a big drinker. I don't like losing control, and that's what drinking alcohol is all about.

Being here tonight makes me anxious, although I'm not sure why. I'd love to run out the door, get in my car, and go home. And that's exactly why I know I need to stay. I'm perfectly safe and surrounded by friends. This is the ideal time and place for me to start my post-Brandon social life. My therapist will be happy when I meet with her next week.

There's a group of about twenty men in the opposite corner of the room. They're watching a basketball game, whooping and hollering. Other than them, the five couples on the dance floor, and a handle of people sitting at the bar, there's no one else here. Still, my nerves are pinging, and I'm slightly jumpy. Rob puts his coat on the chair next to mine and smiles down at me. "Let me get you a drink to celebrate a successful opening night. What would you like?"

I haven't had a drink in months, so I scour my brain for my drink of choice from last fall. "A lemon drop martini."

"Coming right up."

Sylvia gives me a knowing look as Rob and a few of the other guys head to the bar to get drinks.

"Stop," I say as I slide into my seat.

"What?" she asks, feigning innocence.

"I know what you're thinking, but we're just friends."

She bites her lip and nods before turning to one of the local girls next to her. I watch the couples on the dance floor, letting my mind wander to my work on the summer program. Dr. Tyree asked me to draw up an official request for the classrooms for the program, which I'll need to do this weekend. Then I need to draw up a list of possible courses to show the desired scope of the project to prospective instructors. Reed can help me come up with ideas that will interest the boys. Maybe I can even convince him to work in a computer course of his own. He often says that his love of computers and algorithms began in middle school. Perhaps he'll help the boys in the program develop that same interest.

I'm deep in thought when Rob sets my drink in front of me. "Lighten up, Lexi Pendergraft."

I snap out of my train of thought and turn to him. "What makes you say that? I'm here aren't I?"

"There's here and then there's here." He taps my temple with the last word.

He might have a point.

"You need to let loose and have some fun," Sylvia leans across the table with an intent look in her eyes. "No work tonight. No comments or suggestions about the fundraiser. I didn't risk my neck with your brother so you could sit here and think about work or school."

"Okay, okay." I lift my hands in surrender and pick up the glass and take a sip. "Better now?"

"For the moment." She smirks.

The rest of our group joins us and I watch everyone, amazed that the locals from Hillsdale and the students from Southern have blended so well. Rob hits on one of the crew members, an education major who tutors at the charity's after-school center. He sees me watching and winks.

I grin and shake my head. He's a hopeless flirt.

I finish my drink and lean over to Sylvia. "I'm going to get another drink. Want something?"

Her eyes light up as she turns from the crew guy she's talking to and looks at me. "Yeah, another white wine."

I get up and walk toward the bar, passing a table of rowdy guys who watch me as I pass. An uneasiness spreads down my spine, but I try to ignore it. The men are harmless. I need to lighten up.

Two bartenders are behind the bar—a woman who looks like she's in her late twenties and a guy who's slightly familiar although I can't place him. The woman is closer, but she flashes me a smile and calls out something I can't hear. The guy's head lifts and she nods toward me.

He pops the top off a beer bottle and hands it to a guy before making his way to my end of the bar. A grin spreads across his face when he stops in front of me. "What can I get you, darlin'?" he asks with a drawl.

I stare at him, momentarily speechless. He's impossibly good looking with short, dark hair and gorgeous green eyes. A day's growth of stubble covers his lower face.

His smile fades slightly as he leans closer and he asks again, "What can I get you?"

I'm rarely affected by a guy's looks, but he stops me in my tracks. I give myself a mental shake. "Uh...a lemon drop martini and a white wine."

"Coming right up." But he hesitates for several seconds before grabbing a martini glass and starting to make my drink. "I haven't seen your group in here before."

"We wrapped up the first night of our play down the block and we're here to celebrate."

"So, are you an actress then?" he asks as he pours liquor into a martini shaker.

"Me?" I can't help but laugh. "No. I was in the play, but I'm no actress. It was more of an honorary part."

"What do you do, then?"

It sounds like he's just making polite conversation, but there's a slight edge to his question that makes me wonder if it's more than that. Still, I have nothing to hide and networking is part of the game of fundraising. "I work with the Middle Tennessee Children's Charity."

"So the play was a fundraiser for their summer program."

"That's right." I'm surprised he knows this.

He shakes the metal container then pours the contents into my glass. "I heard about how you're adding the middle-school kids. It's a great idea." He sets my glass on the counter. "My brother goes to that summer program. He starts middle-school next year, so this would have been his last year otherwise."

This is my opportunity to get more information. I ignore the fact that I'm grateful for the chance to talk to him longer. "Does he like it?"

He grins and leans his elbow on the counter. "What's not to like? Romping in the park all day with games, swimming, and field trips—it's a kid's summer vacation dreams come true."

His answer worries me. What if I'm wrong? What kid wants to go school while they're on summer break? What if

I'm putting all this time, energy, and money into a program that won't even interest the kids?

A seriousness fills his eyes and he rests both elbows on the counter. "Why do you ask?"

I take a deep breath. "If I tell you my plan, will you give me your honest opinion of whether your brother would want to go?"

His shoulders tense, but his green eyes pierce mine. "Yes, of course."

My stomach tightens. What if he thinks I'm crazy? I shouldn't give so much credence to one guy's impression, but his brother is essentially in my target audience. "The middle-school program we're trying to implement? I want to expand it beyond its original scope." I pause, but he's listening intently. "I'm trying to set up something like a summer school program, but not with the core subject classes kids hate. I want to offer classes they'll *want* to take. Computer programming. How to build your own video games. How to make updated clothing with thrift store finds. Courses on how to build a babysitting business or a lawn mowing service."

He watches me without expression.

My chest tightens. "You think it's a crazy idea."

He shakes his head. "*No.* Not at all…" His eyebrows lift. "Can I ask your name?"

My stomach jitters with nerves. "Alexa," I answer without thinking. Where did that come from?

"Alexa."

My real name rolls over his tongue, sending a shiver down my spine. I've always preferred Lexi to Alexa, but the way he says my name gives me second thoughts.

"Well, Alexa, I think it's a great idea. Honestly, I'm speechless. I would have killed to be able to take part in something like that. I'm just not sure how many kids in Hillsdale can afford it."

Relief spreads through my body. "That's the beauty of the program. Spots will either be available at a very reduced rate or there will be scholarships. If we can get enough funding, the program will be completely free to kids who qualify based on financial need."

"Do you have any idea how much something like that would cost?"

My back stiffens. "Yes."

His face softens as he watches me. "I think it's amazing, Alexa."

Again, his opinion shouldn't matter, but his approval means something to me. "Thanks."

Sylvia sneaks up behind me. "What's taking so long?"

The bartender pushes away from the counter. "Let me get your wine." I realize with surprise that he finished making my martini several moments ago.

She breaks into a huge smile and watches him walk away. "Flirting with the bartender? I approve. He's really cute."

I shake my head and pick up my glass, taking a gulp. "No. I was telling him about the program."

A scowl wrinkles her forehead. "Lexi, I said no work talk."

My mouth parts in protest. "He *asked*, Sylvia. Besides his brother actually *goes* to the summer program and would have aged out this year. His opinion is invaluable."

"Well, no more work. Only fun. In fact, we need to dance."

The bartender returns with the wine and I hand him money for the drinks.

He pushes it back to me. "You can start a tab."

"Oh, I won't be staying—"

Sylvia grabs my arm and pulls me away. "Thank you."

"Why didn't you let me pay?" I ask as she continues to drag me to our table.

"Because you said you were going to have fun with me. You're only getting started."

"Sylvia. I can't get drunk. We have another show tomorrow night."

"You don't have to get passed-out, throwing-up-your-guts kind of drunk." She takes a glug of her wine. "But you can get tipsy enough to loosen up."

I'm the first person to realize that alcohol isn't the answer to my problems, but I can see her point. It might help me relax.

We rejoin our group and I soon find myself caught in the middle of a discussion about welfare and whether it perpetuates poverty or helps families climb out of it.

Sylvia rolls her eyes and pulls me out of my chair. "This is too close to work. Let's dance."

My upper lip curls as I eye the dance floor. "I don't dance."

"Tonight you do. Drink up."

I gulp down the rest of my drink and follow Sylvia. There are more people dancing now, so I feel less conspicuous, but I'm still uncomfortable as I begin to move. The song is a fast-paced dance song I've heard on the radio and I soon find myself letting go of my rigid control.

Several other people from our group join us. I'm laughing and having more fun than I've had in a long time.

An arm slips around my waist and I start to tense when I look up into Rob's smiling face.

"Dance with me, Lexi."

I lift my eyebrows playfully. "I thought I already was."

He turns me so I'm facing him and his hands land on my hips. "Not like this."

I expect to be more nervous, but I'm feeling sassier than usual so I dance with him for several seconds before breaking free. "I need another drink."

When he turns and heads for the bar, I go back to the table, Sylvia following me.

"Look at you," Sylvia says as she takes her seat at the table. "Dancing, drinking, flirting. Who knew you had it in you?"

I laugh. "It's always been in me." But she's right. I'm different tonight, less guarded. Why? Could it be the wig that's helping me feel more in control?

"So why is it always hiding?"

The reminder of the reason is like a kick in the gut, but I'm having fun. I refuse to give into the fear and anxiety trying to claw their way to the surface. "I just needed to remember life isn't all work."

Her smile falters. "It's obvious that Rob's interested in you, but he's not prone to commitment, so tread lightly there."

My eyebrows lift in surprise.

"My cousin goes to Southern too, and she dated him a year ago. He's a great guy and at least he's upfront about his desire to play the field." She pauses. "But you're on the rebound from Brandon and I don't want you to get hurt."

"Thanks, but I'm not looking to date anyone anyway. I'm too busy."

"Says anyone who can't get a date."

I put my hand on the table and lean forward. The alcohol has made me bolder than usual. "I can get a date anytime I want."

"Oh, yeah?" Her eyebrows lift in a challenge. "Prove it."

Rob returns with three drinks—one for me, one for Sylvia, and a bottle of beer for himself. After I've finished half of mine, I flash Sylvia a smile. "Are you coming out with everyone tomorrow night, Rob?" I ask.

He grins and rests his arm around the back of my chair. "It depends on who's coming."

"And if I said I was coming...?"

"Then I wouldn't dream of missing it."

A huge grin spreads across Sylvia's face before I get up and leave him at the table and dance with the rest of our friends. Rob shoots me curious glances until Sylvia and I leave an hour later, and I can't help but wonder if I'm playing with fire.

Chapter Five

Ben

Sabrina is next to me, her long, sleek black hair hanging over her shoulder, the ends skimming her nearly naked breast. I feel myself get hard at the sight of her even though I know I'm not supposed to react this way. Sabrina is a conniving bitch who will use anything and anyone to get what she wants, regardless of who pays the price.

But my dick doesn't care about that.

She reaches for me, her blood-red nails crawling up to the top button of my shirt. Her face leans into mine and her lips part as though she's about to kiss me.

That's when a blaring alarm blasts out of her mouth.

I jolt upright in bed. Five-forty. I turn the alarm clock off and scrub my eyes, trying to convince myself it's a bad idea to lie back down and go to sleep. Who in their right mind thinks showing up for work at six a.m. on a Saturday morning is a good idea? But this is an easy, no brainer job and it pays better than my other two. I don't dare fuck it up.

I climb out of bed, my erection demanding attention. It pisses me off that I'm hard for that bitch, but she knows what to do with that body of hers and my dick remembers every last trick. Thank God I told her *no* the last time I saw her. Otherwise, I have no doubt I'd be sitting in a jail cell right now, awaiting my trial.

I grab a pair of jeans off the floor and pick up a T-shirt, sniffing it before I pull it over my head. The beauty of this janitorial job is that I don't have to wear a uniform. The office building I clean is empty, so as long as I'm wearing clean clothes—questionable at the moment—my boss doesn't care if I show up in jeans and a T-shirt.

I slide my feet into my shoes and grab my phone and keys off the nightstand. If it were a school day, I'd make coffee, but there's an industrial-sized machine in the kitchen at the office. And there will be plenty of refills to get me through the day.

Hillsdale isn't a big town, nor is it affluent, which is why Southern University is a strange fit. One of the two local manufacturing plants has laid off half its work force and, the way things are going, it will soon close its doors. The town's hurting bad and my father's heating and cooling business is hurting right along with it. Before my arrest, Dad wanted to leave the business, Masterson H&C, to Kyle and me, but now he's planning on saving the whole thing for Kyle. I wonder what will be left of it by the time my little brother is ready.

Despite the fact that I hate waking up at o-dark-thirty to go to work on Saturday mornings, once I get there, I usually enjoy it. With no one else around, I can plug in my headphones and listen to music while I clean. And I carry my backpack around, so I can study in between tasks. If I didn't have my notes with me, I'd go insane. Busy work isn't enough to keep my brain occupied for eight hours. I have no idea how my friend Bobby can stand working on the assembly line at the plant. He was one of the lucky employees who kept his job. Although the term lucky is relative, I guess.

I unlock the front door and scan my ID card to get into the building. The door lock pops and I close myself inside, ready for my eight hours away from the world. Coffee is first on my list, and then I'll start cleaning.

The day goes by quickly and I'm actually feeling better about my history exam by the time I head back to my apartment, but I've spent more time than I care to admit thinking about Alexa, the girl from the play. She caught my attention the moment she walked into the bar last night, but when she started to tell me about her work with the charity, I became seriously intrigued.

Alexa was so animated as she spoke about her plans for the expanded summer program, which is obviously much more than a resume booster for her, and several things struck me as I stopped what I was doing to watch her. One, she was in charge of the program, as bizarre as that seemed given the fact she looked all of nineteen or twenty. Two, if I had two functioning brain cells left I would have carded her before taking her drink order. And three, all I could think about were her lips and what it would be like to kiss her.

And that alone is reason for me to worry about my sanity. I've given up women, especially Southern women, and even though she didn't admit to being a college student, something tells me that Alexa is most definitely a Southern woman.

Still, her idea is incredible and I can't help but think about how much I would have loved to attend something like that when I was Kyle's age. Nevertheless, there's no way she can raise that many thousands of dollars, not to offer the courses she has planned while still making it worthwhile for the instructors. And I find myself disappointed, not only for my brother but also for Alexa.

By the time I get off work, I have three hours before I have to be at the bar, and I need a nap. Getting little over three hours of sleep on Friday nights is a killer, but I can do this for three more months. I know I can. All I have to do is keep my eye on the prize: my diploma.

Both of my roommates are sitting on the sofa playing video games when I walk in the front door. I head into the kitchen and grab a bag of chips from the cabinet, stuffing a handful in my mouth. I grab a bottle of water out of the fridge to wash them down.

"You know that game's like ten years old," I say.

"Don't be a hater..." Austin says, his eyes glued to the screen.

"...just because we kick your ass every time," Noah finishes.

"Suit yourself if you want to be losers for the rest of your life," I mumble on the way to my room. They know I don't mean it, mostly. My roommates are socially awkward and I think they like it that way. In the entire year I dated Sabrina, she only came to my apartment once. She met Austin and Noah and stared at them with a blank expression on her face. They reddened under her intense scrutiny, and if I'd had any sense at all, I would have realized I did not want to be caught in the Sabrina Richmond's gravitational pull. But I had no sense and my dick led me down a path to ruin. *What an idiot.* I sigh as I kick off my shoes and lie down on my bed. Live and learn, they say. No more Southern University girls, no matter how beautiful or altruistic.

I close my eyes and sleep isn't far behind, given my perpetual state of exhaustion. I feel like I've only just gone under when I hear Austin calling my name. "Ben!"

I rouse, lifting my head. "*What?* I'm not settling another bet between you and Noah over whether the original Star Trek or Star Trek: The Next Generation is better. Now leave me the fuck alone."

"Then I guess you don't care that your shift at the bar started ten minutes ago."

"*Fuck!*" I jump out of bed, disoriented. The bar. I need my black T-shirt and jeans.

"You're welcome," Austin calls out, his voice sarcastic, and I feel like an asshole.

Not *feel* like an asshole. I am one. I know this. I've carried a fucking chip on my shoulder since that night in late November when the police showed up my apartment. I was hosting a party of about thirty people to celebrate finally cutting the cord with Sabrina. Everyone who knew her knew she was toxic, everyone but me. So when the police knocked on my door, I figured a neighbor must have called in a noise complaint. Imagine my surprise when I discovered they were there to arrest me on rape and sodomy charges.

My life has been a nightmare ever since. I was in too much shock to put up much of an argument when they cuffed my hands behind my back and read me my Miranda rights. The horrified and accusatory stares of my so-called friends will forever stick in my memory. The crowd parted to get a glimpse of the golden boy Ben Masterson, getting arrested for rape.

The police shoved me into the back of a police car, then hauled me down to the station and locked me in a cell. My one phone call was to my father, who hung up on me before saying, "I raised you better than that."

I sat in a jail cell for two days before I was hauled to an arraignment hearing, where I was given a court-appointed attorney. I had no idea who I was even accused of raping until that moment.

Sabrina.

She'd shown up on my doorstep the night before the party, begging me to take her back. I sent her on her way, but not before she slapped me, digging her nails into my cheek. The police loved that piece of incriminating evidence and made sure to take plenty of photos of my face. It was the word of a local boy who went to a snobby school against Sabrina Richmond and her banking mogul father, Robert Richmond. Who were they going to believe?

Sabrina thought she was smart, but she forgot one key piece of evidence in a rape case: DNA. I hadn't had sex with Sabrina in over a week so there was no way my DNA would be in the semen they collected from her as evidence. Sabrina confessed it belonged to some guy she'd picked up at Belvedere's bar, a place we used to hang out. The charges were completely dropped, but my father refused to post bail, so I ended up spending over a week in jail. By the time I was released, it didn't matter that I was innocent. My face had been plastered all over the media. My father lost business because his son was a rapist. I lost my scholarship and was nearly expelled. All because of a selfish, coldhearted bitch.

Carry a chip on my shoulder? Why the fuck wouldn't I? My good friends stuck with me. They all knew what Sabrina was like. They'd seen how controlling she was of my free time. My roommates heard the middle-of-the-night, *paranoid I was with another girl* phone calls I fielded from her. My few true friends never doubted me. But the people who only knew me in passing judged. Whispers and snickers followed my every movement those first few weeks. I'd never felt so ostracized in my life. Cut off from my family and all but a handful of friends, everything I had had been stripped away.

Three more months. Just three more fucking months and I'm out of this living hell.

I really need a shower but I'm not sure I can spare the five minutes to take one. Then I think about all the tips I stand to lose if I don't impress the female customers. After what has to be the quickest shower in the world, I throw on my clothes and jam my feet into my shoes.

Austin is back on the sofa with Noah. Neither of them look up at me, which isn't uncommon when they are absorbed in a video game, but the chill in the air tells me it's for a different reason.

I stop at the front door, my hand on the knob. "I've been a real dick over the last few months, and you guys have born the brunt of it. I'm sorry." My voice cracks and both of my roommates shift their gaze to me. "Only a handful of people have stuck with me through this shit, and you two are in that group. You deserve better from me."

Noah picks up a pillow and throws it at my head. "Yeah, yeah. We love you too. Get out of here already."

I laugh and then sprint out the door, down the steps, and across the parking lot. My apartment is about a block behind the bar, so I never drive my car. I realize belatedly that my hair is still sopping wet and I forgot a coat, but it's too late to turn back. It's going to be cold as a son-of-a-bitch when I go home in the wee hours of the morning.

I slip in through the back door and immediately see Uncle Tony manning the bar.

"Ben." he growls. "Where the hell have you been?" My father's brother might be my boss, but it doesn't get me a pass in the slacker department. I know Uncle Tony took a risk when he hired me after my arrest. He lost a few of his older, more regular customers, and my father is giving him the cold shoulder, but my uncle insists we're blood and blood sticks together. Someone needs to tell my father that.

"Sorry, Uncle Tony."

He reaches up and rubs my head. "You're digging an early grave, Benjamin, running around with all these part-time jobs. Is it worth it?"

I've asked myself the same thing every fucking day since I started this punishing schedule in December, but I'm too stubborn to give up. "I sure as hell hope so."

"You can be thankful that you're such a hit with the young females of Hillsdale. Your presence has increased our revenue by forty percent and makes up for the idiots who left me for O'Malley's after I hired you."

I start checking the glasses and supplies, making sure we're ready for the night. "I'd like to think it's my charming personality and not just my looks that appeals to the ladies."

"More like your notoriety," he grumbles, heading to the backroom.

My smile falls. Surely, he can't be serious.

I don't have time to give it much thought. I'm thirty minutes late, and Tony is going to dock my pay, uncle or not. I need to pour on the charm so that my tips make up for it. The early evening is slow, but I expect business to pick up between eight and nine. Brittany, my co-bartender for the night, shows up an hour after I arrive.

"Hey there, sexy," she purrs as she struts behind the bar.

"Hey, yourself."

Brittany is in her late twenties, a single mother of two toddlers, but you'd never guess it to look at her. She's got dark brown hair with a streak of blue, a nose ring, big tits that catch any guy's attention—particularly in the one-size-too-small T-shirt she wears to work—and a tramp stamp of a heart that's always visible because of her aforementioned T-shirt. She has a job as a nurse's aide at the local old folks home during the week, but as she's admitted on more than one occasion, it doesn't pay shit. The money she makes in one night here supplements her income by twenty percent.

I like working with Brittany. She doesn't hold back and always tells it like it is. She doesn't play mind games like the majority of the women I've met in my twenty-one years of living, my own mother included. Brittany and I have worked out an arrangement that suits both of us most nights. Brittany waits on the guys and I get the girls. While I use my charm and charisma to rake in extra tips, Brittany uses her pure sex appeal.

"There's a Grizzlies game tonight," Brittany says with a grin. "Tips should be good." She definitely has the advantage in a bar that caters to sports. But I choose to see it as more of a challenge.

I hold my hands out at my sides. "You think you can get more tips than me tonight?"

Her eyebrows lift and she gives me a smirk. "*Think?* I know so, little boy."

"Then let's bet on it. Loser closes on their own tonight."

She releases a throaty laugh. "You got a deal. I hope you're ready to stay late."

I shake my head with a grin. "We'll just see about that."

The crowd begins to pick up and Brittany soon has the advantage—there's a good two-to-one ratio of men to women tonight. Thankfully, a group of ten women comes in at around nine-thirty. It doesn't take long for me to figure out that their night out is a bachelorette party. I flash a mischievous grin at Brittany, who's realized the same thing.

She curls her fingers and growls. "Go get 'em, tiger."

I rarely venture out from behind the bar. Brittany's more prone to do it, especially when there's a large group of guys watching a game. They like that she gives them personal attention and tend to show their appreciation with big tips. I usually do just fine behind the bar, but when a group of half-drunk women come in looking for a good time, I know when to leave my comfort zone. Especially if I want a shot at winning this bet.

"Good evening, ladies," I drawl with the accent I used before entering Southern three and a half years ago. The one I dropped to fit in more with my affluent classmates, though now I wish I hadn't bothered. "What are you all celebrating tonight?" The answer is so obvious a blind man could see it, but I need to get the conversation rolling.

"Jenny's getting *married!*" one of the women shouts and the rest of the group screams shrilly. I resist the urge to cringe and flash them my sexy smile. "And which one of you lovely ladies is Jenny?"

They giggle and point to a blonde wearing a tiara.

I press my hand to my chest. "*This* gorgeous woman is Jenny?" I reach for her hand. "Any way you can call off the wedding? No? And to think, I never even got a chance."

The woman blushes and all her friends giggle in a way that tells me this isn't their first stop. "Jenny's taken, but I'm available," one of them says.

I scan the group. "Which one of you said that?"

The girl who raises her hand looks suddenly shy. She's in her early thirties and slightly overweight. Her hair is in a plain bob and there's little to no makeup on her face. She's exactly the kind of woman Sabrina always made fun of toward the end of our relationship. Sure, she never insulted the women to their faces—at least not when I was around—but the victims always knew. I decide I want this woman to feel good about herself before she leaves tonight. I don't even give a fuck about the tips.

When the woman sees that I'm skirting around the group toward her, she turns bright red and tries to look away. I pull up a chair next to her. "What's your name?"

Her mouth opens and closes like a fish tossed onto a creek bank.

"Sophie," the friend standing next to her volunteers with a giggle.

"Hey, Sophie. I'm Ben. I don't think I've seen you in here before."

Her lips part again and she finally says, "That's because I've never been here before."

"Well, that has definitely been my loss." I stand and push the chair under the table. "Ladies, as you may have heard me tell Sophie, I'm Ben and I'm going to take care of you tonight."

They shriek and I wait for a couple of them to make their obligatory *they know how they'd like me to take care of them* remarks.

I tilt my head and give them a pretend stern look. "Now, now *ladies*. The night is young. Plenty of time for that." I shift my weight. "I'm ready to take your drink orders if you know what you want, but I need to check all y'all's IDs first."

The women are all in their late twenties and early thirties, but if I've learned one thing from this job it's that women close to twenty-one hate it when they're carded and women over thirty love it.

They all show me their IDs, and I take particular time with Sophie's. I get their orders and slide back behind the bar. Brittany, who's been watching the show, glares at me.

"Don't fuck with that girl, Masterson."

It takes me a moment to get what she's saying. My anger surges. "You think I'm fucking with her? What kind of asshole do you take me for?"

"An asshole who'll do anything to win a bet."

I shake my head in disgust. "Then I guess you really don't know me." But whose fault is that? I've been so angry these past few months that I've made playing the dick card an art. It's no surprise that she'd think the worst of me. Her eyes fill with guilt when she hears the force behind my words. I lean closer and lower my voice. "I'm not fucking with her, okay? She's the kind of girl that Sabrina used to trash. I don't know why I want to be nice to her. I just do."

"Sorry," she says. "I can be a real jerk sometimes."

Although Britt knows about the rape charges and my bitterness toward Sabrina, I've told her very little about our relationship, other than she was a first-class bitch even before the false accusation. I grin. "No shit."

She flashes me a smile in return before getting serious again. "But be careful with that girl, Ben. If you're too nice to her, she's not going to understand when you don't ask her out. I think it's sweet that you want to help build her self-esteem, but be careful."

Sensing the truth in her words, I nod.

Her smile returns. "And don't worry. I won't tarnish your rep as a dickhead by letting people know that you actually have a soul."

I roll my eyes.

"So we good?" she asks, her eyebrows raised.

"Of course."

I put in the group's order for appetizers and make their drinks. I'm about to take their order to the table when the door opens and a group of people walks in the door, laughing and talking loudly.

Brittany looks up as she's pouring a draft beer.

I recognize this group immediately. They're the theater kids who came in the night before. They stuck together while they were here, tipped well. But I'm kidding myself by pretending I'm not looking for one of their number in particular. I haven't seen her yet.

My eyes are on the door as I put the drinks on the tray, so I'm watching when it finally opens and she runs through it. The guy she was with last night is close behind, and he snags her hand and pulls her back to him. They shut the door and join their group.

"What's the story with her?" Brittany asks, standing behind me.

I look away. "Who?"

"Don't play stupid with me," she says with a laugh. "We both know who. What's the story?"

I shake my head and scowl. "There's no story. They're the cast and crew from the theater down the street. Their play has a two-night run. They came in last night and they're back tonight."

"And...?"

"And nothing." I try to get around her, but she blocks my path. "There's nothing to tell."

"That's bullshit. I saw you talking to her when you took her order, then you watched her for the rest of the night. What's her name? You at least have to know that," she teases.

I press my lips together in irritation. "Alexa. Now get out of my way, or I'm going to blow my tips from the rowdy bachelorette party." I lift an eyebrow. "Or is that your plan?" I try to sound pissed, but we both know I'm on the defensive.

She scoffs and steps aside. "As if I needed any help. Get to it." She smacks me on the ass as I pass by.

The ladies are happy to see me and the band begins to set up while I'm setting their glasses on the table.

The theater group is at the next table and I keep stealing glances. Alexa is sitting next to the guy who escorted her inside and there's a notable change in the way they're interacting tonight. His hand rests high on her upper thigh and she's not brushing it off. Something about her is different too...there's a confidence that wasn't there before.

Why I give a rat's ass is beyond me, yet I do. I'm not jealous, more like intrigued. Something about this girl has crawled under my skin since she burst in the door with her friend the night before. She took in the room with a gaze that said everything she saw was hers to be conquered. Next she intrigued me with her ambitious summer program. Then when she went out onto the dance floor, she caught the attention of every human in the room in possession of a pair of balls. Perhaps she's a siren.

I nearly choke on my own thought. When did I turn into a romantic?

I head back to the bar, but then turn on my heels. I'm already over here. I might as well take the orders for the theater group's table and keep all the tips. Or at least that's what I tell myself as my feet carry me to the table where she's sitting.

"How was tonight's performance?" I ask, trying to not stare at her. Her black hair is a sharp contrast to her pale skin and startling blue eyes. I now worry that this was a bad idea because my eyes are drawn to her, as if I can't control myself.

Look at someone else, idiot.

I tear my gaze away and find her friend, the girl who came to the bar to get her last night, and focus on her. She's pretty and she likes the attention I'm giving her. She was alone then, and I don't see a guy with her tonight either. Unattached. Good choice.

"Great!" is the group's enthusiastic response.

I take their orders, sneaking glances at Alexa, but she's too busy looking at the guy she's with to even notice. What the fuck is wrong with me?

I head back to the bar to get their drinks, an easy order. Most of the guys want beer; a couple of the girls want wine. My mystery girl wants a lemon drop martini. I tell myself that the fact that I remember it's her drink from the night before makes me an attentive bartender, not a stalker worthy of my almost sex-offender label.

"Well?" Brittany asks.

"Well, what?" my irritation is real this time, though it's not necessarily directed at her. More because I don't know a goddamn thing about Alexa other than she's working for the charity and that her electric blue eyes are hypnotic.

Brittany laughs. "Never in a million years would I have thought some random girl could do this to you, Benjamin."

"Fuck off, Britt."

She laughs again and walks away to wait on a customer.

I understand why she's so amused. I've worked here for almost three months, and until now, the only interest I've shown in a customer is in how much I can get her to tip me. Tonight I've expressed an interest in two.

I need to get my shit together.

Chapter Six

Lexi

I'm more nervous than I care to admit. Rob wasn't particularly attentive at the theater tonight, but as soon as we walked out the doors, he snagged my hand and let me know that we were together. Although I was the one who flirted with him last night, I now worry that Rob will expect more than I plan to deliver.

He leans into my ear. "Relax, Lexi. I won't bite." Then he grins. "Not unless you ask."

My breath sucks in and the bartender from the night before returns with our drinks. I tried not to pay him more attention than necessary when he took our order—I'm a bit embarrassed about how much I told him about the program last night—but I turn to him now, when I glance up at him now, he's looking directly at me.

I flush and I tell myself that it's because the room is warm then force myself to turn away. Our group rehashes the night's performance as the bartender finishes handing out our drinks. They talk about getting together to put on a play this summer, but we all know it's unlikely we'll do it, even if we ignore the fact.

Several people get up to dance, but Rob doesn't seem to be in a hurry to join them. Our new semi-privacy encourages me to take the offensive and let him know where I stand. "Rob, I know I was the one to come on to you, but I'm not the kind of girl you usually go for."

His eyes dance with amusement. "And what kind of girl is that?"

My face heats up and I stammer, trying to figure out what to say and not insult him.

He laughs. "Relax. You're right. You're not my usual type. Maybe that's why I'm interested. I just want to have some fun tonight."

"I'm not that kind of girl, Rob." I cringe as the words leave my mouth. I sound like I've come straight out of the 1950s.

"I promise that I'm not trying to get laid tonight, Lexi." He picks up my drink and presses it into my hand.

My eyes widen at his bluntness.

"Hey." He shrugs. "I know I have a reputation. That's why I wanted to put it out there. I figured that if you're not worried about me trying to score with you, you might relax a bit. You're always so intense."

"Rob." Now I feel like an idiot.

He grabs my hand and lifts the glass. "Drink."

I laugh, even though he's being bossy. I take a generous sip of the drink. "Happy now?"

"Not yet, but the night is young and so are you. So let's have some fun." He takes a long drag from his bottle of beer, then lowers it to the table.

Let go and have fun. It's what everyone around me is doing; it's what everyone wants *me* to do. My therapist is constantly telling me to ease up. While she'll be happy that I'm out and interacting in the world, I suspect getting drunk isn't on her list of recommended life choices. Still, Caroline is always harping on about how I need to have a full college experience, and we all know that getting drunk is pretty high on *that* list.

We talk for several minutes and before I realize it, my drink is gone.

"I'll be right back," Rob says as he stands then heads to the bar.

When he returns with our drinks, I ask him to tell me about himself. He's attending a community college about twenty miles away, getting perquisites to transfer to the University of Tennessee in Knoxville while working as a waiter.

"You should be an actor, Rob," I say, feeling the effects of the first drink. Since my first drink in months was last night, the alcohol has gone straight to my head.

"I thought that's what I was doing in your play, little Lexi." He taps my nose.

"No, for real. In New York or in Hollywood. You're really good."

His gaze lands on my mouth before lifting to my eyes. "You're really good too."

I'm not sure what he means. I know the delivery of my line was passable at best, but my head is getting too fuzzy to give much thought to his comment. I turn toward the band and watch the couples gliding around on the dance floor. "You said I need to have fun, and I want to dance."

He gives a laugh and stands, extending his hand. "Whatever the lady wants."

Once I'm out of my chair, I pull him onto the dance floor. It's a fast song and I start moving to the beat. Rob watches me with an amused grin before joining in. We dance for two songs and I'm just getting warmed up when the band changes to a ballad.

Rob stands still, lifting his eyebrows as if asking me what I want to do.

I close the distance between us and wrap my arms around his neck. "I don't want to sit down yet."

His arms wrap lightly around my back. "Whatever you want. It's Lexi's fun night out."

I laugh and sway to the music. About half of our group is dancing and the other half is at the table talking. Sylvia is dancing with a local guy in the crew, the same one who was paying her attention last night. I look up into Rob's amused face. "What's so funny?"

"You. It's like you're a different person when I ply you with a bit of alcohol. Or maybe it's that sexy black wig." He lifts his fingers to caress a few strands of the wig. His gaze lands on my lips. "I like this Lexi."

He's right. I do feel like a different person. More confident. I felt this way the previous evening but even more so tonight. Is it the alcohol or the wig? Maybe it's both. "I like this Lexi too."

"Then we definitely need to let this Lexi out to play more." His hands tighten at the small of my back, but it's feels good…not threatening. We're still loosely connected with only my linked hands on his neck and his at my back.

We finish the song and another fast song plays. Rob leans into my ear. "I need another beer. Do you want another drink?"

Safe, reliable Lexi would say no. But tonight I'm tired of being that way. If I'm ever going to get drunk, tonight is the night. "Sure."

He keeps his arm around my back as he walks me back to the table, then heads to the bar.

Sylvia slides into the chair next to me, her eyes shining with happiness. "You look like you're having fun."

"I am." I try to remember the last time I had fun and come up short.

"At the risk of sounding like your brother, I feel the need to say that you're fast on your way to getting drunk. I have no problem with that, but I need you to tell me when you want me to cut you off. Okay? Tell me how far is too far."

Her words are sobering.

"Lexi." Her tone is direct, which startles me. "I'm not telling you to stop. I don't want you to stop. I just want to know where that line is for you. I don't want you to wake up tomorrow and regret what you did."

I take a deep breath. "I don't want to make a fool of myself." My eyes widen. "Oh, God. I already have."

"What the hell are you talking about?"

"I dragged Rob onto the dance floor and made him dance with me."

"How the hell was that embarrassing? Trust me, that boy is loving every minute of it." She grabs my hand. "Newsflash. Sometimes guys like it when we take charge. There's nothing embarrassing about it. You're a pretty girl, Lexi, and there's nothing wrong with using your looks to attract a member of the opposite sex. And trust me, Rob is very interested."

"But he told me he wasn't looking to get laid tonight."

"Well, I'm sure that was a hard thing for him to say, because that man wants you and he has a reputation for moving fast. But did he say he wasn't looking to get laid *tonight?*"

I nod.

"I think *tonight* is the key word. He's totally interested in you. I've known the guy for a while and I trust him. He may get around, but he's not conniving. Tonight he seems more intent on getting you to let your hair down than anything."

I reach up to my head. "You mean my wig."

"Hair, wig. Whatever. He just wants the same thing I do. He wants you to enjoy yourself." She drops her hold. "So, what'll it be? What's your limit?"

"If I do anything that will make me want to die of humiliation, you have to promise not only to cut me off, but to drag me out of the bar."

"Done."

"And don't let me get so sloppy drunk I can't walk."

She grins. "Call me crazy, Lex, but I seriously doubt you'd ever let *yourself* get that drunk."

I suspect she's right.

Rob is at the bar, flirting with the female bartender who was here last night. She glances in my direction and I hurriedly look away, which is when I see the other bartender, the guy, at the table full of rowdy women next to us. He sets a pitcher of what looks like strawberry daiquiris on the table just as the band starts to play "I Like Big Butts." The women release a collective drunken squeal and rush for the dance floor, leaving one of their group behind. She's slightly overweight, but her clothes make her look even more so. She's not wearing makeup and her thin hair needs a good trim and style. I can't help thinking that Caroline would love to get her hands on the poor woman and give her a makeover to show her how pretty she is, even if she doesn't see it herself.

The bartender sits in the empty chair next to her. She looks down at her lap and he leans into her ear and talks to her for several seconds before tilting his head toward the group of guys watching a basketball game in the corner. She shakes her head, but the bartender gives her a warm smile that lights up his face. He takes her hand and helps her up, then gives her a gentle push toward the dance floor.

He stands in place for several moments, watching her with a worried expression before heading for the guys, stopping next to the chair of a guy who's sitting quietly by himself. He looks close to the same age as the woman— early thirties. When he glances up, the bartender squats next to him and starts talking intently, gesturing toward the dance floor. The guy grins and nods, his face red, and then the bartender slips behind the bar, quickly pouring a glass of wine before he returns to the shy man. The guy hands him a napkin and the bartender moves over to the women's table to place the napkin and the wine glass in front of the woman's seat.

Rob returns and I force myself to look away. Sylvia immediately hops out of his seat, grinning from ear to ear as she returns to the dance floor without another word.

"What's Sylvia so happy about?" Rob asks.

"That I'm having fun."

He clicks his beer bottle into the glass in my hand. "Here's to having fun." He lifts the beer to his lips. I watch him drink, my gaze landing on his mouth, his neck. I watch his Adam's Apple bob as he swallows. When he lowers the bottle it takes me several seconds to figure out that he's watching me. "You're making it really difficult to stick to my promise," he murmurs.

My eyes lift to his, and I'm surprised to see that his are dark with longing.

I laugh before I can stop myself, and to my surprise, his expression fills with amusement. "You think that's funny?"

"You're presuming I would agree to sleep with you and that's never going to happen."

He holds his beer in front of his chest. "Is that a challenge, little Lexi?"

My humiliation with Brandon comes rushing back. I shake my head, sobering. "No."

He senses the change in my mood and sets down his beer, leaning toward me so that his face is just inches away from mine. "I'm teasing. You have nothing to worry about."

I sigh and sit back in my chair, disappointed in myself for killing the jovial mood of the evening. Why do I have to spoil everything?

He stands and grabs my hand, pulling me from my seat. This time he's the one to guide me onto the dance floor. The band is playing a slow song and Rob pulls me closer this time, one hand on my lower back, the other pushing against my shoulder blades. I rest my cheek on his chest as we sway, letting myself enjoy the moment.

Out of the corner of my eye, I see the shy man and woman dancing together.

So my earlier impression was right; the bartender played matchmaker.

I'm not sure why this surprises me. He seemed somehow cynical the night before. But my gaze searches him out and I'm surprised to see him watching me again. My stomach jolts, but then I realize I'm standing next to the couple he set up. *Way to be narcissistic, Lexi.*

I release a sigh and relax into Rob. I'm imagining things that aren't there. I may feel a strange connection with him, but nothing will come of it. The chances of me ever coming back to this bar again are slim to none. I'll never see him again. And even if I did, I have no desire of repeating the nightmare I experienced with Brandon. Better to keep things casual with a guy; better to spend time with someone like Rob. Someone who won't make me want more.

"Somebody really broke your heart, huh?" Rob whispers in my ear.

I look up at him in surprise.

"Not all men are total asses," he says. A grin tugs at his lips. "We're all *partial* asses, but not *total*."

I can't help but smile. I need to relax and enjoy the moment. Rob only wants to have fun. I'm capable of that, despite myself.

With my change in attitude, my mood lightens and we dance for several more songs, laughing and teasing each other. Within an hour, most of the group reluctantly calls it a night and I tell Rob I need to go too.

"I'll walk you to your car," he says.

Sylvia's gaze narrows in question, and I nod before turning to Rob. "Thanks. That would be great."

He helps me put on my coat and takes my hand as we walk back toward the theater. "My car is parked in the next lot over," I say, "behind the building."

We cut through an alley to the parking lot. My white Volvo is the only one left. I stop and search my purse for my keys then look up at Rob and cringe when the memory hits me. "I'm pretty sure I left my keys on the makeup station in the theater. Which is locked." I sigh. "I can probably still catch Sylvia. I'm sure she'll take me home."

"Why not go inside the theater and get them?" he asks.

"Because the key I have for the theater is on the same key ring."

He digs his hand in his pocket and pulls out a key ring. "Good thing I'm here." He leads me to the back of the theater and opens the door, ushering me inside. It's dark except for the glow of a soft light from an open office door. We walk silently to the backstage area, where the makeup table is stationed. He spots my keys right away and picks them up. Sitting on the edge of the table, he places them in my open hand with a teasing grin. "Don't lose these. We don't want you to get stuck here."

"I didn't see your car anywhere. Where is it?" I ask.

"Parked on the street, a couple of blocks down."

"Then this is inconvenient for you."

He puts his hands on my waist, his touch gentle. "Nothing about tonight has been inconvenient," he murmurs before lifting his hand to my neck, lightly tracing my jawline with his thumb.

My breath catches. "Thank you for making me have fun."

"Making you have fun. That's the saddest thing I've ever heard," he says, but he's grinning.

I like being this close to him and I can't help but wonder why. Of course he's an attractive man, but so was Brandon. My lack of anxiety is liberating and all my nerve endings are pinging with awareness.

His gaze drops to my lips. "I want to kiss you. That's all, just kiss you. Is that okay?"

I nod, surprised that I want him to.

His mouth lifts to mine, and I close my eyes, taking in the sensation. Rob's a great kisser and I soon find myself leaning against his chest, losing myself in the moment. If neither of us set any limitations, I would have considered letting this go further, which catches me off guard. When I made out with Brandon, I always felt a sense of anxiety, even when I was turned on. Right now I feel nothing but the desire to take this further.

"What if I want more than a kiss?" I murmur against his lips.

"This is your night, Lexi," he murmurs back. "You take the lead. We'll do whatever you want."

His words are freeing, and I slip my hands inside his coat and slip it down his arms, letting it drop on the table. I run my palms over his shirt, feeling the muscles of his chest as I work my way up to his neck. Grabbing his cheeks, I hold him close as my tongue darts into his mouth.

I wait for his hands to begin their own exploration, but they stay anchored on my waist. I pull back and look into his eyes.

"I told you—*you* take the lead," he says, his gaze full of longing.

I let go of his face and grab his hands and push them down. He cups my ass and stays still, awaiting further instructions.

I plant my palm on his lower abdomen and slowly slide it down, moving it over the button of his jeans until it reaches the bulge in his pants. I press the heel of my hand against it and begin to rub.

A low moan rumbles in his chest. His hands slide down my thighs until his fingertips touch the bare skin of my legs. His hands grip the fabric of my dress, and he lifts it until his palms are pressing against my ass.

I keep rubbing his erection through his jeans until he shifts, uncomfortable. I reach for his belt and zipper, quickly undoing both and spreading the top of his jeans open. I reach into the opening and into his underwear, readjusting him, stroking him again in the process. He groans and leans down to kiss me, his tongue twining with mine as his teeth nibble my lower lip.

"What do you want me to do, Lexi?" he asks.

I grab his hand and pull it in front of me, sliding it between my legs. He rubs me over my underwear and I'm glad I wore a decent pair.

He brushes my hair behind my back and his mouth trails down my neck. We're both panting with need.

"How far do you want to take this?" he whispers.

His words slow down my libido, but only slightly. I'm not a one-night-stand kind of girl. I've always been in a committed relationship before sleeping with someone—or attempting to. But I feel nothing but carnal need right now, no anxiety. No panic. I don't want to question it. I just want to feel this.

"I need to warn you that I'm not a relationship kind of guy. I know you've been hurt before and the last thing I want to do is hurt you more."

I cup his cheek and look into his eyes. "Perfect."

There's enough alcohol still flowing in my veins to give me the courage to kiss him as I wrap my fingers around him.

He continues to rub me through my panties until I can't stand the ache growing there.

"Do you have a condom?" I ask. I want this but not enough to be risky.

He grins against my lips. "Yes." He pushes off the table and continues to kiss me as he guides me backward, toward a prop sofa that's pushed against the wall. He pulls his wallet out of his back pocket and produces a foil wrapper. Before sitting, he pulls his jeans down and steps out of them. He stares up at me then, his amusement falling away. "Are you sure about this, Lexi?"

Lust fills his eyes and I look down at his erection, waiting for my fear to surface. It doesn't. "Yes."

He puts on the condom while I slide my panties to the floor. I straddle his legs, resting my thighs against his.

He grabs the back of my head and pulls me closer, his mouth covering mine. My heat rises as his tongue plunges into mine. I groan as his hand resumes its position between my legs, making me squirm with need. I reach around to unzip the top part of my dress, but he brushes my hand out of the way and tugs down the zipper himself, then pulls the front of my dress so that it puddles around my waist. His mouth lowers to my breast, licking and kissing around the edges of my lacy bra. Within seconds, he has undone my bra and tossed it to the side, his mouth covering my nipple.

My back arches and I grab the back of his head to hold him there.

His mouth drives me wild before he pulls back. "You're setting the pace," he says again. "You're in control."

His words burst open a flood gate of lust and I pull his head up to mine, my tongue plundering his mouth as I rise onto my knees and move closer toward him. I reach down and guide him to my entrance and then lower myself on top of him. I move slowly, waiting for the panic to hit, but it never comes. All I feel is the ache deep inside for something more.

I rest my hands on his shoulders and begin to undulate on top of him as I continue to claim his mouth with mine.

He lets me do the work, resting his hands on my hips to help guide me. I set the pace until I'm panting and desperate for release. He senses I'm close and says, "Come for me, Lexi."

A dam of sensation bursts and my orgasm hits in waves. Rob grabs my hips and takes control, coming within half a minute of me.

I stay on top of him, astounded. I had sex with a man I barely knew and I didn't freak out.

He grins up at me, then places a kiss on the corner of my mouth. "Who knew you were a vixen just waiting to be released?"

He's right. Who knew? Even when I had sex before my rape, I was never aggressive. Tonight I had the best sex of my life. Why?

"I guess you had to help let her out," I say with a smile.

He kisses me again and then lifts me off of him. I stand, amazed that my legs are wobbly. I squat to pick up my panties and step into them, my inner thigh muscles screaming in protest.

Rob disappears into the bathroom and I look at myself in the makeup mirror as I fasten my bra.

The woman staring back at me is definitely not me this time. Long black hair, lust-filled eyes, flushed cheeks, swollen lips. She's sexy and wild. Lexi Pendergraft is none of those things. Is it the wig? Can a wig really have that much of an effect?

Rob comes up behind me and dips his mouth into my neck as I slip my arms into the sleeves of my dress.

I study him in the reflection. "Tonight's the last night we'll see each other, isn't it?"

His face raises and he stares back at me in the mirror. He hesitates, as though he's worried I'll become a stereotypical clingy, post-coital girl. "Probably."

The woman in the mirror smiles, looking sexy and provocative. "Perfect."

Chapter Seven

Lexi

I fold my hands together on the conference room table. It's Friday afternoon and everyone wants to get out of here. "These course ideas are great. Now we need to recruit instructors and, as always, we need to raise money. I'm open to ideas." Raising money is a never-ending chore. I'm used to the task, but the amount we need is daunting.

The original student committee that Dr. Tyree helped me put together to coordinate the summer program now looks at me with blank expressions. Not that I blame them. Four days ago their job was ten times easier. Now that my changes to the program have been greenlit, we have a long road ahead of us.

"Okay," I say with a sigh. "How about we take the weekend to think about it. When we meet next week, everyone should have three to five ideas, no matter how ridiculous they seem."

They murmur their agreement and as they silently stream out of the room, I can't help but wonder if they're sorry they agreed to volunteer, not that I blame them.

"Give 'em time, Lexi," Sylvia says, watching as the last guy leaves the room. "You pretty much dumped a monster project in their laps and told them they had to have it done yesterday."

I sink back into my chair with a scowl. She's right, of course.

"Cheer up," she grabs my arm and pulls me out of the chair. "They'll come around. Between your vivaciousness and can-do attitude, they'll be waving their pom-poms with you in no time."

"Is that what I do? Coerce people into doing things they don't want to with my team spirit?" I grab my bag off the floor and pick up the folder I left on the table.

Sylvia grabs my arm and turns me to face her. "Hey, what's going on?"

I shake my head, refusing to look at her. "Maybe everyone is right. Maybe this is too much, too soon."

She puts her hand on her hip. "Oh, hell no. I can't believe you just said that."

I look up, my jaw set. "Maybe it's time for me to be realistic."

"Stop it. I prefer my friend the dreamer, who doesn't believe in the word impossible."

My shoulders tense. "I'm not sure she exists anymore."

"What's this *really* all about?"

"Nothing."

"Does this have anything to with Rob? I warned you that he wasn't boyfriend material."

A throbbing pain stabs my temple as I follow her out of the room and give her an ornery grin. "Actually…he wanted to keep seeing me and I was the one who told him no." He'd called me a few days later, suggesting we go out again, but regardless of my momentary impulsiveness with him, I'm not capable of a relationship based on casual sex.

Her eyes bug out and her mouth drops open. "What? Why?"

I shrug. "You were right. Rob isn't made for a long-term relationship, or even a short one for that matter. But it was the perfect fling."

All it took was a wig.

I'm not happy about that part. I've spent a lot of time thinking about it. At first I just thought the wig helped me feel free enough to let my guard down. It made me feel like I was someone else. But I couldn't ignore the fact that Rob gave me control. Our encounter had been all under my direction. *I'd* been the aggressor. *I'd* been on top. The rest of my life is all about control. It only makes sense that I would want control in the one area of my life in which I'd been completely helpless and violated. But what if it *was* the wig? The worry wouldn't stop eating my insides.

"You really gave up on Rob because he's not boyfriend material? You couldn't just keep him around for the hot sex?"

My cheeks flush. "Who said it was hot?"

Her face scrunches in disgust. "Uh...it's written all over your face."

"I figured it was better to end it on a happy note, you know? No regrets, only good memories." That and how would I explain needing the wig the next time?

Her eyebrows lift in disbelief. It's obvious she thinks I've lost my mind. "Well, since you're back to having a social life, come out with me and a couple of girls from my dorm."

I stop in my tracks for a second, then keep walking. "I don't know..."

"Why not? You went out last weekend. Two nights in a row."

I shake my head. "That was different."

"How?"

The wig gave me confidence, but there was no way I could explain wearing it tonight. "It was a celebration. We went with a group."

"And you hooked up with Rob. We'll call tonight a celebration too. It can be in honor of your successful committee meeting, although I suspect you could run a successful committee meeting in your sleep."

I roll my eyes. "I have tons of work I need to do."

"You always have tons of work to do. I won't take no for an answer."

"I have to run it by Reed."

"Lexi. You've got to get out from under your brother's control. It's beyond ridiculous."

She doesn't understand why Reed's the way he is. I understand and it's hard enough for me to accept. But the bottom line is that the thought of going out again is terrifying. I'm overreacting, I know, which is reason enough for me to make myself go out with Sylvia. My shoulders sink and I sigh. "I'll talk to Caroline. She'll want me to do it."

"I'm going to ignore your lack of enthusiasm. I'll pick you up at eight." She takes off toward the staircase.

"Where are we going?"

She shrugs. "We'll figure it out." Then she turns around and heads down the stairs.

"Wait! What should I wear?" But she's already out of earshot.

Now I have to talk to Caroline, which opens the door to a lot of potential questions about last weekend. She knows something great happened and she's desperate for details. I should just tell her about Rob, but she'll push harder than Sylvia to find out why I don't want to go out with him again.

I suck at keeping secrets.

It wasn't so hard to hide the secret of why I broke up with Brandon. I couldn't stand the thought of sharing my humiliation with the world. But this is different. Caroline, in particular, can see a change in me. She's been dropping not-so-subtle hints that she knows something's up. I'm sure she'll ask me outright when I tell her I'm going out tonight, and I don't want to lie. I need to come up with a plan of how much to tell her. Only nothing comes to mind. Maybe I should text Sylvia and tell her that I've changed my mind.

But some small part of me screams no.

If I'm honest with myself, now that the cage door has opened, the social part of me isn't willing to go back into hiding. While I'm scared to death to go out tonight, I *want* to have fun. Although Reed has relaxed quite a bit since we first moved here last August, he's still majorly overprotective. I got him to ease up a bit while I was dating Brandon, but seeing my devastation after our break-up was enough to make my big brother go all caveman again. I understand his reasoning. He's taken full responsibility for me, and if something happens, he will have to answer to our parents. But I also know this is his way of trying to make up for not being there when I was attacked last spring.

As always, I'm torn between my desire to appease Reed and my desire to live my life. The only reason I got away with coming home so late last weekend was because Caroline covered for me, telling Reed that the cast party went late into the night. But I know I can't keep relying on Caroline to smooth things over. I've caused enough strain in their relationship, and I don't want to be the source of more.

Reed won't be home until after six, but as expected, I find Caroline home. What's unexpected is that I find her in the kitchen cooking dinner.

"What smells so good?"

She's wearing an apron smeared with tomato sauce and holding a wooden spoon in her hand. She's looking down at her phone on the counter. "Lasagna."

"Yum."

"Well, maybe not. I think I've screwed up the layers." She sounds upset, so I drop my coat and purse on a kitchen chair and head into the kitchen.

She turns to me with tears in her eyes. "I can't even make a damn lasagna."

"Hey!" I try to hide the fact her tears freak me out. It's not like Caroline to cry over something so inconsequential. "It can't be that bad. It smells delicious."

She backs up against the counter, pointing to the stove with the spoon. "First I forgot to put the garlic in the sauce, then I overcooked the noodles. Then I dumped most of the cheese on the bottom layer, and I didn't even put the ricotta down first." A fat tear rolls down her cheek.

"Caroline, who cares? Just throw it together and you know we'll eat it."

She looks up at me. "I wanted to cook for Reed. You both know I'm not capable of making anything more complicated than macaroni and cheese." Two more tears fall.

"And your Kraft mac and cheese is legendary. Who cares? We love you anyway."

She chokes back a sob.

Now I'm really scared. "Caroline, what's really going on?"

Her chin trembles. "I think Reed's having second thoughts." She bites the corner of her mouth. "I think he might be seeing someone else."

My mouth drops open. "Do you have any idea how absolutely crazy that is? Why would you even think that?"

"He's hiding something from me."

"How do you know?"

"Because he told me that he's been working on a project at his office in the evenings. He's been staying late, and I started to miss him." Her voice breaks. "So last night I decided to surprise him. I got some deli sandwiches and took them to him like he did last fall when I was working on my project for the fashion show. Only when I showed up at his office, he wasn't there."

I shook my head in confusion. "He'd already left?"

More tears fall. "When he got home late, I asked him if he'd gotten lot of work done, and he said yes."

"So, he probably took his laptop somewhere else to work."

"I told him that I'd tried to call his office phone and he told me he'd turned off the ringer in the early evening and forgot to turn it back on."

My heart stops. "He lied to you?"

She doesn't answer. The devastation on her face is answer enough.

"There has to be a logical explanation, Caroline. He loves you."

She looks away and moves back to the casserole dish. "I suck at cooking."

"Caroline, Reed didn't choose you for your cooking."

Her mouth twists as she fights more tears. "I worried this would happen."

"What are you talking about?"

Her gaze lifts to mine. "What we felt in the beginning was so intense, so strong, one of my worries was that it couldn't last. That it would cool down and what would we be left with? It looks like my fears are coming true."

"Don't say that." I protest. "Don't you still love him?"

"Of course." Her voice cracks. "More than I've ever loved anyone or anything. I don't know how it's possible, but I love him more than I did in the beginning." She wipes her tears. "But this isn't about whether I love him or not. It's whether he still loves me. And the last two weeks he hasn't been himself. He's colder and more distant...and when I ask him what's wrong, he refuses to tell me."

"That doesn't mean he doesn't love you anymore."

She gives me a wry smile. "But wouldn't he tell me what was wrong if he did?"

I don't answer.

"So I thought I'd cook for him and make a special dinner, but I've fucked that up too." She starts to sob, covering her face with her hands. The solitaire diamond on her engagement ring catches the light.

I throw my arms around her and squeeze her tight. How did I miss all of this? I've been too lost in my own world to pay attention to the two people who are most important to me. "I just can't believe he's seeing someone else. Reed's one of the most loyal people I know." I murmur into her ear. "He loves you. I'm sure of it."

She cries into my shoulder for several minutes before pulling away. "I'm sorry."

"Why?"

"You're Reed's sister. I'm putting you in the middle."

"I'm your friend too." Right now I'm siding more with my friend than my brother, but I'm telling myself not to jump to conclusions. Yet when I examine the last week or two, I have to admit that Reed *has* been different. More distant and more harsh. It's no wonder tutors in the math lab are quitting. I seriously doubt he's seeing someone else, but *something* is going on. "What does Scarlett say?"

"Nothing."

I give her a quizzical look.

"I haven't told her."

"*What?* Why not?"

"She has to work with him. I don't want to make it awkward for her."

"Caroline, she's your best friend. You have to talk to her."

She shakes her head. "I have to deal with this myself."

"No." I lift my chin. "You have me."

"You can't say anything to him."

I shake my head, adamant. "You can't ask me not to."

"Lexi. Please. Let me deal with this on my own."

How can she drop this on me and expect me to not to do anything about it? But then, she didn't plan on telling me—or anyone—in the first place. I just caught her at a weak moment. I glance at the clock and see that it's six-fifteen. "Reed's going to be home any minute. Why don't you go clean yourself up and I'll take care of this."

A guilty look floats across her face.

"Caroline. I've got it covered."

She gives me a quick squeeze and disappears down the hall to the bathroom. Soon I hear the water running.

I'm on the last layers of the lasagna, although they aren't in the usual order, which has made it a bit messy, when the front door opens. When Reed walks in, I fight the urge to pounce on him. Caroline asked me not to bring up her concerns, but perhaps I can get him to share with me by taking a less direct approach.

He looks into the kitchen and surprise flickers in his eyes when he sees the mess. "It looks like a bomb went off in here."

"Rough day at the office, honey?" I joke. There's a jagged edge to my voice that even I can hear. I love my brother, but I love Caroline too. I can't stand that he's hurting her.

Rather than answering, he walks by me to the cabinet where we keep our limited stock of alcohol. He pours a generous drink and downs it in several sips while I openly gawk.

Reed doesn't drink.

"What's going on, Reed?"

He stares into his glass before taking another sip.

"*Reed.*"

He looks up at me, he eyes dark with anger. "With all due respect, Lexi, my life isn't an open book for you to manipulate."

I gasp. This is a not-so-subtle jab at me for setting him up with Caroline on the fashion show committee last fall. I put my hand on my hip. "What the hell is that supposed to mean?"

"It means you don't need to know everything about me."

His words are like gasoline on a fire. "But you expect to know *everything* about me."

He downs another drink. "That's different."

"Why is that different?"

He shakes his head in disbelief. "You *know.*"

I realize it's been an unspoken rule, but the attitude with which he delivers that phrase is my undoing. "You're an ass, Reed."

"Am I?"

My anger fades. He's scaring me. This man is not my brother. He's not the man who saved me from a life of ostracism. Something is really, really wrong. "Reed," my voice softens. "I know you think of me as your little sister, but I'm not a kid anymore. I can help you. Caroline can help you. You just have to tell us what's wrong."

His eyes harden. "What did Caroline say?"

"Nothing."

"Bullshit."

I back-peddle. Caroline asked me not to confront him, but now I've dragged her into this unintentionally. "She knows something is wrong too and she's worried about you. We love you, Reed. You of all people know that worry is part of loving someone."

His face softens and his mouth parts, but he hesitates. I can tell that he's not sure what to say. Then his gaze shifts over my shoulder.

When I look in that direction, I see that Caroline has emerged from the bathroom and is standing at the end of the bar.

He downs the rest of the drink. "I'm fine." Then he brushes past us down the hall. Seconds later, the bedroom door slams shut.

"What did you say?" she asks, tears in her voice.

"He came in and headed straight for the liquor cabinet." I look into her face, pleading with her to understand. "We both know that's not like him, so I confronted him about it and asked him to tell me what's wrong." I sag my hip into the edge of the counter. "Obviously, it didn't go well. I'm sorry."

It's her turn to be the comforter. "You don't have anything to be sorry about. You're right. Last October, that's how I knew the secret he'd kept from me was really bad. We walked in and he immediately poured himself a drink." Tears fill her eyes. "I wish he'd tell us what's wrong."

I sigh. "We both know how stubborn he is." His drinking worries me, but not as much as his indifference and anger. He acted like this once in high school, and I later found out that he'd been accused of cheating on an exam. Was something like that happening now?

Reed reemerges several minutes later and pulls Caroline into a hug, burying his face into the nape of her neck. When it becomes obvious that they need a moment alone, I disappear into the kitchen to check on the lasagna. I come back out a minute later to find them kissing and my shoulders relax. Reed glances up with an apologetic look. "I'm sorry. I had a bad day and I'm taking it out on the two most important people in my life."

"I just want to help you, Reed," I say. "You've done so much for me, and I want to reciprocate."

"I know," he says. "But there's nothing to tell. It was just one of those generic bad days."

He's lying. I can see it in his eyes. Caroline's body stiffens slightly, but Reed doesn't seem to notice. Or if he does, he doesn't acknowledge it.

"Well, Caroline made a delicious lasagna for dinner and I helped, but it will be another hour before it's done. So why don't you two open a bottle of wine and I'll give you some alone time while I get ready to go out tonight."

Caroline perks up. "You have plans tonight?"

My brother's face darkens. "What are you planning to do?"

"Reed, calm down," I say, not wanting to upset the equilibrium we've just achieved. "I'm going out with my friend Sylvia."

"Which one of your friends is she?"

I release a sigh, feeling like a high-school student who's discussing curfew with her father. "She's a business major too. She's also part of the committee for the children's charity. You met her after the performance last Friday night."

He shakes his head. "I don't think this is a good idea."

"Reed. You can't protect me forever. You have to start letting go at some point."

"Not now, Lexi," he says in a low growl.

My timing completely sucks; I know this. I should choose my battles, but for some reason I just can't let this go. "I didn't do anything wrong, Reed. Why am I being punished?"

Exasperation flickers in his eyes. "You're acting like a child, Lexi."

"Maybe it's because you're treating me that way." I'm not willing to get into an argument with him, though, so I go back to my room to get ready. I pray that Caroline lets it go and they don't fight over me. Again.

I have no desire to sit in my room for an hour and a half before Sylvia picks me up. I could get ready and tell Reed I'm going to the library, not that he'd believe me, or I can leave and tell him the truth.

I decide to go with the latter.

I head into bathroom and re-do my makeup—nothing like last week, but more than I usually wear. Unsure what to wear, I settle on pair of jeans, a silky black shirt, and a pair of black stiletto boots. I find my phone and text Sylvia to meet me in the west university parking lot, then I turn my phone to vibrate and put it in under my pillow. The last time I went out without Reed's permission, he tracked my cell phone and found me at a club while I was on my first date with Brandon. I'm not about to let that happen again. After I grab my purse and a leather coat from the closet, I suck in a deep breath, preparing myself for a showdown.

I'm an adult, I reassure myself. I don't need his permission. I'd like his blessing, but I don't need that either.

When I walk out into the living room, Reed is on the sofa watching TV while Caroline is cleaning up the kitchen. Even if tension wasn't hanging heavy in the room, it's easy to see they're not getting along. Ordinarily, Reed would be helping her.

Reed looks over at me, his face hardening with anger. "Where do you think you're going?"

"I told you that I'm going out," I say, keeping my tone neutral.

"Like hell you are."

"I'm an adult and I'm perfectly capable of taking care of myself. I'll be home later." I reach for the doorknob and Reeds stands up. For a moment, I think he's actually going to try to physically stop me.

"I'm warning you, Lexi: Do not walk out that door."

I hesitate, hating that it's come to this, but it's time to take a stand. I open the door and walk out as Reed shouts behind me.

I've finally crossed the line.

Chapter Eight

Lexi

I sit in my car in the west university parking lot, the car Reed took me to buy only a month ago. I feel incredibly guilty, but I tell myself I have no reason to feel this way. Reed's overprotectiveness borders on ridiculousness. It's time to cut the cord.

But as I sit and wait for Sylvia, I realize I didn't wait to get a response from her. I have no idea if she received my text. Thankfully, she pulls up five minutes later. I hop out of my car and get into the front passenger seat.

"Did you tell Reed you went to a study group? Is that why we're meeting here instead of the apartment?" She knows my usual cover stories.

"No. I told him the truth. And then I left, so he wouldn't try to lock me in my room."

"You can't be serious."

I wouldn't put it past him.

"So what do you want to do?"

My eyes widen in disbelief. "Go out, of course. I didn't go through all of this for nothing." I sure as hell hope our night out is worth it because I'll have hell to pay when I go home.

"Well, okay." She pulls out of the parking space. "Do you want to go to Voodoo Lounge? There's supposed to be a great band tonight."

"Are your friends still going to join us?"

"They'll meet us there."

"Sounds good." But when we pull into the parking lot of the bar, my stomach is in knots.

Sylvia turns off the car and takes the keys out of the ignition but makes no move to get out. "Are you okay?"

"Yeah, just give me a minute."

She rests her hands on the bottom of the steering wheel and stays silent for a few seconds. "We don't have go out," she finally says. "We could go back to my dorm room and watch a movie."

I know Sylvia thinks Reed is strange and overbearing, and it hurts me that she thinks so badly of him. Part of me would like to tell her everything. I could share my conflicted feelings with someone who's not caught in the middle. But Reed's given up everything for our anonymity; he even risked his relationship with Caroline last fall because of it. I can't break his trust.

I grab my purse. "No. I'll be fine." I open the car door. "Let's go in."

"Okay."

We walk across the parking lot and I keep telling myself I've done the right thing. That no other nineteen-year-old girls let their brothers treat them like they're twelve. Then why do I feel so guilty?

There's a cover charge since there's a band, so we hand over our money and find Sylvia's friends, who have already grabbed a table. We make our introductions and Sylvia goes up to the bar to order our drinks. The band is still setting up, so we sit and chat for the next twenty minutes. I can't help comparing tonight with last weekend, even though it's an unfair comparison for so many reasons. I ignore my strong desire to go home and force myself to smile and pretend like I'm having a good time. Worst case scenario, if

I want to go home before Sylvia, I can call Caroline and have her pick me up. Except then I'll get her into even more trouble with Reed, not to mention the fact that I don't have my phone. Leaving it behind had seemed like a good idea at the time.

The music starts and after two songs, Sylvia is ready to dance. I finish my second drink and follow her onto the dance floor. Not many people are out here yet, so I feel conspicuous. As we start to dance, Sylvia leans into my ear. "Lexi, lighten up. Maybe you need another drink."

I'm not driving, so why not? I need something to take away the dull ache in the pit of my stomach. I walk up to the bar and order a cosmo, leaning my arm onto the counter and watching the crowd as I wait for my drink.

A hard, warm body presses against my back and a man drops his mouth next to my ear, his breath warming my neck and sending shivers down my back. "Hello there, beautiful."

My body stiffens, but I refuse to turn around and give him any more attention than necessary.

The bartender places my drink on the counter and the man behind me places cash on the counter.

"That's really not necessary," I say.

"I insist." He doesn't sound like a typical college student, so against my better judgment, I turn around to look at him.

I was right, there's no way he's a college student. He has a dark complexion and hair and deep brown piercing eyes that remind me of a predator's. He has to be at least thirty and he's creeping me out.

The bartender is taking the man's money, but I call out, "Wait."

He stops, raising his eyebrows in question.

105

I dig money out of my front pocket and hand it to him. "I can pay for my own drink." I don't even wait for my change before heading back to my table. Unfortunately, the man follows me. I turn around to confront him. "I'm not interested."

His face scrunches into a sneer. "You think you're too good for me?"

The words echo through my head. *He* said the exact same thing to me before he violated me.

I will *not* fall apart.

I force myself to take a deep breath. I was helpless that night, but I can stand up to this asshole. "No, I'm too *young* for you."

He calls me a couple of obscene names before sulking off toward another table of university students.

I sit in my chair, shaken from the encounter. I want to go home, but Sylvia is having a good time. I should have listened when my instincts told me not to come out tonight. Then I wouldn't have argued with Reed. But that argument had been a long time coming. If it hadn't happened tonight, it would have happened in the near future. And even though I'm upset over our fight, I know that's not the true source of my anxiety. I've been on edge since I walked in here tonight. I feel naked and exposed and it pisses me off. Have things really gotten so bad that I can only have fun when I'm not myself?

Sylvia comes back to the table after a couple of more songs. "You're not enjoying yourself."

I try to smile. "I'm good."

"No, you're not. I don't understand what the problem is. You had fun last weekend." She pauses for a second. "Although that might have had something to do with Rob."

I can't hide my amusement. "You're terrible."

"We could give him a call."

"I am not going to call him." I shrug. "Look, I'm just tired, and I'm upset over my fight with Reed."

"Do you want to go home?"

I do, but I figure I should suck it up until Sylvia is ready to leave. "No. I just got hit on by an old guy. Give me a moment to get over the shock."

She scans the crowd and spots him. "That one?"

I see where she's pointing and nod.

"God, I'm sorry. What a loser."

I try to relax, but I'm on edge for the rest of the night. A group of three guys from Southern comes over to our table to talk and everyone pairs off except for me, not that I'm complaining. I purposely avoid eye contact with any of them. I feel completely out of control in this situation, which only adds to my anxiety.

It's a little after midnight when I see a girl I recognize, heading toward the exit with a group of friends. It takes me a moment to put together how I know her. Tina. She works in the math lab with Reed and she used to live with Caroline.

I sort of know her and she's leaving. Since I helped move Caroline out of her apartment to move in with us, I know she lives close to campus. I jump up from my chair.

Sylvia shoots me a startled look.

"I see someone I know. I'll be right back."

She looks dubious. "Well, watch out for that old geezer. He's still wandering around, trying to screw his way through his mid-life crisis."

"He'd be more fun than she is," one of Sylvia's friends whispers with a smirk. Their other friend laughs.

Sylvia shoots them a glare as I turn around and hurry after Tina and her friends. I catch them right before they leave.

"Tina!"

She hears her name and looks around, passing over me in her scan.

"Tina," I say again, moving closer. "Hi! I'm not sure if you remember me, but I'm Lexi, Caroline's friend." Knowing that Reed is widely considered to be a bastard on campus makes Caroline's name the safer choice.

Recognition lights up her face. "Oh! I know you! You're Reed's little sister." She gives me a sly grin. "I hear you're quite the little match-maker."

I shrug. "You know..."

"You're pretty good at it. Have you ever considered going pro? I could work up some statistical probabilities for you to help you make more accurate matches. For a cut of course."

"What?" I shake my head in confusion.

"Well, you're a business major, aren't you? You'd think that would be right up your alley."

She knows more about me than I expected. I'm not sure if this is a good thing or a bad one.

"I haven't really given it much thought." I move closer, ignoring the curious stares of her friends. "Say, I see that you're leaving and I need a ride back to my car. It's parked in the west campus parking lot. I know where your apartment is, so—"

"Why don't you call your brother? I'm surprised he let you out of your glass cage." She laughs and her friends laugh with her.

My back stiffens. "Never mind. I'll just take a cab." I spin around and am heading back to my table when fingers dig into my arm and pull me back.

"Hold on, Curly Sue." She's grinning like she's up to something devious. "Why don't you want to call Reed? I'm sure he'd drop everything to come and get you. Or does he not know you're out." When I don't answer, her face lights up. "He doesn't know!" She laughs. "Hell, yeah, I'll give you a ride. Let's go."

I'm not sure I like that she's so enthusiastic about the idea that I snuck out behind Reed's back, but she's offering me a ride and I'd hate to refuse it. "Let me get my coat and purse."

She thumbs toward the door. "We'll meet you outside."

I nod and then hurry back to our table to scoop up my things.

Sylvia's eyes widen. "What are you doing?"

"I found Tina, who works with Reed in the math lab. She's leaving, so she's going to take me to my car."

Concern wrinkles her forehead. "I don't know…I should take you."

"Sylvia, I'm fine," I say forcefully. "You're having fun. Stay." Before she can protest, I hurry through the exit, grateful for the fresh air when I make it outside.

Tina and her friends are standing beside two cars, laughing and shouting and clearly inebriated. I realize I hadn't really thought this plan all the way through. There are seven people in Tina's group, three girls and four guys. I glance at the cars, both mid-sized sedans. "You know, I feel bad just inserting myself into your plans. I can find another way to get to my car."

One of the guys snickers. "She just said *insert*." The rest of them start laughing and I resist the urge to tell them to grow up. But they're drunk, and most drunks act like three-year-old kids.

Tina shakes her head and loops her arm through mine. "Come on now, Lexi. We're practically family, you and me. Between Caroline and Reed, we're closer than in that damn Kevin Bacon game."

"I know, but I don't want to interrupt—"

Tina shoves my head down and pushes me into the back of the open door, sliding in beside me as a guy gets in on the other side. My chest tightens. I don't want to ride in a car with a drunk driver, but to push my way out at this point would make a scene. I watch as one of the guys gets into the driver's side. Thankfully, he seems more sober then the rest.

I grab the seat in front of me and lean over his shoulder. "How much have you had to drink?"

He looks over and laughs in my face. "Calm down. I don't need another DUI. I'm the designated driver. I haven't had a drink in over an hour."

His breath in my face confirms his statement.

I ease back in the seat while Tina and the guys laugh.

"You're an uptight little virgin, aren't you?" Tina asks, resting the back of her head on the seat.

"I'm not a virgin," I murmur before stopping to consider what I'm saying.

Tina sits up, narrowing her eyes as she studies me with this new piece of information. "You're just full of surprises tonight, Curly Sue." She reaches up and bats one of my curls. "I might just keep you around for entertainment purposes."

"I just want a ride to my car."

"We'll get there." She leans back again, closing her eyes.

The car backs out and we pull out of the parking lot and head toward the university campus. We ride in silence and I think Tina has fallen asleep until we approach the west edge of campus. "Take Curly Sue to her car," she murmurs, her eyes still closed.

The car turns into the parking lot and I point out my car, one of the only vehicles left.

Tina sits up again, chuckling. "A *Volvo?*"

I clench my teeth. I can see why Caroline didn't have very many nice things to say about her.

The driver stops next to my car and I wait for Tina to move so I can get out, but she just keeps watching me. "I like you, Curly Sue." She turns serious and looks deep into my eyes. "I think a part of you is tired of being the good girl. When you want to have a good time, call me and I'll take you out."

I push on her arm. "Thanks for the offer. I'll consider it."

She laughs as she gets out of the car and I slide out of the seat and head toward my Volvo.

"Your secret is safe with me," she says.

I stop. "What secret?"

"Where you were tonight. You don't want Reed to know, otherwise you would have called him." When I don't answer, she shakes her head in disgust. "Come on, Curly Sue. I've played this game before. I'm the master at. But against my better judgment, I'll keep this between the two of us."

I narrow my eyes in suspicion. "Why?"

She shrugs and hangs onto the car door. "Call it solidarity." Before I can ask her what she means, she gets in and the car drives away.

Chapter
Nine

Lexi

Reed is waiting for me when I get home. He's on the sofa, his eyes glued on the television, which is providing the only light in the room.

I shut the door and take off my coat before he finally focuses his attention on me. "I hope you had a good time tonight, Lexi, because you won't be going out again for a long time."

I'm too tired to argue with him, but can't let him think I'm willing to kowtow to his wishes. "Reed, I love you. You know that." I take several steps toward him. "But I can't keep doing this. *We* can't keep doing this."

"I'm glad we agree on that."

"No, Reed. We don't. You can't shut me away in this apartment for the rest of my life."

He rolls his eyes. "It's not for the rest of your life, Lexi."

"Then how long, Reed? How long until I can be like everyone else in the world?"

"*Lexi.*"

"No, it's a legitimate question." My voice is soft and controlled. "How long?"

He closes his eyes and rubs his forehead. "I don't know."

"I need a parole date. Do I get time off for good behavior?"

His shoulders stiffen. "Now you're acting like a child again."

"And you're acting like a parent. But you're not my father and I'm not a child." I take in a breath. "I know you threw everything away for me—"

"Lexi, I didn't throw everything away for you."

"But you did. You gave up Stanford—your dream. You did it for me. And I understand how scared you must have been bringing me here. I was a mess…I know that. But I'm better now, Reed. I'm stronger than you give me credit for."

He takes in a deep breath and releases it.

I sit on the sofa next to him and take his hand. "Reed, I love you more than you can possibly know. I will never in a million years be able to repay you for what you've done for me, but I can't keep living this way. So I'm asking you: When are you going to let me live without these restrictions?"

"I don't know," he finally says. "Until I feel comfortable letting you go."

"That's never going to happen and you know it."

He stiffens and pulls his hand from me. "Don't push me. Not tonight."

He's angry anyway, so I decide to go for it. "Why have you been on edge over the last few weeks?"

"Lexi." He's shut down again, but he's hurting me, and he's hurting Caroline. We deserve some answers.

"Does it have anything to with Mom and Dad?"

He turns back to face the TV. "We'll discuss relaxing your restrictions tomorrow."

This is more than I hoped to get from him tonight, but I just can't let this go. "I know something's seriously wrong. I've only seen you act like this one other time, back in high school when you were accused of cheating on a test. Has something like that happened here, Reed?"

Anger hardens his face as he turns back to look at me. "I'm not discussing this with you. Now go to bed."

I realize his voice has risen several times now and Caroline still hasn't emerged from their bedroom. "Where's Caroline?"

"Gone."

My stomach falls to the floor and I feel lightheaded. "What do you mean *gone*?"

"She left and said she didn't know when she'd be back."

"*Where did she go?*" My voice rises with my panic.

"She didn't tell me."

My anger bursts loose. "You'd follow me to a club and make me leave, *but you won't even track down your own fiancée?*"

"That's different and you know it."

I shake my head, tears burning my eyes. "How is it different, Reed? Are you saying you don't love her anymore?"

"This is none of your fucking business, Lexi. Now go to bed."

"It *is* my business! She lives with us. She's like a sister to me. I want to know what you did to drive her away. And I want to know where she is."

Reed lunges from the sofa and turns to face me. "You'd choose her over me?"

"Does there have to be a choice? You've been impossible to live with over the last few weeks, you know, and you drove her to tears this afternoon. She tried to make lasagna for you, because she's worried that you might have found someone else. We both know that she hates to cook.

Did you even acknowledge that she went to all that trouble?"

The color drains from his face.

"For the love of God, stop being so stubborn and tell me what's wrong."

"Why would she think I've found someone else?" The way he asks it sends terror racing through my veins.

I've said way more than I should have, so I can't tell him about Caroline's visit to his office. "*Have* you found someone else?"

Tears fill his eyes. "How can you even ask me that?"

"Answer the question, Reed."

He turns away, looking devastated. "This is between Caroline and me."

"That's not fair."

Anger blazes in his eyes. "Life's not fair, Lexi. Get used to it."

"You know what Reed? I got an up close and personal view of how unfair life is last April. *When I was raped.*"

He cringes.

"I was raped...and while we've dealt with the fallout from that night for months and months, we've never addressed what actually happened."

"And we never will."

"Reed!"

He shakes his head violently. "Don't you see, Lexi?" His voice breaks. "I can't. I don't think I can hear the details and survive it."

His words hit my chest and steal my breath away.

He turns off the television, then rubs a hand over his face. Dark circles underscore his eyes. "When you were a baby, you had a nanny. I'm sure Mom never told you that, because you didn't have one for very long." He looks into my face, his cheeks splotchy. "I wasn't like most boys my age. I actually wanted a baby sister. I was excited when Mom and Dad brought you home and I loved to see you every chance I got. But whenever I went to the nursery, the nanny would shoo me away. One afternoon, I camped outside your door and refused to leave until I got to see you. I stayed there for hours, and you cried the entire time. Finally, I ran into the room and saw that the nanny wasn't even in there. She'd slipped out the terrace door after propping a bottle on a pillow in your bassinet. It had rolled off, though, so you couldn't drink it. Somehow I managed to pick you up and take you to the rocking chair and give you your bottle."

My mouth drops open in disbelief.

"You stopped crying the minute I gave you the bottle. You were starving. I had finished feeding you by the time the nanny came back. She was furious that I was holding you, but I think she was more concerned about having been caught. She tried to take you from me, but I kicked her in the leg and threatened to hurt her if she ever came near you again." He looks up at me. "Amazingly enough, Mom actually believed me when I told her what happened. Maybe it was because I was still holding you when I found her."

I shake my head. "Reed, you were four. What four-year-old kid does that?"

He shrugs, looking defeated. "The nanny was fired, but I was upset with myself that I'd let you cry so long before intervening." He pauses. "I made a promise to you that day. I promised you that I would always be there for you when you needed me, that I would *never* let anyone hurt you again." He voice breaks. "I failed you, Lex. Someone hurt you in the most vile, disgusting, dehumanizing way and there wasn't a fucking thing I could do about it. I had no idea that it had even happened until after the fact."

I grab his hand, tears clogging my throat. "You can't protect me from everything, Reed."

"Maybe not, but I can try."

I pull him into a hug, squeezing my arms around his back. I cry onto his shoulder, and he holds me tight. After a minute or so, I pull back and look into his face. "Reed, I mean it, you have no idea how much I love you."

He smooths the hair back from my wet cheeks. "Go to bed. We'll talk more in the morning."

I kiss his cheek and then head toward the hall.

"She's with Scarlett."

I stop and look back at him. He's staring at the dark TV screen. "Caroline went to Scarlett and Tucker's. That was the first place I called."

Fresh tears burn my eyes as I head down the hall. I have no idea how to fix this, but I have to find a way.

***

I try to talk to Reed on Saturday like he promised we would, but he spends most of the day out of the apartment. Caroline doesn't return until Sunday afternoon, and that's only after Reed finally goes to get her. When she comes home, they disappear into their room.

I spend the weekend focusing on my homework, the summer program, and brainstorming fundraising ideas. The play was the perfect way to get the university and the town to come together. We ended up making nearly eight thousand dollars, which is amazing, but we still need so much more. I can't ignore the fact that many of the university students have deep pockets. I need to figure out how to get them to spend some of that money.

I decide to call Sylvia to run a few ideas by her, but I haven't talked to her since Friday night besides texting to tell her that I made it home okay. I'm worried it will be awkward. The only way to address this is head-on. As soon as she answers, I launch right into my apology.

"Sylvia, I'm sorry I ditched you."

"No. Don't say that. I forced you to go and I knew you weren't having fun. I should have left instead of making you find another way home."

"I didn't want to ruin the night for you. Did the guy you were talking to ask you out?"

She hesitates. "Well...yeah."

"That's awesome! Tell me all about him."

She spends the next five minutes telling me about Ken. She has a date with him tonight and she's trying to figure out what to wear.

"Do you want me to come over and help?"

"You know my clothes. Just suggest something."

"Where are you going?"

"Dinner and a movie."

I make a suggestion and then tell her a bit about the brainstorming I've been doing. "I need something that will make Southern students spend their money."

"An event with lots of beer."

"I'm serious, Sylvia."

"So I am."

"I was hoping to keep it legal."

"So I guess prostitution is out."

"Very funny." But the thought jogs a memory. "When Tina figured out who I was the other night, she mentioned that I should start a match-making business. She offered to put together some probability charts to help."

"You're thinking about starting a match-making service?" she asks in disbelief.

"No, but what if we did something similar? Like a bachelor auction or something."

She's silent for a moment. "That could actually work. The key is to get some really hot guys to participate."

"True."

"But we should include girls as well. Guys are just plain stupid around sexy girls. They'll pay out the nose to go out with a hottie."

I believe that. "Let's bring this idea up at the committee meeting tomorrow. I think we're onto something."

"Sounds good."

"Have fun on your date."

I hang up and then work on homework until it's time for bed. The only time I see any sign of my brother or Caroline is when Reed emerges from his room to get some food for them. No one's more happy that they're back together than I am, but this makes it painfully obvious that it's past time for me to move out.

Now I just need to break the news to Reed.

Chapter Ten

Ben

Monday's are a bitch. My history class is still kicking my ass, but at least I feel semi-prepared for the exam. When I walk out of the room, I'm certain I've made a C. Not ideal and not up to my 3.8 GPA, but I'm letting a lot of things slide this semester. All I need is my damn diploma. No one will give a shit if I got a C in American History.

I'm at the Higher Ground coffee shop studying for my thermal stress class when someone sits in the chair across from me. I look up, and this time I'm not surprised to see Tucker.

"Hey," he says. "I hear you got the math lab job."

I give him a wry smile.

"Does that grin mean you want to thank me or kick my ass?"

I snicker. "The jury's still out."

He laughs too.

"Seriously, Price," I say. "Thank you. The pay is great and they work around my schedule, even if Pendergraft's a dick."

"After what happened this weekend, I agree with you about Pendergraft, and don't sweat it, I helped you for purely selfish reasons," he says. "My girl was working too much before they hired you."

I'm curious about what happened this weekend, but not enough to ask. "Well, thanks nonetheless," I say.

He stands and ruffles my hair. "You're welcome."

I push his hand off my head with a snort and turn back to my homework. After my class, I grab a quick lunch and head to the math lab. Scarlett and Tina are at separate tables with an empty table between them, each sitting with someone. Tina's quite the enigma and I'm still trying to figure her out. She's not like any other math major I've ever known, and in her case, that's not necessarily a good thing.

"I think it's a great idea," Scarlett says to the blonde girl across from her. "I'd love to help, but I'm not sure about my summer school schedule yet."

"That's okay," the girl says. "What I really need right now are volunteers for the auction."

Her voice sounds familiar and I scour my memory trying to place her, but her back is to me and I can't see her face.

Scarlett laughs. "Well, we both know that I'm out, but Tina might be available."

The blonde turns to look at Tina and her face scrunches. "Yeah, I don't know."

Tina's talking to the student at her table and doesn't seem to notice.

I take a seat at my table and try not to be too obvious about checking out Scarlett's friend.

"You need guys too, right?" Scarlett asks.

"Definitely."

"What about Ben? He's attractive enough," Scarlett says this as though she's listing the periodic table.

"Wow, I might get a big head if you keep giving me compliments like that," I say, turning my attention to the girl now that she's looking at me. She's petite, with a fair

Business as Usual

complexion. Loose blonde curls hang slightly past her shoulders, but it's her striking blue eyes that catch my attention. I've seen her somewhere before, but I can't place where yet.

The blonde looks up at me, confusion flickering in her eyes, followed by something that looks like panic. Why would she panic? Icy realization shoots through me. She probably recognizes me from my brush with infamy. But I quickly realize I'm wrong. She seems nervous but not fearful. It's as though she's worried I'll find out something about *her*.

"We're still sorting through the details," she finally says, shifting her gaze back to Scarlett.

"I might be able to help if I knew what you were talking about." I slide my chair next to her. I'm certain she's recognized me, but I still can't place her. While I'm not usually drawn to blondes, I'm sure I would have remembered this girl.

Scarlett starts to talk, but the girl hushes her by putting a hand over hers. "We're still in the planning stages so let's keep this quiet," she says. "I want to make sure it has the maximum impact when we announce it."

Scarlett's eyes narrow. "Okay..."

I'm dying to know more about this girl, and the one sure way to get her to tell me her name is to introduce myself. I reach out a hand. "I'm Ben Masterson. Obviously, I work with Scarlett here in the lab."

She smiles, but it wobbles. She's still nervous. "Nice to meet you, Ben," she says, shaking my hand with a firm grasp.

The fact that she purposely omitted her name doesn't escape my notice.

123

She stands and picks up her leather bag, casting a wary gaze in my direction. "Scarlett, can I talk to you out in the hall?"

Surprise flickers in Scarlett's eyes. "Sure. I don't have any students waiting for me." She gets up and follows her out the door.

I wheel my chair back to my table and pull my homework out of my bag. That's another benefit of this job—I can work on homework when we don't have anyone to tutor. I've started on an equation from my last class when Scarlett returns and resumes her seat.

"Who was that?" I ask, not caring if I sound nosy. I've seen the girl before and my brain won't rest until I put it together.

She looks down at her own work. "Reed's sister."

"*That's* Reed's sister?" And suddenly, I've figured out where I saw her last. The day I started, Reed was explaining how the lab worked when a cute blonde walked in. He stopped everything to go talk to her, but I barely got a glimpse of her before they ducked into his office. They look nothing alike, so I figured she was his girlfriend.

"Stay away from her, Ben." Scarlett's tone tells me she's serious.

My mouth drops in confusion. "What are you talking about?"

"I can tell that you're intrigued, but Reed will skin you alive if you ask her out. He takes overprotectiveness to his own extreme level."

I hold up my hands in surrender. Reed's already made it clear he's only tolerating my presence here until I screw up somehow. "No worries. Not interested." I am, but if she's Reed's sister, I'm not interested enough to lose my job.

"Good."

The student at Tina's table leaves and Tina scoots her chair next to mine. She's made it clear she's interested in getting to know me better and I've made it as clear as possible that I'd prefer a raging case of herpes. The girl doesn't take a hint.

"Personal space, Tina," I growl.

"Easy there, Virgin Ben. I'm not going to rape you."

I cringe at her word choice. So far no one in the math lab has shown any sign they know about my arrest last fall and I hope to keep it that way.

"Wasn't that Reed's sister in here?" Tina curls a hand around my arm. "You should hook up with her. She's virginal too."

Scarlett shoots her a glare. "That's enough, Tina." It's obvious that she cares about this girl more than she would about someone who was just her boss's sister.

"God, Scarlett. You need to loosen up. I told Virgin Mary that Friday night when I took her home. Imagine my surprise when she busted out with the piece of intel that she's not a virgin after all." She leans back in her chair and crosses her arms under her breasts. "I bet fifty bucks Reed doesn't know that."

"And you're going to keep it that way," Scarlett says, her tone harsh. Scarlett is a mild-mannered girl, but I can tell she'll bear her claws if Tina keeps pushing. "And what do you mean you took her home Friday night? Caroline said she was supposed to be out with her friend on the committee."

Tina shrugs and gives a smart-ass grin. "Hell if I know. All I know is that I was leaving the Voodoo Club with my friends when Curly Sue comes running up, asking if I can give her a ride back to her car."

"Stay away from her, Tina."

"Ben can't play with her. I can't play with her. What's the fucking deal?"

"I mean it, Tina. Stay. Away."

"Damn, Scarlett. No need to be such a bitch. It's not like the two of us were going to become besties anyway. I took her to her car and dropped her off. I even offered to help her open a match-making business, but she flat-out turned me down."

God help me, this conversation is making me even more intrigued with the girl. Despite my better judgment, I find myself asking, "Why would she start a match-making service?"

"Haven't you heard?" Tina asks.

"Would I ask if I had?"

Tina releases a throaty, sexy laugh. "I like you, Masterson. I think we should keep you around." She leans forward on the table, looking into Scarlett's face. "We're a bit *incestuous* around here." She lingers on the word. "You see, Scarlett used to be roommates with Caroline Hunter until she moved in with Tucker last summer."

"After he quit the Chicago Fire."

"Don't encourage her, Ben," Scarlett grunts.

I know I shouldn't, yet I'm curious.

"Yep," Tina says. "That's right. So Caroline was left without a roommate and Scarlett and I were *friends*." The way she says the word makes me question it. "Anyway, I wanted out of the dorms, so Scarlett suggested I move in with her bestie."

"Okay…" I say, wondering where she was going with this.

"Here's where it gets interesting." She sits up and turns to face me. "Reed moved here last August with his baby sister. They came to the party Tucker threw Scarlett for her high GRE scores and Caroline was there. The sparks that flew between Caroline and Reed were strong enough to start a raging inferno, only Caroline was too busy looking for a rich boyfriend and Reed was too busy being a stuck-up prick. Baby sis decided to take matters into her own hands and got the Monroe Foundation to sponsor the fashion department's fall fashion show because she knew Caroline would be working on it. And she got Reed to be the head of the committee." She grins. "You would have thought getting laid regularly would mellow the guy, and it did until a couple of weeks ago."

"So Caroline and Reed hooked up?"

"Keep up, Masterson. I didn't think you were slow-witted. Yes, they hooked up, and those two..." she releases a low whistle. "Let's just say that the walls in our apartment are thin and I heard things most people don't want to hear." A slow, evil grin spreads across her face. "Good thing I'm not most people."

Scarlett rolls her eyes in disgust.

"Reed Pendergraft is a dirty, *dirty* boy," she drawls.

"*Enough, Tina.*" Scarlett looks close to blowing up.

I hold up my hands. "Yeah, I have no desire to hear about his exploits in the bedroom."

She lifts an eyebrow coyly. "They say the apple doesn't fall far from the tree. I bet Virgin Mary is a freak in the bedroom too. Maybe you want to find out."

"That analogy refers to offspring, not siblings," Scarlett says.

Tina shrugs her indifference.

"Yeah, no thanks," I say. Yes, I'm interested, but I need to keep Reed on my good side. "I've had enough freaks to last a lifetime."

She leans forward and curls her fingers around my thigh. "I want to hear more about your freaks."

I brush her hand off. "Not a chance. Don't you have work to do?"

She looks up at me through thick, black eyelashes. "Nothing more interesting than what's in front of me right now."

"Leave Ben alone or I'll write you up for sexual harassment," Scarlett says, turning a page in her notebook.

Tina rolls her chair back to her table. "God, I realize you're all a bunch of math nerds, but can't you have fun like *ever*?" Grabbing her purse, she stands. "I'm taking a smoke break."

I expect Scarlett to stop her—Reed has specifically forbidden smoke breaks—but her lips just press together in irritation as she watches Tina walk out of the room.

"She didn't always used to be like that," Scarlett says after a moment. "And she's right, we used to be friends. But she's changed so much in the last year and I can't figure out why. When I try to bring it up, she changes the subject." Releasing a sigh, she rubs her temple. "Sorry for her behavior."

"Hey, it's not your fault. I can handle her, but it makes it difficult since we work together so much."

She sighs again. "Well, Reed's just about had it with her, so I'm not sure how much you'll have to put up with her."

"Damn, he's firing people right and left."

"He wasn't like this until the last month or so. He's always been a perfectionist, but something's going on with him. I thought it was about his sister, but Caroline says it's not. Tucker is over him, saying he's upset Caroline one too many times… I'm willing to give him the benefit of the doubt, though. I think he's acting out because he's under some kind of pressure."

I release a bitter laugh. "You're nicer than most people. I could have used you as friend last fall."

She looks up, her brow wrinkling with confusion. "What?"

I shake my head. "Nothing."

If Scarlett's right about Reed, things are bound to get rockier in the math lab.

Chapter Eleven

Lexi

I stare at the message on my phone and my breath catches.

Come to the math lab. I have some information.

When Scarlett and I spoke in the hall outside the math lab several days ago, I asked her to let me know if she heard of anyone looking for a roommate. She insisted Reed would pitch a fit.

"That's why I really need for you not to tell him," I said. "But you and I both know it's time. Me living with Reed and Caroline isn't helping their relationship."

She sighed and leaned against the wall. "I think they have more problems than you living with them."

"I know. Something's going on with my brother. Do you have any idea what it is? He won't tell me."

She shook her head. "After Caroline showed up on my doorstep Friday night, she told me what was going on, including how she went to his office and didn't find him there." She scowled. "Tucker was ready to go beat him up."

"Again?"

She grinned. "Well, technically, last time he only punched him for making Caroline upset. He claims Reed's out of strikes. The only reason Tucker hasn't gone after him is that I threatened to deck him if he did." She shook her head and frowned. "Obviously that won't help anything. If it did, I'd be tempted to let him have at it."

I grinned despite the fact that she was talking about her boyfriend hurting my brother. "Caroline's lucky that Tucker looks out for her like that."

"He considers her my sister since we're so close. And you're lucky to have a brother who cares so much about you."

"I love Reed, but he's a little over-zealous."

She lifted an eyebrow and grinned. "You mean like Tucker."

There was no comparison between the two, but I knew it would be pointless to argue that fact. "Look, I want to help Reed, but I can't unless I know what's going on. Will you let me know if you hear anything?"

She nodded. "Even though I'm not a fan of eavesdropping and spying, I'll keep an eye out. I'll let you know first if I find anything out."

And with that, she left.

Four days have gone by without a word, and now she's sent me a message. Is it about an apartment or Reed?

Reed has his own classes to attend on Friday morning, so I know I won't run into him. Scarlett is waiting for me in his office, a serious expression on her face.

It's about Reed.

I'm nervous when I enter the math lab, mostly about why Scarlett wants to talk to me, but also because I'm worried about running into Ben. I recognized him right way when I was talking with Scarlett the other day, and I don't want him to figure out that I was the woman he talked to at the bar. Not that he probably remembers anyway. He meets tons of people at his job and I was wearing a wig. But he works with Reed, and if he tells my brother about me dancing and practically making out with Rob on Saturday night, Reed's liable to lock me away in an ivory tower for the rest of my natural life.

Unfortunately, the other person I was hoping to avoid is sitting at a table. A grin spreads across Tina's face when she sees me. "Hey, Curly Sue."

I ignore her as I walk into the office and close the door behind me. Scarlett is resting her butt against Reed's desk, waiting for me. "What did you find out?"

"Nothing definite, but there's something I think you should know about."

"Did you tell Caroline?"

Scarlett doesn't answer, which is answer enough.

I take a deep breath. "Go on."

"It may be nothing, but I've seen Reed take two phone calls while he was with a student, and he left the kid he was tutoring to take the calls in his office."

"That doesn't sound like him."

"It's not. And when he came back out, he wasn't in a good mood."

I'm grateful that I'm not imagining things, but I don't know what to do with this information.

"Lexi, that's not all." Scarlett says, her forehead wrinkled with worry.

I take a deep breath. "Okay."

"I saw him with a woman."

I feel lightheaded and my heart seizes. "What do you mean saw him with a woman?"

She shakes her head, looking upset. "It's not how I made it sound, but it still doesn't look good."

"Tell me."

"After one of the calls, he kept looking at his cell. About thirty minutes later, he looked at his phone and then announced he was taking a break. He hadn't finished tutoring the student at his table."

My heart stutters.

"I'm ashamed to admit that I did this...but I wasn't tutoring anyone at the time, so I followed him."

"It's okay, Scarlett," I force myself to say.

"He went to the first floor and a woman was there waiting for him. They embraced and then left together."

Tears burn my eyes. "I don't understand. There has to be a logical explanation, Scarlett. I know Reed. I *know* him. He would never cheat on anything—a test, his taxes, and most of all, he would *never* cheat on Caroline."

Scarlett's face is flushed. "God, I hope so, Lexi. If he is, it will kill her."

I nod, tears clogging my throat. "I know."

"I'll keep watching."

"Okay. I will too." Although I suspect Scarlett is now looking for proof that he is cheating while I'm looking for evidence that he *isn't*.

Scarlett opens the door to leave.

"I'm just going to sit here for a minute." I settle into his desk chair.

"Stay as long as you want. I'm sure Reed won't mind."

I hear her tell Tina she's taking a break, and then she leaves the room.

I need to figure out what Reed is up to. Why would he meet a woman and then leave with her? Maybe she's a fellow graduate student, and Reed is studying with her? If so, Scarlett would probably know her, though, and he wouldn't lie to Caroline about the whole thing. I'm truly at a loss.

I'm deep in thought when Tina startles me. "What's going on, Curly Sue?"

"Not now, Tina," I grumble.

She barges into Reed's office and sits in the chair across from his desk, leaning back as she stares into my face. "What's got you down, little one?"

"None of your business." I start to stand.

"Is it about your brother and what he's up to?"

I sit back down. "What do you know?"

She laughs. "I make it my business to know things. You never know when you might need to pull out some information."

"Then tell me."

She shakes her head. "I don't just hand over information. People have to earn it."

"You don't have anything."

She laughs. "Oh really? Scarlett might know that Saint Reed met a woman yesterday, but I bet she doesn't know her name."

I suck in a breath. "You're bluffing."

She shrugs, looking bored. "Suit yourself."

When she stands and takes a step toward the door, I say, "Wait."

A mischievous grin spreads across her face. "I knew you'd see things my way."

"What do you want?" I ask, gripping the arms of the chair.

She taps a fingernail on the corner of Reed's desk. "What do I want..."

A student walks into the lab, and he looks confused when he sees only one tutor.

"Duty calls, Tina."

"He can wait." She leans to the side in her chair. "What do I want? I want so many things. The question is: What do *you* have that I want?"

"You want me to list my assets?" I ask sarcastically. "How about I email you my portfolio later this afternoon."

She releases a belly laugh. "Oh, Curly Sue. You are so much more fun than I expected. Not to worry. I already know what I want."

The fact that she's given this thought worries me. I stare at her while I wait for her to deliver her demand.

"I want you to go out with me tonight."

"Sorry, Tina," I say. "I prefer guys."

"Oh really?" she laughs. "As far as I can tell, you're damn near virginal, even if you insist otherwise. Who's to know which way you swing?" Her smile fades. "But not with me. I just want you to go out for a night of fun with me and my friends. And at the end of the night, I'll tell you her name."

"Why?"

"Because you live up to your end and I'll live up to mine."

"No." I shake my head. "Why on earth would you want me to go out with *you*?"

She leans forward, her gaze intense. "Because I think you're capable of having a really fun time. You just need help."

While my friends have told me this so often it's become a mantra, hearing it from Tina feels slimy. "And if I'm not interested?"

She shrugs. "Suit yourself." She starts to leave again.

She probably doesn't know anything. Tina is a conniving bitch who likes to stir up trouble. But what if she really does have information? Her stipulation doesn't make any sense, but I'm willing to play along if I can get answers.

"Fine." But the thought of going out at all, let alone with Tina, makes me anxious. Before I even realize what I'm saying, I burst out, "But I get to pick the place."

She stands in the doorway, hanging on the frame. "Funny, Curly. But we're going to a bar. Not the park."

"It is a bar," I say. "But Southern students don't go there. I found it when I went out with the cast from the play."

She narrows her eyes. "Go on."

"There's nothing to tell. It's half a block from the theater downtown, full of locals." She looks skeptical. "And not old farts either. There were a ton of good-looking guys."

"What's it called?"

"Tony's Bar and Pub."

A slow grin lights up her face. "Okay, we'll go to your place. But if it's a bust we leave. Deal?"

Did I have a choice? "Fine." It was a spur of the moment decision. If I get into trouble, I hope that Ben is working and will help. I'll pull out the *I'm your boss's sister* card if need be.

"Don't sound so eager, Virgin Mary. Don't worry, I'll get you laid yet." She walks out, singing Madonna's *Like a Virgin*.

I cringe. Is that her game? I told her I wasn't a virgin, and she's determined to prove I'm not lying? One thing is clear: I'm treading on dangerous ground. I only hope it's worth it.

Chapter Twelve

Lexi

I feel like I'm walking through a landmine field. Caroline and Reed might have made up, but things are far from okay. Reed's secret is destroying us all. Caroline looks like she's lost weight from worrying so much and I've made a devil's bargain with the Southern University wild child. But the sooner I can get to the bottom of this mess, the sooner life can get back to normal. If it's not too late...

I'm not sure how to tell Reed I'm going out. But I've decided to wear the wig again. If I see anyone I know, they hopefully won't recognize me. And if I'm truthful with myself, it's an experiment. I want to see if it makes me feel different from how I did last Friday night.

After a dinner of take-out pizza, I head to my room to get ready. I take my wig into the bathroom, along with a hat. I pin my hair up and put the wig on, pinning it securely into place. Again, I'm amazed by the transformation and I haven't even darkened my eyebrows or put on more makeup. While I'm applying dark eye shadow to the crease in my eyelids, Tina texts me.

Be at my apartment at 8:30

That gives me forty-five minutes to finish getting ready and drive to her apartment. More than enough time. I finish my makeup and put the hat on, stuffing my black hair inside before walking the few steps from the bathroom to my room. Once I have the door closed, I look at the clothes in my closet, trying to figure out what to wear. I want this night out with Tina to fulfill her requirement, but I don't think I can be as wild as she wants me to be. I decide to go with a black knit dress that's clingy, but not too slutty, with a pair of gray tights. It's short enough that I can wear my coat over it to hide what's underneath. I pair it with a pair of black stiletto leather boots.

I still have twenty minutes.

I don't want to go out without my phone again, but Reed can still track me down if he figures out I'm missing. I figure out the best way to ensure he can't do that is to bring my phone but turn it off unless I need to make a call.

I leave a note on my desk saying that I left for a little while, but will be back. With any luck at all, I'll slip out undetected. Then if Reed comes to my room looking for me, he'll know I left of my own free will and wasn't abducted, because Lord knows that's where his paranoid mind will jump.

When I slip out the door and down the hall, Caroline is snuggled on the sofa, watching Gossip Girl, a pudding cup in her hand. Things are worse than I thought.

She glances up at me, taking in my hat and coat, and then turns back to the TV.

"Caroline?" I ask, sitting next to her. "Where's Reed?"

"He went out." Her voice breaks.

"He's not cheating on you," I say. "I know it."

She nods. "The Reed I know wouldn't even consider it. But he just took off after getting a phone call."

I don't say anything.

She keeps her gaze on the TV. "I heard a woman's voice on the phone."

"Caroline." I fight the tears burning behind my eyes. "I'm doing everything in my power to find out what's going on with him."

She turns to me. "Lexi, I know you helped get us together, but it's not your responsibility to *keep* us together. I love him more than anything, but I can't deal with these secrets. I think I'm going to move in with Scarlett for a little while to sort things out."

I grab her arm. "No. Please. Just give me a week, okay? Reed loves you so much."

"I used to think that too. Now I'm not so sure."

She sinks back into the cushions, looking sad and alone, and I vow to call Scarlett as soon as I get outside the door. "Aren't you going to ask where I'm going?"

"I don't want to know." She turns to me. "But have fun. And be careful. And if you need a ride home, please call me and not that bitch Tina."

If she only knew.

She takes in my stunned expression and turns back to her show. "Scarlett told me."

I give her a hug, hanging on longer than usual. "I love you, Caroline."

She gives me a squeeze. "I love you too."

On my way to Tina's, I call Scarlett. "Caroline's in bad shape."

"How bad?" she asks.

"Gossip Girl, second season. She was eating pudding cups since we don't have Ben & Jerry's."

"Oh, God. That is bad. Where's Reed?"

I hesitate.

"Lexi, where is he?"

"Caroline said he got phone call from a woman and left."

She curses for several seconds and I gasp because it's so unlike her. "I'm bringing her to my apartment, Lexi."

"No, wait, Scarlett. I'm sure he's not cheating on her. Give me the chance to prove it."

"Lexi," Scarlett says with forced patience. "If he's not cheating on her, then why won't he tell her what's going on?"

"I don't know." My heart is breaking into pieces.

"Caroline loves you almost as much as she loves Reed, but I can't let him continue to hurt her this way. I'm going to go get her."

"Scarlett, please. I asked Caroline to give me a week to get to the bottom of this."

"I know you mean well, Lex, but you're hurting her more by asking her to stay."

I want to cry.

"You can come stay with me too if you want. Tucker won't mind."

"I can't," I choke out. "I can't leave Reed." He's going to be devastated if Caroline moves out, not that he hasn't brought it upon himself.

"We're here if you need us."

"Thanks." I hang up and wonder how awkward it will be on Monday when Scarlett shows up at the lab for work. But I can't worry about that now. I'm pulling up to Tina's apartment and I need to focus on getting through tonight. I need the information she has more than ever.

I park my car and take off the hat, finger combing the tangled strands of my wig. When I think I look presentable, I get out and lock up my car, then climb up the steps to her second floor apartment.

I've barely knocked on the door when a large, muscular guy with tattoos and multiple ear and facial piercings opens it. He steps back and looks me up and down, his eyes lingering on my chest and legs before returning to my face. "Well, hello there, sugar."

My back stiffens. "Tell Tina that I'm here."

His pierced eyebrow lifts with a smirk. "And who might you be?"

"Alexa." The name is out before I realize I've said it. "She knows me as Lexi."

He opens the door wider. "Little Lexi. I've heard all about you. Come on in."

I'm not sure I like the sound of that and I sure don't like the way he's eying me. Against my better judgment, I walk into the apartment. Several guys and girls already here. The designated driver from last weekend is in the kitchen mixing himself a rum and Coke.

"Hey, Virgin Mary," he calls out when he sees me. "Let me make you a drink."

I cringe at the name. "No thanks, I'm good."

"Have a drink, Curly Sue," Tina says from behind me. When I turn around, her mouth drops open. "Whoa. What happened to your hair?"

"Nothing," I say.

She stands next to me, and grabs a strand. "This is the real thing, not some cheap drugstore knock-off. What's the deal?"

Caroline got it for me and while she can work magic with a budget, I'm sure it's high quality. But there's no way in hell I'm telling her the real reason I'm wearing the wig. I shrug. "You want me to channel my wild side. It seemed like a good first step."

She walks around me, looking me up and down. "I like it. Tonight's going to be *fun*." She grabs a red plastic cup from the guy who's making drinks and hands it to me. "Bottoms up, Curly."

My curls might be gone, but the nickname hangs on. I suppose it's better than Virgin Mary.

I stand next to the counter and take small sips of my drink while I wait for them to leave for the bar. Unfortunately, no one seems in a hurry.

"Have a seat, Alexa," The tattooed guy pats the space next to him on the sofa.

I lift my cup and give him a tight smile. "Thanks, I'm good."

"You might as well relax, Lexi," Tina laughs. "We're going to pre-game here for a while."

It takes all my inner strength to keep from rolling my eyes in disgust.

She sits on a bar stool close to me and takes another cup from the in-house bartender. "You gave me double rum, right Mikey?"

He holds out his hands. "Please. Of course."

She grins. "Good boy." She takes another gulp and then turns to me. "Let's lay down some ground rules."

I cross my arms, still holding my cup, and lift my chin. "That's a great idea."

"You will get drunk. If you don't, the deal's off."

"What the hell do you care if I get drunk?"

A slow grin lifts the corners of her mouth. "How can you have fun if you're not drunk? And that's the entire point of this endeavor—for you to have fun."

"Fine, I'll get drunk. What else?" I have no intention of getting drunk. There's no way I'm going to let myself lose control with this group. But Tina will have no way of knowing if I'm drunk or just acting that way.

"You have to sleep with somebody to prove you're not a virgin."

I set the cup down on the counter. "Then we're done." I spin around and head to the door, fully expecting her to call me back. This is far from the first negotiation I've handled, although it's undoubtedly the sleaziest.

As I expect, she grabs my arm and pulls me back. "God, you're so fucking touchy."

I jerk out of her grasp. "I'm not having sex tonight."

She picks up the cup and places it in my hand. "Drink." Her eyes are hard and the word is definitely an order.

I take a generous gulp and lower the cup. Give on the little things, hold firm on the deal breakers. "I'm still not having sex tonight."

She tilts her head with a grin. "Fine, it's not a requirement, but it's highly recommended."

"What else?"

"It's all business with you, isn't it, Curly?"

I take a sip to prove I'm following the rules. "I *am* a business major."

"Well, business as usual then." She laughs. "If you don't have sex, you have to make out with someone."

"A guy of my choosing."

"A guy or girl of mine."

I shake my head and look her in the eye. "A guy of my choosing. Or I walk."

"You really want the name of Reed's new girlfriend, Curly?"

"You know I do." But for some reason she really wants me to go out tonight—and in a big way—so I have some bargaining chips as well.

"Fine. A guy of your choosing, but he has to kiss you *and* feel you up."

The rum in the coke has hit my stomach, making a toxic brew with all the pent-up anxiety that sits there. "You're disgusting."

She laughs, but it's a hollow sound. "So I've been told."

I would feel sorry for her if she weren't so intent on making me do things I don't want to do. "Is that all?"

"I guess. We've got to start you off slow. There's always next time."

Next time? She actually thinks we're going to hang out again. "My turn."

She laughs. "You think you're in a position to make demands?"

"I'll stay out with you until midnight, and if I meet all of your requirements, you'll give me the name."

She shakes her head. "Midnight? We're just warming up. One."

I expected her to say two or three. "Fine."

"What else?"

"We go to the downtown bar I told you about."

"I already agreed to that this morning. Anything else?"

"No."

Her grin turns cold and hard. "Good, then finish that drink."

And that's when I know it without a doubt: I'm in deep shit. I drain the cup and Tina hands me another, even stronger than the first. "Are we ever going to leave?" I ask.

I'm sipping, but Tina is impatient. "We'll go as soon as you finish your drink."

I gulp it down. "Let's go."

Tina and her friends laugh and even though she told me we'd leave, it takes everyone fifteen minutes to get ready. When we walk out the apartment door, I question the wisdom of my stiletto boots, but it's too late to do anything about it now. I stumble on the steps and the guy who made my drinks steadies me before I fall on my face. He tries to grab my ass and I push his hand away.

"The night is young," he whispers in my ear.

I freeze at the bottom of the stairs, watching as Tina and her friends walk toward two cars. What the hell am I doing? I don't even know if she has real information for me.

Tina turns around and holds out her hands. "Come on, Curly. Let's go to your bar."

At least the bar is a public place. I hope more than ever that Ben will be there. If I order my own drinks, I can make sure they're non-alcoholic. I don't doubt that he'll help. Taking a deep breath, I join the group, proud of myself for not falling over.

I climb into the back of the car and Tina slides in next to me. The guy with the tattoos and piercings gets in next to her and they start making out before we leave the parking lot. He slides his hand up her thigh, under her skirt. My face flushes and I look out the side window when she begins to moan.

"Lexi," she calls my name.

I ignore her, but she calls my name again, more insistent this time. When I finally turn to look at her, her eyes are hooded and her breath is coming in short pants as he continues to rub her. "Are you into threesomes?"

"You're disgusting," I say again, turning toward the window as she moans louder. I'm sure she's doing this to make me as uncomfortable as possible and it's working. Maybe that's what this night is all about—humiliating me.

"Does that feel good, baby?" the guy asks her.

"Get me off and then you can play with Lexi," she pants.

"You touch me and I'll cut off your balls." My voice is deadly calm.

Tina laughs. "God, I think she means it. Curly Sue has some backbone after all."

It's not an idle threat. I'm shaking as the guy who's driving parks on the street half a block from the bar. As soon as the car stops, I open the door and stumble out onto the sidewalk. Tina's still in there, her moans increasing in volume as she comes.

There's no way in hell I'm ever getting in a car with her again. Ever. I'll have to find another way back home. Caroline offered to get me if I need help. I'll call her.

But that's hours away and now I'm stuck in this untenable situation. The thought of spending the next four hours with Tina and her friends makes me want to throw up. I gulp in deep breaths, fear and disgust rushing through my veins. I just need to get into the bar, and then I'll be safe. Ben will be there. If I feel threatened, I'll ask for his help.

I don't wait for Tina and her disgusting friends. I practically run into the bar and nearly cry with relief when I see him behind the counter.

Chapter Thirteen

Ben

Every time the damn door opens, I look up, hoping she'll walk in. You think I'd give up after two weeks, but hope fucking springs eternal. Apparently, I've become an asshat who spouts clichéd platitudes.

I'm an idiot.

Brittany thinks it's hilarious. She noticed what I was doing the night after she lost our bet. "Who you looking for, Masterson? Your dream girl?"

When I didn't answer, she grabbed my arm and literally squealed like a damn girl. "You are!"

"Shut up, Britt."

Of course she hadn't shut up, and was still teasing me mercilessly. So tonight, I've been fighting the urge to watch the door, which has proven harder than expected.

I'm pulling a draft beer when the bell on the door jingles and a cold wind gusts into the room.

Brittany stares at the door, her body stiffening. "She's here."

I instantly know who she's talking about. She's faked me out before, but this time something's different.

"Ben, I'm not joking," she murmurs, "and something's not right."

I spin around and see Alexa standing in the doorway, scanning the room with fear in her eyes. I'm about to go around the bar to check on her when the door burst open behind her and Tina walks in, her face flushed. An evil smile lights up her face as she loops her arm through Alexa's and drags her to a table. Three guys and a couple of girls join them, each one of them looking like they're full of piss and vinegar. They put Alexa between Tina and a big guy with tattoo sleeves on his arms and his neck. His ears are pierced and he has gauges. A dumbbell in his eyebrow reflects the light.

"I'm going over to check on them," I say, my anger rising.

"I was about to suggest the same thing," Brittany says.

I'm not a huge guy, but at six foot and one-eighty-five, I'm not a shrimp either. Still, it's easy to see that the big tattooed guy could take me out with one hand tied behind his back, never mind his friends.

How in the world did Alexa get mixed up with this group and how does she know Tina?

I stop at the edge of the table. "How is everyone tonight?"

"Well, I'll be damned," Tina says. "If it isn't Virgin Ben. What a coincidence. I was telling you all about Reed's sister—"

"It's good to see you again, Ben," Alexa interrupts. Her startling blue eyes lock onto mine and I suddenly know who she is, even if she desperately doesn't want me to. Her black wig has thrown me off. But I can tell it's not the only thing that's going on with her. She's genuinely upset about something.

"You sneaky devil, Curly Sue." Tina asks, leaning forward and looking into my face with a sly grin. "Is Ben the guy of your choosing? Because I wouldn't blame you. He's quite yummy." She licks her lips in a slow seductive manner.

I resist the urge to shudder. I'm not sure what Tina's talking about, but Alexa looks horrified. "I'm glad you came in. You left your scarf the last time you were here." I gesture to the back room. "I have it in back. Why don't you come get it?"

She starts to get up, but Tina grabs her arm and pulls her down. "Wait a minute." Her gaze travels from me to Alexa. "Whatever goes on between you two needs to happen within my view." She winks at Alexa. "I'm sure you're not surprised to find out that I like to watch."

Alexa blushes.

What the hell is Tina up to?

Tina crosses her arms on the table and rests her boobs on top of them, making her cleavage into an even deeper vee. "Why don't you just bring the scarf out to her?"

I refuse to visibly react. "She has to come back and describe it to me while I look at it. It's one of the bar rules."

Tina's grip on Alexa's arm tightens. "Lexi needs to get another drink in her first. She's falling behind. Maybe later."

Alexa glances away, resignation darkening her eyes.

I'm torn. I can tell she doesn't want to be with Tina, but she's not taking the opportunity to get away either. Still, I'm not ready to let this go. Something's definitely off. "So, what are you all doing here tonight? Don't you usually hang out at the Voodoo Lounge, Tina?"

She laughs and surprise widens her eyes. "Good memory, Benjamin. I invited Curly out with us and she demanded that we come here. Now I know why."

I'm curious about why she wanted to come here, but getting her away from Tina seems like the more important goal. "The band's about to start in thirty minutes. You owe me a dance, Alexa." I wink playfully, even as I resist the urge to clench my fists.

She looks up into my eyes. "Oh yeah. I'm counting on it."

Tina grins. "Remember, when you two crazy kids make out, I get to watch."

Alexa blushes again and the tattooed guy scoots closer to her.

"What can I get you guys to drink?" I fight to keep my voice even.

"*Alexa* and I will take a rum and Coke, double the rum in both."

Alexa shoots me a look of desperation again. Is this some hazing ritual? I'm pretty damn sure Tina's not in any sorority or even club for that matter. So why does she seem so intent on getting Alexa shitfaced. This is just wrong.

I finish taking the rest of their drink orders and head behind the bar.

Brittany sides up next to me. "Well?"

"Damned if I can figure out what's going on." I tell her what Tina said and how Alexa reacted. "She obviously doesn't want to be there, but she's not leaving either. I tried to give her an excuse to leave the table, but the only one Tina would accept was for her to dance with me. But if I actually do that, Tony's gonna have a coronary."

Brittany narrows her gaze on the table. "Don't you worry about him. First of all, he's not here, so he'll never find out. But even if he did, he's a big softie and he'll understand. How about I go in the back and offer the band a free round if they start sooner?"

"Good idea."

Brittany heads into the back while I take the drinks over to the table. I'm careful not to mix them up. "Double rum, on the house." I wink at Tina, hoping she doesn't check Alexa's drink. I only put enough rum in it to make it smell like alcohol.

"Careful, *Alexa*," Tina says. "I just might insist on a threesome after all."

Alexa looks like she's about to puke.

"I'm afraid I can only handle one woman at time." I force out a laugh.

"I'll be gentle." Tina laughs and her friends laugh with her.

"Yeah, I have the claw marks to prove that's a fucking lie," says a guy directly across the table from Alexa.

I serve the rest of the drinks and start a tab. To my relief, the band has come out and begun to warm up.

Brittany is back behind the bar wearing a shit-eating grin.

"They did this for a free drink?"

She shrugs. "I flashed 'em my tits too."

My mouth drops open. "You did *what*?"

She puts a hand on her hip. "It wasn't a big deal. Half of them have seen them anyway."

I'm shocked speechless and it takes me a couple of seconds to respond. "Thanks, Britt."

She shrugs again, looking uncomfortable in face of my gratitude. "Hell, it was nothin'. I'm pretty damn proud of these tits. I breast feed two kids and they're still perky."

I laugh. "That they are."

"You totally check them out, don't you?"

"I have balls and I'm still breathing. *Of course* I check them out."

When the band starts to play, everyone who wants a drink has one. It's the perfect time for a break.

"Go get her, Romeo," Britt says.

"Yeah." I wipe my sweaty hands on my jeans, surprised by how nervous I am. I walk around the counter and stop next to their table. "Alexa, I'm taking a break. Let's do this." I try not to sound too eager because I'm sure Tina will latch onto it and use it to her advantage.

"Yeah." She starts to get up, but Tina pulls her down again.

"She has to finish her drink first."

What the fuck is her deal?

The drink is half-gone and Alexa gulps down the rest. Tina belly laughs. "Damn girl. Don't be so eager."

She just pushes her chair back without saying anything and walks around the tattooed guy. He reaches out to grab her ass and she spins around, her face contorting with rage. "Don't you ever touch me again or I really will cut off your balls. Then I'll shove them down your throat." I have no doubt she would follow through on her threat.

The group at the table laughs and I grab her hand and pull her away to the dance floor. Britt has watched the entire interaction and she looks worried.

The band's first song is the furthest you can get from a ballad, but I need answers, so I pull her close, resting my hands lightly on her waist. Her hands lift and she seems unsure of where to put them. They land on my shoulders, trembling.

Now that we're here, now that she's in my arms, everything flees from my head and all I can think about is holding her. I breathe in her scent, a combination of apples and honey, and I realize I'll never smell this scent again without thinking about her. I'm the furthest you can get from a romantic, so the thought catches me by surprise.

"Thank you," she finally says.

Her words bring me back to reality. "Why are you with Tina when you obviously don't want to be?"

"It's a long story." She sighs and rests her cheek against my chest.

Her touch is electrifying and I suck in a deep breath. What the fuck is wrong with me? "I can wait you out all night," I say, "but I'm not letting you go back until you tell me." I'm not sure this is the right way to handle it, not after watching her threaten Tattoo Guy. She obviously bites when backed into a corner, but she has to know that I'm on her side.

She relaxes into me a bit and stumbles. My grip tightens on her waist to keep her upright.

"Sorry," she says. "Tina tried to get me drunk before we even left her apartment." She looks up at me, her blue eyes wide with gratitude. "Thanks for not putting very much rum in my drink."

I stare down at her, lost in the depth of her eyes. I give myself a mental shake. "You seem too classy for Tina and her group, so what's this all about?"

She continues to study my face as though she's trying to determine my trustworthiness. "She has something I want. Apparently, I have something she wants. Mutual need is the cornerstone of all business transactions." Her face has changed with this statement, as though she's weary.

"I know her from working with her in the math lab. Maybe I can help you and save you the grief."

Hope flickers in her eyes before resignation replaces it. "If it were that easy, I'd jump at the chance."

She won't tell me what she wants, so I decide to find out what Tina wants. "So she's giving you something in exchange for getting you drunk?" I ask. "That seems bizarre, even for someone like her."

Alexa looks away, her cheeks turning pink. "She thinks I'm repressed and wants to loosen me up. Why she cares, I have no idea. I'm not sure she knows either, other than that it's a game to her."

"What else does she want?"

The pink in her cheeks darkens. "I have to make out with some guy tonight. She has to see it."

"*Why?*" I knew Tina was sleazy, but this is unbelievable. Then a new thought bursts into my mind. "Who with? That guy you just told off?" My rage catches me by surprise.

She shakes her head. "No. I insisted it had to be a guy of my choosing. If it was him..." her voice softens. "I want this information, but I don't want it that bad."

I place a finger under her chin and tilt it up so I can study her face. "What makes this information so valuable to you that you'll go through with so much humiliation to get it?"

She hesitates. "Have you ever loved someone so much you'd give up everything for them?"

Have I? No, it's a sad fact, but there it is. I never really loved Sabrina. She forced the relationship on me, not that I fought it after we slept together at the frat party. She was good in bed and it was easy in the beginning, before her true colors started showing through the cracks of her lacquered persona. For a while I ignored the neediness and the constant bitching, expecting her to break up with me since I was no longer fulfilling her expectations of constant attention and socializing. And then when I ended it I paid the price for all those months of complacency. But when I look into Alexa's face, I realize I want that kind of love for someone. The all-encompassing, all-consuming, you can't think about anyone or anything else kind of love. This girl makes me think that kind of love is possible, especially with someone like her. And that scares the shit out of me. "No."

"Neither have I. I'd like to think I do, but honestly I don't think I would have done what he did for me. He gave up everything and this is my chance to make it up to him. So one night of humiliation is nothing. I can endure it to help him."

My chest constricts and I feel like I'm drowning.

She loves someone else.

I want to ask her who he is, but I don't want to know. Is it the guy she was with two weeks ago? It seems unlikely. They seemed too casual and he's not with her now. I'm more confused than ever.

The song ends and I look across the room, hatred filling every pore of my body for the person who's putting Alexa through this charade. Tina's watching us with amusement. I look down into Alexa's face and she steps away from me. Our song is done. Our commitment is up.

Only I'm not ready to let her go yet. Maybe I can save her at least part of her embarrassment.

I cradle her cheeks and stare into her eyes, looking for any sign that she finds my touch revolting. But her breath comes in short bursts and her pupils are dilated. My thumb strokes her right cheek bone, and it amazes me how smooth her skin is. I should stop prolonging my torture, but I don't want to hurry this moment. I want to sear it into my brain.

I lower my face to hers and her mouth parts in anticipation. Our lips touch lightly and I run my tongue along her upper lip. Her hands return to my shoulders as she takes a step closer, pressing her chest to mine, her mouth parting as she sighs. My tongue accepts the invitation, twining with hers.

Her arms tighten around my neck and I slide a hand behind her head. Blood rushes to my groin and the way she's pressed against me, she has to know I'm getting a hard-on, yet she doesn't step away. She presses closer instead.

Still, I take my time with the kiss, making it last. I want more, so much more, but we're on a dance floor, surrounded by at least thirty people, being watched intently by a group of perverts in the corner. I want to keep this pure. I want to take the thing Tina meant as a punishment for Alexa and turn it into something meaningful. At least for me. But the way Alexa clings to me tells me the experience has power for her too, even if it's just because she's sacrificing herself for some other guy.

I finally lift my head and stare into her lust-filled eyes and I want to curse the gods who put her in my path only to take her away.

"Thank you," she breathes out with a sigh.

"Do think that was enough to appease her?"

Her eyes cloud with momentary confusion. "Oh...yeah."

"If it's not, I want you to promise me that you'll ask me for help." I sound like a pervert myself, but the thought of someone like Tattoo Guy pawing her nauseates me.

She seems to understand my intention because she gives me a grateful look. Tears fill her eyes. "Thank you."

I want to kiss her again, to take her out the back door and away from Tina and her vile crew, but that's not what Alexa wants. I step back and interweave my fingers with hers. It takes every ounce of fortitude in my body to take her back to that table. When we get there, I pull out her chair to show this table full of disgusting low-lifes how to treat a woman.

Tina claps her hands. "I think there might be hope for you two yet." She waggles her eyebrows at Alexa, then looks up at me. "I told you Reed's—"

Alexa leans forward, her eyes wild. "I think I need another drink."

I stare at her in disbelief. She's trying to interrupt Tina because she thinks I don't know who she really is—Alexa Pendergraft, baby sister to that asshole Reed Pendergraft. And with a sigh, I realize it's better this way, all around, because I would throw everything away to get one shot with this girl.

Chapter Fourteen

Ben

I stuff down my disillusion and disappointment. This is for the best and the sooner I let her go, the better off I'll be.

Brittany shakes her head when I walk around the end of the bar. "Damn, Ben. That was ..." Her voice trails off.

I lift my eyebrows and she remains silent. I snort. "In all these months working together, I've never seen you at a loss for words."

She leans an elbow on the counter and looks at me with appreciation. "After that kiss, you make me want to rethink my rule about not dating coworkers."

"Drop it, Britt," I mutter.

She moves closer. "Why aren't you happy? Not only did your mystery girl come back, but she danced with you *and* you two shared one helluva a kiss."

"She's in love with someone else." I shake my head with self-disgust, my chest heavy. I've never felt this way about a girl before, and it's just my luck that I turn into a love-struck moron over a girl who belongs to someone else. Maybe it's karma.

Brittany tilts her head to one side and scrunches her face in disbelief. "Uh...I saw that kiss, Masterson. There's no fucking way that girl is in love with someone else."

"She says she is. That's why she's putting herself through this humiliation. Because Tina has some kind of information and Alexa's trying to find out what it is to help some guy."

Brittany's eyebrows furrow as she gives the situation thought. "You realize that makes absolutely no sense, right?"

"Tell me something I don't fucking know."

Tattooed Guy walks up to the bar and I swallow the urge to jump over it and beat the shit out of him. Not that I could.

"I need a couple of rum and cokes and another beer. And be sure to really load them up with rum." He looks over his shoulder with a leer. "After seeing you with her, I need to get her more eager, if you know what I mean."

"Perhaps it's the company that matters, not her level of intoxication." My statement is harsh and direct.

His smile fades. "What did you just say?"

Brittany pushes me aside. "Ben, I need you to go in back and bring out another CO_2 bottle. You know I can't lift those heavy things." Her southern accent is heavy as she leans forward, pointing her tits, which are hugged by her too-tight T-shirt, in Tattoo Guy's face. "I'll be more than happy to help you out, sugar."

I continue to glare at the fucking asswipe in front of me.

"*Now, Ben.*"

Brittany is right to make me leave, which only pisses me off more. Cursing under my breath, I head into the back to lug out a CO_2 bottle. Too heavy for her, my ass. I've seen her carry two canisters without breaking a sweat. She's learned how to move heavy objects around from transferring patients in and out of bed in the nursing home.

The storage room is too small, the air too stale. I can't believe I took her back to that table and left her there. With that fucking pig who wants to get her drunk and eager.

I'm suddenly desperate for air.

I leave the canister in the hall and step out the back door into the coolness of the night, hoping it will ease my mood. Why do I feel responsible for this girl? She's not mine and she's where she wants to be, but I suspect she's gotten herself into a more serious situation than she realizes. The real question is why do I care? I barely know her other than a couple of interactions. I sort through my head, trying to remember what Tina and Scarlett have said about her. I didn't pay much attention then, and I curse my short-sightedness. How could I see her in the math lab days ago without figuring out how I knew her? How could those blue eyes belong to anyone else?

Focus, Masterson.

Every time I've seen her here in the bar, she's worn that black wig, yet at Southern she's a blonde. Why the disguise, especially since she doesn't want me to know who she is?

She lives with her brother and his fiancée in an apartment and Reed keeps her on a tight leash. It's obvious he has no idea she's out with Tina tonight. In fact, I'm tempted to tell him and let Tina take the heat. But that would implicate Alexa, so for now I'll keep her secret. I know she's a sophomore business major and the student liaison for the Middle Tennessee Children's Charity, and that she's determined to establish a program for middle-school kids that I would have killed to attend at that age. She throws herself wholeheartedly into whatever she loves, whether it's a project or a person.

As I finish my list of what little I know about Alexa—Lexi—Pendergraft, I feel worse instead of better. It makes me want a shot with her even more.

Down, boy. She's taken.

So where the fuck is the asshole? Where was he two weeks ago when that actor from the play was ready to screw her on a table? Where is he tonight when she's putting herself in danger? For *him*? I don't know jack-shit about the fucktard other than he doesn't deserve her.

Instead of cooling off, I'm angrier than when I first came outside.

I take a deep breath. So what am I going to do about any of this?

No, the real question is what do I *want*?

But that's not a question, not really. I know I want her. I want to protect her from Tina and her group of miscreants. I want to get to know her better and to kiss her again, in private this time so it can go further. I hardly know her, and I'm not a love-at-first-sight kind of guy, yet I know deep in my gut that if I had a chance with her, we would have something amazing.

But she's Reed Pendergraft's little sister, and no matter how honorable my intentions are—four words not usually uttered in conjunction with my name—Pendergraft will never approve. He'll fire my ass before I can utter a word of protest, especially when he finds out about my arrest. Because I'm sure he'll dig that gem out and polish it until it's nice and shiny, blinding everyone within a two-mile radius with the glare.

No, Alexa Pendergraft is off limits. I've already let one girl nearly destroy my life. I can't make that mistake again.

I close my eyes and take a deep breath, trying to blow my tension away. Then I go back inside, determined to put her out of my mind. Hopefully her evening with Tina is a one-time venture. Chances are I'll never see her again unless she visits Reed and up until now she's only dropped by twice, once for him and once for Scarlett. If I make it through tonight, I can be free of her.

As I lug the CO_2 tank behind the bar, Tattoo Guy is walking back to the table, juggling the drinks and his beer.

"You didn't really put more alcohol in her drink did you?" I ask Britt as I start to replace the can.

She rolls her eyes. "I can't believe you even asked. And you're welcome for saving your ass. That guy would have beat you to a bloody pulp, not to mention that your uncle would have fired you."

I grumble my thanks.

"She won't be getting drunk *here* tonight, but what happens to her after she leaves is out of our control."

I nod. I hadn't thought that far ahead. Was she really going to leave with them? I don't like it, but there's nothing I can do.

Brittany leans against the counter, watching Tattoo Guy with a scowl. "But I don't trust that snake who got her drink. We need to watch him like a hawk."

More patrons enter the bar and we're working double time to keep up, making it harder for us to keep an eye on Tina's table. Alexa is still between Tattoo Guy and Tina and they've ordered quite a few drinks. I'm making a pitcher of margaritas for a group of mommies who look desperate for a night out when I see Alexa head back toward the restroom while Tattoo Guy makes his way to the bar. He sets one of the drinks I've made on the bar and pushes it toward me.

"Are you sure you're putting enough alcohol in these drinks? My girls aren't getting very buzzed."

I shrug as I wipe a spill off the counter with a rag. "Maybe they have a high alcohol tolerance."

"Well, they're switching to Long Island Iced Teas. And you better not be cheating me."

My stomach drops. I have no idea how to fake the alcohol content of a drink made almost entirely out of alcohol.

Britt casts a glance my direction, hurries to finish making the drink she's working on, then heads to the back. She returns just as I'm handing the new cocktails to the guy.

He's walking back to his table when she whispers in my ear, "I've warned her. I don't know what else to do. I tried to talk her into going home, but your girl is a stubborn thing. She refuses to consider it."

Your girl. Why do those two words catch my breath?

"I told her if she feels unsafe to let one of us know."

She makes her way toward a customer who's waiting at the bar, but I grab her arm. "Britt, thanks. Seriously."

She shrugs and grins. "I feel inclined to help because you're stuck on her, and this is the first time I've ever seen you show any interest in a woman since we started working together. But I also can't stand jerks like that who try to prey on vulnerable women. I'll bash in his head before I let her leave with him."

I'm not sure how Brittany plans to put this statement into action, and I'm afraid to ask.

We're so distracted by Alexa and Tina's group that we get behind, but we bust our asses to get caught up and get a few minutes to breathe. I look up the clock on the wall. Twelve forty-five. Only another hour and fifteen minutes until we can close. The stress of the evening has made me more exhausted than usual.

Britt is at the other end of the bar when she suddenly stiffens. I automatically turn to Alexa's table. She's trying to get out of her chair but Tattoo Guy is pulling her back down.

I'm around the bar and at their group before I even stop think about how to handle the situation. But when I reach the table, Alexa's trying to pull out of his grasp. "It looks like the lady wants to get up." I say, my back tense. "I suggest you let her."

Tina bursts out laughing. "Benjamin Masterson, wanna-be hero." She moves her hands in a shooing motion. "There's nothing to see here, so why don't you run along and leave us alone."

My gaze lands on Alexa. "Alexa, do you want to leave?"

She looks up at me with unfocused eyes, panic etched on her face. "Yes."

Tattoo Guy stands and puffs out his chest. "She came with me and she's leaving with me. I'd like to see you try and stop me." He reaches down and grabs her arm, pulling her up.

My vision clouds with my rage when she cries out. I start to lunge for him, but Britt's voice stops me.

"Let go of her *now*."

I cast a look at her out of the corner of my eye and see that she's holding a baseball bat.

Tattoo Guy hesitates, looking from Britt to me. I can see why. Britt looks deadly serious. Her eyes are steely focused and she's holding the bat like she's about to swing it at his head.

Tina stands and groans, rolling her eyes in disgust. "She's not worth the effort. Leave her."

The guy hesitates before releasing his hold and Alexa drops back into the chair, her body limp.

"Sorry, Curly Sue," Tina sneers, leaning over her. "You didn't fulfill your end of the bargain, so no name for you." She scoots around Alexa's chair.

"I suggest you don't step foot back in here," Britt says, following the group as they head toward the door. "Or I'll beat your sorry asses before I call the police."

"Yeah, don't you worry your pretty little head over it," Tina says over her shoulder. "This place is a *bore*."

They stomp out the door, slamming it behind them as I slide into the chair next to Alexa. Her head is floppy, her hair hanging in her face.

A guy in his twenties slinks over from a couple of tables away, his expression wary. He looks at the door, then back at me. "I think I saw him dump something in her drink."

He roofied her?

Britt lowers the bat and lets it dangle at her side. She plants her feet apart and glares at the customer. "*And you didn't think to tell someone?*" Several customers look over at her.

He cringes. "I wasn't totally sure, and if I falsely accused him, I doubt he would have let it go."

He's right and I wonder what I would have done in his situation. Damn if that doesn't stick in my craw.

"How long ago did it happen?" Britt asks.

"I don't know." He looks scared. He should be. I'm about to kick his ass.

She bangs the bat on the table. "Think harder."

His face pales as his gaze drops to the bat. "I don't know. Twenty, maybe thirty minutes."

"Come on," Britt grabs Alexa's arm. "Help me get her to the back room."

When I take her other arm and we lift her up, her legs are like noodles, barely supporting her weight. I sling her arm around my neck and we drag her down the hall to Tony's office. I set her in the desk chair and kneel in front of her. "Alexa, I'm going to call the police."

Her eyes fly open in panic. "No! No police."

"We have to report this, sweetheart," Britt says, leaning closer. "We can't let them get away with this and we need to get you to the hospital."

She shakes her head wildly and tries to stand. "No. Reed can't find out. *Please.*" Tears fill her eyes as she pleads with me.

"Who's Reed?" Britt asks.

I stand and lower my voice. "Her over-protective brother," I say. "And my boss at the math lab. He's already looking for a reason to fire me. If he finds out, I suspect he'll try to pin this on me somehow."

"Shit."

"Yeah."

Alexa is slumped across the desk. We're running out of time.

"What do you want to, Ben? Your call."

"If he drugged her, she needs to go to the hospital."

Britt leans her shoulder against the doorframe. "If he really gave her a roofie, she'll sleep it off in about eight hours. You could call a friend of hers to pick her up, but you're going to need to do it soon. At the rate she's going, I give her ten minutes tops before she's comatose for several hours."

I brush Alexa's hair off her cheek. Her eyes are closed, but she flinches at the contact. "Alexa, I want to call a friend to come get you. Who should I call? Scarlett? Caroline?"

Her eyes open, but her pupils remain dilated. "No. Please. They'll tell Reed."

"Ben," Britt's voice is low. "Take her home and end your responsibility in this. I'll grab her purse and we'll look up where she lives."

"Okay." I stay squatted next to Alexa, watching the rise and fall of her chest. She doesn't seem to be in any respiratory distress, thank God.

Britt returns moments later and hands me her small bag. "I need to get back out there. I'll check on you in a minute."

"Okay."

I dig through Alexa's purse and find her cell phone, a wallet, keys, and a tube of lipstick. I open the wallet and am surprised to find a Massachusetts driver's license with a Boston address. Alexa Nicole Pendergraft. According to her birthdate, she's twenty-two. I'd bet my ass it's a fake ID, but I have to admit that it looks legit. The wallet only has some cash and a debit card with her name on it. I pick up her cell phone, but the access is password protected.

I should call Reed and tell him she's here, but she begged me not to let him know, and I still suspect Reed will somehow try and pin this on me. I'll lose my job at the math lab. I tell myself it's an irrational fear, but I'm not so sure.

If I don't call Reed and can't call one of her friends, what am I going to do with her? Britt's right. I'm quickly running out of time before she completely passes out.

"Alexa?"

Her eyes remain closed.

"Alexa." I give her a shake and she rouses. "I don't know who to call to come get you. Who can I call?"

She tries to look at me, but her eyes look glazed and fill with tears. "No one. There's no one."

I'm at a loss and panic starts to claw at my chest. I definitely can't leave her in the office, and I can't dump her out on the street. Before I stop to think this through, I say, "I live a block from here. I'm going to take you to my apartment, okay?"

"Thank you." A tear escapes and falls down her cheek, and I feel more protective of her right now than I've ever felt about anyone.

"I have to tell Britt I'm leaving. I'll be right back."

She nods and leans back in the chair.

I run out front and look for Alexa's coat, which is still in the chair where she was sitting, and stop at the bar. "I'm going to take her home."

"Good call. I'll cover here," Britt says. "Be careful."

I realize she's misunderstood *which* home I mean, but I nod before rushing to the backroom. My apartment is a block away and I'm not sure Alexa can make it that far.

I pull her up. "Alexa, we have to get your coat on so I can take you to my place."

She tries to help, but her movements are loose and uncoordinated. Once we get it on, I button up the top buttons and hoist her to her feet. "Come on, Sleeping Beauty."

Once she's up, she leans into me and I guide her out the back door. The cold air seems to jolt her awake, so I take advantage of it and hurry her as fast as her feet will move in her skinny, high-heeled boots. Ordinarily, I'd appreciate her footwear, but right now it's a hindrance. If it weren't so cold, I'd take them off so we could move faster.

We've made it to my gravel parking lot when she starts to fade again. "Come on, Alexa," I say. "Stay with me. We're almost there."

She looks up at me, her eyes half closed. "I'm sorry."

"Don't say you're sorry, baby. Just help me get you to my apartment."

But her knees buckle and she's falling. I catch her before she hits the ground and it's apparent she's not walking any farther. I scoop her legs up with one arm and support her back with the other, then carry her toward the stairs. By the time I get to the second floor, I'm heaving and my arms are burning. Once I get to my apartment, I kick the door three times in rapid succession, praying my roommates are still up playing video games.

Seconds later, Austin opens the door, irritation on his face. "What the—" his gaze drops to the girl in my arms and his voice fades "—fuck."

"I'm about to drop her."

He moves out of my way and I carry her to my bedroom.

"Quick," I shout. "Grab a clean blanket and throw it on my bed." I can't remember the last time I changed my sheets and I'm not about to set her on disgusting bedding.

Austin disappears and returns with a blanket that he quickly spreads out over my comforter.

I lay her down as gently as possible, resting her head on my pillow. I unbutton her coat and wrangle it off her, tossing it in my ratty recliner in the corner. Her black dress has hiked up and I try to tug it down, but there's only so much fabric and it's not going any lower. I glance toward the hall and Austin and Noah are standing in the doorway, ogling her—their eyes wide, their mouths hanging open.

"Where did she come from?" Austin asks.

"Can we keep her?" Noah whispers.

I pick up a pillow and throw it in his face. "Hell, no we can't keep her. She's not a pet." I don't like how they're looking at her legs. They're covered in tights, but still...
"Get another blanket."

They continue to stare.

"*Now.*"

They jump and Noah goes this time, returning with a small quilt that he throws at me. I catch it and spread it over her, starting at her chest and stopping at her knees. Her boots look uncomfortable. Given her current drugged state I'm not sure removing anything other than her coat is a good idea, but in the end, I decide they have to come off. I've grabbed her right calf and am starting to unzip when Noah comes over and reaches for her other leg.

"Don't even think about touching her," I growl.

"I just want to help," Noah mutters.

"You just want to touch her, jackwad. Get away." I slip off the first boot and move on to the other leg.

"Seriously, Ben," Austin says. "What the fuck is going on?"

"Her name's Alexa. She's been in the bar before, so I kind of know her." Talk about stretching the truth. "She showed up tonight with a sleaze-ball I work with in the math lab and one of the girl's friends roofied her."

"Shit. Why is she here? Why didn't you call her roommate?"

"Because her roommate is Reed Pendergraft. She's his sister."

After Austin's run-in with Reed last fall, they know all about Reed Pendergraft's legendary surliness, just like everyone in the math department does. "Shit."

"Fuck." Austin moans. "You know how protective he is of her."

"Yeah," I sigh. "I know."

"So you plan on keeping her *here?*"

"I told her I wanted to call the police or take her home and she begged me not to tell her brother."

"Damn."

"Wait," Noah says. "I thought his sister was blonde."

I sit in my chair, watching her. "She is. Every time I've seen her in the bar, she's wearing a black wig. I have no idea why, but she thinks I don't know who she really is."

"But you said she asked you not to tell Pendergraft."

Leaning my elbows on my knees, I rest my chin on hand. "She was semi-conscious. I suspect she wasn't aware of what she was saying and won't remember in the morning." I glance up at them. "And if you ever speak to her, you will pretend like you never saw this and that you don't know who she is." I narrow my gaze. "Do I make myself clear?"

They hesitate and then nod.

"I'm going to watch her sleep and make sure she doesn't stop breathing." A cheery thought. Soon another one joins it. A girl who's been drugged has passed out in my room. If her brother finds out, I'm liable to end up back in jail and I may not get out this time. Sure, I didn't drug her and I have witnesses who'll testify that I'm innocent, but I didn't call the police. I didn't call *anyone*. I just took her back to my apartment. Where I could have done anything to her. The skin on the back of my neck prickles and I take a deep breath.

What have I done?

"Don't you have to go to work in five hours?" Austin asks. "I can take over watch duty."

The thought of him or Noah watching her sleep unfurls something dark and ugly inside me. I shake my head. "I'll call in sick or tell them I'll be in later."

"I didn't think you could afford to miss work," Austin says.

I get up and turn on a lamp on my dresser, flipping off the overhead light. "Don't you two have something else to do other than stand there and mentally undress her?"

They shake their heads. At least they have the decency not to deny it.

I shove them into the hall. "Well, I don't like it. Out." I shut the door and sit in my chair, watching the rise and fall of her chest under the blanket. Thank God she doesn't seem to be struggling to breathe. I lean back the recliner and try to stay awake, but my exhaustion soon takes over. As I fall asleep, I think about the irony. While I've imagined Alexa in my room a hundred times, this wasn't how I pictured it.

Chapter
Fifteen

Lexi

When I start to wake up my head is pounding and my mouth is dry. Pins are jabbing my skull and I realize I'm still wearing my wig. I try to roll over, but I feel uncoordinated and clumsy, like my brain isn't connecting to the nerves in my limbs. My eyes blink open and a moment of panic washes through me.

I have no idea where I am.

I try to sit up, but the pain in my head is too piercing. I lie back down and close my eyes, taking a moment to recover. I can feel clothing on my body, so I know I'm not naked, which gives me a small sense of relief. When I finally pry my eyes open, I see I'm lying on a bed and covered in a quilt. The room's a mess and it smells of guy and dirty socks. In the corner, a guy is sleeping in the ugliest recliner I've ever seen. I start to panic again until I realize who it is.

Ben.

An afghan covers only his chest and upper thighs and he's lying on his side.

How did I end up in Ben's room?

Surprisingly, I'm not frightened. I hardly know Ben, but I'm already certain that he would never hurt me. I close my eyes and try to remember what happened last night.

The first memory that hits me is dancing with Ben and his kiss, his incredible kiss. The mixture of disappointment when Tina said the kiss wasn't enough and the thrill of excitement when she told me that he needed to feel me up. Not because I have voyeuristic tendencies like she so obviously does, but because I wanted the chance to touch and kiss him again. But when she pressed me, I couldn't bring myself to ask him. He did me such a huge favor by kissing me. I couldn't embarrass myself or him anymore. I'd hoped Tina would relent and change her mind.

I was an idiot.

I was an idiot about lots of things. The last thing I fully remember is Ben telling Tina's friend to let me go, then everything else is a blur. Somehow Britt had a bat, and I remember Ben walking with me in the cold. But I have no memory of getting here. Looking around, I'm sure this is his room.

He brought me to his apartment.

He stirs in his chair, releasing a small groan. Guilt quickly replaces my initial feeling of panic. He spent the night in a chair instead of his bed. He could have slept next to me, but he chose the chair instead. My chest warms with gratitude and something else I can't figure out. Respect? Admiration? It goes deeper than that.

Before I can give it more thought, Ben stirs again and his eyes blink open. He jolts as though he hadn't meant to fall asleep, and sits up when he sees me watching him. "You're awake." He sounds relieved. "How do you feel?"

"I'm awake," I say, my voice scratchy. "I'm still trying to determine the rest."

He collapses the foot rest of recliner. "You need water." Hopping out of his chair, he opens the door and disappears down the hallway, returning with a glass of ice water. He sits on the edge of the bed, slowly as though he's afraid of startling me. "Can you sit up?"

I nod, but pain stabs my temples when I try. I close my eyes.

"Let me help." He sets the glass on the table and slides his arm under my upper back, gently pulling me into an upright position. "Let's take this slow."

When I'm sitting up, he doesn't drop his arm, just leaves it there to make sure I don't fall down again.

"Are you okay?" he asks.

"My head's pounding, but I can live with it."

He picks up the water and hands it to me. "You need to drink this. But not too much. I have no idea if it's like a hangover. For all I know, you might get sick."

I nod and take a sip, waiting to see if my stomach's going to stage a revolt. When it seems to react fine, I drink more.

After I finish, Ben takes the glass and sets it on the nightstand. "Do you remember what happened last night?"

I close my eyes. I want to go back to sleep and stay there forever. To take the humiliation of last night with me. I cringe. "God, I'm an idiot."

"Hey." Ben's finger is under my chin, tipping my face up. I open my eyes and stare into his green ones. "Don't do that."

"Do what?"

"Act embarrassed."

"It *is* embarrassing."

He cradles my side against his chest, his forehead against my temple. "You didn't do anything wrong."

I try to laugh, but it hurts my head. "I was stupid. Something very, very bad could have happened to me." And when I let myself think about what could have happened, I feel nauseated. "Thank you," I say and it seems so inadequate. Ben saved me from being raped, I'm positive

175

of it. I'm not sure I could emotionally survive something like that again. I know Reed couldn't.

"Right time, right place," he finally says, his forehead still resting against my temple.

"How did I end up at your place? I'm assuming it's your place."

"You begged me not to call the police. You said you were worried about your brother finding out. I didn't have any numbers to call since your phone's password protected and I didn't know what else to do, so I brought you home with me. I only live a block from the bar. I hope that's okay."

Reed. He's probably freaked out. How am I going to explain being gone all night? Maybe he didn't notice. Since Caroline started living with us, he's stopped knocking on my door to make sure I'm still breathing. For all I know, he never even realized I was gone.

I sneak a glance at Ben. He could have called the police and been done with me, but he helped me even though he owes me nothing. "Why are you being so nice?" My voice is husky. "You don't even know me."

"Maybe I want to get to know you better."

I want to get to know him better too. But there's the problem. I'm incapable of having a relationship. Brandon taught me that. Apparently, meaningless sex is all I'm capable of, and only when I'm pretending to be someone I'm not. I sag against him, disappointment shooting through my body.

"Are you still tired? Do you want to go back to sleep?"

My traitorous mind imagines lying on the bed with Ben. His comforting arm around me. The thought is dangerous. "What time is it?"

"Uh…" He looks around for his phone, finds it in the recliner and leans over to grab it. "Seven-thirty."

If Reed *has* figured out I've been gone all night, he's probably flipped his lid. The longer I put this off, the harder it's going to be. "I should go."

He doesn't say anything for a moment, instead his fingertips make slow back and forth movements under my shoulder blades. "Do you feel up to driving?"

"I do, but my car isn't here. It's in Tina's parking lot."

"*Tina's* parking lot?"

"I met her at her apartment."

"That reminds me." His hand stops its movements and I already miss it. "I have some bad news." His arm tightens around my back. "Tina wasn't happy when she left last night. She said she wasn't going to give you the name because you hadn't met all the criteria."

I close my eyes and suck in a breath. All that humiliation for absolutely nothing. Ben's finger resumes its soothing motion and I resist the urge to sigh. No, it wasn't for nothing. I'm here with Ben. And I can appreciate that at some level even if all I've done is inconvenience him.

"What name was she supposed to give you?"

"It's not important now. I suspect she never had one to begin with. She was just playing some sick, perverted game with me." But what if she *did* have a name? I blew it, yet I can't imagine handling everything differently.

"I'm sorry."

I don't say anything. There's nothing to say. I toss the blanket off and slide to the edge of the bed. Staring down at my stockinged feet, I try to remember what shoes I wore.

But Ben's already picking up my boots and handing them to me, looking like he's worried he's going to say the wrong thing.

I take them and stuff my feet inside, zipping them up. When I stand, I take it slow, trying not to wobble on the spiky, three-inch heels. Ben is standing next to me, holding his hand out as though he's afraid I'll fall.

"You okay?" he asks.

"Yeah." *No.* I don't want to leave him, but that's my selfish desire. I search his eyes. I'm not sure what I'm looking for, maybe some sign that he feels as drawn to me as I do to him, that he enjoyed our moment last night too. The room is charged and my hair stands on end and I ache for him to kiss me again. But he looks down and releases a barely audible sigh.

He hands me my coat next and I put it on, feeling an overwhelming sadness. I really like him and I'm not ready to leave him yet. But Reed's probably had a stroke by now, and I can't bear to keep him waiting any longer.

"I can just take a taxi to my car, Ben," I say, unable to look into his face. "I've inconvenienced you enough already." I cringe. "My keys are in my purse. Do you happen to know where that might be?"

He groans, rubbing his face with his hand. "I left your purse at the bar. And it's closed and I don't have a key. I'm sorry."

"Hey, you saved me from a group of barbarians. I don't expect you to be responsible for all my personal items too."

"I was glad to help you," he says. His hands are by his sides and he clenches them into fists and then shoves them into his jacket pockets.

"You didn't have to help me at all, but now your responsibility is done. So I'll just go home and come back later to get my purse."

A flicker of hope passes through his eyes. "I'm off on Mondays and Wednesdays. But I'll be there tonight and tomorrow night."

I can't stop the smile that warms my face. "Good to know. I'll make sure I stop by on a night when you're working." Although I suspect what little social life I've had is now history after this all-night stunt.

"Good," he says quietly, studying my face. "I'd like to see you again."

Heat fills my abdomen and spreads into my chest and lower. *He wants to see me again.* What I feel between us isn't in my head. Just my luck considering that Reed will probably lock me in my room for the next two years. Disappointment floods me again and I head for the door. "I really can call a cab, Ben. I don't want you to have to do anything else for me."

He's shoving his feet into the shoes by his recliner. "I've taken care of you for this long. Do you really think I'd drop my responsibility now? I offer door-to-door service." He tries to sound light-hearted, but I can tell how freaked out he was last night. And who could blame him? Some random girl gets drugged, begs him not to call the police, then he gets stuck with taking care of her. My cheeks blush with embarrassment. How is he not shoving me out the door already?

"Alexa." His voice is soft and he's standing next to me.

I look up at him, suddenly fully aware that I have to have the nastiest breath on the face of the planet.

"Please, don't be embarrassed. I wanted to help you. You have to trust me on that."

Why? Because Reed's his boss at his other job? But he's calling me Alexa, the name I gave him on closing night of the play. Surely he'd call me Lexi if he knew who I really was. In some twisted way, it makes me feel better that he's helping me for me and not because of Reed.

"Okay," I finally say softly.

"Are you hungry? Do you want something to eat before you go?"

I'm standing here wearing my coat, which means he's stalling. He really does want to be with me. Part of me really, really wants to stay here with him, but I can't do that to my brother. "No, I need to get home."

"Okay." He grabs a jacket and shoves his arms in the sleeves, then leads me to the front door. His apartment is older and it kind of smells. A stack of dirty dishes and plates fill the sink and counter in the kitchen. He follows my gaze and cringes. "I have two roommates. They're both slobs. I'm the neat freak…or at least I used to be before I started working three jobs in December along with my fifteen-hour course load."

My mouth falls open. "You work three jobs?"

His eyes widen like he's said something he didn't mean to say.

"I don't mean anything bad by that. Honestly, I'm in awe. I only have school."

"That's not true," he says, opening the front door. "You work with the charity. You're expanding their summer program and raising money for all the changes. That has to be worth two of my part-time jobs."

I step outside under a covered walkway and turn to stare at him. "You remember all of that?"

"Of course I do. How could I forget?" He takes the lead again, holding my forearm. "Be careful on the steps."

I haven't had any trouble walking since I left his room, but I like his hand on my arm, so I don't complain or try to pull out of his reach.

We walk toward an older sedan and Ben opens the passenger door for me. He waits until I'm all the way in before shutting the door and circling to the driver's side. After he starts the car, he scrunches his eyes shut. "I should have warmed the car up for you. I'm sorry."

"I don't mind."

He shifts the car into drive and stops at the exit to the parking lot. "Where to?"

I give him the simple directions to our apartment and then we drive in a silence that makes me both edgy and sad. "What's your major?" I ask.

"Mechanical engineering. This is my last semester, thank God."

"That explains the math lab job."

"Math nerd," he laughs. "Guilty as charged."

"I know two of your jobs—math lab tutor and hero bartender," I say. "What's the third?"

"I'm a janitor." He hesitates and I can tell he's embarrassed. "I clean at the Garrison building on Saturdays and a couple of other office buildings owned by the same janitorial service on Sundays."

Horror drains the blood from my head. "Oh, my God. You're supposed to be at work right now, aren't you?"

He gives me a soft smile. "It's okay. I can just go in late."

"I'm sorry." It seems so inadequate, but it's all I have to offer.

"Don't be. I'm not."

My chest warms again and I resist the urge to take the hand he's not using for steering and link our fingers together. I feel a connection to him that I haven't felt with anyone else. Is it because he saved me? Is this displaced hero-worship? As I sneak a glance at him, I know it's more than that. His kiss left an imprint on my lips that can't be explained away so easily.

I hope I haven't gotten him into trouble with his boss by making him late to work.

As I think about Ben's three jobs, I realize how lucky I have it. The only job I've ever had is working for my mother on her charity committees, but I never even got paid for those. Instead of waiting for permission from my parents to move out on my own, perhaps I should grow up and take care of it on my own. But Ben is right—my work with the charity takes fifteen to twenty hours of my time on any given week. How would I fit in a real job? Would it be better for me to work with the charity under the tyranny of Reed's rules or get a job and move out on my own?

Ben pulls into the parking lot of our building and turns off the engine. Before I can thank him for bringing me home, he gets out of the car and walks around to open my door.

"You don't have to walk me in, Ben," I say as he reaches down to take my arm and help me out.

"It wouldn't be door-to-door service if I let you out in the parking lot, now would it?"

The air is cold enough that I can see my breath and I shiver. He wraps an arm around my back and before I realize what I'm doing, I'm pressing myself into his side.

I'm glad he's walking me to the door. I'm not ready to leave him yet.

He stops at the outside door and waits for me to key in my security code. Instead, I turn to face him, grabbing his lapels in both hands. "You better not come up. My brother is bound to be...intense." I swallow. Talk about an understatement. "You've helped me so much. I really don't want you to get caught in the fallout."

He hesitates, then a soft smile lifts the corners of his mouth. "Okay."

I look up into his face, wanting to kiss him, but fearing I won't be able to give him anything more.

His hand lifts to my cheek, tucking my black hair behind my ear. "I want to see you again."

"You will," I force myself to tease him. "When I come back for my purse."

He glances inside the lobby. "Maybe I should go in with you. Just in case."

I shake my head in amazement. "If you had any idea what you're suggesting, you would turn around and run away as fast as you can."

An intensity fills his eyes. "I don't scare off that easily."

"No, I don't think you do."

We continue to stare at each other for several long seconds before I shift my gaze. I'm putting off the inevitable.

"Thanks again, Ben."

He kisses my forehead, his lips lingering before he pulls back. "I'd do it again in a heartbeat."

His tenderness is too much for me to resist. I stand on my tiptoes and kiss him. He's hesitant, as though caught by surprise. I slide a hand up his chest and behind his head and pull his mouth down to mine. One of his arms encircles my back and pulls me close; the other cups my cheek. Carnal need rushes through me, stronger than I've ever experienced with anyone, and I'm desperate to feel more of him.

He takes charge, his mouth demanding on mine, and I want to cry out of relief and happiness. He wants this too. He wants me.

Then he lifts his head, his pupils dilated with lust. He tugs on the loose strands of hair around my face. "If you need help with your brother, call me. I'm serious."

He tugged on my hair. My wig.

Oh God. He has no idea who I am. "Thanks," I force out, and my shaking finger keys in the code.

He grabs my arm loosely before I can disappear into the lobby. Ordinarily, the move would fill me with anxiety, but instead I have the urge to throw myself at him again. But I've deceived him with this stupid thing on my head. What will he say when he finds out the truth? Will he think it's some horrible trick?

He smiles down at me. "Try to come get your purse tonight."

I'm not sure how to tell him who I really am, but what I feel with him is worth pursuing. I'll figure it out. The biggest issue at the moment is how I'll get out of the apartment, but I'll move in with Scarlett if need be. Reed's overprotectiveness is a thing of the past. I offer him a shy smile. "Okay."

He pulls me into his arms again and kisses me as though tonight is twelve years away instead of twelve hours. When he releases me, a grin spreads across his face and he takes several steps backward. "Until tonight."

"Tonight." Without thinking, I touch my fingers to my lips, wondering how I'll go that long without seeing him. Then I realize the ridiculousness of the thought as I step into the lobby and push the button for the elevator.

I watch him walk back to his car before the elevator doors open and I step inside the empty car. When the doors shut, I pull the wig off my head, my hands full of bobby pins. I try to fluff out the mess pinned to my head as the doors open. I can't face Reed wearing this thing.

When the elevator reaches our floor, I step out and stare down the hall. Our apartment door looms ahead and I square my shoulders, ready to face the firing squad.

Chapter Sixteen

Lexi

When I reach for the door knob, I realize I can't walk in holding the wig. How am I going to explain that one to Reed? In fact, I have no idea what I even look like. I haven't looked in a mirror since last night.

Oh, God. What if Ben saw me with smudged mascara or drool crust on my face? In a panic, I reach up to wipe around my mouth and then run my index fingers under my lower eyelashes to wipe off smudges. Thankfully, nothing comes offs. I still have to deal with the wig, though. A fake plant stands in the corner by the hallway window. I stuff the hair piece and pins into the corner behind the pot, vowing never to wear it again. I fluff my real hair with my fingers, knowing it has to be a disaster. Great, when I walk in Reed's going to assume it's after-sex hair. I groan. There's no way this will end well.

Time to suck it up.

I don't have my keys, so I try the door knob, not surprised to find it locked. I knock on the door, cringing during the three seconds it takes Reed opens the door. His mouth drops open and he sucks in a breath, relief in his eyes. He pulls me into a tight hug. "Oh, my God, Lexi. I was so scared," his voice breaks.

"I'm okay. I'm fine." Now I feel like an ass for not calling him as soon as I woke up.

He hugs me for several seconds before pulling away, his hands bracketed on my arms. "What happened?"

I grit my teeth and offer him a tight smile. "I was just being a college student, Reed. Sometimes we hang out at parties all night and drink too much."

His eyes narrow. "Did you drink too much?"

"Yes, but I—"

"You can't do that, Lex." His voice rises in anger. "Do you have any idea of the danger you're in?"

For one brief moment, I think he somehow knows about Tina. But there's no way he could. Is he talking in general? Somehow the look of genuine terror on his face tells me no. "What are you talking about?"

He runs a hand through his hair and when he lowers his arm, he looks years older. "Lexi, there are things going on that you don't know about."

"No shit, Reed!" I shout, my temper flaring. "Why don't you start with the woman you've been talking to and meeting?"

His eyes widen and he gasps. "How do you know about her?"

I stumble backward and tears sting my eyes. "How could you, Reed?" I start to cry. "How could you cheat on Caroline?"

He shakes his head. "What are you talking about? I would rather face a firing squad than cheat on Caroline. How can you both think so little of me?"

"Then who is she?"

He turns away and shakes his head.

"Reed!"

"I want to keep it to myself for now. I don't want to involve you two."

"So you'd rather destroy your relationship with Caroline than tell her the truth?"

Tears fill his eyes and his expression pleads with me to understand.

"Reed, I'm begging you. Tell me what's going on."

He reaches for me and pulls me into a hug, his chin resting on top of my head. "Lexi, you can't disappear on me again. I was scared to death. I called the police to file a missing person's report, but they said I had to wait twenty-four hours. I would have needed to give them your real name."

I hadn't considered that. "You didn't need to call them at all. I'm a college student, for God's sake! I'm supposed to stay out all night."

"Not you, Lexi. Not now of all times."

This is the second time he's alluded to some special kind of danger. "Why not now? What's going on?"

"Lexi…"

And then I know. I know what he would keep secret even at the risk of losing Caroline. I blink, fear washing through me. "Why am I in danger?" He doesn't answer and I collapse into a chair at the kitchen table. "It's *him*."

Reed pulls a chair next to mine. Picking up my hand, he searches my face. "You have to trust me, Lex."

Tears sting my eyes again and I fight to catch my breath. I refuse to give into panic. "Is he *here?*"

Reed drops my hand and takes my face in his palms. "No, I promise Todd Millhouse is not in Hillsdale. The woman I've been meeting with is kind of like a private investigator. She knows where he is at all times. He's not here."

"Where is he?"

He wipes the tears from my cheeks and kisses my forehead. "Not here."

"Reed!" I jerk out of his grasp. "I'm not a child. You have to stop treating me like one. I have a right to know."

His face hardens. "Lexi, I know I've been unfair and unreasonable in my treatment of you. But if you can just bear with me a little while longer—"

I stand. "I have a right to know!"

He looks up at me, his face heavy with exhaustion. "He's not here, but he might get desperate enough to seek you out. Ms. Pembry thinks he knows where we are." He sits back in his chair. "The Monroe Foundation's involvement in the Southern fashion show probably clued him in. The national press coverage was great for the charity, but it didn't help us stay undercover."

"This is all my fault."

He grabs my hand again. "No. It's *his* fault. He's the criminal and he got away with it. But now he's looking for you and you have to lie low."

I take a deep breath. What have I done? "Why is he looking for me?"

He shakes his head.

"Reed!"

"He thinks you broke the confidentiality agreement."

That damn confidentiality agreement. When my parents convinced me not to press charges, I signed a statement saying that I would keep what happened a secret forever. I agreed because I had no desire to share my experience with anyone, but I've regretted it ever since. "I didn't! I swear!"

"I know, Lex. I know." He tugs on my hand. "And for the record, I'm not sorry you pulled the Monroe Foundation in for the fashion show. If you hadn't, who knows if Caroline and I would have figured things out? But it makes me feel guilty that the very thing I'm grateful for is what's putting you in danger."

My nails dig into his hand. "You have to tell Caroline! Why would you keep this from her? Or me? I can handle it, Reed, and so can she."

He pulls out of my grasp. "I can't, Lexi. I'm handling it and I don't want either of you to be complicit."

Complicit? My heart stutters. "What are you doing?"

"It's safer if you don't know."

"You're doing something illegal."

He stands. "Lexi, let it go."

I jump up and grab his arm. "Reed!"

He gently shakes me off. "Now you know why I was so scared. And now I have to call Ms. Pembry because she has a team of people looking for you. They found your car in the parking lot of Caroline's old building." He turns to me and his voice breaks. "Did you go try to find her?"

"No." I shake my head. "She's really gone?"

He swallows. "She packed a bag this time."

"You have to tell her the truth!"

"I don't want her to know *anything*. If there's some kind of backlash, the less she knows the better. We're not married and she would be forced to testify against me. And worst case scenario, if she knows some of it, they won't believe she doesn't know all of it and they'll charge her too."

I swallow a sob. "Oh, Reed. What are you doing?"

"I'm taking care of you. Just like I promised." He starts for the hall then stops. "I have to call Ms. Pembry. I'm begging you: Don't leave the apartment this weekend."

"Okay," I say, numb with fear and guilt. How did this turn into such a tangled mess? But as soon as Reed closes his bedroom door, I immediately break my promise and open the front door and rush to the planter to grab my wig. If I'm in real danger, this disguise might be the way to escape notice when I see Ben again.

Because, no matter what, I have to see Ben again.

Chapter Seventeen

Ben

I'm watching the damn door at the bar again, but this time my heart feels a lot lighter than it did before.

Lexi's coming to see me tonight.

Ignoring the fucking fact that seeing her *at all* will endanger my math lab job, I'm ecstatic. Optimistic. Hopeful. Which isn't like me. Not since Sabrina.

But Lexi is different. Tonight I'll tell her that I know who she is. I want her to know I don't care what color her hair is or what nickname she uses.

Britt steps around the bar, thirty minutes late. "Thanks for picking up the slack."

"You covered for me last night. We're good. But you're not usually late." I look up at her. "Everything okay?"

"Yeah. Of course." But she doesn't look at me. "The kids' dad is watching them tonight, and he was late."

My mouth drops open. Never in the months I've known her has she mentioned their father. "They have a dad?"

She scrunches her nose and snorts. "Of course they have a dad. They weren't hatched from spores, you idiot."

I shake my head. "Well, of course they have a father… It's just…"

She whacks my arm. "Yeah, I know. He's a lowlife, but he says he had a *come to Jesus* moment and wants to be part of their lives." She narrows her eyes. "And yeah, I know, it's not a great sign that he was late."

I hold up my hands in defense. "Hey, I'm the last person to judge. Especially after what happened with Sabrina."

She raises her eyebrows in surprise. I don't usually mention her name. I prefer to pretend she doesn't exist. Which is impossible, given that my entire life changed because of her.

A customer approaches the bar and Britt takes his order.

I whip around when the door opens again, but my shoulders sag when a couple walks in.

"What's got you so freaking uptight?" Britt asks, pouring a glass of wine.

She's going to figure it out soon enough, so I might as well tell her. "Alexa's coming by."

She finishes pouring and sets the wine bottle on the bar. "Did you tell her friends your name and number?"

My back stiffens. "No."

She takes a step closer. "So, you left her a note explaining what happened?"

I hesitate. "No."

Her eyes narrow as she looks into my face. "Then how do you know she's coming in tonight?"

"She told me this morning. After I took her home." I prepare myself for her tongue lashing.

"You told me you were taking her home."

"I did. You just misunderstood which home."

She shudders and moves closer. "Fuck, Ben. Do you know what serious shit you could have gotten yourself into?" Her voice lowers. "After your arrest—"

"I know. But I didn't know what to do. And my roommates were there all night—"

"You were putting them in danger too!" She shakes her head. "Damn it, Ben."

I take a deep breath and release it, then rest my hands on her shoulders. "I know. You're right. But Alexa knows what happened. She thanked me for helping her and not calling her brother." I've been thinking about her all day, worried about Reed's reaction. Why didn't I think to get her cell number so I could call and check on her? Once she shows up at the bar tonight, she's not leaving until she gives it to me.

Britt stabs her finger into my chest. "You're damn lucky."

A grin spreads across my face. "I know."

Horror fills her eyes. "Oh, my God. You didn't screw her did you? Even if she consented, she was still drugged—"

I take a step back. "What? *No!* God, no. Do you really think I'm a perv?"

She closes her eyes and blows out a breath as she opens them. "No. But I saw that kiss and I know how you feel about her."

"She slept on my bed. I slept in my recliner in the corner. After she woke up, I took her home."

Britt lifts an eyebrow with a smirk. "And? Because you look far too happy to have just driven her home."

My cheeks start to feel hot. Good God. Am I *blushing*? I turn my back to her. If she sees me blushing, I will *never* hear the end of it. "She kissed me goodbye and told me that she wants to see me again. She's coming in tonight because I forgot her purse in the office."

She elbows me. "Did you forget it on purpose?"

I shake my head. "No. I was worried about getting her to my apartment before she completely passed out more than anything. I had to carry her upstairs."

"Ben Masterson, savior of swooning women."

"Shut up, Britt," I say, but there's no bark behind it. I'm feeling good. She might have been here for another guy last night, but she kissed me this morning and told me she was coming to see me. Maybe she realized the asswipe isn't worth her sacrifice.

A couple of hours later, Lexi still hasn't come in, but I tell myself not to worry. It's only nine o'clock and maybe she wants to spend time with me after I get off work. That's a *good* thing. She's probably coming in later.

But after another ten minutes go by, the door opens and I suck in my breath when I see who's there. Turning my back to the door, I lean into Britt's ear. "I need you to cover for me. Lexi's brother just walked in."

She scowls. "If you're serious about this girl, you're going to have to deal with her brother eventually."

"I know. I'm not a complete idiot. But I need to make sure Lexi's ready for him to know. He's likely to give her extra grief if he knows that we're involved. Not to mention, I have no idea what she told him about last night."

"Just say you didn't see anything," she grumbles.

"And that's a fucking lie. I don't want to do that."

"This is not a way to start a relationship, Benjamin," she hisses. "You are not fucking Romeo and Juliet."

"God, I hope not. They both died at the end."

Reed has been standing at the counter for several seconds, and although I'm certain he hasn't heard us, I wouldn't be surprised if he's pissed about waiting.

"Go take care of him and I'll go in the back and check on..."

"Shut up." She scowls. "*Go.*"

I hurry in the back and find Lexi's purse on the desk where I left it. I wish I could enter my number into the contacts on her cell, but I have no idea what her password might be. I consider putting a note with my number in her purse, but I'm worried Reed will find it. I wasn't lying when I told Britt I didn't want him to know about me before Lexi tells him. The fact that he's here and she's not is telling enough.

Britt comes back in a couple of minutes with an exasperated look on her face and snatches the small bag from my hands.

"That bad?" I ask.

She shakes her head and disappears down the hall.

I go out a few minutes later, checking first to make sure the coast is clear. Reed is gone and Britt is busy making a drink.

"Well?" I ask.

She tilts her head to the side. "He doesn't seem that bad."

"*What?*"

She glances over her shoulder at me. "He's a big brother, worried about his little sister. He knew her purse was here. He produced ID to prove he's her brother. She told him that she came here with friends and then left and went to a party. He asked if I remembered her." She pauses and doesn't continue.

"*And?* What did you tell him?"

"I told him that I remembered her dancing with a guy, but I didn't see her leave." She makes a face. "Both the truth."

"I owe you."

"You're damn fucking right you do."

We get slammed shortly after our conversation and I don't have time to think about Alexa until we're close to last call. I know she's not coming to see me tonight. I hope it's because Reed has grounded her in some way—though it's crazy to think her brother would have that power—and not because she's changed her mind.

When she doesn't come Sunday night, I begin to worry.

Scarlett's quieter than usual when I show up at the math lab on Monday. When Reed comes in, he ignores her. In fact, he ignores everyone, heading directly for his office and shutting himself inside.

"Is it just me or does he seem frostier than usual?" I ask.

"It's not your imagination." She pauses. "It's bound to get worse. His fiancée left him this weekend and moved in with me and Tucker."

"Fuck," I whisper. Now I'm really worried about Alexa. "Is Lexi okay?" I ask.

Scarlett gives me a curious glance. "When I talked to her on Friday night, she seemed upset that Caroline was leaving, but she understood." She pauses. "I didn't realize you and Lexi had become friends. You didn't even know who she was when she was here last week."

Shit. How can I explain this one? "She seems like a sweet girl. I just know Reed has a temper... I'd hate for him to take it out on Lexi."

She releases a low laugh. "You don't have to worry about him hurting Lexi. He wouldn't touch a hair on her head. The only problem between them is that he smothers her to death. And though I understand why he does it, he can't guard her forever."

"Why does he treat her like that?"

Her face pales and she gives a nervous shrug. "Oh, you know. He's just a typical protective big brother."

She's lying. Scarlett's the last person I'd expect to lie. What doesn't she want me to know?

"So why did his fiancée leave?"

Scarlett bristles. "That's a personal question."

"I can wait and ask Tina. I'm sure she'll tell me."

"Fine," Scarlett grumbles. "I'd rather you hear the truth. Not Tina's whacked-out version. Caroline suspects that Reed is seeing someone else. So she left him and moved in with me." She lowers her voice. "Lexi is devastated. She loves Caroline like a sister."

I remember Scarlett and Tina talking about how Lexi got the Monroe Foundation involved with the fashion show to get Reed and Caroline together. My chest tightens as the pieces fall into place. "I bet she'd do anything to get them back together," I whisper.

"Yeah. She probably would."

Oh, Alexa. Tina must have offered to tell her who Reed was seeing. She was trying to help her brother and Caroline. I suspect that Tina doesn't even have a name, but I plan to find out the truth.

The realization follows that *Reed* is the person she was trying to help last night, the one for whom she risked everything.

She's not in love with someone else.

Relief and something like happiness flood through me, but more questions than answers storm through my head. Before I have time to give it more thought, several students pour into the math lab at the same time to look for assistance. While Scarlett and I help the first two students, the others wait in chairs against the wall.

Reed comes out and waves a student over, ignoring Scarlett and me. We all stay busy answering questions and helping the students with equations.

Tina saunters in about an hour later, a wicked look in her eye. She sucks on the tip of her finger then drops her bag and takes a seat.

My heart thuds against my ribcage. She could easily rat me out. Of course, she'd implicate herself in so doing. She has much more to lose, but she acts like someone who doesn't give a shit. And that makes her dangerous.

When Reed's student leaves, Tina leans away from the kid she's tutoring, an ornery grin on her face. "Say, Reed. I bet you can't guess what I was doing Friday night."

My breath becomes shallow and it's hard to concentrate on the student I'm helping.

Reed scowls. "Your personal life is none of my concern…or interest."

She rolls her chair closer to his table, stopping on the opposite side. The student she was helping is watching with confusion. "I hear Sweet Caroline has flown the coop." She rests her elbows on the table, folding her hands underneath her chin. "After hearing the nightly Reed and Caroline sex show in my apartment for weeks, I decided I made a mistake by cutting you loose so soon."

I can't hide my shock. *Reed and Tina dated?* I mouth to Scarlett.

She cringes then holds up one finger. *One time*, she mouths

That's one date more than I would have expected.

"This is neither the time nor the place, Tina."

"The things you say in the bedroom, Reed Pendergraft." Her eyes twinkle. "You are a *very* naughty boy." She laughs. "I suspect little Caroline is too sweet for you."

I shake my head. I can't believe she's saying these things. In front of all these students. In front of *anyone*.

Reed's body stiffens. "Tina, I suggest that you think carefully about what comes out of your mouth next, or I'll slap you with sexual harassment charges faster than you can blink."

She stiffens, then shoots a wink in my direction. "Then I guess you don't want to hear my juicy gossip about Lexi."

Reed's cold gaze doesn't waver from her face. "*No*. I do not."

Tina gives him an exaggerated pout. "That's too bad. Because it's all about..." She pauses and winks at me again before turning back to Reed. "The charity fundraiser she's organizing. She wants to auction off people for dates." Her eyes widen in mock disgust. "Auctioning people off as though they're cattle. What kind of behavior is that?" She tsks. "You should talk to her about sexual harassment."

Reed's eyes darken with anger, but he stays silent.

"I hear she wants a representative from every department." She smiles wickedly. "I was going to suggest Ben, but if you're really single now, maybe *you* should climb back on that horse." She leans forward, lowering her eyelids in a seductive pout. "And some of us horses *love* to be ridden hard."

Scarlett gasps and I'm surprised I haven't gasped myself. Tina is in full-on self-destruct mode.

"Tina," Reed says in his coldest, most formal voice. "You may collect your things. You service is no longer required here."

Her eyes narrow. "I don't think you want to do that."

His face remains cold. "I just did."

I find myself in the unique position of cheering Reed on.

Tina rolls back to her table and picks up her bag as everyone stares at her with dropped jaws. "This isn't over, Reed." She turns her gaze to me with a steely look. "This is *far* from over."

Chapter
Eighteen

Lexi

I'm such an idiot. Why didn't I think to get Ben's phone number before he left on Saturday morning? Now that I know I might be in actual danger, I'm more understanding of Reed's paranoia. Even so, I'm tired of being under house arrest by Monday morning. I know Ben works in the math lab. I just need to find out when.

I know just the person to ask.

The problem is that Scarlett doesn't know that Ben and I have gotten to know each other. Is she going to think it's weird if I ask her about his schedule? Then I realize I have the perfect excuse. The charity auction I'm organizing. The committee meeting I've just left has decided to move forward with the auction. We're putting it on an accelerated track, with the goal of making it happen in two weeks. Right before spring break. We've received permission to use the student union on Thursday night and we plan to auction off thirty students, equally divided between men and women. Now we need to get attractive students to take part. It makes me feel shallow to even think about that, but we'll make more money if the participants are cute.

I don't get a chance to contact Scarlett until later in the afternoon. I know she's working, so I text instead of calling.

How's Caroline?

I haven't contacted either of them since Friday night, partly because I'm worried I'll confess Reed's secret. I hate to admit that I understand his reasoning, even if it hurts Caroline. I spent all of Sunday trying to get him to tell me what his illegal plans are, but he just pressed his lips together and refused to answer. I pleaded with him to stop, to realize that revenge wasn't worth the risk, but his eyes turned cold and hard.

"This isn't about revenge, Lexi. It's about ensuring that you're safe and that you remain that way."

I need to figure out a way to stop this madness before he ruins his life, but I'm at a loss. The one person who loves him even more than I do can't know any of it. I have no idea who can help.

I watch my phone for ten minutes before Scarlett answers.

As well as can be expected.

That tells me precisely nothing. Caroline's probably a distraught mess and all because of me. I text back.

Can you call me when you get a chance?

It takes her another minute to answer.

Yes, I need to warn you about something that happened today.

My heart jolts and I force myself to take a breath. I can think of half a dozen things she might need talk to me about and none of them are good. Did Tina tell Reed I went out with her on Friday night? Does he know about Ben? Reed didn't mention anything when he came home with my purse the other night, thank God, but Tina might have blabbed. I won't be able to deal with the guilt if Reed fires Ben because of me.

The only thing I can do is wait.

I go back to our apartment and it feels lonely and sad. Reed has a late class on Mondays and Caroline is usually here when I get home, keeping me company while I make something for dinner. My heart is heavy with the loss of her cheerful smile. I've spent so much time thinking about moving out that I never gave any thought to how much I would miss my brother and his fiancée.

My phone rings as I'm making myself a sandwich. I answer on the second ring, relieved to see that it's Scarlett.

"Hey, Scarlett. How's Caroline really?"

"She's a mess. She went to classes today, but she's barely functioning."

"Reed's not cheating on her," I say, hoping my words are emphatic enough to convince her. "I know it."

Scarlett sighs. "Lexi, I know you mean well, but your insistence isn't helping Caroline. So unless you have actual proof, please let it go for now."

I do have proof—Reed's word—but I know that won't mean anything to Scarlett. And I can't tell her about Ms. Pembry's real identity. It would only lead to questions I can't answer right now.

"I was going to call to give you a warning," Scarlett says, an edge to her voice. "Tina went nuts when she came in to work today."

She pauses and my stomach knots. "What did she do?"

"She knew that Reed and Caroline were on a break, although I'm not sure how she found out. In any case, she told Reed she was sorry she let him go after one date—as though he would have gone out with her again anyway," she says in disgust. "He only went out with her that once because he was upset that Caroline wouldn't date him."

Her words only make me sadder.

"She told him about your charity auction and how you want to include someone from each department. She said she was going to suggest Ben until she heard that Reed was single again. She made some very rude and inappropriate statements. Reed warned her to stop or he'd file sexual harassment charges against her."

"Oh no."

"Tina seems determined to commit academic suicide lately, but I still wasn't prepared for what happened today. She said something else disgusting and Reed fired her. Ben and I spent the next hour giving statements to human resources to back up Reed's claim that he was harassed."

I hesitate. "Did she say anything else? Anything about me?" I worry about piquing her curiosity, but I'll be sick with worry if I don't find out.

"No...wait, she did. Tina said she had some juicy gossip about you, but Reed said he wasn't interested." She pauses. "What does she know about you?"

Crap. "She saw me out at a bar getting drunk on Friday night," I say. "She probably wanted to tattle on me."

"Be careful, Lexi." Scarlett's voice lowers to a whisper. "I know you want to break free of Reed's overprotection, but don't swing too far the other way."

Scarlett would freak out if she knew I was out with Tina that night. I know Caroline would. But Tina seems to have kept my secret. For now. I suspect she will use it to her advantage somehow. How could I not foresee this? Especially since Tina didn't get what she wanted. "I won't, Scarlett. I was just being a college student. Caroline is always saying she wants me to have the full experience. Getting drunk and partying is part of it." Little does she know that I spent Friday night doing everything in my power to *avoid* getting drunk.

"We're still your friends, you know," Scarlett says softly. "Caroline misses you."

My throat burns. "I miss her too." I swallow the lump that's become lodged in my throat. "Say, do you happen to know Ben's math lab schedule? Or maybe his phone number?"

She's silent for a moment. "Why do you ask?"

I take a deep breath, hoping I sound convincing. "Tina was right about the charity auction. I want to ask Ben if he's willing to participate."

She goes quiet again. "I'm not sure that's his kind of thing."

"You never know." I try to sound cheerful. "He might be willing to do it since it's for a good cause." I stop myself from telling her that he seemed interested in the expansions to the charity's summer program when I told him about it at the bar.

"Don't get your hopes up. Ben doesn't seem the joiner type and he's pretty busy with all his jobs."

"We'll see."

She laughs. "You don't like hearing no, do you? I don't have his phone number, but I can tell you his work schedule. He works Monday, Wednesday, and Friday from two to five-thirty. And Tuesdays from ten to noon."

"Thanks, Scarlet."

Now that I have his schedule, I just need to figure out a time when Reed won't be there. Tomorrow morning will be my first opportunity.

But after class the next day, my advisor sends me a short e-mail saying that he needs to see me right away. I'm nervous when I show up at his door. Am I in trouble?

"You want to see me, Dr. Tyree?" He looks up and smiles and I let myself relax.

"Yes, I have some great news. We almost have enough funding to start accepting applications for courses from instructors. And this has all happened in less than a month. Great work, Lexi."

My face stretches into a grin. "Thank you."

We discuss more logistics of the program—the actual applications process for both the instructors and the students. When we finish, I promise to drop by the charity to tell the director the great news.

When I leave his office, I realize it's after noon. I've probably missed Ben, but I decide to stop by the math lab anyway in case he's running late. He's not there when I show up, but Reed is in his office, staring at the wall.

"Reed?"

He blinks before turning to look at me. "Oh, Lexi." He offers a smile, but it's forced. "What are you doing here?"

I sit in the chair across from him. "Checking on you." I feel badly about lying, but seeing him like this has me worried.

He sighs and leans back in his chair. "I wanted to talk to you anyway. I've set up a document that will take effect if something happens that prevents me from staying with you."

Fear stabs my chest. "Reed, stop talking like that."

He turns to look at me. "I've set it up so that my trust fund will continue to pay for your education and the apartment until yours kicks in at twenty-one. In case Mom and Dad decide to pull rank and make you come back home."

I swallow a sob.

"I'm sure Caroline will come to stay with you. If not..." His voice fades.

I drop to my knees in front of him and grab his hand. "Reed, whatever you're doing. Stop. I need *you*, do you hear me? *I need you*."

He shakes his head. "It's too late."

One of the tutors I don't know stands in the door. "Reed, I need to ask you about that tablet you ordered."

Reed stands and pulls me to my feet. "Go to class and then head home. I don't think I'm going to be back tonight." Then he walks out of his office, leaving me in a state of shock.

Since Reed is one of the most level-headed guys I know, I had hoped he would come to his senses, but I should have known better. He won't stop until he's sure I'm safe. I have to do something.

If Reed won't listen to me, maybe he'll listen to Uncle Robert. Reed has always been close to our uncle, but the two grew even closer when my brother disappointed my parents by announcing he intended to teach college math instead of joining the family business. Uncle Robert could relate all too well; he had forsaken his birthright, handing the CEO position of Monroe Industries to our father so he could pursue his dream of becoming a wildlife photographer. If anyone can talk sense into my brother, it's Uncle Robert. The only problem is getting ahold of him. He's often out of the country for his job.

As I walk out of the building, I pull out my cell phone and pull up his number. I nearly cry with relief when he answers.

"Hey, Lexi," he says, sounding cheerful. "How's my favorite niece?"

In most cases, this would be an oxymoron, but my father and Uncle Robert have a sister with two daughters. "You know you're not supposed to say things like that, Uncle Robert," I tease.

"Why not? The truth will set you free, Alexa. Now what's got you so down?"

I can't help but smile. "How'd you know?"

"I know you, girl, you and that rapscallion brother of yours."

"He's what's got me down, actually. I'm hoping you can help."

He pauses and sounds more serious. "What's going on?"

I tell him everything... I know Reed will be furious, but at this point I really have nothing to lose. "I'm hoping maybe you can talk to him," I say through my tears. "I can't let him ruin his life this way."

He releases a heavy exhale. "I'll call him, Lexi, but you and I both know that once your brother makes up his mind about something, there's little chance of changing it."

"But you have to try. *Please*, Uncle Robert," I beg.

"I'll do better than call him. I'll come see him."

My tears fall down my cheeks. "I don't think he'll be here. He said he didn't think he was coming home tonight."

"Where's he going?"

"I don't know."

"I'll try to get to the bottom of this. I'll let you know as soon as I find anything out."

"Thank you," I say before I hang up. Though I'm still worried—desperately so—I feel as if a giant weight has been lifted from my shoulders. At least someone else knows, at least someone else is trying to fix this mess.

The rest of the day is a blur. So many people are suffering because of me and I don't know how to fix any of it.

The apartment is lonely and I make sure the alarm is set. Reed's paranoia has seeped into my psyche since he told me Todd Millhouse is trying to locate me. What will I do if he finds me? How will I defend myself?

When I finally go to bed, I still haven't heard from Uncle Robert. I'm tempted to call him, but I know he'll be in touch as soon as he can. I need to be patient, difficult though it is. I feel like I need to do something else—anything—but I'm at a loss.

I try to get some sleep, but I toss and turn for hours. With everything weighing on my mind, one person rises to the top.

Ben.

I want to see him. Does he think I changed my mind? Did he change his? My world is crashing down around me, but he's all I can think about.

I think about our kiss on the dance floor and the way he brought me home. I want to kiss him again. I want to tell him who I really am and, amazingly enough, I'm tempted to seek out his help. Maybe it's because he went out of his way to help me last weekend, or maybe it's because I know he's interested in me, but I'm sure he'll help even though we haven't known each other for long. But if I ask him for help, I'll have to share everything. There's no way I can do that, is there?

I glance at the clock on the bedside table. One-thirty. Ben's probably just about to get off work at the bar.

I want to go see him.

It's crazy, and I know it. It's one-thirty on a Wednesday morning, and Reed told me to stay at the apartment. I *cannot* do this. Yet I'm climbing out of bed anyway.

I go into the bathroom and look in the mirror. My blonde hair is a mess from rolling my head around on my pillow and my face is free of makeup. I can't go to him looking like this.

I can't go to him at all. The last thing I should do is involve anyone else in this mess that my life has become.

Grabbing the counter, I close my eyes and take a deep breath. Maybe what I felt with him was in my imagination. What better way to find out than to go see him?

It's not safe, I remind myself. Disappointment settles in my chest, stealing my breath, but some rebellious part of me rises up. Yeah, a crazy asshole *might* be in Hillsdale, but he's probably not. And a million other awful things might happen that I have absolutely zero ability to control. I might get hit by lightning. Or a car. Or drop dead of a heart attack.

I'm tired of hiding, of letting my life be defined by this apartment.

I take a breath as excitement ignites in my stomach. I'm doing this. I'm really going to sneak out in the middle of the night to see Ben. But I need to be as safe about it as possible. I'll wear my wig, which will give me some protection and keep Ben from going into instant shock.

It takes me twenty-five minutes to get ready and five of those minutes are spent trying to figure out what to wear. I settle on a pair of jeans and an ivory sweater since it's cold outside. I stare at myself in the mirror. I look like me, but not. More exotic and less girl next door. What if Ben doesn't like the real me? What if he prefers Alexa and the wig?

There's only one way to find out.

Chapter Nineteen

Ben

I'm exhausted as I walk out the back door of the bar. Uncle Tony still hasn't replaced the second weeknight bartender. He's been staying past his day shift into the evening to help, but after seven, it's just me and the dishwasher and the part-time cook. Thankfully, there weren't many late-night customers tonight, so I started to close the place early. But now it's ten minutes after two and all I can think about is my bed. The cold air jars me awake as I briskly walk the block home. My gaze is on the ground as I start up the steps to my apartment, but something draws my eyes up. I stop mid-step.

Alexa is standing at the top of the stairs.

She doesn't say anything as I climb toward her, and I take slow steps in case she's a mirage and will disappear as soon as I reach her. Her hands are stuffed in her coat pockets and she twists them as she watches me climb. She's nervous.

When I reach her, I'm not sure what to do. I know what I want to do. I want to take her in my arms and kiss her. But I can't ignore the fact that I haven't seen her since Saturday morning. I need to wait and find out why she's here. It's two o'clock in the fucking morning. Not a normal time to show up on someone's doorstep.

She looks up and fear and longing alternate in her eyes. Fear. Why is she scared?

"Alexa? What's wrong?"

She shakes her head and wraps her arms around my neck, pulling my body against hers. She looks into my eyes before her eyelids sink closed and she presses her mouth to mine. She's tentative, as though she wonders if I want this too.

My exhaustion vanishes and I'm caught by surprise, but it doesn't take my body more than half a second to catch up. I pull her close as I take over the kiss, telling myself to slow down before I scare her. But telling myself to slow down is like using a garden hose to put out a raging inferno.

I want her like I've never wanted anyone in my life.

The thought is both exhilarating and frightening. But I still can't ignore that it's two o'clock in the morning. How did she escape from her brother? Maybe the more important question is *why*.

I make myself drag my mouth from hers and look down into her face. Her eyes are still closed and her breath escapes in rapid short bursts of white vapor. "Alexa."

She releases a heavy breath, and then her eyes flutter open and she looks up at me through thick dark lashes.

"Why are you here?"

Her cheeks flush and fear flickers in her eyes again before she looks away.

I grab her face and lift her chin. My gaze pins hers. "Are you in trouble? Why do you look scared?"

Her eyes turn glassy. "I worried you wouldn't want me anymore. I didn't come to get my purse and I—"

I pull her against my chest as my mouth claims hers again. The saying *action speaks better than words* seems appropriate here.

Her hands thread through my short hair and hold me pressed against her, as though I would ever dream of pulling away.

My own hands roam her back, one of them capturing the back of her head. I can't get enough of her. I'm like a man who's been starved for days and then given a feast.

She lets go of my hair and lowers her hand to my waist, slipping it under my shirt. I jump from the cold and try not to tense as her fingertips slide up and dig into my back.

I pull away and disappointment covers her face, but I drop my hold on her and snag her hand in mine. "Let's go inside."

She doesn't say a word, just follows me through the front door. I stand in the thankfully vacant living room, unsure how far she wants to take this. If we sit on the sofa and things get carried away, Austin or Noah might come out and find us, but if I take her to my room she might think I only want her for sex. While the dominant thought in my head is to strip her naked, a rational part of my brain tries to rein me in. I don't want this thing between us to just be about sex. I want something more with her. Talk about a one-hundred-and-eighty degree change from Sabrina.

She senses my hesitation and takes the lead, tugging me down the hall to my room.

I flip on the light switch just inside the door and my bedside lamp turns on. Alexa pushes past me and shuts the door behind her. As she looks at me, her fingers rise to her coat, unfastening the buttons, top to bottom. I watch in fascination as she tosses the jacket behind her. It lands on the floor, but she doesn't pay attention as she pulls her thick sweater over her head, leaving her in jeans and a black lacy bra.

My breath catches in my throat as my blood rushes south. My erection strains against my tight jeans and I ache to unfasten my zipper, but I'm too hypnotized by the striptease in front of me.

She kicks off her shoes and then unfastens her jeans. Hooking her thumbs in the loops, she pulls them down and lets them drop to her feet.

Then she looks at me with a question in her eyes, as though I would find her lacking. As though she might not be beautiful enough for me.

I want to tell her she has nothing to worry about. She's gorgeous. Her wig frames her face and falls lightly over her shoulders. The black of her lingerie is a sharp contrast to her pale skin. Her face has less makeup on it than the other times I've seen her with the wig, but she doesn't need it. I want to tell her she doesn't need the wig either. I know who she is and I don't care. I don't care that Reed is her brother and that I'm risking my job by getting involved with her. I don't care about anything but making her mine.

But my tongue lies at the bottom of my mouth, thick and useless as a slug. I can only take in her beauty and thank God she came to me. That I have this shot with her.

She must see the longing in my eyes because she lunges for me, pulling my face down for a kiss.

I kiss her back, my arms reaching around her back and pinning her to my chest. She frees her arms and grabs the bottom of my shirt, tugging it up and over my head before her mouth claims mine again and her hands start to play with the waistband of my pants.

I reach to help her, but she bats my hands away and pushes me back against the door with a thud. I barely have time to hope my roommates don't wake up before she grabs my hands and presses my palms forcefully against the door.

I'm about to come in my pants.

She takes a step back, her eyes on my face. I keep my hands in place, watching and waiting to see what she'll do next.

She reaches for my jeans, taking her time as she unfastens the button on top and slowly unzips them, her thumb rubbing along my erection.

I try to hold back a groan, but she hears and looks up at me with a hesitant smile that turns seductive. She tugs my pants to the floor and I'm left standing pressed against my bedroom door in my briefs.

She looks at my bulge and smiles before reaching down and taking me in her hand. After several strokes, she releases me and pulls my briefs to my thighs. When she bends down, I expect her to pull them off and one hand does, but her mouth finds the tip of my dick. Her tongue circles it as the rest of her mouth closes around me.

This time I don't try to stop the groan that explodes from my chest. I reach for the back of her head out of instinct, but she grabs my wrist and pins it to the door as her mouth continues to drive me insane.

This is like every fantasy I've ever had rolled into one. I have no idea how long I'll last, but now that she's here and more than eager, I want to bury myself in her. But if she keeps teasing me this way, I won't last another minute.

"Alexa." I reach for her shoulders and pull her back up. "I want to be inside you." But as soon as I say the words, I wonder if that's not what she wants. Maybe she was hoping we would get off this way.

But when she stands, she kisses me and then leads me over to the bed. I sit down and she pushes me onto my back.

I have to be dreaming, There's no way she's in my room, taking total charge. But she slips off her bra and panties and straddles me, rubbing herself over my erection.

Oh fuck.

I try to roll her onto her side so I can rub her, but she digs her knees into the mattress.

Okay, she really wants to be on top.

I'm sure as hell not complaining. Instead, I sit up and move my legs over the edge of the bed. Grabbing her hips, I lift her up and reach between her legs to rub her. "God, you're so wet already." Grabbing her shoulders, I pull her breast to my mouth, my tongue finding her nipple.

She moans and her body tenses as she starts to lower herself on top of me.

"I need to get a condom." I grab her ass with both hands and stand, setting her on top of my dresser while I pull out the top drawer on the side and grab one. Thank God I still have some. I didn't use them for the last several months I was with Sabrina.

Alexa takes it from my hand and opens it, pulling me close so she can roll it over me. Then she wraps her legs around my waist. I'd take her right here, but the height is wrong. Instead, I pick her up again and sit on the edge of the bed with her on my lap.

She puts her knees on either side of my spread-apart thighs and cups my face with her hand, looking into my eyes with a longing that is nearly my undoing. Then her mouth lowers to mine and her tongue teases my lips as she sits on the tip of my erection and slowly begins to lower herself.

The feeling is both tortuous and elative. I grab her hips as she begins to move, taking more and more of me inside her with each movement. Soon I'm buried inside her as our tongues become tangled and it's not enough, not nearly enough. I'm not sure I'll ever be deep enough inside of her to feel complete.

I slide my hand up her back, my fingers digging into her shoulders and pushing her down. I'm not sure how much longer I'll last, but I think she's close from the sounds she's making and the intensity of her movements. I feel her tense and her nails dig into my arms as she releases a sound that tells me she's coming.

And that's my cue to let loose. I want to turn her over and get even deeper, but she seems adamant about her position. Instead, she pushes me on my back and partially lies on top of me, her knees still straddling me. I grab her hips and help guide her, pushing deeper and deeper until I come with a loud groan.

Alexa continues to move and I hold her still. Finding her mouth, I kiss her with a passion I don't usually have after sex. It's as though I can't get enough of her.

She's still on top of me so I ease her off and onto her side. She looks up at me with a mixture of lust and uncertainty. How can she be uncertain of anything after that?

"I'll be right back," I say, pushing into a sitting position. "Don't go anywhere."

She doesn't say anything as I climb out of bed, a difficult task given the fact that I'm sated and my exhaustion has returned with a vengeance. I want to lay down and fall asleep with her in my arms.

I clean up in a hurry and head back to my room. Alexa's still on her side, but she's put her bra and panties back on and she's propped up on her elbow, her head in her hand. She watches me with those intense eyes as I lie down next to her, my fingers trailing down her arm.

"I was starting to worry that I wouldn't see you again," I finally say, lying back on the pillow and closing my eyes. Sleep has already grabbed hold of my brain and is sucking me under. I wrap an arm around her back and pull her head to my chest. "Not like *this*."

"Ben," she whispers. "There's something I need to tell you."

But her words are becoming jumbled in my sleep-hazed state. The next thing I know, the alarm on my phone is going off.

And Alexa is gone.

Chapter Twenty

Lexi

I let myself into the apartment and head to my room, stripping my wig and throwing it onto the dresser. I've begun to hate it. It has given me freedom in so many ways, yet it now makes me feel trapped.

I tried to tell Ben about the wig and who I really am, but he fell asleep within seconds of laying his head on the pillow. I watched him sleep for at least ten minutes, my fingertips smoothing the worry lines around his eyes. He works three jobs and goes to school, which is obviously exhausting. I robbed him of precious sleep by going to him tonight, but I'm not sorry. Perhaps that makes me a terrible person, but I'll live with it. I wouldn't trade our night together for anything.

I pull all the pins out of my hair and dump them on the dresser, then strip out of my clothes and climb in bed naked, pulling the covers to my chin. This is unlike me too, but tonight I've given myself over to carnal pleasure.

I close my eyes and remember touching Ben…and the way his hands and his mouth felt on my body. Heat spreads through my abdomen and lower, and I suppress a groan. Now I wish I hadn't left him. But I have no idea when Reed will be back and I don't want him to worry. Not now.

The truth is, I didn't plan what happened with Ben. I wanted to talk to him and tell him the truth, but once I saw him standing in front of me, I suddenly worried he'd be pissed when he found out about my lies. And in that moment, I realized how upset I would be if he walked away from me. So I went with my instincts and kissed him. And then I did so much more.

When I examine my behavior in his room, I wonder if I should be embarrassed. The way I took charge isn't considered normal. Women are supposed to be submissive, right? Yet I enjoy sex most when I have the power. No, *enjoy* is the wrong word. Sex with Rob was enjoyable. Sex with Ben was *euphoric*. I know it's because I'm developing feelings for him. I'm fairly certain he feels something for me too. All the more reason I can't let this deception continue. The longer it does, the more likely he'll be upset.

The guilt and worry of my deception make it difficult to sleep. My body still tingles with awareness and I wish again that I hadn't left Ben. He was naked when he climbed into bed, and I spent time exploring his body and his face before getting up to leave.

As I think about pushing him down on the bed and straddling his legs, my breath comes in short pants. Before I realize what I'm doing, my hand is reaching between my legs. My therapist has suggested that I try masturbating to regain power over my sexual feelings, especially after my experience with Brandon, but this is the first time I've done it. It's funny that I can take charge sexually with two different guys without feeling shame, yet I hesitate to pleasure my own body.

Forcing my tense muscles to relax, I start to touch myself as I think about my experience with Ben. I'm so sexually charged that it doesn't take long for me to come. I lie on my bed, concentrating on my body's reactions—my thudding heartbeat, my shallow breath, and the contractions that shake my body—I'm amazed at the progress I've made.

But do I still need the damn wig?

I'm not wearing it now and I've achieved an orgasm after only a couple of minutes. But what if I freak out with Ben if I try having sex with him without wearing the wig? I'll be even more humiliated that I was with Brandon.

I finally get to sleep and when I wake it's around seven-thirty. I put on a robe and search the apartment for any sign of Reed, but his bed is still made and it doesn't look like he came home at all last night.

What could he be up to?

My head is full of worry as I take a shower and get ready for the day, yet there's nothing I can do now. I still need to figure out how and when to tell Ben. I need to stop Reed from whatever madness he has planned and get him to tell Caroline the truth. I pray she'll still be willing to listen.

When I get out of the shower, I see that I have a missed call from Caroline. She's also sent me a text message asking me to call her back as soon as I can. Curious, I dial her number immediately.

"Caroline, is everything okay? " I ask when she answers.

"Yeah," she says, sounding distracted. "Everything is… okay." She pauses. "Reed called me this morning and asked for a favor. It concerns you, so obviously I said yes."

"What is it?"

"He said he had to go to Boston for a few days. He wanted to know if I'd come back to the apartment and stay with you."

"Oh." Boston? Why hadn't he told me? Did this have something to do with whatever illegal activity he had planned? "You don't have to do that, Caroline." I want nothing more than for her to come back to the apartment, but Scarlett was right. I need to put her needs before my own. She still thinks Reed is seeing someone else and coming back here would hurt her. "I'm a big girl. I can stay by myself."

"He seemed more…insistent than usual."

"Really, Caroline, you don't have to. I'm protected by two alarm systems—one on the outside door and one in the apartment. What's going to happen? If I get a paper cut, I'll be sure to call you and ask you to take me to the hospital."

"I would hope you'd call 911 first," she says in a teasing tone.

"Seriously, Caroline. I'm fine. I miss you like crazy, but I'm a big girl."

"I miss you too." Her voice breaks. "Maybe we could meet for lunch this week."

"Yeah, I'd like that."

"I hear you're making progress with the summer program for the charity."

"Yeah." I force myself to sound cheerful. "I can't believe how well it's coming together."

"Well, I can," she says. "You're probably the most determined woman I know. If you want something to happen, nothing stands in your way."

Everyone says that, so why can't I stop Reed? "Yeah," I say. She's right. Why am I sitting around waiting to find out what Reed's up to? It's time for me to take charge. "Thanks."

"Let me know when you can meet for lunch."

"Okay." But as I hang up, I'm already rushing down the hall to Reed and Caroline's room. I'm not surprised his laptop isn't here. It's like an appendage for him, but I don't need the laptop itself. Just the passwords to access his accounts, which I realize won't be so easy to figure out. But surely there's clue somewhere—all I need is a single bread crumb—to point me in the right direction.

I feel like scum for invading his privacy. In spite of all his protectiveness, he'd never search my room like this. I tell myself that this is different, that Reed's life is on the line. And I know that's not an exaggeration. His future rides on whatever plan he intends to carry out. And I need to stop him.

After ten minutes of searching, I find a torn off piece of graph paper in the pocket of a pair of dirty jeans in his laundry basket. A long distance number is written in Reed's neat handwriting. Could this be Ms. Pembry's number? It could just be the number to a math department in another university, but my gut tells me that it's not.

I head back to my room and open my laptop, then run a search for the number. It's for a cell phone based in New York City. Deeper investigation shows the area code is for Manhattan. I suspect it belongs to Ms. Pembry, there's only one sure way to find out.

I dial the number.

I hold my breath while the phone rings and I worry that I'm calling too early. It's only 8:30, but New York is Eastern Time, making it an hour later. Still, I'm not prepared for the voice on the other end of the line.

"Hello?" He sounds groggy, like he's just woken up.

I don't answer. I can't. I'm too numb with fear.

"Who the fuck is this?" he asks, sounding more awake and irritated.

I still don't respond, but I can't make myself hang up either. I just hold the phone to my ear like a dazed idiot.

He pauses. "Why does the area code 931 look familiar?"

Oh God. He has my number.

That snaps me to attention and I pull the phone away from my ear, pressing the end button.

I've given the man who raped me my phone number. He has enough money to connect the dots, so I've practically led him to my front door.

My phone starts to ring and I drop it on the bed, filled with the irrational fear that he can reach through the line and grab me. I force myself to take a deep breath. He doesn't know it's me. Why would I call him? He's only calling back because he's curious about who called and hung up. That's all.

The phone stops ringing and I watch it for several minutes, waiting for the ding that indicates an incoming voice mail. But it never happens. I nearly collapse with relief. There's no way he knows it's me. My voice mail message is just the generic automated recording with my number.

It was close call, but it's over.

I glance at the time on my phone. It's already 8:45. I'm going to be late for my nine o'clock class and I still haven't finished getting ready. I pile my hair into a bun and pull a knit hat over it, swipe on a bit of mascara and blush, and then grab my bag and run out the door.

I arrive five minutes after class starts, but the teacher doesn't seem to notice my late entry. I sit in my usual place next to Sylvia. She leans close with a smirk. "I suppose you want the first three minutes of lecture notes you missed."

"Uh…yeah." I say, taking out my notebook. I need to focus, but all I can think about is that phone call.

"Are you okay?" she asks. "You look like you've seen a ghost."

"What?" I shake my head. "No. I just overslept and I'm running behind."

"Okay…" She doesn't look convinced, but soon we're both busy taking notes. Thankfully, by the time class is over, I've gotten ahold of myself and Sylvia seems to have forgotten.

"We have an hour until our next class," Sylvia says as we walk out of the room. "Do you want to go to the Higher Ground and copy my notes?"

"Sounds good." I was planning to call Reed, not that I expect him to tell me anything, but I need the notes and I'm cold. Coffee will warm me up and help revive me.

There's a line when we get to the coffee shop, not that I'm surprised. But after we get our drinks, there's nowhere to sit. I turn to Sylvia to suggest we return to the business building when I hear Ben's voice.

"Alexa."

My back stiffens. He's here and he knows who I am. But does he really? My hair is stuffed inside my hat. Even so, to see him like this—after last night…

Sylvia peeks at him from over my shoulder. "It's the bartender from the bar we went to after the play. I didn't know he went to school here. And did he call you Alexa?"

I shrug and lower my voice. "Sometimes I use full name—Alexa—because it sounds more professional."

She narrows her eyes as though she isn't sure whether to believe me.

"Can you give me a moment?" I ask. "I need to ask Ben if he'll take part in the auction to represent the math and engineering department. He seems kind of hesitant, so it might be better if we don't gang up on him." I have no intention of asking him to do this, but it's a good enough excuse to justify talking to him alone.

Sylvia gives him another look and a slow smile spreads across her face. "Okay. Although you might want to save him for yourself. He's pretty cute."

My cheeks start to burn. Great, I'm about to turn around to face him and I'm blushing. "I'll keep that in mind." I give her arm gentle push. "Now go. I'll see you back in the business building."

She heads for the door and I take a deep breath before turning around. He's sitting at a table with an open book and a notebook. His eyes are on me as I move toward him, but his face is expressionless. What is he thinking?

I stop at the side of the table. "Hi," I say, softly. My heart is about to leap out of my chest.

"Can you sit for a minute?"

I take the chair opposite him and set my coffee cup on the table. Is he surprised to see me? As Alexa I never told him I went to school here, but he never told me that he did either.

He looks down at his notes and licks his lower lip. He's nervous. For some reason that puts me more at ease.

"History, huh?" I ask.

A slow grin spreads across his face as he looks up at me. "Yeah. It sucks to take one of your worst subjects the second semester of your senior year. No pressure."

"Oh. Maybe I should let you study."

He grabs my hand when I start to get up. "No. Please stay," he pleads.

"Okay." I settle back in my chair, but he doesn't let go of my hand.

He swallows, looking nervous again. "I'm sorry about last night."

My heart stops. I think I'm going to die right here in the middle of the campus coffee shop.

He sees my expression and his eyes widen in panic. "No! That's not what I meant... I'm not sorry about last night." He pauses and lowers his voice. "I'm sorry that I fell asleep." He closes his eyes and cringes. "God, I sound like an idiot."

I flip my hand over and weave my fingers through his. "No, you don't."

His gaze falls to our joined hands and then flicks up to my eyes. "I'm still sorry about falling asleep. And I'm sorry that you were gone when I woke up."

I break eye contact with him. "I had to get back."

"To your brother?"

I look up. "Yeah." I should tell him. This is a good cue.

He licks his lips again, the color draining from his face. "Alexa. I know."

My breath catches.

"I know who your brother is."

I'm frozen in place.

"I don't care." His eyes search mine. "I don't care what he says or if he fires me for going out with you."

The tension in my chest eases and I tell myself to think this through. "How? How did you know?"

His hand lifts to my face, but then he looks around and lowers it. "Your eyes, Alexa," he said, leaning close over the table. "No one has eyes like you. I know you recognized me in the math lab. I knew I'd seen you before, but didn't put it together until I saw you with Tina that night."

"Why didn't you say anything?"

He looks down at our joined hands and then gives me a hesitant smile. "Because you seemed so desperate for me *not* to know. Every time Tina mentioned Reed, you cut her off and changed the subject."

I sigh. "I was afraid you'd tell him I was out with her."

"That name Tina was keeping from you—it's the name of the woman Reed's cheating on Caroline with, isn't it?"

I try to jerk my hand back, but his grip tightens. "He's not cheating on her. There's a logical explanation for the whole thing."

"I'm sorry." His voice softens. "I only know what Scarlett told me."

But I can tell he doesn't believe me. I'm sure Scarlett's made a convincing case. "I know what you think, but it's true. I know what he's doing. He's in trouble, but it's not an affair."

"What kind of trouble is he in?"

I release a breath. "I can't tell you."

"Reed can be a dick, but I wouldn't use whatever you tell me against him, even if half the math department would like to bring him down after how much of an ass he's been this semester."

I gasp and his eyes widen.

"Shit. I'm sorry. He's your brother."

I shake my head. "It's okay. I know he's hard to deal with sometimes. But he's been really stressed out over this last month or so and it's because of me."

"Why is he so overprotective?"

I stare at him. There's no way I'm going to tell him.

"He was the guy you were talking about when we were dancing. The one who gave up everything for you."

I try to pull away again, but he won't release me.

"Reed's presence here is sort of a mystery. His background is sketchy. What happened? What did he give up for you?"

I tug hard to escape his hold. "I have to go."

"Alexa."

I get up and grab my bag, then rush out the door into the cold wind, leaving my drink behind. But Ben follows me and reaches me within seconds. "Alexa, *wait*."

"Why are you still calling me Alexa if you know who I really am?"

"You introduced yourself as Alexa the first time we talked. Everyone else may call you Lexi, but you're Alexa to me."

I shake my head. I want to stay with him, but he's asking too many questions I can't answer. We haven't known each other long, but I know him well enough to know he won't accept vague answers. This is never going to work.

"You haven't said anything about my wig."

He shrugs and wraps his arm around my back, pulling me closer. "What about it?"

"Aren't you curious why I wore it?"

"I don't care."

Anger rises up inside me. "You don't care why I've worn a black wig almost every time you've seen me, but you *do* care about Reed's mysterious past?" I pull out of his grasp. He called Reed a dick and said half the math department wanted to bring him down. Is he part of that half? What if he's using me to hurt Reed? "I have to go."

"Alexa. *Please*. I'm sorry." I start toward the business building, but he blocks my path. "I don't care about Reed. I'll never even mention his name again. I just want a chance with you."

I stop, my resolve softening. I want a chance with him too. I worry that his ultimate goal is to hurt Reed, but part of me wonders if that's just because I have trouble trusting men.

He sees me weaken. "I swear—I don't give a rat's ass about your brother. If you want, I'll quit my job in the math lab to prove it."

I gasp. "But you need that job."

"I know, but I think you and I could have something amazing. I'm willing to stop working there if that's what it takes to get a shot with you." His jaw squares in determination.

I shake my head. "No. Please don't quit because of me."

His hand slides to the back of my head, and he pulls my face towards his until our foreheads touch. "I'll do it. I want to be with you."

"I want to be with you too," I whisper.

He kisses me, his lips pressing softly against mine, as though he's worried I'll change my mind if he's too aggressive. When he stops kissing me, his hand is still behind my head, our foreheads touching. "I have to get to class. I'd skip it but I have a test. I want to see you later."

"I…" Reed is gone and I can take advantage of his absence.

"I'm off tonight. I'll take you out to dinner."

He's working three jobs. He can't afford that. "I have a better idea. Reed's out of town. Come to my apartment and I'll cook for you." Indecision flickers in his eyes. "That way we can be alone." I add in a husky voice.

He pulls me to his chest and kisses me senseless. "Okay," he says when he finally pulls back. "What time?"

My last class is over at three, but I have a committee meeting for the charity at four that will last at least an hour. "Seven," I say. "That will give me time to get home and make something."

"Don't go to too much trouble." He kisses me again. "I'm far more interested in the company than the meal."

"Okay," I say against his lips. "Any allergies I should know about? Any dislikes?"

He gives me one last kiss and then pulls back and grins. "I'm allergic to penicillin and I hate cold feet on my legs."

My lips lift into an ornery grin. "Okay, no moldy bread and I'll make sure to wear socks."

His eyes darken with desire. "Skip the socks. And you can put your feet anywhere you want."

He reaches for me again, but I step back. "Nope, you need to go take a test, and I'm not going to be the reason you're late."

"You're a harsh woman, Alexa Pendergraft."

"You haven't seen anything yet."

"God, I hope not," he says as he starts to walk backward to the coffee shop.

I narrow my eyes and smirk. This is the second time he's walked away from me like this. "Is this a talent of yours? Walking backward?"

He shrugs, still grinning. "How am I supposed to turn my back on such a beautiful woman?"

And just like that, Ben Masterson has slipped his way into my heart.

Chapter
Twenty-One

Lexi

Sylvia and I use our lunch period to go over the logistics for the auction.

"Did Ben agree to take part?" she asks.

I stare at her for a moment before I remember my excuse for talking to him. "Uh...no."

"You told him why, right?"

It's a ridiculous question. I'm like a barracuda with this project. I'm about to answer, but my phone rings and I snatch it up quicker than usual. My eyes widen at the name on the screen. "It's my uncle. I really need to take this."

Her gaze narrows with concern. "Are you okay? You look nervous."

"Yeah, I'm fine." I get out of my chair. "Excuse me for a moment." I walk into the hall, trying not to hyperventilate. "Uncle Robert, please tell me that you have good news."

"I wish I did, kiddo."

My back sags against the wall as my eyes sink shut. "What happened?"

"I had a devil of a time finding him, for one thing, but I finally tracked him down in Boston. He wasn't staying with your parents; he was in some hotel. And although he's left Boston, I have no idea where he went next."

"What's he up to?"

"He refused to tell me a damned thing. He swore he knew what he was doing and that it was the only way of handling the situation."

My throat burns. "I'm scared for him, Uncle Robert. There has to be something we can do to stop him."

"I'll keep trying to think of something, but I'm fresh out of ideas. I guess we just hope he comes to his senses."

To hell with that. I'm going to try to stop him myself.

I hang up and immediately call Reed, but he doesn't answer. He doesn't answer my next three phone calls over the next few hours either, but he finally picks up on my fifth attempt, while I'm walking to my car after the committee meeting.

"I wish you'd left Uncle Robert out of this, Lexi. You're only complicating things."

"I had to do something. I can't watch you throw your life away."

"I know what I'm doing." His voice is steely.

"Do you?" When he doesn't answer, I push on. "Reed, come home. Stop this craziness," I say, my words drenched in fear.

"This is going to take another day. I'll either be home tomorrow night or the next morning. Is Caroline there yet?"

I want to tell him that I don't need a babysitter, but I suspect he'd actually call a nanny service and have someone sent right over. Or worse yet, he'd call a body guard.

So I dodge the question. "It's Wednesday. She has a late class."

"Oh, yeah. You're right," he says absently. He sounds sad and lonely. "Tell her..." His voice trails off. "Never mind."

"Come home and talk to her. *Please*."

"I'm not done here yet." There's no hesitation, just his firm response. I know that he's not going to come home until he completes whatever mission he's assigned himself. If he's not thrown in jail first.

"Reed, you're scaring me."

"Oh, Lex," he says with a sigh. "Don't be scared."

We're talking in circles and not getting anywhere. "I love you, Reed. Please don't try to sacrifice yourself for me. I *need* you."

"I love you too. I've got to go."

And just like that he hangs up.

I sit in my car for several minutes, letting the engine warm as I think about what Reed could be doing. I need to let myself consider all the possibilities. Reed suggested that whatever he was doing was illegal and possibly dangerous. Is he going to have Todd Millhouse killed or beaten up? It doesn't seem like Reed's style, even if he hired a "firm"— Ms. Pembry—to do it. No, Reed seems like a *bring someone down from behind the scenes* kind of guy. Todd Millhouse and his family have money, loads of it, and I suspect that's Reed's angle. Maybe he's using his genius computer knowledge to attack their money, their corporation, or both. Thankfully, Reed is enough of a mastermind to pull it off without getting caught.

Oh, God.

The blood rushes from my head as I realize I have tied Reed and myself to Todd Millhouse with a neatly trimmed bow. My phone number is on his cell phone.

I rest my forehead on the steering wheel. What have I done?

There's a rap on my passenger side window and I jump, releasing a shriek. Caroline has squatted, and is watching me through the window with wide eyes. I roll it down and she leans into the opening. "Lex, are you okay?"

Tears fill my eyes. I'm eager to tell her the truth. All of it. I need advice. But I can't confide in her. Reed will be furious and as much as I hate to admit it, I think he's right to want to keep her away from this mess. I wipe a tear that escapes. "I'm fine. I just want things to go back to the way they were."

She reaches in and unlocks the door, then opens it and slides into the passenger seat. After closing the window, she turns to me. "Maybe I should come stay with you after all."

I shake my head, forcing myself to smile. "No, I'm fine." I shrug. "It's probably hormones. You know, that time of the month and getting weepy."

Her brows lower. "Only you don't get like that."

Most people dismiss Caroline's intelligence because of her beauty. She's always impeccably dressed, and most people would never guess that she makes her own clothes or repurposes thrift-store finds, something she learned to do growing up in a trailer park with little money. With her long, thick blonde hair, blue eyes, and high cheek bones, she's gorgeous enough to be a model instead of the designer who makes the clothing they wear. Reed and I saw both aspects of her, right from the beginning. "I've got a lot going on, Caroline. I'm just overwhelmed."

My tone is snippier than I intend, but Caroline doesn't back down. "You're right. You do have a lot going on and if anyone deserves a meltdown from time to time it's you. But I know you, Lex. You're worried about something. I can see it in those beautiful eyes of yours."

I drop my gaze to my lap.

"Why is Reed in Boston?"

My head jerks up in surprise.

Her face is expressionless. "So you *are* worried about Reed."

"Caroline..."

"Is he really in Boston?"

Despite the fact that I've strutted around with a black wig on my head a handful of times this month, I hate lies and deceptions. "I don't know. I know he *was* there, but Uncle Robert doesn't think he's there anymore."

"Why did he go? What's he doing?"

I turn to look out the front windshield. "It's about me. That's all I know."

"You?" She's silent for a minute. "And the woman he talked to?"

I don't answer and tears prick at my eyes again.

"She has something to do with you, doesn't she?" I swing my gaze to her determined face. "I know he's not having an affair, Lexi."

"But...why...how...?" A million questions march through my head.

She shrugs. "I doubted him at first. Why else would he take secret calls from a woman and then run off to meet her? But the more I thought about it, the more I realized he wouldn't cheat on me. He'd break up with me before he ever did something like that." She wipes a tear from her cheek. "Say what you like about Reed Pendergraft Monroe, but he's an honorable man."

"But if you know he's not cheating, why haven't you come home?"

"Because he's keeping secrets again, Lexi. After he finally told me who you two were, he promised he wouldn't do that."

"He's trying to protect you, Caroline!"

"From *what?*"

I suck my lower lip into my mouth. I've said too much.

"People in a committed relationship share everything with each other," she says. "Reed didn't tell me about your past because he didn't trust me and I understand that. I had to earn his trust, especially after our rocky start." Anger fills her eyes and she clenches her hands in her lap. "But why doesn't he trust me now? What more can I do to prove that I love him and want what's best for all of us?" Her voice softens. "I almost wish it was another woman. It would be easier to understand."

I grab both her hands. "Oh, Caroline! He does trust you! He's trying to protect you."

"You keep saying that, but protect me from *what?*"

I clench my jaw. Damn my need to fix this.

Her body tenses and her eyebrows rise. "So you've known all along and you kept the truth from me too?"

I shake my head emphatically. "No! I didn't find out until this past weekend."

"Why didn't you call me?"

"Reed doesn't want you to get hurt."

She throws her hands up. "Again with the overprotectiveness." Her eyes narrow. "I understand his practically caveman need to do anything and everything in his power to watch over the people he loves. But it's insulting for him to keep this to himself when he knew it was tearing us apart," she spits. "It's as though he thinks my feeble brain can't handle the truth."

"That's not it, Caroline. I swear."

"Then what is it?"

I take a deep breath. I'm losing this argument, but I'm not sure how else to handle it. "I can't tell you."

Caroline reaches for the car door. "I thought more of you Lexi. I thought we were a team and that you'd help me just like I've tried to help you. But I guess that was stupid of me. Of course you're going to side with your brother."

A sob explodes in my chest and I grab her arm. "Caroline, that's not it!"

My rising hysteria stops her and she turns to me. "I love you, Lexi. You're like a sister to me. I love you more than I ever loved my brother or my parents. I may rot in hell for that fact, but it's the truth." Her lips tremble as tears fill her eyes.

I force myself to calm down.

"But I'm a grown woman and I have a right to know the truth, especially when it's destroying my life. I can understand why Reed would act this way—as much as I detest it—but I expected better from you." She tilts her head and sighs. "If either of you are ready to tell me the truth, I'll listen and consider moving forward, but the longer it waits, the harder that's going to be." She swallows. "Surely, you of all people can understand that."

I nod. "I do." I just don't know what to do about it.

"But no matter what, even if Reed and I stay apart, I'm here for you. I meant what I said about you being like a sister to me. Sisters fight, but they make up. You're stuck with me, Lex."

I throw my arms around her and press my cheek to her shoulder. "I love you, Caroline."

She pulls back to kiss my forehead. "I love you too." She's getting out of the car when she stops to look over her shoulder. "And I'd appreciate it if you two would get your shit together sooner rather than later. It's getting a bit crowded at Casa de Lovebirds," she says in a teasing tone.

She really does want to come back.

A grin spreads across my face. "Now you know how I feel."

She smiles back. "Which means you really *do* need to move into your own apartment." Then she gets out and waves before walking away.

I've got a lot of work to do.

Chapter
Twenty-Two

Lexi

The fact that Caroline is still willing to take Reed back gives me hope. But now I need to concentrate on making dinner for Ben, which produces a whole new level of anxiety. Before I was worried about his reaction to my wig, but now that that's out in the open, a new worry haunts me. If I look at what we have together, it's mostly sex. What if his attraction to me is just physical? But I remind myself that he didn't have to help me after Tina and her friends drugged me. He could easily have called the police or Reed. Surely the fact that he went so out of his way to do me a favor carries some weight. Ben's a very good-looking guy and I'm sure he wouldn't have to put so much effort into just getting laid.

I guess tonight will be a good test.

I stop at the grocery store and pick up some chicken and pasta along with a loaf of French bread and a cheesecake. Ordinarily, I'd make dessert, but it's already 5:30, so I'm running out of time. My cell phone rings as I'm checking out, and I grab it out of my purse and answer, "Hello?"

Silence greets me on the other end and when I look down at the caller ID, terror creeps up my spine. It's him. I drop the bag of fresh tomatoes in my other hand on the conveyor belt with thud.

"*Lexi?*" he asks in amazement.

I continue to hold the phone to my ear as the cashier asks, "Paper or plastic."

I need to answer. I need to hang up. Instead, I'm paralyzed with horror.

"Lexi?" he asks again. I press end and drop the phone to the floor.

"Miss, are you okay?" the cashier asks.

I watch her for a couple of seconds. *Get it together, Lexi.* I bend down and pick up my phone, forcing myself to smile as I stand. "I'm sorry. Long day. I kind of zoned out."

She smiles and nods her understanding. "Oh, honey, I know all about it." Then she holds up a plastic bag and raises her eyebrows.

I shake my head. "Paper, please."

"You one of those eco-friendly university students?" she asks with a smirk.

I could give her any number of retorts about the state of our environment. Instead, I take the easy way out. My fight has fled at the moment. "I save them for the afterschool program for the kids at the Middle Tennessee Children's Charity. They use them for projects."

A grin lights up her face. "Oh, well that's a great idea. My niece's kids go there."

"Really?" I make myself say. Ordinarily, I'd ask a million questions, but right now I'm dying to run home and lock my door. "It's a great organization."

She finishes checking me and places several extra folded brown bags into the bag containing my groceries. "Anything to help the kids," she says with a wink.

"Thank you," I say. This is the type of community spirit I still need to tap into.

But I can't think about the summer program right now. I'm eager to get home and... What do I plan to do? I should call Reed and confess my betrayal of his privacy, but I keep thinking there has to be a way out of this. As I force myself to calm down, I decide if Todd calls back, I should talk to him. Perhaps I can reason with him.

I recognize that it's the craziest plan I've ever hatched, even more so than going out with Tina, but I'm at a loss. I could take the offensive and call him first, which is probably the best way to handle it if I really plan on going through with this—but I can't make myself go that far. I'll wait until he calls me.

When I get home, I prepare the chicken and put it in the oven, then start to heat the water for the pasta while I practice what to say.

Hey, Todd. Let's call a truce.

Really? That's all I've got? That's never going to work.

No, I can do this. I'm the queen of negotiations. I've dealt with bigger assholes than this.

Really, Lexi? Bigger assholes than the jerk who raped you and told everyone it was consensual? Then threatened to sue you for slander if you continued to press charges? There are bigger assholes in the world than *that?*

I'm having an argument with myself. Maybe I've finally lost my mind.

I find a bottle of wine in the refrigerator and decide to open it even though Ben's not here yet. I need some courage. In fact, I've begun to wonder at the wisdom of having him come here at all. I'm clearly distracted and distressed. This evening could turn out horribly.

But anger bursts inside of me, filling every cell in my body.

No!

I'm done playing the victim. I'm done cowering in fear. I'm done letting that jerk ruin my life any more than he already has. I want to see Ben tonight. I'm not going to let Todd Millhouse take this from me.

By the time dinner is under control, I have twenty minutes left. I go into my room and stand in front of my open closet. What do you wear on a first date with a man who's already seen you naked?

Oh, my God. This is a first date.

I'm not sure why this strikes me as a surprise. Again, he's already seen me naked, so this should be so simple.

I pull on a pair of jeans and a silky blue shirt. The color is close to the shade of my eyes and makes them look darker than usual. The blouse clings to my curves and is low cut enough to show off what little cleavage I have, but not too low cut to make me look slutty.

Too late for that one, Lex.

I shake my head, refusing to listen to my negative thoughts. I look through my closet for shoes to wear and then remember our conversation about cold feet. I decide to go barefoot.

After I finish touching up my makeup, I pull my hair out of the bun from this morning and am relieved that it's not a total disaster. I pull the sides back with two clips and call it good.

I stare at my reflection, worrying anew. My face it still the same, but I'm definitely not as exotic looking as a blonde. What if Ben doesn't like me this way?

I lift my chin. Then it's his loss.

As I'm leaving the bathroom, the buzzer to the exterior door fills the apartment. I press my hand against my stomach, hoping to calm the butterflies flapping around inside.

When I answer, Ben's confident voice responds. "Alexa, it's Ben."

"Come on up," I say. "Apartment 306."

"I'll see you in a few moments."

And he's knocking on my front door less than a minute later. My paranoia from earlier still lingers because I look through the peephole to verify that it's him. When I open the door, he's standing in front of me with a wine bottle in his hand, looking good in jeans, a solid dark gray T-shirt, and a brown leather jacket. He stares at me, taking me in from the top of my head to the tips of my feet. A smile spreads across his face. "No socks."

I shrug and give him a playful grin. "I like a challenge."

His smile lights up his eyes. "I'll be sure to remember that."

I step back. "Come on in. The chicken's still baking, but the water's boiling and I need to add the pasta."

"Let me help." Ben steps inside and I close the door behind him, making sure to fasten the deadbolt.

"Making it harder for me to get away?" Ben teases as he takes off his jacket.

"What?" I shrug. "Reed's gone so it's a habit."

"It's a good one," he says, following me into the kitchen. "Better to be safe."

He notices my nearly empty wine glass on the counter. "Got a head start?"

"Oh." I clasp my hands together and look up into his face. "I was nervous." I'm not sure why I feel the need to be this honest with him. Perhaps it's because I know how much I plan on keeping from him.

He grabs my left hand with his right, pressing our palms together and linking our fingers. His gaze lands on my face, shifting from my mouth to my eyes. "I'm nervous too…which is why I *brought* the wine."

I smile. "You don't seem like a wine guy."

He winks, the first sign of a devilish charm I'm sure he possesses. "I was trying to impress you. Beer didn't seem like a good choice for that task."

"Good call." We're still linked together, but I can't bring myself to let go of his hand.

"You're beautiful, Alexa." His free hand reaches up to my hair, grabbing several strands and rubbing them between his thumb and index finger. "I think I prefer you as a blonde."

"Really?" I ask in genuine disbelief.

His eyebrows lift. "Why do you sound so surprised?"

Embarrassment creeps in. "Well… I guess because the wig makes me look so much different…more…"

"Older?" he asks, studying my lips.

"That too," I murmur.

"I'll agree that you look more…sophisticated in the wig. But this—" his fingers comb through my locks "—is the real you. And I'd prefer the real you any day."

I'm speechless, unsure of how to respond. "Thank you," I finally say.

"No, thank you," he answers, his eyes darkening. "I keep worrying that I've blown it with you, yet you keep giving me another chance. That's all I ask—for a chance."

The timer goes off for the oven and I jump, dropping his hand. "The chicken's done."

He puts his hands on his hips and looks around. "What can I do to help?"

"You were serious?"

He scoffs. "Hell, yeah, I was serious."

I slide a wooden cutting board toward him and hand him the loaf of French bread. "Then you can cut this into slices for garlic bread."

"Yes, ma'am," he drawls in a thick southern accent.

"You southerners are so polite," I say as I pull the chicken out of the oven. "Yes, ma'am. Yes, sir. And all the thank yous and excuse mes."

"What?" Ben asks, looking over his shoulder with a grin. "They aren't polite on the upper east coast?"

I start to bristle—*he knows that I'm from the east coast*—but he works with Reed. Of course he knows. "Let's just say they have their own type of formal politeness. You southerners take it to a whole other level."

I cook the pasta as he finishes up the bread. We talk about our childhoods and our experiences in high school. When Ben speaks of his family, at first I think I imagine the pain in his voice. I've been through enough to recognize such things, though, and before long I'm certain. His family has hurt him and it happened recently.

As I set the table, I say, "This is unusual. We rarely eat at the table."

"You live with your brother and his fiancée, right?" he asks, setting silverware next to the plates I've put down on top of placemats.

"Yes," I say, refusing to address the fact that Caroline doesn't live with us right now. "And we do eat together a lot—Reed's an excellent cook—but we usually sit at the bar."

He motions his thumb over his shoulder. "We can eat at the bar if you want to."

I shake my head as I fold a napkin. "No, I want this to be special."

He sets the wine glass in his hand down next to a plate. "Alexa, we could be eating hot dogs in a parking lot. It would be special as long as I was with you."

I search his face for a sign that he's bullshitting me, but he seems genuine. "Thank you," I finally say.

We stare into each other's eyes for several seconds and even though we're on opposite corners of the table, I wonder if he's going to kiss me. But he grins, his face lighting up. He looks like he's full of happiness and sunshine, and I'm amazed to realize that's exactly how I feel too. Like anything is possible when I'm with him, even love.

Another timer goes off and I laugh. "I'm beginning to regret not going with hot dogs." I brush past him into the kitchen and turn off the buzzer.

He winks. "I'm not. I get to see your culinary skills at work."

"Interviewing for potential wife material?" I ask before I think. Then I cringe and my cheeks start to burn.

He reaches around my waist and pulls my back to his chest. "Maybe I am," he whispers into my ear. "Maybe I'm one of those guys who wants my woman barefoot, pregnant, and slaving in the kitchen. Lucky me, I've got two out of three right now." He laughs.

I spin around in his arms, giggling, and swat at his chest. Cocking an eyebrow, I give him a mischievous grin. "Maybe I have an ulterior motive of my own." But I'm hyperaware that our chests are pressed together and he's holding me close. He smells good and I resist the sudden urge to taste the skin on his neck, right under his jaw.

His voice turns husky. "If it's anything like what transpired last night, consider me your willing victim." His arms tighten, but then he releases me. "We're going to burn my delicious garlic bread. Someday when you're taking an inventory of all my good traits versus my bad ones, the deciding factor could boil down to this very moment."

"Whether or not your garlic bread burned?"

"Exactly." His eyebrows rise playfully. "Some women love a man who can cook in the kitchen. It could be the deciding factor on whether to cut me loose or keep me around. I think I need all the help I can get."

I laugh. "Cook in the kitchen? Isn't that redundant?"

He lowers his voice and presses a kiss to my earlobe. "I know plenty of places to cook." His tongue traces the edge of my jaw. "On the patio with a grill." He grins against my cheek and trails kisses back to my ear. "Grilling at a tailgate party."

He's teasing me, but his mouth is still making my breath come in shallow pants. "Why am I noticing a grilling theme here?"

He takes my earlobe into his mouth and gently bites and licks the tender skin. A white hot bolt of lightning shoots from my abdomen to between my legs and I resist the urge to gasp. "My cooking involves a trifecta of skills."

"And the first is grilling?" I ask, my voice breathless.

"Yes." His mouth is moving downward again, to the side of my neck.

"The second is garlic bread."

"Do not underestimate the effects of the perfect garlic bread on a beautiful woman." His hand is in my hair, tilting my head to the side to give him better access.

"And the third?"

His mouth trails back to my ear. "I'm saving that one for later."

"Does it involve dessert?"

"Oh, it *definitely* involves dessert." He raises his head and grins. "So you can see how imperative it is for me to present you with the perfect garlic bread."

"Yes," I murmur, staring at the pair of lips that just drove me mad with need. "I can see that." But he's still holding me in his arms.

"I'm about to say fuck the bread and hope my other two skills speak for themselves."

I step back, breaking free of his hold. "No," I say with a laugh. "I think you're right. At some point in the not-so-distant future, our relationship could hinge on your garlic bread. Are you willing to take that risk?"

He laughs and places his hands over his heart. "I'm wounded. You've used my own words against me."

"Let's let your garlic bread speak for itself."

We put the food on the table and Ben finds a corkscrew in a drawer and starts to open the wine he brought.

I remember his earlier statement about bringing beer. "If you'd rather have beer, Reed has a couple in the fridge."

He shakes his head and laughs derisively. "Somehow I don't think Reed would appreciate me drinking his beer." He pours the liquid into my wine glass. "I'll just drink wine with you."

I'm starting to sit down, but I stop and look up at him. "Does he really dislike you that much?"

Ben sighs as he pours wine into his own glass. "It's not so much that he dislikes me, Alexa. He seems to hold a grudge against the world. He thinks everyone is untrustworthy until they prove otherwise."

I look down the table, my stomach sinking. I could see how others would read him that way.

"Hey." He's next to me, wrapping an arm around my back. His other hand tips up my chin. "I'm sorry. Let's not to discuss your brother. Forgive me?"

I shake my head. "There's nothing to forgive." I offer a smile. "Let's eat."

He pulls out my chair. I sit and watch as he takes the seat beside me.

We start to eat and an awkward silence hangs over us. Ben takes a bite of the chicken and makes an "mmm" sound. "This is delicious."

"Thanks."

"Did I mention I can grill?" he gives me a teasing grin. I laugh. "You might have."

"Next time I'll grill steaks and bake potatoes."

"But it's freezing outside."

He looks at me like I'm crazy. "So?"

"You grill in thirty-degree weather?"

He cuts a piece of chicken and stabs it with his fork. "Hell, *yeah*."

"Okay," I say, suddenly feeling shy. "You can cook next time."

"You're agreeing to a second date when we're not done with the first one yet?" A grin spreads across his face. "I feel like one of those bachelor dudes on TV who get a rose on a date."

"*You* watch The Bachelorette?" I ask in disbelief

"Oh, yeah." He nods in mock seriousness. "Every Friday night. I own the first five seasons on DVD."

I laugh. "I may have to reconsider that second date."

He holds up a hand. "Wait. Don't cancel yet. They belong to one of my roommates. He tied me up and forced me to watch them. It was a form of torture for missing my turn with the dishes."

"I'll let it slide this time, although I'm still slightly troubled that you know about the Bachelorette."

We continue eating and joking around and I'm amazed that I can feel this elation considering everything else that's going on around me.

"That was delicious, Alexa," Ben says, pushing his plate away from him. "Although I may need to have more to be sure. Two helpings wasn't enough to completely convince me."

"That can be arranged."

He looks up at me, his expression turning serious. "We'll have to wait until next week for me to cook for you. My nights off are Monday and Wednesday."

"How long have you kept this crazy schedule?" I ask.

He tenses, the smile falling from his face. He picks up the wine glass and studies it. "Only since December."

While I'm relieved to hear that, I'm curious too. "So why start right before your last semester?"

He takes a deep breath and looks into my face. "I had a full-ride scholarship, but they took it away from me at the end of last semester."

"Budget cuts?" I ask. When he doesn't answer, I shake my head. "I'm sorry. That sucks. So you're working to pay for your last semester?"

He nods. "I could have transferred somewhere cheaper, but not all of my credits would have counted." He takes a sip of wine and then raises his glass. "Either way, I would have been in debt. So I sucked it up and took the six months of hard labor." He looks at me. "I figured I could do anything for six months."

"And you're halfway done."

"Yeah." His face softens. "That's a good way of looking at it."

I stand and pick up my plate. "Do you want dessert?"

He shoots me a devilish grin as he stands too. "Not yet."

I shake my head. "Then you can show me your dishwashing skills. Have I mentioned how sexy it is to see a man washing dishes?"

"Will there be dirty talk involved?"

I put a hand on my hip, smirking. "Do you want dirty talk to be involved?"

"Ah, I guess we'll see." He picks up his plate and carries it into the kitchen then he stands in the middle and looks around, gesturing the plate toward the dishwasher. "Now I'm a bit rusty, but if you put dirty plates and silverware in there, I think it will miraculously clean them for you."

"No wonder your roommate tortured you."

He moves past me and grabs both wine glasses and the half-full bottle.

I start to rinse off my plate, but he reaches around and takes it from my hands. "Oh, no, Ms. Pendergraft. You put on a show for me last night that nearly made ejaculate before you even touched me. Now it's my turn to return the favor." He puts the plate in the sink and lowers his mouth to my neck, wrapping one arm around my waist and planting his palm on my lower abdomen. His other hand skims my waist, brushing against the underside of my ribs.

"You want me to ejaculate prematurely?" I ask as a tingling shoots to my pelvis.

He laughs and spins me around and happiness spreads through me with a fizzy effervescence. "You have no idea how much I need you."

Before I can figure out what he means, let alone how to respond, he's gripping my waist and lifting me up. I shriek and grab his shoulders. "Now you sit there," he says, setting me on the counter. "You said watching a man doing dishes was sexy, so I aim to please." He grabs the wine bottle and pours more into my glass and hands it to me.

"Are you trying to get me drunk?" I ask, chuckling.

"Yes, if it helps."

I turn serious. "I don't need to be drunk to want to be with you, Ben."

His grin fades and a certain gentleness fills his eyes. "Are you still nervous?"

Am I? "No. Everything's perfect."

His eyes fill with lust and I'm sure he's about to kiss me, but he grabs my glass. "Then I need your wine." He takes a gulp.

"You're nervous?" I tease.

"Hell, *yeah*," he says as though I've lost my mind. "Do you know how many sexy dishwashing shows I've put on?"

I laugh. "Two?"

"Ha!" He points a finger at me. "See! I've fooled you into thinking I'm an expert, when really I'm a virgin."

I cock my head to the side. "You don't have to do this, Ben."

"Just stacking up those bonus points."

"Then let's get this show on the road," I say. "Why do I think I'll need dollar bills?"

His eyes bulge in mock-insult. "Dollar bills? I'll have you know I'll accept nothing less than a five."

"Good to know, but so far all I see is talking, no washing."

He turns on the water and picks up a plate, then looks at me with hooded eyes. "There's a way to washes dishes and a way to seduce a woman with them."

"And which are you going for now?" I ask.

He picks up the wine glass and shoves it in my hand again. "If you're going to talk smart, you might as well drink some wine to keep your mouth busy," he says with a smirk to let me know he's joking.

Narrowing my gaze, I say, "I can think of better things to keep my mouth busy."

Ben leans forward and grabs the edge of the counter in front of the sink. "If you keep talking that way, I'm going to say fuck the dishes."

"Maybe I want you to fuck something else." I'm astounded by my boldness, but Ben brings out a confidence in me that I didn't even know existed.

He stands up straight and spins around, then steps between my open legs and pulls my body flush against his. His erection is pressed firmly against my crotch.

His eyes darken as his mouth lowers to mine. "As I said, I aim to please."

Chapter Twenty-Three

Lexi

Ben kisses me as though he's a dying man and I'm his lifeline.

He scoops his arms under my butt and picks me up off the counter. His mouth lifts long enough to ask, "Where's your room?" But then he's plunging in again before I can answer, dragging me under a wave of lust.

When he comes up for air, I force out, "Down the hall. Second door on the left." Then he's kissing me again, but he's on the move. I wrap my legs around his waist and my arms around his neck.

My bedroom door is open and I left the lamp on next to my bed. He unwraps my legs and slides me down the front of his body. "God, Alexa. Do you have any idea what you do to me?"

I smile up at him. "It's probably somewhat similar to what you do to me."

He grabs my face and kisses me with tenderness this time. "I want you to know this isn't just sex to me. I want more with you." He kisses me again, then lifts his face, a grin lighting up his eyes. "Don't get me wrong, I want the sex, but if you told me you wanted to wait, even after last night, I'd do it."

I shake my head. "I don't want to wait." I grab the bottom of his shirt and pull it up. He tugs it over his head and drops it on the ground. I place my palms on his chest and slide my fingertips up to his shoulders. "About last night…" My voice trails off. "I'm not sure what you think of me after that." I look up into his face. "But I want you to know that I don't sleep around."

His eyes soften. "Alexa. You don't have to—"

"Yes," I say firmly. "I do. I've had sex with four guys. One in high school and two other guys in college." I take a deep breath. "And you." Does it make me a liar that I didn't include Todd in that list? I don't care because I refuse to include him.

His hands slide up and down my arms. "Alexa. We both have experience. I didn't expect you to be a virgin." He grins. "Hell, I don't *want* you to be a virgin."

My fingertips glide across his chest, exploring. "That's just it. I've had sex before, but I'm not that experienced." I pause. "Contrary to what I may have insinuated with my actions last night."

He doesn't say anything for several seconds. "I don't expect anything from you, if that's what you're worried about. I just want you to be you."

"I just want you to know that I'm not usually like that."

"Then I'm even happier that you felt safe doing it with *me*." He hands reach for the buttons on my shirt and start to unfasten them from top to bottom. "I love this color on you. It makes your eyes even more beautiful, something I didn't think was possible. All through dinner I couldn't figure out whether to look at your eyes or your cleavage."

My shirt hangs open, exposing my lacy navy blue bra. His fingertips slide from my cheek, down my neck, and to the valley between my breasts.

"It's almost a shame to take this shirt off." He grins as he slides it off my shoulders and down my arms. "Almost."

I laugh softly, loving that he's taking his time and that he's taking charge. I'm shocked by how comfortable I feel.

He reaches for the button on my jeans and I close my eyes, reveling in the joy of having him undress me...and the fact that I'm actually enjoying it. He pulls down my zipper and slides the fabric over my hips until the jeans fall to my feet. I step out of them and reach for his, which I remove in a matter of seconds.

We're both standing in my bedroom in our underwear, something I never even imagined would be possible without that damned wig. I trail my fingertips up to his face and across his lips and then stand on my tiptoes to give him a gentle kiss.

One of his hands lifts to the back of my head and the other wraps around my back. He's holding me firmly against him, trapping my mouth against his, but I feel no anxiety, only electricity humming across my skin.

Desire rises up in me, making me hungry for more. My tongue becomes bolder as it explores his mouth, tempting his tongue to join mine.

His grip tightens as he groans, and then he's pushing me down to the bed. He lies next to me and rolls me onto my side to face him. He tugs the straps of my bra from my shoulder and unfastens the hook in the back. After he tosses the lingerie to the side, he stares my breasts before meeting my eyes again. "God, Alexa. You're so beautiful."

I smile as his fingers skim across my chest, making me squirm as they outline my areola.

"Am I driving you crazy?"

"Yes." My answer comes in a breathless rush.

"You drive me crazy even when you're not with me." Then his mouth finds my nipple and his arm wraps around my back, holding me in place. His other hand slides down my abdomen and inside the front of my panties.

I gasp and sink my hand into his hair, overwhelmed with sensation. I reach down to touch him through his underwear and rub the heel of my hand up and down his length.

Groaning, he rolls me onto my back and props himself on an elbow. He tugs my underwear down and I lift my hips to help. Then he pulls his own off and we're both naked.

He's still on his side when he presses his right palm on my abdomen. Anxiety prickles the back of my neck, but before I can begin to panic, his hand slides between my legs and finds the spot that makes me ache for more.

I roll onto my side and stretch my neck to kiss him, taking his erection in my hand and beginning to stroke.

A low rumble emits from his chest. "I want to be inside you."

His words shoot a jolt of desire to my core.

Ben sits up and leans over to pick up his jeans. Within seconds, he's holding a condom package and ripping it open. He quickly puts it on and spreads my legs apart.

The panic that floods my head catches me by surprise, but I recognize the reason why. "I want to be on top."

He hesitates, then smiles. "Okay." He drops to his side and rolls onto his back. I straddle his waist and lean over him to kiss him and then reposition myself and guide him to my entrance. As I lower myself on top of him, he releases a low groan and his pelvis rises so that he sinks deeper.

We begin to move, quickly becoming attuned to each other's bodies, and soon I'm climbing. I need him deeper. He grabs my hips, pulling me down as he grinds into me.

Soon we're both panting and I'm soaring higher, close to coming. When he gives another deep thrust, it pushes me over the edge. I cry out and he takes over, becoming more desperate in his thrusts until he releases a loud grunt and pulls my hips down, holding me on top of him. Seconds later he loosens his grip and pulls me onto my side, rolling with me, still inside me.

He touches his forehead to mine. "My God, Alexa. You are so perfect."

I grin and kiss him. "You're not so bad yourself."

We lay still, staring into each other's eyes. After a while, Ben releases a sigh. "I need to clean up. I'll be right back."

"Okay."

He gets up and disappears around the corner and I realize we were lying sideways on the bed. I crawl to the top and pull the covers down, then slide inside and lie down, my head on the pillow.

He returns within seconds and crawls into bed next to me, taking me in his arms. His hand strokes my hair, fingering my curls.

"You're really not curious about why I was wearing a wig at the bar?" I ask.

The corners of his mouth tip up. "I am and I'm not."

"That's not really an answer."

"Yes, I wondered why you would hide your beautiful hair, but I was mostly curious about who you were."

"The first two times were after the play. Caroline did my makeup and hair for my very small part and she put me in a wig. She thought it would be fun. I was kind of in a rut, so when I saw how different I looked, I liked it. But the real reason I wore it to the bar was because my hair would have been a disaster if I took the wig off. So I did it out of necessity."

"Why did you tell me your name was Alexa?"

I shrug. "Honestly? It's my real name for one, but I've never felt like an Alexa until you started calling me that. Lexi's my nickname and what everyone except for my grandmother calls me. But the wig made me feel like someone else, more confident. Sexy."

He groans. "God, Alexa. Do you really not feel sexy as you are?"

I shrug again. "I was in a dark place when I first wore it. It gave me the confidence to be brave and reach out of my comfort zone."

"And the guy you were with the second night?"

There's no accusation in his voice, but I'm still a bit uncomfortable. "He was a one-night fling. He was exactly what I needed to regain my confidence after my ex-boyfriend and I broke up before the start of winter break."

"What guy would be stupid enough to break up with you?" He kisses me.

"I broke up with him." I'm surprised that I actually want to tell him why we broke up, even if it opens a topic that he might not be able to handle. But when I look into his adoring eyes, I think he can. The real issue will be keeping him from boarding a plane and flying to New York to kick the shit out of Todd. But tonight is not the night. We need to share more intimacy, more passion and fun before I bring something so serious into the mix. But what's amazing is that I actually *want* to tell him.

He releases an exaggerated sigh. "You broke up with him? That makes sense, but now I wish I hadn't abandoned my sexy dishwashing act."

I laugh, feeling happier than I have in longer than I can remember. "Well, there's plenty of time for *that*."

"Does that mean you're going to keep me around for a while longer?"

"Are you kidding? At least until I see the show."

He cocks an eyebrow and smirks. "All the more reason to keep putting it off. I'm already becoming quite attached to you, Alexa Pendergraft."

My grin softens. "I think we need dessert."

His grin turns wicked. "I thought we just *had* dessert."

"Real dessert. I bought a cheesecake."

"Oh, Alexa. If I were forced to pick between you and cheesecake, I would pick you every time."

I sit up and look over my shoulder. "As virile as you are, I'm sure you need a few minutes to recover. I'm going to eat some cheesecake while you do."

He sits up laughing and wraps his arms around my waist, pressing his chest to my back. His mouth finds my neck. "Is that a challenge? Did I mention that I like a challenge?"

I look over my shoulder at him, giggling. "Take it as a challenge if you must, but I still want cheesecake."

His grin softens. "Then I'll go get it. Stay where you are."

I lean back on my elbows as he climbs out of bed. He stops and looks at me, his gaze darkening as he takes in my naked body. I can see from his growing erection that he's already recovering.

"Are you sure you want cheesecake?"

I lower my eyelids. "If you get some for me, I'll give you a dessert of your own."

He grins. "I'll be right back." He heads out the door, completely naked.

"You're not going to put on any clothes?" I call after him.

"Why bother when I'm going to take them off in a matter of minutes?"

True enough, he's back within a couple of minutes with the entire cheesecake and a fork, along with a glass of water.

"The entire thing?" I ask with a laugh as he sits beside me.

"I want to make sure you're satisfied."

"Then I'll definitely keep you around."

He smiles and uses the fork to get the first bite.

"Where's *my* fork?"

He shakes his head and lifts the fork to my mouth. I grin as I take a bite.

He scoops off his own piece. "I have to say, this was a good call."

"Never doubt me."

"I'm learning that." He takes a bite, then scoops another for me. "What's your favorite dessert?"

"Chocolate cake. You?"

"Boston Crème Pie."

I laugh.

"What's so funny?"

"*I'm* from Boston."

He leans over and kisses me, long and slow. "Go Boston."

"Favorite food?" I ask.

"Fried chicken. You?"

"Lasagna."

"Favorite drink?" he asks.

"Diet Coke."

"Diet Coke?" he snorts. "That's not a real drink."

"It most certainly is. What's yours?"

He curls his lip as if I've insulted him. "Lemonade." He lifts an eyebrow. "Homemade."

"Favorite vegetable?"

He takes a bite. "French fries."

"French fries are not a vegetable."

He drops his fork, his eyes widening in disbelief. "Um, hello. It's a potato, aka a vegetable."

"There is little to no nutritional value in French fries."

He pierces another piece and holds it to my lips. "You never said it had to have nutritional value. Only that it had to be a vegetable."

A grin spreads across my face as I take a bite. I know it's a goofy grin by the way it stretches my face, but I don't care.

He smiles back. "Why are you smiling like that?"

At the risk of looking like an idiot, I decide to tell him the truth. "I'm just so happy. I can't think of the last time I felt like this."

Ben puts the cheesecake on the nightstand, then rolls over to me and pushes me down on the bed, kissing me until I'm desperate for more. We take our time, exploring each other and what we like, and when we finish—me on top again—I lie on my pillow, exhausted.

"You wear me out, Ben Masterson."

He leans over me, propped on his elbow. "Consider me your personal trainer."

I close my eyes and grin. "So we have to wait until next Monday night to do this again?"

He tucks several strands of hair behind my ear. "Unless you come see me or I come see you after I get off work at two a.m."

My eyes fly open. "How do you keep going? You should be catching up on your sleep right now. And you should definitely get sleep after work instead of fooling around with me."

"What if I'd rather fool around with you?"

I shake my head. "Priorities."

He grins. "*Exactly.*"

"You only have to work three jobs until you graduate right?"

He sighs. "Yeah. It sucks."

"I'm working with the chancellor on the charity's summer program. He actually likes me. I can put a good word in for you, see if he'll reinstate your scholarship retroactively."

His eyes fly open wide. "No. Don't do that."

Why is he acting so weird? "It's really not a problem, Ben."

He kissed me. "I appreciate the thought Alexa, really I do. But I don't want you talking to him on my behalf. It's emasculating."

I'm not sure how I know, but he's not telling me the full truth. I can't get angry, though…that makes two of us. "Okay. I won't say anything."

"Thanks."

"I know you're upset about losing your scholarship, but at least you got seven paid semesters you wouldn't have had otherwise, right? I know several students who are thousands of dollars in debt from student loans. Caroline's one of them. You only have this semester to worry about."

A slow grin of wonder spreads across his face. "I need you around Alexa Pendergraft."

My eyebrows furrow in confusion. This is the second time he's said that.

"You make me look at things differently. I've been so pissed about having my scholarship pulled that I haven't let myself feel grateful for everything that I do have. You put things in perspective."

I watch him to see if he's mocking me.

"I mean it." He strokes my cheek. "At the risk of scaring you off, I feel the need to tell you something."

I take a breath and release it, suddenly nervous. "Okay."

He turns my hand and traces a lazy pattern on my palm with his fingertip. "I've been in a dark place for a couple of months, but since you burst into my life, all that darkness has been fading away."

"You mean like a depression?"

"Maybe. I don't know." He shrugs. "More like feeling sorry for myself, since I lost my scholarship for reasons beyond my control. I'm more like Reed than I care to admit." He holds up his hands when I stiffen. "Hear me out."

I press my lips together.

"I've been holding a grudge, a bad attitude, whatever you want to call it for months. And truth be told, the people close to me have paid the price." He pauses. "But you've made me realize how selfish that attitude is."

My shoulders stiffen. "I come across as preachy, don't I?"

"No!" He shakes his head. "For the first time in a long time, I don't want to be the type of person who holds grudges. I want to be free of all that baggage. I want to be happy. And it's because of you."

"But you hardly know me."

"God, Alexa, I know you better than you think." He places his hand on the side of my face, tipping it up to look into my eyes. "You have this fire for living that so few people have. You throw your entire self into the things you care about, whether it's the charity's summer program or the relationship between your brother and his fiancée. There's a sweetness about you that's one hundred percent genuine. You deserve a man who is worthy of being with you. And as much as I hate to admit it, I'm so not that man. I know it deep in my gut, but I can't help myself. I want you. So I'm trying my best to be the kind of guy who deserves you."

I shake my head. "Ben, I don't want you to be anyone other than who you are. You can't change for me. I'm not asking for that and even if I was, it wouldn't work."

"Don't you see?" His eyes burn with intensity as he tries to convey his meaning. "I used to *be* that person until all this hate and resentment pulled me under. You're helping the real me come alive again."

I'm still not sure what to make of what he's said.

"I'm sorry. That was probably TMI," he says.

I look into his eyes. "No. Thank you for your honesty." I offer him a grim smile. "And I've wrestled with demons of my own, so who am I to judge?"

He lies down and wraps his arm around my back. I burrow into his side, resting my head on his chest.

"Is it okay if I spend the night?" he asks.

"I'd be disappointed if you didn't." But I don't know how we'll make this work this with his schedule and our current living arrangements.

He kisses my temple and I slip my feet between this calves. He jolts. "Holy shit, woman. Have you had those feet set on ice?"

"Don't be such a baby," I murmur, already drifting off to sleep. "Just warm up my feet."

"Don't you know?" he asks. "I'd give you just about anything you could ask for."

Before I can think about what he's said, I succumb to sleep.

Chapter Twenty-Four

Ben

I'm dreaming that I'm with Alexa in her bed, her sexy backside pressed against a now growing part of me. I blink my eyes to see I'm in a dark room and she's really here next to me. My arm is draped over her side, my fingers sprawled across her abdomen. My hand starts to explore, gently skimming across her skin and cupping her breast. She stirs as my thumb brushes over her in sweeping half-circles, moving closer and closer to her nipple. I lower my mouth to her neck, placing soft kisses on her throat and along her clavicle. I gently pull the covers down to expose her from the belly button up. A soft light filters through the blinds and casts a pale glow on her skin. I watch her nipple harden.

God, I want her.

The intense need I feel for her scares me. We've hardly spent any time together, yet I know deep in my gut that I could search the world and never find a more perfect fit for me. She's fun and funny, light-hearted and cheery. She brings out a fun-loving side of me that's been hidden for over a year, since before I started seeing Sabrina. I never realized how much Sabrina changed me until I stepped into Alexa Pendergraft's life. Her devotion to her family and friends, and even children she's never met, astounds me. To be included in that inner circle has become a driving force since I saw her this morning.

I study the outline of her breasts as my fingers continue their exploration. My erection presses against the soft flesh of her ass and primal need sends my hand searching lower, under the blanket. My fingers slip between her legs and my erection jolts when I feel that she's already wet.

I want to wake her up and fuck her right now.

But part of me likes that I can still turn her on when she's asleep. I want to take my time and watch her body react. She moans and rolls toward me as my hand continues to make gentle strokes over her body

I lower my mouth to her nipple and when she spreads her thighs apart, I can tell she's rousing. She grabs my head and pulls it up to her mouth. She kisses me as she reaches for me, taking me in her hand and beginning to rub. I'm not going to last long—and part of me is annoyed as shit over that, like I'm a fucking teenager—but she makes me more excited than any other woman ever has. I can only hope that my dick will settle down the more time we spend together.

I lean away and grab a condom off the nightstand. Alexa had laughed at me when I'd put several there during our second round last night, but look who knew what he was doing at the time. I quickly get it on with her help and she's climbing on top of me, plunging down without any warning.

I grit my teeth at the overwhelming urge to grab her hips and pound into her. She likes to set the pace and I let her.

She's straddling me, her gorgeous naked body upright in the moonlight. She closes her eyes and leans her head back, exposing her throat as she rides me. She starts off slow, but she's quickly picking up the tempo as she grinds herself into my pelvis. I reach up to fondle her breast, watching her in utter amazement. This has to be a dream, but if it is, I never want to wake up.

"God, you are so fucking beautiful." I say the words out loud without intending to.

But the words seem to encourage her and she comes within seconds, crying out, her spasms putting delicious pressure on my erection. I clench my teeth to keep from coming. As soon as she's somewhat recovered, I grab her hips and flip her on her back, my mouth finding hers as I begin to thrust deep inside her.

But she stiffens beneath me and I stop, lifting myself on one elbow. "Alexa, are you okay?"

She's pushing on my chest, and even though her face is drenched in shadows, I see the terror in her eyes.

What the fuck? I instantly roll to my side and slip out from inside her.

She's scrambling to get up, but I pull her back, which makes her even more frantic, so I let go. Before I can register what has happened, she's sitting on the edge of the bed, sobbing.

Panicked, I reach up and turn on the lamp, then crawl across the bed to her and grab her face. She stiffens again, so I release my grip, but not before I get a good look into her eyes. She's terrified.

"What happened?" I ask, keeping my voice calm even though I'm totally freaking out inside. Both of us flipping out won't help anything. "Did I hurt you?"

She closes her eyes and shakes her head. "I'm sorry," she forces out between sobs.

"Alexa, baby." I stroke her cheek with my thumb. "Don't say you're sorry. Just tell me what happened."

She pauses, calming down a bit. I can see she's trying to figure out how to answer. "I don't know."

She's lying and that sort of pisses me off. Why would she lie to me? "You don't know why you freaked out?"

Taking a deep breath, she tries to stand. I grab her arm and pull her back down, but her eyes widen in fear and she stiffens again.

"Why are you afraid?" I ask calmly even though I'm anything but. "Are you afraid of me?"

She shakes her head, her eyes pleading with mine. "No. I'm so sorry." Fresh tears fall and she makes a move to get up again.

"Alexa, please," I beg. "Don't leave me right now. I need you to stay." It's a dick move, and what's more, I know it. She's too sweet to go if she thinks I need her. I do, even though a guilty part of me wonders which of our needs is stronger—her need to get away or mine for her to stay?

She sinks back down on the mattress, an utterly devastated look on her face.

It's obvious she's embarrassed by what happened and doesn't want to talk about it, but I'm desperate to figure out what's wrong. "I'm going to ask you some questions—a"

She cringes and her eyes squeeze shut.

"—all you have to do is answer yes or no? Okay? That's all." I keep my voice gentle but I'm still panicking inside. I can feel her distancing herself from me. We're so new that I wouldn't be surprised if she decides to cut me loose rather than face this—whatever it is—head-on.

She sits there for several seconds before taking a deep breath and slowly nodding. "Okay." But she keeps her eyes closed.

I've never been more nervous in my life. Somehow I know the questions I ask—never mind the answers she gives me—might determine whether she'll stay with me. "Okay," I finally say, reaching up and wiping the tears from her cheeks. She flinches.

I lean over the side of the bed and grab my T-shirt. "Why don't you put this on so you don't get cold?" That's not why I want her to wear it. It occurs to me that sitting next to me naked probably makes her feel more vulnerable.

"Okay," she whispers and opens her eyes. She pulls the shirt over her head and slips her arms through the sleeves.

I tug the covers over the lower half of my body, but leave my chest exposed. I gently pick up one of her hands and begin to roll up the too-long sleeve. "Did I hurt you? You have to know I would never want to hurt you."

She shakes her head and her eyes are open, but she's not meeting my eyes. She's watching me work on the first sleeve. "No. You didn't hurt me."

That's good. She gave me more than a one-word answer.

But if I didn't hurt her, I'm even more confused about what happened. I reach for her other hand and begin to roll up the sleeve.

"Did you not want to have sex? You can always tell me no, Alexa."

Her face lifts and she looks into my face, astonishment in her eyes. "No. I wanted to have sex," she says, dropping her gaze. "And I'd tell you no if I didn't."

I slowly reach my hand toward her face and she doesn't flinch this time. "Good, because fair warning: I plan on having lots and lots of sex with you until you're so sick of it you'll beat me off with a broom."

A grin quirks the corner of her mouth. "I guess I better get a broom then."

I resist the urge to let my shoulders sag with relief. She's not going to send me away.

"So, I didn't hurt you and I didn't force you to have sex," I say, thinking out loud.

But her body stiffens as though I've slapped her.

I didn't force you to have sex.

She likes to be on top and in control.

She freaked out when I pinned her to the bed.

The blood drains from my head and pure and unadulterated panic washes through my body, followed by so many thoughts I can hardly sort through them, but the largest and most horrifying pushes to the surface.

Alexa has been sexually assaulted at some point.

And suddenly it all makes so much sense—Reed's notorious overprotection, their sudden move here, her need for control in bed.

I stare at this woman in front of me, who's so absolutely and stunningly beautiful, both inside and out— and white-hot rage blazes through my body. I want to kill the motherfucker who did this to her. I want to rip his fucking head off and beat the ever-loving shit out of him and I'm not thinking metaphorically. I literally want to torture him before I murder his worthless ass.

I don't realize my breath is coming out in short bursts until Alexa looks up at me in confusion. Her eyes widen in horror when they meet mine.

"You know," she whispers.

Get your shit together, Masterson.

This moment could be the tipping point, the moment when she decides whether or not to kick me out. And I need to put my own need for revenge—justified or not—

aside and make sure she's okay. She's been through enough without me adding to her trauma. But what can I possibly say to ease her discomfort?

"I'm not going anywhere."

Tears fill her eyes and she scoots back from me. "You say that now, but you won't look at me the same way now. You'll look at me with pity like Reed and Caroline do. You'll always be thinking 'poor little Lexi' or wondering what really happened that night."

"Are you fucking kidding?" I ask, trying to temper my anger. "Why would I look at you with pity? You're a fucking fighter and you've never been 'little Lexi' to me anyway. Reed's your older brother and he's always going to think of you as his kid sister. I'm sure Caroline sees you the same way he does." I grab her hand and hold tight. "But I see you as Alexa. That's the only way I've ever known you. And Alexa is a strong, independent woman who fights for what she wants and the people she loves. What in God's name is there to pity?"

Her mouth drops in disbelief.

"As far as wondering what happened *that night*, as you referred to it, I want you to tell me what you want me to know. Nothing more. I will never ask you to share anything you don't feel comfortable sharing. I'd like to know some details, like how long ago it happened and whether you knew him, but I'm afraid if I know too much, I won't be able to keep myself from going after the guy."

Her eyes widen and then fill with tears again. "How can you want to be with me after I freaked out like that?"

"Have you listened to what I've been telling you?" I say, my voice softening. "You are an amazing woman and I feel so unworthy of you. But I'm a selfish son-of-a-bitch, so I want you anyway." My eyebrows rise. "You think the knowledge that some motherfucker hurt you is going to change my feelings about *you?*"

"But I'm broken." Her gaze drops to the bed.

"I'm broken too. I'm a total fucking mess. So, we'll be broken together."

She's still for several seconds and then she lifts her arms and wraps them around my neck, weeping softly into my shoulder and relief washes through me. I rub her back as she cries herself into exhaustion.

"I'm going to lay us both down, okay?"

She nods into my shoulder and I gently lower her to the bed.

"Don't treat me differently now. Please," she begs.

I tuck the covers around her and sink my hand into her hair, searching her eyes. At least she's looking at me now. "First of all, if you cry like that—no matter what the reason—I'm going to treat you gently and make sure you're okay."

"Even if it's over something stupid?"

"If you're upset enough to cry, then it will never be over something stupid."

"And what's second? You said *first of all.*"

I gently rub her head. "Second is that you are already very precious to me, Alexa Pendergraft, and I will always try my best to make sure you know that. Please don't ask me to stop."

She closes her eyes. "Okay."

I turn off the light and watch her sleep for several minutes before carefully slipping out of bed. I pull on my underwear and go out into the kitchen. Resting my hands on the counter, I lean forward and give in to my own personal freak-out.

I was accused—and arrested—for the very thing that happened to Alexa. There's no way I can keep that a secret forever. At some point, she's going to find out. What will she do? What will *Reed* do?

I force myself to take several deep breaths. This is out of my control, as hard as that is to admit. I finally—*finally*—found someone I can see risking everything for and there's a very good chance I've already destroyed it.

Anger burns white-hot in my gut. *I* didn't destroy it. That bitch Sabrina did. Her false charges may not have stuck, but the stench of her accusation still clings. If Sabrina were a guy, I'd beat the ever-loving shit out of her. But she's not, and that's a line I'll never cross—no matter how angry I become. Sabrina may deserve to be pummeled, but I won't be the one to do it.

But there's another factor in this equation. The guy who did this to Alexa. What he did was far, far worse than Sabrina's accusations. Tomorrow, the first thing I plan to do is find Reed. He'll know what motherfucking piece of shit hurt Alexa, and if he's the brother I now know him to be, he'll help me bring the bastard down.

Chapter
Twenty-Five

Ben

I wake up before Alexa does. Maybe it's because she cried herself into total exhaustion or it could be the need to avenge what has happened to her, which kindled inside me the moment she confirmed the truth. I can tell that it won't die down until I do something. Maybe if I'm proactive in my quest to avenge the wrong that's been done to her, I'll prove myself incapable of doing what I was accused of.

She's lying on her side, facing me with one hand under her pillow, the other draped across my waist. She's still wearing my shirt and an unfamiliar warmth spreads through my chest at the sight.

How has she so quickly wormed her way into my heart?

The *how* is superfluous at this point... The real question is what will I do about it? My schedule is insane and I know I'm going to want to be with her every possible moment. But then again, maybe my schedule will help us ensure that we don't take things too fast.

As I'm watching her, Alexa stirs, sighing before settling closer to me. My hand is draped around her back and I lower it to cup her ass. The now familiar jolt of need strains my growing erection.

Taking this slow is already not an option.

But I need to be careful. She doesn't want me to treat her any differently, yet I want to be sure to respect whatever boundaries she has, because she obviously has them. I just don't know what all of them are yet.

"Good morning," she murmurs with a soft smile, her eyes are still closed.

"I thought you were going to sleep all day," I say. "I thought I was going to have to wake you up with a kiss."

"How can you be sure it would work?" she asks, quirking an eyebrow, her eyes still closed. "Maybe you should practice."

I lean over and kiss her tenderly, but her tongue runs along my lip and I groan and deepen the contact. She grabs the back of my head, holding me in place as my tongue begins to explore her mouth.

I pull back and ask with a grin, "And how was that?"

She smiles and stretches, arching her back. Her chest thrusts out when she does that, and my shirt clings to her breasts, making it impossible to look away.

"I have an hour and a half until I have to get to class. How about you?"

"What time is it?" She tries to prop herself up to look at the clock next to her bed.

"Seven-thirty."

She flops back down on her back, her curls spilling around her face. "What day is it?" she asks, grinning.

"Thursday." Unable to resist, I lean over and kiss her.

"Nine," she says breathlessly when I start to caress her neck.

"Then we have time for this?" I murmur, licking the soft area behind her ear.

"Yes." I love when she answers like that, all breathless and low.

We make love, starting slow and tender, but I can sense that Alexa thinks I'm being gentle because of her revelation. I want to tell her that I'm being tender because that's how I feel about her, but I know that's not what she wants to hear or what she needs. She needs to know that I don't see her the way she sees herself, that I don't think she's broken. I up the intensity in my kiss and grab her leg, wrapping it around my waist as I reach between her legs.

Soon she's panting and pushing me on my back.

Afterward, she lies against me, her head in the crook of my arm. "Thank you," she says softly, her finger absently tracing figure eights on my chest.

"I told you last night, I aim to please," I tease.

She props her head up and studies my face. "I'm serious Ben. Thanks for...dealing with me."

I laugh and lift my eyebrows in an exaggerated manner. "Is that what we're calling this? If so, I'll deal with you any day, any time."

"Ben, I'm—"

"Serious," I finish. "But you're inferring that I did something special. All I want is the chance to be with you. I should be the one thanking you." I stretch up and kiss the tip of her nose.

She stares at me, tenderness in her eyes then she finally says, "I need a shower. Want to join me?"

"Sure. But first I need a cup of coffee or I'll never keep up with you." Then I pause for dramatic effect. "Please tell me you have coffee."

She sits up and the sheet falls. I reach up and run my fingertips along the curve of her back. I could touch her every moment of the rest of my life without getting enough of her.

"Yes, we have coffee. The machine is Caroline's and it's her baby." She pauses. "I'm surprised she left it here.

But I know she hopes to come home. She's waiting for Reed to confide in her."

"She left because she thought Reed was seeing someone else, but you said he's in trouble."

She looks over her shoulder at me, as though weighing her options. I wonder if I've overstepped my bounds, but then she says, "Yes. Reed won't tell her because he's doing something illegal and he's worried that if Caroline knows about it, she might be implicated too."

I sit up, shock jolting through my body. "Your brother—*Reed Pendergraft*—is doing something illegal?" I shake my head. "I don't buy it."

She turns around to face me, but she doesn't look angry like I'm worried she will. She looks scared. "He told me so himself, Ben. He says she'll be forced to testify against him if she knows anything."

I try to keep my mouth from sagging open. "What is he doing? And why would he tell you?"

She swallows. "It's *because* of me."

I watch her for several moments before I put it together. "You said he was out of town. Where did he go?"

"He called Caroline and told her he was going to Boston. He asked her to come stay with me while he was gone, but I convinced her I didn't need a babysitter, that two security systems would be enough. But my uncle says Reed left Boston yesterday. I think he's in New York City."

"What's he doing?"

"I don't know." She shakes her head with a sigh. "He told me that Todd has been trying to find me." She pauses. "I need to tell you the whole story."

Is Todd the name of the motherfucking bastard? I put my hand on her shoulder and rub lightly. "Alexa, you don't have to."

"Surprisingly, I want to," she says softly. "I realized that last night, and it astounded me. I've never wanted to tell anyone, especially my last boyfriend." She tilts her head to the side with a wry smile. "Whom I incidentally broke up with just minutes after freaking out when we had sex."

I slide my arm around her back and tug her into the crook of my arm, then gently kiss her. "Thank you for not breaking up with me, not that I would have let you." I give her an ornery smile. "I'm not sure if you've noticed, but I'm pretty damn...stubborn."

"I was going to say sweet," she says, kissing me back. Then she looks down. "That was the first time I had sex after being raped last April. We tried multiple attempts. At first I didn't understand what the problem was because I felt fine most of the time...at least when he wasn't holding me down or anything. He felt terrible," she whispers. "And I felt terrible about putting him through that. He's a really nice guy. He didn't deserve it."

I squeeze her shoulder. "And you didn't deserve it either."

She's silent for a moment. "The wig is what helped me figure it out, although at first I wasn't sure if it was the wig or the fact that I took charge with Rob."

"The guy you were with at the bar?"

"I knew it was short-term. He seemed safe." She releases a nervous laugh. "You probably think I'm a slut."

"Uh. No."

"I felt like I was more sophisticated in the wig. It gave me a confidence I didn't have."

"Is that why you wore it when you showed up at my apartment the other night?"

She's silent for a moment. "Well... I wasn't sure if you knew who I really was, so I didn't want to just show up as a blonde. I was actually there to tell you the truth. Only I was scared that you'd be angry. That's why I kissed you." She takes a deep breath. "But I wore the wig when I left in case someone was watching our apartment. I figured they wouldn't know it was me if they saw me leave."

I try to keep my arm from tensing. "Who would be watching your apartment? The guy who raped you?"

She doesn't answer.

"Is he around? *Are you safe?*" My breath comes in short bursts. "Why the hell would Reed leave you alone?"

She turns to me and grabs my hand. "Ben, calm down. I'll tell you everything. But you can't freak out."

I nod, hoping I can live up to my agreement.

She tells me that she went to a small private college out east her freshman year. She knew the Todd guy was interested because he kept asking her out, but she found him arrogant and conceited, so she turned him down every time. So he turned into a secret admirer, only Alexa didn't put the pieces together. It started out as notes, then gifts— the tokens left in her classes or outside her dorm room door. But one night, when her roommate was gone for the weekend, Alexa went back to her room and he was waiting for her there. He raped her multiple times before he left that night. She immediately called the campus police and then her brother. Reed had been waiting in the ER when she arrived. She pressed charges and then the shit hit the fan. His family had money, and they threatened to slap Alexa and her family with a slander suit. Her parents' corporation was undergoing an investigation for fraud, and her parents couldn't handle the media storm of a *he said, she said* public spectacle. So they made her drop the charges and quit school to protect her from further contact with him. Reed was livid when she called him. He convinced her parents to let him bring her somewhere with a new identity, so that she could live a normal life, free of media scrutiny.

"So, you're not Alexa Pendergraft?" That explains the fake ID from Massachusetts.

"No, I'm sorry. I'm Alexa Monroe. Pendergraft is my great-grandmother's maiden name." Worry fills her eyes. "Are you mad?"

"Why would I be mad? Your last name could be Jingleheimer Schmidt for all I care." I cup her face with my hand. "You did it to be safe, right? To hide from that psycho. How could I be upset over that?" My back stiffens. "You said he's trying to find you?"

She nods, not looking at me. "That's what Reed said. This has been going on for over a month."

Fuck, no wonder her brother has been such a dick. I'm about to become one too.

"Reed told me that the woman he's been talking to is like a private investigator. And I know he's doing something illegal. He said he was going to make sure I was safe this time."

"And you don't know what he's doing?"

"No, although when I think about it, physical violence isn't Reed's style. I suspect he's doing something with his computer."

"Like what?"

She shrugs. "I don't know. I was hoping you might have an idea since you're a math guy too. But knowing Reed, he's going to go after their money, their corporation, or both."

I close my eyes and release a heavy breath. "If he gets caught, the charges would be federal."

She sniffs and turns to me, tears spilling down her cheek. "Will you help me stop him?"

My eyes widen in surprise. "How?"

She starts to cry. "I don't know, Ben. All I know is that Reed gave up his entire life to come here with me. He was supposed to go to Stanford to work with his lifelong idol, but he gave it up for me. And now he's about to give up the rest of his life too." She starts to cry harder. "I've known this for days, but I didn't know who to turn to for help. I called my uncle thinking he could talk some sense into Reed, but he wouldn't listen to him either. I can't let him destroy his life, Ben. I can't."

I pull her against my chest and stroke the back of her head. "Shh. Don't cry, Alexa. We'll figure something out."

She pulls back, her eyes wide. "You'll help me?"

She really thinks I could deny her? "Of course."

"Thank you." She throws her arms around my neck again and kisses me.

"Hey," I grin. "How can I turn down a job with such great perks? Now I need to know everything that could possibly help us figure out where he is and what he's up to." I slide to the edge of the bed. "But first I need coffee." I reach for her hand and pull her to her feet. "And you need a shower."

She stands. "There's one more thing."

I wait for her to continue.

"The reason I think Reed is in New York City." She looks up at me. "When I was looking for clues to help me figure out what Reed was doing, I found a phone number in the pocket of his dirty jeans."

Something about the way she's saying this has me on edge. "And it was a New York City number."

"Yes." She seems nervous.

"What aren't you telling me?"

"It's *his* number."

I try to control my temper, but rage spills out with my words. "The motherfucking asshole who hurt you? You have *his* number?"

She nods.

"I want it *right now*."

Her shoulders stiffen. "Ben, stop. There's more."

"*There's more than that?*"

Her eyes narrow. "If you can't control yourself, I won't tell you anything else."

I take a step away from her and suck deep breaths through my mouth, pushing them out again with force. I don't think I've ever been so angry in my life, but Alexa's been through enough grief. I will *not* add to it. "I'm sorry. You have no idea how much I want to hurt that guy."

"I do. I've seen it in Reed."

Who would have thought Reed Pendergraft—Reed Monroe—and I would have so much in common?

I take another breath. "Okay, I'll try not to react so strongly."

"All I found was the number," she says in a quiet voice. "I looked it up and the only information I could find indicated that it was a cell number from Manhattan. I called it thinking it was Ms. Pembry, but it was him."

I suck in a breath.

"He tried calling back immediately after I hung up without speaking. And then he tried again yesterday when I was at the grocery store." She shakes her head with a shrug. "I almost missed the call, so I just grabbed it out of my purse and answered without checking who it was. He figured out it was me. I hung up, but he knows I have his number."

Fear races up my spine—if he has her number, he can easily find her.

"Ben, don't you see?" she asks. "If Reed does something to sabotage them, the fact that I just called Todd will tie my brother to whatever happens."

"We need to call Reed, Alexa. We need to stop him."

"I've tried!" She says, frustration filling her voice. "After Todd called me, I tried calling Reed again, but he wouldn't answer. He still won't. And I've been leaving him voice mails telling him to call me, that it's important, but he still hasn't gotten in touch."

I place my hands on her shoulders. "We'll figure this out. I promise. Why don't you take your shower? I'm going to skip my class and let's go to his office in the math lab to see if we can find something that will help us."

Tears fill her eyes. "Thank you."

I take another breath. "Don't thank me yet. He doesn't seem like the kind of guy to leave a paper trail, but it's worth a shot. Are you sure you searched his entire room?"

She hesitates.

"Then we'll search it again before we go."

"Okay."

"Get in the shower and I'll be there as soon as I get my coffee IV going."

She disappears in the bathroom and I head to the kitchen, thanking God that Caroline not only left her coffee maker, but that it's a one-touch system. I grab a cup and press the button when I hear a cell phone ringing.

It's coming from Alexa's purse. Ordinarily, I'd let it ring, but it could be Reed. I dig out the phone, but Reed's number isn't on the screen. It's just a number and it's not local.

Is it the motherfucker?

Knowing what I'm doing is wrong on every level—I could stir up even more shit by doing this, but I can't stop myself. I want him to know that Alexa has people who will protect her, that we will not allow him to intimidate her. "Who is this?"

There's silence, then a low laugh. "The question is who is *this*?"

"Leave her alone, you asswipe."

"Lexi's the one who called me," he says in a cultured voice. I'm used to his kind. There are a few hundred of them running around the campus of Southern University.

"It was an inadvertent mistake," I say. "So do yourself a favor and lose this number."

"No can do, muchacho," he laughs. "Lexi called me for a reason." He pauses and lowers his voice. "I know she likes to play shy and hard to get. But it's all an act." He chuckles. "Maybe you've figured that out by now."

"The only thing I've figured out is how to treat a woman with respect, which means comprehending what the word *no* actually means."

"You're funny," he says. "I like you."

"The feeling is so *not* fucking mutual."

"Tell Lexi I know where she is and that I'll be seeing her soon."

I grit my teeth and force out, "Over my dead body."

He laughs. "That can be arranged."

And then the connection is broken.

Chapter Twenty-Six

Lexi

Ben never joins me in the shower.

I tell myself that it doesn't mean anything. But I've dumped a ton of crap at his feet in the last few hours—what if he's having second thoughts?

I'm amazed that I told him at all. No, I'm amazed by his reaction. He didn't run when I freaked out. He didn't freak out himself. In fact, he helped me regain control of my own rollercoaster emotions. But what if it's all too much? My freak-out, Todd's reappearance, Reed doing something to stop him, and me begging Ben to help—he even said he was going to skip his class this morning to search Reed's office. Ben's a wonderfully thoughtful guy, but what if the cold light of day is making him reconsider? If so, I couldn't blame him.

When I get out, I get dressed and find him in the kitchen. He's sitting at the bar with a notebook and pen, making a list. He looks up when I come around the corner, then gets out of his chair and pulls me to his chest, his arms tight around my back.

"I think we should skip everything today and just focus on finding Reed."

I pull my head back. "What?"

His jaw is tight and determination fills his eyes. "I think he's in trouble and we don't have time to waste."

"But you don't even like Reed very much." He starts to protest, but I place my fingertips on his lips. "Don't argue. I just want to know why you want to help him."

He offers me a grim smile. "Reed and I aren't best friends. Hell, we aren't even friends, but of course I want to help him. He's trying to help you. And he's your brother."

I look up at the intensity in his eyes and I shake my head. "Ben, you hardly know me."

"It's like I told you last night—I might not have known you for a long time, but I *do* know you. Are you telling me that you aren't the person I think you are?"

I was embarrassed when he listed my traits to me last night, but I have to admit that everything he said was true. "Okay, but I don't think you should skip anything. We'll both go to our nine o'clock classes first. Then we can go to the math lab."

"Do you have a test in your first class or anything you can't miss?"

"Well, no…" I can always get notes from Sylvia.

"Then let's get started right away. I have a really bad feeling about this."

He's serious.

"So we skip our first classes to get started, we don't need to skip the entire day."

He starts to say something, but then he gives me a soft kiss. "We'll see how it goes." He grabs his coffee off the counter and drains it. "I'm going to grab a quick shower, and then we can get started. We'll start in Reed's room."

"Okay."

He starts down the hall, then stops and turns. "Don't leave the apartment, okay?"

My eyes narrow in confusion. "Why?"

His mouth parts and he hesitates. "You said the guy tried to call you last night and I'd rather err on the side of safety. Just humor me, okay?"

"Okay."

I make a cup of coffee and am starting to clean up the kitchen from last night when I notice the paper Ben was huddled over. I lean over the counter and realize he's created a list of things to look for, along with places to look. He's thought of things I haven't, like a sequence of numbers and binary code. I'm still studying the paper when he comes back into the kitchen, his hair dripping wet.

"Anything to add?" he asks, swiping his empty cup from the counter and putting it under the coffee maker.

"No, in fact, I would never have come up with some of these."

He grins, but it's not as playful as usual. "I was trying to think like him. He's a computer geek, though. I'm more a trig and calculus guy."

"Do you think we'll find anything in the lab?"

He takes a deep breath and releases it. "Honestly, I don't know. Like I said, he doesn't seem like the kind of guy who would leave evidence lying around. He's meticulous to a fault. I think he's going to have done a damn good job of covering his tracks."

I nod, trying to hide my disappointment.

"Hey," he says, trying to sound lighter. "No one's perfect, though, so maybe he fucked up somewhere."

I shake my head and laugh. "I'm not sure which one to hope for."

"Yeah, I know."

"I'm going to make eggs for breakfast," I say and open the refrigerator to pull out the carton. "How do you like your eggs?"

His eyebrows lift and a grin spreads across his face as he takes a sip of his coffee. "Why do I think this sounds like a test?"

"It's not. It's a simple question. Fried? Sunny side up? Scrambled?"

"What if I want eggs Benedict?"

I put a hand on my hip. "Then you're out of luck."

"Scrambled," he mutters over the rim of his mug. "And I'm more than a little afraid of what that says about me."

I walk over and pull a bowl from the cabinet. "It means you like scrambled eggs."

He holds his cup out and away from his body but snags his free arm around my waist, pulling me to him. His face lowers until it's just inches from mine, and he stares into my eyes. "And how do you like your eggs, Ms. Pendergraft?"

"Scrambled. Just like you."

His grin spreads, lighting up his eyes. "See? The stars have aligned. We were meant to be together."

I kiss him again and then pull out of his grasp. "On a planet with nearly seven billion people, what *are* the odds of finding someone else who likes scrambled eggs?"

He tilts his head to the side with a smirk. "Mock me if you'd like, but I notice you're barefoot and working in the kitchen again, so who gets the last laugh?"

I'm happy to see his lightheartedness has returned. When I'm done, we sit side by side at the bar as we eat and there's a familiarity I don't expect. The beginning of a relationship is usually full of awkward moments and pauses, but I realize I've never experienced that with him.

I find myself staring at him for lengthy stretches of time and he notices. He leans forward and gives me the most gentle of kisses, butterfly soft. "Let's get moving."

I put the plates in the dishwasher as Ben reads his list. "Ideally, I'd love to crack his passwords, but I think we have a better chance of a meteorite striking the earth and sending us into an ice age."

"I could ask Caroline, but I'm worried she'll ask questions. It's a suspicious request."

His eyebrows lift in surprise. "Do you think he would have told her?"

"I don't know." I give a half shrug. "They were really, really close. They spent almost every spare moment together until Reed started pulling away when this whole mess started."

"That's pretty sad."

"Yeah." The guilt eats at me.

He leans across the counter and grabs my hand. "Alexa, don't do that. You are not responsible for your brother's relationship."

"Aren't I? If it weren't for me, they'd still be together."

"If it weren't for you, there's a good chance they wouldn't have been together at all. Does that make you responsible for the health of their relationship for the rest of your life?"

"No, but they split up because of me. Because Reed is trying to protect *me*."

"No, they split up because Reed kept secrets from Caroline. Granted, he did it to protect you both, but that's the real reason."

I stare into his eyes. "Don't keep secrets from me, okay? Even if you think they'll hurt me."

He hesitates, and then a goofy grin spreads across his face. "My heart is laid bare for you, Alexa."

I shake my head. "Come on. Let's get started."

We start searching Reed and Caroline's room. When Ben opens a drawer full of Caroline's lingerie, he takes a step back and lifts his hands in the air. "Whoa. Nothing makes you feel more like a creeper than going through your boss-slash-girlfriend's-brother's-fiancée's lingerie. You look through it."

"I don't want to go through it. I don't want to think about her wearing it with my brother."

"Well, *someone* has to and it's not going to be me."

I realize what he's just said. "You called me your girlfriend."

He looks up from the next drawer he's begun searching and then straightens to standing. "Do you like me?"

I shudder in surprise. "Of course. How can you even ask that?"

"Do you want to be with me?"

"You know I do."

"You know how I feel about you, so what's the big deal?" He shrugs. "It's a title. A label."

I can't help but chuckle. "You have no idea how much you sounded like Reed just now. I'm going to chalk it up to left brain domination."

He cringes. "Wow. I'm not sure whether to feel horrified or flattered."

I smile and wrap my hands around the back of his neck. "Shut up and kiss me."

"You are a demanding woman. Is this what I have to look forward too? You ordering me to kiss you?"

"I guess you'll have to stick around and find out." I cock an eyebrow. "And you still haven't kissed me."

His mouth lowers to mine, hovering less than an inch away. "Like this?"

"No."

His mouth moves to the corner of my mouth. His lips brush along my cheek, his warm breath sending shivers up my spine. "Like this?"

"No," I say, breathless.

His mouth returns to mine, his tongue barely outlining my lips. "Like this?"

A jolt of desire spreads through my abdomen and my knees weaken. "No," I moan.

His mouth finds mine, hard and demanding as one hand grips the back of my head, the other pressing firmly on my back.

I cling to him, wanting more.

"I have absolutely no will power with you," he murmurs when he lifts his head. "You have no idea how much I want to take you to your room and strip you naked. All from just a kiss."

A shiver of desire spreads across my skin.

He stares into my eyes. "But we have to find clues about Reed." His arms drop and he places a chaste kiss on my lips. "So no seducing me, you siren."

"Ever?" I ask, mischievously.

"No, just the next hour or so."

We spend about forty-five minutes searching without finding anything. Ben shakes his head as he takes a final look around the room. "This isn't a good sign. I'd expect any clues to be in here."

"But we're still going to look at the math lab, right?"

"Of course, just don't get your hopes up." He pauses. "Maybe it's time to call Caroline."

"Yeah." I know he's right. But I did such a bad job of deflecting her questions the last time we spoke that I worry how I'll manage now. "I need to get my cell phone. I think I left it in my purse."

Ben follows me to the kitchen.

My phone is at the top and I check the screen for any missed calls, finding none. The last call received was Todd's number. I have Caroline's number on speed dial, so it only takes a second to make the call. "Hey, Lex. Is everything okay?"

"Yeah," I hedge. "I have an unusual request."

She answers hesitantly, "Okay."

"You'll want to ask questions, but I'm begging you to wait until later for an explanation."

"No, Lexi." Her voice is firm. "Enough secrets."

My shoulders sag with disappointment and I look up at Ben.

"Tell her," he says.

My eyes widen and I cover the mouthpiece. "I can't! What if she's called to testify?"

"Hopefully, we'll stop Reed before he does anything. Tell her. She still won't really know anything and she deserves to know."

"Lexi?" Caroline asks in my ear.

"Okay," I sigh. "I'll tell you what's going on."

"*You will?*"

"Yes, but I want to do this in person."

"Meet me at Panera in fifteen minutes."

"Okay."

I hang up and look up at Ben and tell him when and where I'm meeting her.

He looks grim. "Okay. Do you need to do anything else before leaving?"

"I need to do something to my hair. I'm sure it's a mess."

"It's perfect."

I laugh and kiss him before heading to the bathroom. "You just want to get laid later."

"That too."

We take Ben's car to Panera. He pulls into the parking lot and turns off the engine. "Is it okay if I come in with you?"

I turn to him in surprise. "Of course. I need your help."

"Okay." He gets out of the car and comes around to the passenger side. "Are you going to start off by telling Caroline what's going on? That's probably the best way to handle it, since she'll probably be more on board with helping us."

"Yeah, good idea."

Caroline is sitting at a table with a coffee cup in front of her. She looks up as we approach, her eyes widening with surprise when they land on Ben.

"Hey, Caroline." I put my arm around Ben's back. "This is Ben Masterson."

She's still staring.

"We've been seeing each other," I add.

Ben steps forward and shakes her hand. "Nice to meet you, Caroline. If you want references, I work with Scarlett in the math lab," he teases. "I'm pretty sure she'll vouch for me."

Recognition spreads over her face. "Yeah, Scarlett's mentioned you. She likes you, especially after the Tina freak-out on Monday."

Ben leans down and kisses my cheek. "I'm going to get a coffee. Do you want anything?"

I look up at him and smile. "No. I'm good." My voice softens. "Thank you."

He nods and heads toward the counter.

Caroline's gaze follows him and then shifts to me as I sit across from her. "He's in love with you."

"*What?*" I watch him at the counter. He turns around to check on me and when he sees me watching, he lifts his hand and waves, a grin spreading across his face.

Caroline is watching too. "Yep, he's a total goner."

I shake my head. "No, he can't be in love with me. We haven't been together for very long."

"Maybe not, but it didn't take Reed very long either." She laughs as she gives him another look before returning her gaze to me. "Well, the boy is smitten, we'll leave it at that."

I blush. "Fair enough."

"For the record, Scarlett really does sing his praises. What does Reed think about this?"

My smile falls. "He doesn't know. Yet."

"Understood," she says. "Sorry I haven't been there to run interference."

"That's not why I miss you, Caroline. I miss *you*." A lump fills my throat and I try to swallow it.

"I miss you too, Lex." She grabs her coffee cup with both hands and her eyes turn serious. "So, you said you were going to tell me what's going on."

I nod. "Reed's going to be furious, but Ben agrees that you need to know."

Her mouth lifts on one side. "I like this Ben already."

I tell her everything about Reed and what I know. Somewhere in the course of my explanation, I decide to tell her *everything*, including going out with Tina and Ben helping me when I was drugged. She's furious with Tina, but grateful that Ben was there to help me. And when I finally finish, she grabs my hand, tears in her eyes. "Why didn't you and Reed tell me?"

"I told you. Reed was trying to protect you. He was worried that you'd get in trouble with the cops if you knew everything."

Anger fills her eyes. "Damn him and his need to protect everyone. I'm not some delicate flower that's easily crushed!"

"No, you're not."

Her voice rises. "And neither are you!"

"I know."

Ben has been hanging in the periphery, but Caroline's outburst draws him back to the table. "Is everything okay here?" His wary gaze moves from me to Caroline.

"Relax. She's fine." She smirks, turning her attention to me. "He's a lot like Reed." Then she smiles at Ben. "Why don't you sit? Lexi and I have reached the part where you're about to pump me for all the information I have that might help us stop Reed."

Ben slides in next to me and takes my hand in his. Caroline's mouth lifts into a soft smile.

Ben taps the table with his free hand. "We're trying to figure out what Reed's up to and where he actually went. Alexa says he told you he was going to Boston."

She nods. "Yes, but he didn't say why. I presumed it was family stuff since that's where he and Lexi are from."

"Do you have any clues that can help us figure out the passwords to his email accounts or a travel site where he might have bought his plane tickets?"

"I can do better than clues," she says. "I have access to the site he uses to book his travel. He wanted me to check airfare for our honeymoon." Her voice breaks.

I reach over and grab her hand with my free one. "Everything's going to be okay, Caroline. We're going to stop him."

Tears fill her eyes as she shakes her head. "Don't you see, Lexi? Stopping him isn't going to fix everything. What's to stop him from doing something like this again?"

Fear grips my heart. "But you said you wanted to come home."

"I *do*, more than I've ever wanted anything. But we have a few other things to resolve before everything's okay."

"Let's just concentrate on finding him," Ben says. "Caroline, can you try calling him? I know he's been a fucked-up mess since you left. I bet he would answer if you reached out to him."

She gives him a wary glance. "How do you know he's been a fucked-up mess?"

He smirks. "I worked with the dick—" he stops and clears his throat "—the *guy*. We all experienced the fallout of you leaving him."

"Sorry," she says.

He shrugs. "Nothing I couldn't handle."

"So will you call him?" I ask.

Her face softens. "Lexi, I still love him more than anything. I want to help him as much as you do. Of course I will."

Ben leans forward. "If he answers, be sure to tell him that Alexa has been in contact with the asshole who hurt her. Let Reed know that he can protect her better here than from somewhere else. It's imperative for him to come home."

I turn to him and narrow my gaze. "Why do you want him to think he needs to come home to protect me?"

Concern lowers his brow. "Alexa, this guy called you yesterday. I'm worried, and if *I'm* worried, your brother is going to flip out. This is what will drive him home."

"But how do you know it won't drive him to do the very thing we're trying to prevent?"

"Call it a hunch. Your immediate safety takes precedence over your long-term safety. If what he's up to was so easy to set into action, he would have done it already."

My stomach is a bundle of nerves. "I hope you're right."

He leans over and kisses me gently. "Trust me."

"Okay." I stare into his eyes for several seconds before I remember Caroline is watching us.

She's already holding her phone in her hand. "While you two cuties had your tête-à-tête, I looked up Reed's travel account. You're right. He flew into Boston the day he left, and then he landed in JFK yesterday. He's staying in a hotel in Manhattan."

Ben's mouth presses together. "Maybe he's there to try and dig up dirt on Todd's family's corporation."

Caroline shakes her head. "I'm going to call him and put an end to this nonsense." She gets up from the table and walks away.

I don't realize I'm holding my breath while I watch her until my chest begins to burn. It looks like he's answered and Caroline's voice floats across the restaurant. She pushes through the doors and starts pacing on the sidewalk, shaking her pointed finger as though he can see her.

"That Caroline is something else," Ben murmurs. "No wonder Reed was so upset when she left him. I bet she keeps him on his toes."

I lean my head against his shoulder, praying that Caroline can talk some sense into my brother. I'm watching her when she suddenly stops pacing and turns her back to us, huddling with the phone. After several minutes, she wipes tears off her cheeks, lowers the phone, and comes back inside.

Her eyes are red from crying when she sits down, so I'm not sure what to expect.

"He's coming home."

I feel close to crying myself. "Thank God."

"He wouldn't tell me exactly what he was doing, but I think you guys were on the right track. It had something to do with their corporation. He's coming back tonight. He booked a flight while we were on the phone, but it won't get in until really late."

"Does that mean you're coming home?" I ask, wondering if I've gone too far.

She looks sad. "Not tonight. We're going to hash things out tomorrow." She gives me a grim smile. "Don't worry, Lexi. I'll probably be home tomorrow night. I can't make it too easy for him, though, can I? I have to make sure he never keeps secrets like this from me again."

She's right. I nod my understanding.

She grins at Ben. "He was very surprised to hear about you and Lexi. He wants to see *you* tonight and expects you to be there when he gets home. I'm sure he'll have unearthed a full debriefing of your entire life by the time his plane lands in Knoxville. Knowing him, he'll dig up everything, down to the number of times you were tardy in the third grade."

Ben's back becomes rigid and his face turns pale.

My anger rushes to the surface. "I'm going to call him back and tell him to stop. He thinks he can investigate anyone I meet. It's insulting." I say, gritting my teeth at Reed's audacity. "And he can't just order Ben to be at our apartment when he gets home. He has to work tonight."

"I can get off, Alexa." His voice is quiet.

"The hell you can. You already skipped your class to come meet Caroline with me."

He doesn't answer, but he seems distracted.

"Reed loves you, Lex," Caroline says softly. "You know why he is this way."

"I know." The very fact that he was willing to risk everything to protect me—again—is evidence enough of that, but he and I are going to have to reach a compromise. He can't keep prying into my personal life whenever he wants.

She picks up her purse and grabs her coat. "I have to head to class. Let me know if you need anything else."

Ben gets up and shakes her hand. Caroline shakes it back, looking amused.

"Thank you for helping Alexa."

"Thank you for insisting that she tell me the truth. These Pendergrafts can be pretty hard-headed."

He grins, but he looks nervous. "I've already figured that one out on my own."

"Let me give you some inside advice." She leans forward and lowers her voice. "Reed might bark a lot, but once you earn his loyalty and trust, you've earned it for life—unless you screw up, of course. He'll be a hardass on you at first, but once he sees how important Lexi is to you, he'll back off."

Ben's eyes are serious as he nods. "Thanks. Good to know."

I give Caroline a hug and watch her walk out the door before I turn to Ben. "What time is your next class?"

"Let's just skip our classes today."

My eyes narrow in suspicion. "Why?"

He snakes an arm around my back. "Because I haven't had nearly enough of you yet."

"We can't hide forever."

"No, but we can for one day."

"As much as I love the idea, I can't. I have a test this afternoon, and then I have to go by the charity to talk to the director about the current status of the summer program."

"I'm off this afternoon. I'll come with you."

He's making me anxious. I never would have struck him as the clingy type. "Why are you being so insistent? You're acting like this is your last chance to be with me or something." Then I realize what's happening. "This is about Reed, isn't it? You're worried he's going to convince me to stop seeing you."

He blinks then nods. "You know how persuasive he can be. What if he convinces you that I'm not good enough for you?" He lowers his voice. "You're a Monroe for God's sake. I'm no one."

I lean closer to him. "Caroline is 'no one,' as you say, and yet Reed's with her."

"That's different, Lex. He's the guy."

I put my hand on my hip. "Are you going to get chauvinistic on me now?"

"No! Look." He shakes his head. "The bottom line is that Reed will never approve of me. Ever."

"He'll never approve of anyone." I take a deep breath. "Ben, I know you. You're sweet and protective and you make me happier than I've been in ages. Reed's not going to make me change my mind about you."

He nods but doesn't look convinced. "Maybe I need the rest of the day to plead my case."

I kiss him softly. "You seem so certain that there's going to be a Judgment Day. Why can't you just accept that I like you and want to be with you?"

"I can accept it," he says with a sad smile. "I only hope it's enough."

Chapter
Twenty-Seven

Ben

I'm man enough to admit that I'm scared shitless.

One way or another I'm going to lose her. She's begged me to not keep secrets from her and my arrest last fall is like an albatross around my neck. How will Alexa react when she finds out that I was charged with the very crime that was committed against her? Will she think the charges were dropped for similar reasons? Granted, I don't have money, but victims are coerced into dropping charges for a host of other reasons, all unsavory.

Will she believe me?

I need to be the one to tell her, because if Reed really is creating a dossier on the Life and Times of Benjamin Masterson, my arrest is going to be on top, probably bedazzled. But if I tell her and she's horrified, she'll send me away, which will leave her unprotected—not an option. Because I'm certain that asshole is coming to Hillsdale to see her. There's no way I'm going to leave her alone until Reed comes home. And telling her that her rapist is coming for her is absolutely out of the question. She's upset enough over Reed and everything else. I'm not about to subject her to more trauma.

So my only option is to stay close to her all day and keep my mouth shut.

We head back to the university and I'm glad I drove her to Panera. She's dependent on me for transportation now, which is a good excuse for sticking by her side. The biggest monkey wrench in all of this—besides getting her to let me stay—is getting off work. I need to call my uncle as soon as possible.

I keep my backpack in my car, thankfully, so I don't have to leave her to go back home.

She doesn't realize she's without transportation until we're walking across campus, discussing our schedules. "Oh, Ben! I'm so sorry!"

"I really don't mind driving you to the children's charity, Alexa. I'll probably get to see my little brother."

She stops and smiles, that dazzling smile that fills all the dark corners of my heart. The thought hits me again, just like it's been doing all morning. I can't lose her. I can't lose the way she makes me feel.

"Ben?" she asks. The puzzled look on my face must be a dead giveaway because she smirks. "You didn't hear a word I just said, did you?"

"Sorry. I was too busy admiring you."

Shaking her head, she continues walking.

I grab her arm and pull her to a halt. "I hope you get used to repeating things because it's probably going to happen a lot." I give her a wicked grin. "Now what did you ask?"

"I wanted to know if you had any other siblings."

"No. Just Kyle."

"There's quite an age difference between you two."

"My parents' last-ditch effort to save their marriage. The fact that my brother's eleven and my mother's been gone for a little over ten years should be some indication of how well that one worked out."

"Ouch."

"Yeah."

She slips her hand into mine and peace fills me just like that, along with a feeling that catches me by surprise: home.

It makes my imminent loss all the worse.

We both have an hour until our next class, so we go to the Higher Ground for coffee.

"How much coffee do you drink?" she asks as we sit at a table with our drinks. "You have to be caffeinated enough to power an electrical substation."

She's sitting across from me and the sunlight shines behind her, making her golden hair glow like a halo. "I need it to stay awake. Some nights I only get three hours of sleep."

Her eyes widen in horror. "You can't keep going like that, Ben. You're going to get sick."

"I borrowed money to buy my books and I've got living expenses, Alexa. I'm barely making do as it is."

She closes her eyes and groans. "Now I feel like a bitch for telling you to be grateful for the semesters when you had your scholarship."

I reach across the table and grab her hand. "No. You were right."

We both have work to do. I study history since I have another test tomorrow, and she pulls out her statistics homework. When it's time for our next class, I walk her to her classroom and stop outside the door. "I can't believe I still don't have your cell phone number," I say as I drop her off.

We exchange numbers and I smile down at her. "Wait for me after class and we'll have lunch together, okay?"

"Okay."

I'm distracted through most of my engineering lecture because I spend a good part of my time on my laptop, searching the internet for information about Todd

Millhouse, heir to Millhouse International, a big corporation with lots of fingers in lots of pies. Young master Todd has already earned himself a reputation as a party boy. I have to wonder why he's spending his spare time chasing down Alexa. I can understand why his sick and twisted mind might justify what he did to her, but why is he trying to find her now? What does he care? From the photos plastered across the internet, he doesn't face a shortage of available women.

Perhaps he's one of those little rich boys who doesn't like to be told no. I wish I knew what he planned to do with Alexa. I stiffen. I have a good idea. Let the motherfucker try.

I leave class early and jog across campus to make sure I'm at Alexa's class when she gets out, but the room is empty. My heart slams against my ribcage. Where is she? I'm about to panic when I see her at the end of the hall talking to her friend, the one I saw at the bar with her after the play.

I take a deep breath to calm myself, then head toward her.

A smile lights up her face when she catches sight of me.

"You got out early," I say, stating the obvious.

"You too, I see." She turns to her friend. "Sylvia, this is Ben. Ben, Sylvia."

Sylvia is clearly evaluating me and she seems to approve.

"You work with Alexa on the charity, don't you?" I ask.

"Yeah."

Alexa turns to me with a grimace. "I told Sylvia I would eat lunch with her today to work on the charity dating auction."

"How about all three of us have lunch together?" I suggest.

Alexa looks worried. "You don't have to do that, Ben."

Sylvia waves her hand. "We can talk about it another time."

"No, this will be great. You guys can work on your auction stuff and Sylvia can grill me." I wink. "Isn't that what a girl's friends do when they meet the new man in her life?"

Alexa laughs and kisses me. "Have I told you how amazing you are?"

I wink. "No, but since I already know, it's okay."

She rolls her eyes, then takes my hand. "We were just going to eat in the student union."

"Sounds good to me."

We head to the student union and find an empty table after getting our lunch. I take a seat and Alexa sits next to me, with Sylvia across from us. I stay quiet while Alexa and Sylvia discuss the auction. They have almost everything set up, but they still don't have enough participants for the auction.

"Lexi was supposed to ask you to be a bachelor." Sylvia says. "Instead she kept you for herself."

"I didn't go after Ben," Alexa says. "He went after me."

"It's true," I tell Sylvia. "But she dazzled me with her beauty and her charm, so I didn't stand a chance."

Alexa rolls her eyes.

"Well, we still need someone to represent the math and engineering department," Sylvia says.

I shrug. "I know a few guys who would do it."

Sylvia leans forward, her voice stern. "They have to be cute. No geeky nerds."

"That's discriminatory," I tease. "But the two guys I'm thinking of have no problem getting dates. I have a class with both of them tomorrow. I'll ask."

Sylvia seems pleased and hints that if I want to fix her up with one of them, she's open to it.

After lunch, I walk Alexa to her next class. "You go to the charity after this, right?"

"Yeah, but I can get a ride from someone else, Ben. You don't have to take me."

"I already told you I want to go. I might get to see Kyle there."

I cut my next class and call Uncle Tony to tell him why I need to skip work tonight. He tells me he has it covered. Britt has hinted that she needs some extra hours, but I worry it has something to do with her sleaze-ball ex who's recently reemerged from somewhere dark and creepy.

One problem at a time, Masterson.

Next I call the Hillsdale police department to find out if there's anything Alexa can do legally to stop Millhouse. They tell me she can file a restraining order, but a vague threat over the phone isn't enough of an incentive.

Which means we're on our own.

I'm nervous as we drive to the charity. I hope Kyle will be there, although I can't imagine why he wouldn't be. He's been going to the afterschool program since I started college four years ago. But I haven't seen Kyle since Christmas. Will he be angry? It hasn't been by my choice, but he doesn't necessarily know that.

When we pull into the parking lot, I study the buildings that make up the charity. They've purchased five older houses and converted them into their headquarters. Alexa heads for the office, the farthest building on the left, and I follow along. The director greets her with a smile, which is when I realize something.

Everyone loves Lexi Pendergraft.

Including me.

I expect the realization to shock me. I've never been in love before, and there's no arguing the fact that I haven't known her very long, but I know enough about her to know I'm damn lucky to be part of her life.

Alexa introduces me to the director as a fellow Southern student. "I think Ben would really like to go to the tutoring center to see his brother while we talk, if that's okay."

"Who's your brother?" she asks.

"Kyle Masterson."

She beams. "Kyle is such a delight. I'll call the center to tell them you're heading over." When she completes the call, she takes me to the front porch and points. "It's the house on the end. You can't miss it."

"Thank you." I give Alexa a smile before I leave.

One of the volunteers is a girl I know from school. In fact, several of the staff members are Southern students. "So you're Kyle's brother?"

"Yeah."

"He's going to be excited to see you. He talks about you all the time." She leads me past several rooms and stops at what used to be a large bedroom. Now it contains a table with student-sized chairs, along with about eight students and a volunteer who's working with two of them.

I see him before he sees me. He's bent over the table, pencil in hand, as he fills out a worksheet. My breath catches in my throat and I suddenly worry how he'll react. Will he accuse me of abandoning him?

But when he finally looks up, his face just about bursts with happiness. "Ben!" He jumps out of his seat and nearly tackles me. "I've missed you."

"I've missed you too."

The volunteer leads Kyle and me to the kitchen so we can talk privately. She winks at me after handing him two pudding cups and a plastic spoon. "Just don't tell the other kids or there's bound to be a riot."

Kyle sits across from me at a small table, working on opening his first pudding cup. He looks so much older than when I saw him last. How could I have missed so much in two months?

"How's fifth grade going?" I ask.

His upper lip curls. "Okay, I guess. Math sucks since you're not around to help me with it. Susanna Baker has a crush on me," he says out of nowhere.

I cross my arms and watch him. "Is that a good thing or a bad one?"

He shudders. "It's gross."

"Good. You have a few years left before girls will become a serious issue for you." I pause and continue watching him, drinking in his presence. "I hear you're rocking the basketball court."

He looks up in surprise.

I grin. "I have my sources."

"Coach Tucker told me that he saw you."

"I wish I could come and watch you play, but I work one of my new jobs on Saturday mornings."

He shrugs. "It's okay."

"No," I say firmly. "It's not. But I want you to know how much I'd like to be there."

313

"Thanks." He takes two bites, then keeps his gaze on the pudding cup as he says, "I really miss you, Ben."

A lump fills my throat. "I miss you too, bud."

He takes another bite and sniffs.

Even though Dad turned his back on me after my arrest, I realize now that I handled things badly as well. I was so mad about his lack of support that I let our relationship slip, which took my brother from me too. There's plenty of blame to go around. "I'm going to talk to dad to see if I can spend some time helping you with math."

He stares at me with eyes wide with hope.

"I'm going to talk to dad about a lot of things."

"I think he misses you, but he won't tell me why you guys are fighting."

"We said some stupid things to each other. We both thought we were right and neither of us apologized. You were caught in the middle, and I'm sorry for that." I pause and lean forward, lowering my voice. "And for the record, I miss him too." And I'm surprised I mean it. My father isn't a touchy-feely guy, but we became close in our own way after my mother left. It's funny how differently I'm looking at things now that I know Alexa.

We're talking about what he's been up to at school when Alexa walks in the back door, her hair windblown, her cheeks pink from the cool breeze. I give her a bright smile as she approaches us and sits in the chair between Kyle and me.

I sit up straighter. "Kyle, I'd like for you to meet someone. This is my friend Alexa."

He shrugs. "I've seen her before. Only she's not Alexa. She's Lexi."

Alexa laughs and looks surprised. "I didn't realize any of the kids knew my name. Caroline is usually the hands-on person, while I'm more behind the scenes."

Kyle shrugs again, looking unimpressed.

"Well, I bet when you saw her before you didn't know she was my girlfriend."

His eyes bug out and he gives Alexa a big smile before looking back at me. "I like her. She's a lot nicer than your old girlfriend."

"You've got that right, bud."

Our exchange piques Alexa's interest, but she doesn't ask any questions. We stay for about ten more minutes and Alexa quizzes Kyle on what living with me was like. "It was awful when he moved out a few years ago. He used to do all the laundry and cooking because Dad sucks at it. So Ben would come home every Sunday and hang out with me and we'd do the laundry together and cook dinners for the week." A scowl puckers his mouth. "Until around Thanksgiving. Now he never comes home."

Alexa shoots me a grin. "I know Ben's pretty busy with all his new jobs, but maybe we could come help out sometime. Then we could hang out."

I'm nervous that Kyle's going to contradict her timeline. The coming around stopped before the new jobs, but he ignores it.

"That would be awesome!"

When we leave, Kyle gives me a long bear hug. He pulls away and stands on his tiptoes. "I think Dad would like Lexi," he whispers.

I grin and rub the top of his head. "Me too."

After Alexa and I get in the car, I sit behind the wheel for a moment to get my shit together. I really miss my little brother, and I've only realized how much right this moment.

"Are you okay?"

"Yeah, I haven't seen my Kyle since Christmas."

Her mouth drops open. "How is that possible? You live in the same town."

"My dad and I had a huge fight. But seeing Kyle has reminded me that some things are worth eating humble pie for. I'm going to go see my dad and apologize."

Her hand covers mine. "Do you know how many people are never able to do that? I'm so proud of you, Ben."

Her statement could have been condescending, but it's anything but. I give her a soft kiss. "Thanks. Now let's go eat dinner. I'll cook but we have to stop at the store on the way home."

"What do you plan on making?" she asks.

"Hot dogs."

She laughs. "Sounds perfect."

Chapter Twenty-Eight

Lexi

I could get used to this.

True to his word, Ben buys hot dogs and buns, baked beans and coleslaw. When he tells me his roommates will be gone at an overnight gaming party, I suggest we hang out at his place.

"No, Reed will feel better if you're home when he gets there."

I have to admit he's right, but I'm worried that Reed will overreact to how quickly Ben has become a part of my life. But whether tonight or tomorrow, I have to face it sometime so I might as well get it over with.

While Ben's preparing the food, we play another round of "What's your favorite…?" and I tell him that my favorite TV show is Sherlock.

"Which one?" he asks.

"The one with Benedict Cumberbatch. Caroline got me hooked on it."

"Never seen it."

"This must be rectified." So we eat our hot dogs on paper plates and watch a full episode of Sherlock before Ben grins and declares it's time for dessert. His hand skims up my waist and an anticipatory shiver runs up my spine.

I laugh. "I'm surprised you lasted this long."

"I don't want you to think I only want you for your body." He lowers his mouth to my neck. "Even if it's true."

Ben makes me give him my "ground rules" as he calls them—a list of things that make me anxious and uncomfortable—before we even remove any of our clothes. He smooths the hair away from my face. "I never want you to feel uncomfortable with me. If you ever do, you have to promise to tell me immediately, okay?"

I nod.

"Good, now I get to ravage your body."

We spend the next hour in my bed. After we've made love, I catch Ben checking the clock.

"Don't be so nervous about facing Reed," I say. "Granted he might not be nice at first, but he'll learn to accept you."

He kisses my temple. "Yeah." But he sounds distracted.

We get dressed and go back out into the living room. Ben looks like he's preparing for his execution.

"Ben, if you're this nervous, you don't have to talk to him tonight. We'll do it some other time."

"No." He's emphatic. "I'm staying."

Ben puts his arm around my back and I lean into him, snuggling against his side. I doze off as we watch TV, but when the front door starts to open, I rouse. Ben sits up, his body stiff.

Reed slams into the apartment, livid. He points a shaking finger at Ben and shouts, "Get the *fuck* away from my sister!"

I'm instantly awake. "Reed!"

Ben stands and clenches his hands at his sides. "Reed, I know it looks bad, but I can explain."

Reed bolts across the room and grabs a handful of Ben's shirt, jerking him forward.

"Reed!" I jump up and grab his arm. "Stop!"

"Do you know?" he asks me, his face red. Veins bulge on neck. He looks like he's about to have a stroke.

"Know *what*? What are you talking about?"

"Your *boyfriend* here is a *rapist*."

"*What?*" I drop my hand from his arm in shock, and just like that, Reed is dragging Ben across the room. "Reed! *Stop!*"

My brother shakes Ben by his shirt, and I can't believe it, but Ben isn't fighting back. "Deny it, you fucking asshole. Deny that you were arrested for rape last November."

"Reed!" I scream. "What are you talking about?"

He shakes Ben again. *"Deny it!"*

Ben searches my eyes. "Alexa, I didn't—"

Reed slams him against a wall. "Don't you *fucking* talk to her, you lying piece of *shit*. You're lucky I haven't killed you yet." I've never seen my brother this angry before.

I start to sob with fear. "Reed! Stop!"

Reed's eyes are wild. "He was arrested for rape, Lexi! He raped a woman last November!"

"No!" I shake my head, struggling to breathe. "No."

Reed turns his attention back to Ben. "Have you hurt my sister?"

Ben's mouth opens, but no sound comes out.

Reed shoves him into the wall again. *"Have you hurt her?"*

"No!" He shakes his head. "I would never hurt her. I'd rather die than hurt her."

"You fucking liar!" Reed shoves him again. "Deny that you were arrested for rape!"

Ben stays silent.

Fear seeps through my body with an icy chill. "Ben?"

Tears fill his eyes. "Alexa, listen to me. I would never hurt you, I swear to God. I love you."

Reed flips his shit and punches Ben in the face. Ben still doesn't fight back.

"Reed! Stop!" I sob. "Ben, is it true?"

His lip is split open and blood drips down his chin. "Alexa."

Oh God. This can't be happening. "It's a yes or no question, Ben."

"Yes, but—"

Reed punches him two more times and I'm sobbing, trying to pull my brother away. He grabs Ben by the shirt and drags him to the open door. "You get the fuck out of my apartment *now*. If I find out that you've come within fifty feet of my sister, I will beat the shit out of you."

"Alexa, I didn't do it. I swear to you!" Ben pleads.

But Reed has already pushed him into the hall.

"Alexa!"

Reed slams the door and locks it, but Ben is pounding on the door and shouting my name. I stand by the door sobbing as he continues to call out to me. "I swear to God, Alexa! I didn't do it!"

Reed grabs my arm and pulls me to his chest. "I'm so sorry, Lexi. I should have been here. I should have protected you instead of going off on my own mission. I failed you again."

I cling to him, wondering how this happened. How has my world turned so completely upside down?

He pulls back from me and looks into my face, his eyes hard. "Did he hurt you?"

I shake my head. "No." It doesn't make any sense. The Ben I know is so respectful of me. Why would he have been so angry about Todd if he's a rapist himself? "Are you sure, Reed? Are you really, really sure?"

He nods. "I'm so sorry, Lexi. My phone died on the plane, so I didn't see the arrest report until I was almost back to Hillsdale. I tried to call you, but it went straight to voicemail. I was scared to death. I'm amazed I didn't get pulled over for speeding."

I shake my head. "He's not like that, Reed. He's so nice to me. He's so sweet..."

"He was arrested, Lexi. I can show you the report."

"Then why isn't he in jail?"

"The charges were dropped."

"Then he didn't do it!"

"Lexi!" he shouts. "You and I both know that doesn't mean a fucking thing!"

Oh, God. "No." I wail, my knees collapsing.

Reed holds me up and pulls me over to the sofa.

"No. No! It can't be true. I don't believe it." I remember how gentle he was with me. How protective. Ben can't be a rapist.

"I'm so sorry, Lex."

Ben has given up and is no longer outside my door. For some reason that upsets me even more.

"Let me get you something to help you sleep." Reed disappears into the kitchen and comes back with a bottle of pills and a glass of water.

This scene is so familiar. How many nights has Reed calmed me after I had a nightmare about Todd? It fills me with gratitude. I can never, ever repay my brother for everything he's done for me. But it fills me with anger too. Not at Reed. At Todd. At our parents. I'm angry that once again, I feel like a victim.

I'm done. I'm done being a victim.

"No," I say, forcing myself to calm down. "I don't want any pills."

"Lexi, it'll make you feel better."

"For a few hours, sure. But not tomorrow morning."

"We'll figure out tomorrow morning later," he says. "Let's just get through tonight."

"I don't need anything," I say and take a deep breath. "I'm better."

"Lexi—"

I look at his hands. His right hand is covered in blood. "Reed, your hand."

He looks down at his knuckles. "I'm fine."

I stand up and drag him into the kitchen. "No, you're not." I wet some paper towels and start to dab at his knuckles. He flinches and I hold his hand still. "I thought you were going to kill him."

"I wanted to kill him."

"Where did you learn to hit like that? You were never a fighter." His knuckles are split open. I don't think he needs stitches, but his knuckles have already begun to swell.

"Tucker might have taught me a thing or two."

I look up at him in surprise.

A grin tugs at his mouth. "On the receiving end."

I open the freezer and grab a bag of frozen corn. I wrap it in a kitchen towel and put it on top of his hand. "Reed, if Ben is what you claim he is, why didn't he fight you? Why didn't he defend himself?"

He's silent for a moment. "I don't know... But who knows what he was playing. He was still denying the whole thing as I shoved him out the door."

"Maybe it's because he was telling me the truth."

His eyes harden. "There's no denying the fact that he was arrested. I have proof."

"And he didn't deny that part."

Reed sighs. "Lexi, I know you don't want it to be true, but he was charged with rape."

"But what if he didn't do it?"

"I'm sure people believe that about Todd Millhouse too."

"That's not fair!"

"Isn't it?"

"No, it's not. Because Todd Millhouse was a first-class ass long before he attacked me. Still is. Ben is anything but. Name one thing that he's done in the math lab that makes him suspect."

Reed is silent for several long moments. "He's got a mouth. He was borderline rude when he applied for the job."

"Anything else?"

He scowls. "No, but that doesn't mean a thing."

"He didn't do it." The sudden certainty almost staggers me. I feel like an ass. Oh god. Will he ever forgive me?

"Lexi, you don't know that."

I shake my head. "But I do! I know it in my heart. I've made a terrible, terrible mistake." I step around Reed and grab my purse off the table.

"Where are you going?" Reed asks in disbelief.

"I'm going to find the one good thing that's come into my life this past year, and I'm going to beg him to forgive me." And before Reed can protest, I run out the door.

Chapter
Twenty-Nine

Lexi

How could I have been so stupid?

I understand why Reed would believe the worst of Ben, but I have no excuse. Ben has never given me any reason to doubt him. He could have taken advantage of me any number of times, yet he's always treated me with the utmost respect.

And how did I treat him? I let my brother beat him up and kick him out of our apartment. Even worse, I believed—if only for a few minutes—that he was capable of a horrific crime.

There's no way I can make up for this, but I'm going to try.

I run across the parking lot to my car, amazed that Reed hasn't tackled me yet. But by the time he leaves the building, I'm already in my car. I pull out of the parking lot and turn in the opposite direction of Ben's apartment. I want to make sure I don't lead Reed there, so I make multiple wrong turns. When I'm sure my brother's not behind me, I head downtown.

I blindly reach in my purse and pull out my phone. When I find it dead, I realize I forgot to charge it last night. No wonder I didn't get Reed's phone calls. If Reed had gotten a hold of me, this entire scene could have all been avoided. I could have talked to Ben without Reed influencing me. And I never would have believed the worst of him. Or so I'd like to think.

I plug in my phone as I go over what I'm going to say to him. *I'm sorry, I'm an idiot,* seems like a good place to start. I can say that Reed swayed me, but the bottom line is I betrayed Ben. He gave me everything and I threw it back in his face.

I'm close to Ben's apartment when I notice a car following me. I chalk it up to paranoia. I'm on a city street and the car is going the same direction, but when I turn down the side street toward Ben's complex, the car turns with me.

I grab my phone, my heart racing, but it's still dead. What if it's Todd?

I hope to God that Ben's home.

I pick up my speed, but the car that's tailing me speeds up too. My heart racing, I turn into Ben's parking lot. His car is parked in front of the building, thank God. I lay on the horn for several seconds before I jerk the car to a stop and throw my door open. The car that's been following me pulls into the lot before screeching to a stop.

"Ben!" I shout as I sprint for the stairs.

The voice behind me nearly brings me to my knees. "Where are you going, Lexi?"

Todd.

Refusing to give into my rising hysteria, I force myself to focus on getting to Ben's door. I've just reached the top of the stairs when Todd lands on the bottom step.

"Don't make this more difficult than it needs to be, Lexi. I only want to talk."

I skid to a halt at Ben's doorstep. "I don't want to talk to you."

Todd hits the top of the stairs, laughing as though he's heard a particularly funny joke. He probably thinks he has. In his mind, *no one* tells him no. What happened last April is proof enough of that.

I bang on Ben's front door. "Ben! Ben!" I shout again.

Todd is twenty feet away now, sauntering toward me slowly, as though he has all the time in the world. He's wearing a pair of dark, tight jeans with a black, form-fitting sweater. His dark blond hair is trimmed close and he's just as good-looking as ever. He's always used his money and his good looks along with his sporadic charm to get what he wants. He looks the same as when I knew him in school, except for one thing—the wild, out-of-control look in his eyes.

I'm in serious trouble.

Terror explodes in my head and I pound on Ben's door with renewed force. "Ben! Ben!"

Todd takes slow purposeful steps. Why won't Ben open his door? Does he hate me that much?

Todd laughs. "Give it up, Lexi. Your boyfriend isn't going to help you. Did you lead him on too, telling him *yes* with your body but *no* with your mouth?"

"I never did that!" A sob rises up, but I force it down as I start banging on the door again. "Ben! Please! Help!"

Todd's only six feet away. "He's not going to help you, Lexi. Not all guys are as understanding as I am." He reaches a hand toward me. "Come with me."

"No!" I beat on the door again, fear threatening to overtake my senses. "Ben! *Please!*"

Todd starts to advance, slow easy steps, and I back away from the door, scrambling for another plan. I've hinged everything on Ben helping me.

Think Lexi, think.

I keep backing away, but I know the end of the landing is behind me. What I am I going to do when I reach the end? I'll be trapped. "Just go away and leave me alone, Todd. Please."

"I can't do that, Lexi."

"Why?" My back hits the railing and I release a gasp of fear.

"Do you have any idea what your brother's been up to?" He's in front of me now, but he's not touching me, just watching me with a soft smile.

Calm down. You'll figure some way out. I force myself to take a deep breath. "No." I shake my head. "I don't know."

"He's been digging into my past, finding some of my old girlfriends."

Was that what he was doing while he was in New York? Were Caroline, Ben, and I wrong after all? "I didn't know. I swear. I agreed never to talk about what happened and I haven't. Reed said you were the one who was trying to find me."

He reaches a hand toward me and I flinch, fighting the urge to close my eyes.

"Are you afraid of me?"

That's what he wants. He wants me to be afraid. Though he told the cops we had consensual sex, this is what got him off—this power over me. The harder I fought, the more he enjoyed it. Well, he's taken enough of my life. I'm not giving him anymore.

"No."

He laughs and touches my cheek. "I don't believe you."

Reed enrolled me in a self-defense class after we left home. Now I struggle to remember any of what I learned. My biggest worry is that I'm pressed against a railing, twelve

327

feet over the ground. Even if I hurt him, how will I get around him?

I know one thing: I have to try.

He's looking down at me with a grin on his face. "We're going to go down to my car and then find someplace to talk."

"Okay."

If I feign compliance, I can bolt as soon as we reach the parking lot.

He seems surprised by my agreement—disappointed, even. He grabs my upper arm and drags me to the staircase. I resist the urge to look at Ben's door as we pass. It's better that he didn't come out. Todd is clearly out of his mind. How could I live with myself if he hurt Ben? Reed's hurt Ben enough as it is.

Todd tugs me down the stairs, his fingers digging into my flesh with more force than necessary.

I need a plan... I search my memory for details from the self-defense class. What were we told about breaking free of this kind of hold? When we reach the bottom step, I squat, and his wrist bends at an awkward angle. He loses his grip when I thrust my arm straight up, and I take off running, shouting for help as I go. But there's little hope of anyone hearing or helping. We're downtown and it's well after midnight. No one's around to hear me.

The bar. The bar's still open.

He catches me within seconds, grabbing my shoulders from behind. "Where do you think you're going?"

I lift my left arm straight up and swing around, breaking his hold, and slam the side of my hand into the base of his neck. He grunts and bends over as I take off running again. I won't be able to make it to the front of the building, but I think I can make it to the back door.

I'm in the lot behind the bar when Todd catches me and slams me face-first into the brick wall of the bar. I'm still several feet from the back door.

"That wasn't nice, Lexi."

"You think?" I shout. Rage unfurls inside me and all I can think of is hurting him...hurting him badly enough that he'll never hurt me or anyone else again. I lift my foot and scrape it down his shin before stomping on his foot. Then I swing my hand to his groin, hitting him with all my force. His hold loosens as he shouts, "You bitch!"

"Get away from me!" I scream at the top of my lungs as I spin around and shove the heel of my hand into his nose.

He stumbles backward, blood gushing from his nostrils.

I finally make it to the door and I beat on it frantically with my palms. "Help! *Help me!*"

Todd stumbles toward me, holding his nose, the look in his eyes murderous.

I move away from the door as he approaches.

"I'm going to mess you up now, Lexi."

But the back door swings open as Todd advances me and Ben is standing in the opening, holding Brittany's baseball bat. "*The fuck you will.*"

I nearly drop to my knees with relief. "Ben."

Ben bursts through the door, wielding the bat as though he's about to swing it into Todd's head. "You back up now and get away from her."

"Ho!" Todd laughs, taking several backward steps with upraised hands. "So you're the boyfriend."

Ben ignores him and moves forward.

Brittany appears in the doorway, a phone in her hand. "The police are on their way."

"Did he hurt you, Alexa?" Ben asks, his voice tight.

My cheek stings from being shoved into the bricks, but I realize I'm in the shadows and Ben hasn't taken his eyes off Todd. If I tell Ben that he hurt me, God knows what he'll do with that bat. "No," I lie. "He just grabbed me."

"See?" Todd asks. "She wanted me. You need to butt out of this."

His statement infuriates Ben. The bat shakes as he lifts it higher.

"Don't, Ben," I plead. "Let the police take care of it."

"I can make sure that he never hurts you again, Alexa." Ben's voice breaks.

"It's not worth it if I lose you in the process."

Sirens wail in the distance.

Brittany, who has clearly clued into the danger here too, approaches Ben, reaching for the bat as she keeps her eyes glued on Todd. "Give me the bat, Ben. Go check on Alexa."

"Listen to the women, you pansy," Todd taunts as he steps closer. "You haven't got it in you."

Ben's chest rises and falls more rapidly as his hold on the bat tightens.

I grab his arm. "Don't listen to him! He wants you to do something stupid so he can use his money and power to make you pay for it."

Ben glances at me and sees my cheek. Rage fills his eyes as he turns back to Todd. "I'm going to kill you."

Todd falters before wiping his bloody nose with the back of his hand and grinning. "You're not going to kill me. Even a hick boy like you isn't that stupid. Lexi mentioned money. You want money? How much will it take to make you put down that bat? Then we can all go our separate ways."

"There isn't enough fucking money in the world to let you get away with this." Ben's voice is tight and he starts to advance.

Britt moves in front of him, her face stern. *"Give me the bat, Masterson.* Do not throw your life away over this scumbag."

When Ben refuses to comply, I grab his arm again. "Ben, *please.*"

He reluctantly releases his hold.

Todd tries to bolt, but Brittany blocks his path, holding up the bat. "I'd love an excuse to bang up that pretty face even more. Just try me."

Ben rushes over to me and pulls me into his arms, holding me tight. "Are you okay?"

"Yes."

He leans me back to study my face. "Your face is bleeding."

"He shoved me into the wall, so I gave him a bloody nose. I guess those self-defense classes came in handy after all." I try to laugh, but my adrenaline is crashing and I start to shake.

A police car screeches to a halt at the entrance to the parking lot, the flashing lights bouncing off the buildings.

Ben takes a deep breath, and his expression practically shouts his feeling of relief. He pulls me to his chest, his arms encircling me as the police approach. "I can't live without you, Alexa. Please. You have to believe me. I didn't do it."

I look up at him. "I know."

But we don't have time for a longer conversation about it because the police begin to ask questions. I tell what happened, including the truth about my rape last year. Todd tries to talk his way out of this mess, but the Hillsdale police are used to rich kids thinking they can get away with whatever they want and they're sick of it. They handcuff him and are leading him to the police car when Reed's car pulls up. He runs out of the car toward me. He's furious when he sees Ben's arms around me.

"Reed!" I say firmly as he approaches. "Stop right now. If you can't control yourself then leave."

"What?"

"Ben just saved me from Todd. He's not what you think he is. He'd never hurt me. I know it."

"Todd? Todd Millhouse?"

"They just took him away in the police car. Why did you think it was here?"

"I don't know. I saw Ben touching you and...." He shakes his head, looking pale. Then he sees my face and his anger returns. "Who hurt you?"

I grab his arms and get in his face. "Todd, but Ben stopped him and Britt called the police. I'm fine."

Reed's breath is coming out in short bursts.

I throw my arms around his neck. "I'm fine. I promise."

His arms tighten around me and he starts to shake. "Oh, God, Lexi..."

"I'm fine."

We hold each other for several long seconds before he lets me go and turns to Ben, his eyes hardening. "While I appreciate how you helped Lexi, I still don't trust you."

"I do." I square my shoulders. I'm not backing down. "I want you to like Ben. But he's going to be part of my life whether you like it or not. So you have two choices right now: You can calm down and be civil with Ben, or you can leave."

He releases a huff. "Fine." He crosses his arms, but he doesn't look happy.

I can't believe it worked.

The three of us spend the next couple of hours giving statements at the police department. Ben has refused to leave my side, so I'm not surprised that as we're walking to our cars he announces we're staying together tonight.

He stares Reed in the face, clenching his jaw. "I don't want to fight you Reed, but tonight has freaked me out so much that I can't leave her."

Reed studies Ben's beaten and swollen face. "Fine, but she's coming home because I'm freaked out too."

My mouth drops in disbelief that they've come to a mutual agreement.

I ride to my apartment with Ben. He holds my hand the entire way. When he parks outside my building, he turns off the car, but doesn't make a move to get out. "I need to tell you what happened last November."

I shake my head. "You don't owe me anything."

He looks into my eyes. "But I want you to know."

"Okay."

He takes a deep breath and tells me about Sabrina, how he went along with their relationship until he couldn't take her attitude anymore. She was furious when he broke up with her, which was why she accused him of rape. He was stuck in jail for a week and many of his friends and family believed the worst of him, even after the charges were dropped.

I cringe in horror when I remember my own behavior. "I'm no better than the rest of them."

"No," he insists. "Your situation is different. I was arrested, Alexa, and Reed came blasting in, ready to beat the shit out of me. Why wouldn't you believe I did it?"

"Because I know you. You would never do that. I'm so utterly ashamed of myself. I almost lost you due to my own stupidity."

He cups my cheek. "Alexa. Please don't beat yourself up about it. And you wouldn't have lost me. I wasn't about to give up on you that easily."

"Thank God."

He kisses me gently, wincing. "I might not be able to give you a proper kiss for a few days. Your brother throws quite a punch."

"Sorry about that too."

He shrugs. "I can't blame him. He loves you. He was protecting you."

I lean my head on his shoulder.

"Let's go inside and go to bed. You're exhausted."

I lift my head and give him a grin. "You just want to get me in bed."

"Always."

Chapter
Thirty

Ben

Alexa's in full-on control mode, and I stand back and watch in awe as she directs the people who are working behind the scenes to pull off her bachelor and bachelorette auction. She's incredibly sexy when she's in charge like this and it makes me even more eager to take her home when the event is over.

My backstage job is simple: I stand out of the way and offer moral support. Alexa and Sylvia have this thing under control with the exception of one problem. They're missing one of the guys they plan to auction.

Sylvia's about to freak out, but Alexa directs the MC— a communications major—to start the show. "Seth was supposed to be auctioned toward the end of the program," she tells the guy, who thankfully seems willing to go with the flow. "We'll figure out what to do by the time you get to him."

He nods. "Sounds good. Just let me know." Then he walks around the dividers they've set up to block the audience from the backstage. Cheers and catcalls percuss from the audience and I hear his voice booming over the racket. "Welcome to the Southern University Bachelor and Bachelorette Auction. Tonight you'll see thirty of Southern's finest available co-eds, so run to the ATM or ready your checkbooks." He pauses. "Do they still have those? Well, never mind because Lexi Pendergraft, the

335

organizer for this event, has set it up so you can use your Gold Card to buy a date with the man or woman of your dreams." His voice lowers. "And guys, there's a couple of girls back there I plan on bidding on myself." He laughs. "Remember that the proceeds from tonight go to Southern's first ever Middle School University, so bid high and bid often. Let's get this show started."

There's a lull while the first guy walks around the divider, soon followed by loud applause.

"He's in the *program*, Lexi." Sylvia is saying to Alexa. "I know half a dozen girls who are out there right now, waiting to bid on him."

Alexa grabs her arms and looks into her eyes. "Take a deep breath. We'll do the best we can."

I walk over to them and Sylvia turns her attention on me. "This is all your fault."

I'm momentarily stunned. "How do you figure?"

"It's one of *your* guys who didn't show."

I hold up my hands in protest. "Hey, I just gave you a couple of names. That's when my responsibility ended." Still, I feel bad—the last thing I want to do is stress out Alexa.

A guy joins us, a cell phone in his hand. "Seth was in an accident. There's no way he'll be here in time."

Alexa gasps. "Is he *okay?*"

"Yeah, but he's stuck. He needs to give a police report and arrange for a tow truck."

I feel vindicated, even if the poor guy smashed his car.

Sylvia throws up her hands. "What are we going to do?"

Taking a deep breath, Alexa turns her gaze to me. "Ben will do it."

A chill runs down my spine. "Do what?"

"You'll take his place." She looks down at her clipboard. "Even Scarlett said you were attractive enough."

"Oddly enough, it was more of a compliment coming from her."

She looks up and grins. "Are you seriously questioning your looks? Please." She shakes her head.

"Let me get this straight—you want me to go up on a stage and let Southern girls bid on a date with me?" I look her in the eyes. "Is this your not-so-subtle attempt to break up with me?" I tease.

She steps closer and places a kiss on my lips, lingering for several seconds. "Let them bid as high as they want. I'll outbid them by double."

I lift my eyebrows. "I think that's technically bid rigging."

"It's for a good cause. I think we'll be fine." She winks and pats my chest. "Besides, you're presuming that someone else will bid on you." She laughs as she walks away.

"Ouch."

Sylvia eyes me up and down. "Good thing you dressed to impress Lexi. I suspect it will work on the other girls too. I think we'll get a lot of money off you."

"You're serious?"

She curls her upper lip. "I wanted Lexi to get you for the auction in the first place. Hot and smart? Girls eat that shit up."

I snort. "Now you tell me. Where were you freshman year?"

She laughs, but my stomach twists into knots. They really want me to do this, but I'm sick to my stomach. I've never liked public attention to begin with, and I got more than my fair share last fall. But I tell myself this is different. I'll be helping Alexa and my brother Kyle.

"I still haven't agreed, you know," I call over to Alexa, but she waves a dismissive hand.

I wait thirty minutes before I begin pacing. Alexa has been running the event with a masterful hand and has paid little attention to me up until now. "We've auctioned off twenty-two bachelors and bachelorettes and already made eight thousand dollars," she says, her eyes shining with excitement. "And we saved the ones we thought would bring in the most money for last."

I swallow my nausea. "I hope I don't disappoint."

Her hand drapes over my wrist and her eyes widen. "Ben...are you nervous?"

"Hell, yeah I'm nervous. Girls are going to be checking me out and bidding money on me."

"They're not actually going to *win* you."

"Still..."

She laughs. "How about we get a few bids, and then I'll bid some outrageous amount to end your torture?"

I release a sigh of relief. "Thank you."

"Let's just hope it doesn't go over ten thousand or we're both screwed," she teases.

"Lexi," Sylvia calls. "There's a problem with the credit card reader."

"Coming," she says then turns to me. "Duty calls. Listen, you're up after the girl who's out there right now, so why don't you go stand at the edge of the stage and Chuck will let you know when it's time to go on."

"Okay."

As she walks toward Sylvia, she looks over her shoulder. "And we'll talk about what I expect from our date later."

I want to laugh, but I'm still nervous. I barely have time to think about why when I hear the emcee bang his gavel. "Sold to the guy in the plaid shirt for eight hundred and seventy-five dollars."

The girl who just pulled in the big bucks walks offstage, grinning ear to ear. "Good luck," she says. As she passes me, she looks me up and down. "You should get at least five hundred."

Five hundred dollars to go on a date with me?

Chuck puts a hand on my shoulder. "When he calls your name, you're going to walk onto the stage and stand on the giant X taped next to him. Then when he starts to talk about you, you'll walk down the short runway, turn around, and come back to the X. You'll wait there for the bidding to end." His voice lowers. "We've found the guys tend to get more money if they flirt with the girls as they walk."

"You're shitting me."

"No." He shrugs. "Pretty awesome, huh?"

Awesome is not the word I'd use and I hope they don't expect me to follow suit. Surely, Alexa wouldn't be happy if I did.

"Bachelor number twelve is Ben Masterson, a replacement for Seth Holkum."

I find myself climbing the steps to the temporary stage and standing on the X. I look to the side, hoping Alexa is watching, but I don't see any sign of her.

"Ben is a senior mechanical engineering major, which means he's not only smart and good-looking, but most likely good with his hands."

My eyes widen in terror as the girls in the audience shriek and catcall. I look back at the curtain behind me and see that Sylvia has popped around the edge, an ornery grin on her face. Now I know who wrote the copy. But I still don't see Alexa and I try not to panic.

The emcee laughs. "Ben, start strutting your stuff down the catwalk." When I take a few steps, he continues. "Ben's six-foot-two and one-hundred and eighty pounds. He works out three days a week at the Southern gym and can bench press two of you beautiful girls at one time."

Where the hell did Sylvia come up with this stuff?

"Ben's a hometown boy, born and raised in Hillsdale. He loves long walks, lemon cream pie, and puppies."

A collective ah ripples through the room.

I'm at the end of the stage, thank God. When I turn around, Sylvia is still peeking around the corner of the curtain, giggling behind her hand. I'm going to kill her, but I'm too freaked by the fact that Alexa is nowhere in sight to focus on being mad.

I mouth to Sylvia. "Where's Lexi?"

Her eyes widen as her head swivels around. Panic floods her face when she apparently sees no sign of Lexi.

Oh shit.

"Ben's ideal woman is a girl who's confident in herself and her looks. Who has a strong sense of who she is, and keeps physically fit and thin."

I can't hold myself back when I finally end up back on the X. That last sentence makes me sound like an ass. "I didn't say that last part."

"What's that?" the emcee asks, sticking the microphone in front of my face.

My palms are sweaty and the room is suddenly very warm. "I didn't say that part about keeping physically fit." He keeps the microphone in front of me. "Well…" I stammer. "If I want a woman who has a strong sense of who she is, why the hell would I say she has to be thin? That seems counterintuitive, doesn't it?"

"So you're saying you don't care if your date isn't thin."

"I'm saying she should be happy with herself, inside and out, without letting society dictate who she is."

The room fills with the women's yells and I worry that I've pissed them off.

"Let's start the bidding at fifty dollars," the emcee says, staying next to me.

"Fifty!" a girl screams.

"One hundred!"

"Two hundred!"

"Two fifty!"

Oh shit, in my need to defend myself, I've made them actually want to date me.

The emcee lifts the hand that isn't holding the microphone. "Whoa, whoa, slow down there, girls. I know he's a hot commodity, but he's not going anywhere yet." He starts the bidding again and the figure soars up to a thousand dollars.

I turn to the side to get a look at Sylvia. She's frantic. Still no Alexa.

"Five thousand dollars," a voice calls out.

The crowd quiets and the emcee asks, "Who made the last bid?"

"I did." The crowd parts as a girl makes her way to the stage.

Oh, fuck. It's Tina.

She stops at the end of the stage, eyeing me like it's Easter Sunday and she gave up men for Lent.

"Does anyone want to bid more than five thousand dollars?" the emcee asks.

The room is quiet.

"Going once, going twice—"

I'm about to have a stroke. There's no way in hell I can go out with that bitch, but I can't break the rules either. I'm screwed.

"Six thousand," Lexi calls out, walking toward the stage.

I release my breath and my shoulders sink with relief.

Tina lifts an eyebrow. "Eight."

Alexa is next to her now, pinning her with a deadly gaze. "Really, Tina? You actually have that much money?"

She holds out her hands. "Trust fund baby. *Surprise*," she singsongs.

"Ten thousand," Alexa says, her voice firm.

"That's ten thousand dollars, ladies. *Ten. Thousand.* Anyone else want to jump in?"

Ten is Alexa's limit. When she teased me about it minutes ago, I never dreamed it would become an issue.

The two girls engage in a staring contest, but Tina breaks her gaze and looks down at the stage before glancing up at me and licking her lower lip. "Twelve thousand."

Alexa's mouth drops open and she looks up at me in horror.

I'm fucked twice over.

"Twelve thousand going once… going twice…"

"Twenty thousand dollars," Caroline shouts from the back of the room. She kisses Reed's cheek and makes her way toward Alexa.

I've never passed out in my life, but the thought of someone paying twenty thousand dollars to go on a date with me—for anything, really—makes me lightheaded.

Tina shakes her head in disgust. "Go back to your man, Caroline. You need to learn to share."

"You only want him because Lexi does." Caroline steps closer, her eyes deadly. "But I'm warning you to back off, because while Lexi might not bite, *I will*."

Tina turns back to me and narrows her eyes. "I had planned to make a man out of you, Virgin Ben, but Caroline steals all my fun. Again." Then she turns around and walks away.

"Twenty thousand going once, going twice... Sold to the blonde in the black dress."

"Thank you," I mouth to Caroline before I make my way to the steps at the corner of the stage.

"The rest of the bachelors have a lot to live up to after that," the emcee murmurs before he announces the name of the next bachelorette.

Alexa meets me at the bottom of the stairs. "Ben, I'm so, so sorry."

I turn my gaze to Caroline, who's standing behind her. "So, Caroline, when do you want to go out?" I joke. "And for twenty thousand dollars I'm sure you're expecting a private jet *and* an island."

She grins.

"Seriously, thank you."

"Don't thank me. It's Reed's money and his idea. He's using his trust fund."

Alexa and I both stare at her in amazement.

Caroline laughs. "You're lucky it was Tina betting against you. If it had been anyone else, he probably would have stood back and let it happen." Caroline lowers her voice as we move to the backstage area. "The truth is that you never should have put him in at all, Lexi. You took a huge risk."

Alexa scowls. "How was I to know that the bidding would go over ten thousand?"

I hold my hands out at my sides. "Hello."

"Shut up," she says with a grin. "Ten minutes ago you were worried no one would bet on you at all."

"Reed's going to write the check—" She winks at me. "—so technically, you and Reed should be the ones who go on a long walk and cuddle puppies."

"Sylvia wrote that," I protest.

"*Sure* she did."

I can't believe Reed saved my ass. He still barely tolerates being in the same room with me. And yet he just forked out twenty thousand dollars to help me.

Reed walks up behind Caroline and wraps an arm around her waist as we walk to the backstage area.

I have to admit that I admire Lexi's older brother, and not just because of what he did for us at the auction. Reed's multilayered plan to shut down Todd Millhouse was impressive and then some. His ultimate goal was to get the guy arrested on multiple charges that would put him away for a very long time. Reed's private investigator had been investigating other sexual assaults, most of which were never reported, at both the college Alexa had attended and Todd's old high school. Once the list was ready, Reed flew to Boston to meet with the women—along with a female attorney he'd hired—promising them quality legal representation if they chose to press charges. Many of the girls were too scared and some had been paid to keep quiet, but Reed managed to convince three of them to cooperate. Alexa wanted to reopen her own case, but the agreement she'd signed made that impossible, although Todd was still facing assault charges for what he did in Hillsdale.

Ms. Pembry's investigation had been going on for several months when Todd got wind of it. He threatened Alexa's safety in an attempt to force Reed to stop. Which is when Reed began to withdraw and spend all his free time working on the second piece in his plan for revenge.

We'd been correct about Reed developing a plan to attack the corporation. It was his Doomsday plan. He still refuses to elaborate on what it involved. Thank God it never got that far.

I hang in the back until the auction's over, not wanting any attention from Caroline's outrageous bid. When Alexa finishes her duties, she wraps her arms around my neck, pressing her body against mine. "What can I do to make this up to you?"

An ornery grin spreads across my face. "I can think of a few things." I pause. "But I think Reed is waiting to take our walk."

She swats my chest. "Very funny. Take me home."

"You're awfully bossy for a woman who almost lost her boyfriend to a psycho nymphomaniac and *then* lost him to her brother."

"You're never going to let me forget that are you?"

"Not as long as we both live."

We walk across campus to my car and Alexa tells me how much money she made for the charity tonight. "Without Reed's bid, we made fifteen thousand dollars."

"He doesn't really have to pay that does he?"

She grimaces. "If he forfeits, the next highest bidder gets a date with you. And we both know who that was."

"That's a hell of a lot of money."

She shrugs. "It is, but it's a tax deduction, plus I plan to pay him back with my own trust fund money when I turn twenty-one and get access to it."

"Good, God. How much money do you have?" I scrunch my eyes closed and shake my head. "Scratch that. I don't want to know."

Alexa stops and I nearly stumble to stop my forward momentum. "I have money, Ben. I can't help that and I won't apologize for it."

"I know and I don't want you to, but I'll never make that kind of money, Lex. I'll never measure up."

She shakes her head. "I don't care how much money you make. I want to be with you, not your money. Besides, I doubt I'll make much money working for non-profits my whole life. The trust money won't last forever."

I'm momentarily stunned. "But I thought you were going to work for Monroe Industries after you got your MBA.

"I think I've changed my mind. Working with charities is what I love."

I grin and pull her into my arms. "Then we'll be middle-class together."

"I can think of worse things."

I kiss her long and slow for several seconds. "Let's go," I finally say.

The drive to her apartment complex is short, but it's agony. All I can think about is stripping her naked.

When I park, she's out of the car before I can get around to open her door. "Come on," she says, excitement in her voice. "I have a surprise for you." She grabs my hand and practically runs across the parking lot.

"Does it involve the removal of clothing?"

Her mouth twists to the side as she punches in her code at the door. "Let's say it will most likely lead to the removal of clothing more often."

"Then I'm definitely intrigued. Lead the way."

We enter the lobby and I'm thankful there's an available elevator. I press her against the wall and claim her mouth with mine. I need to slow down because Reed will probably be in their apartment and I can't walk in with an obvious hard-on. It's awkward enough spending the night there when I know that Reed and Caroline are only separated from us by a bathroom.

The elevator opens and I drag myself away from her and grab her hand. "Come on."

We step into the hall, but instead of walking to the far end, Alexa pulls her keychain out of her purse and stops in front of another apartment.

I squint in confusion. "What are you doing?"

She inserts a key into the lock and opens the door. "Surprise. I got my own apartment."

"*What?*"

She pulls me inside and I look around at the empty space, still feeling baffled.

"When...? How?"

"Caroline. She called the manager and found out that a one bedroom was available on the same floor as her place and Reed's. She paid a deposit to hold it until I could sign the lease."

"Can you afford this?"

She nods. "My parents have agreed to pay for it since I'm only going to be two doors down from Reed."

"Is Reed okay with this?"

She grins. "He's getting there."

"Why didn't you tell me?"

"It all happened so fast. I signed the lease yesterday and got the keys today. I decided to surprise you."

"You definitely did."

She grabs my hand again. "Come see the bedroom."

When she pushes the door open, I'm surprised to see her bed, dresser and nightstand. "Did you move this?"

"Caroline and I did most of it this afternoon, but Reed helped with the dresser."

"I would have helped." I stare at the bed. "You should have been worrying about the auction."

"I can think of better uses for your time." She kisses me, her lips soft on mine.

Wrapping my arms around her, I pull her close and deepen the kiss, my tongue searching for hers.

Within a minute, we're both out of breath. I reach for the zipper on the back of her dress and pull down. Grabbing the fabric at her shoulders, I tug the dress until it falls and puddles at her feet. She's standing before me in sexy black lingerie.

"This hardly seems fair," she murmurs before she pulls my shirt over my head. My jeans are next and when I step out of them, she sits on the bed and pulls me down with her.

I wait for her to show me what she wants. Alexa likes to take the lead and I let her do it since it makes her feel in control. But she looks up at me through lowered eyelashes. "You're in charge tonight."

I shake my head. "Alexa, no. It's one of your boundaries, and I'm fine with it."

She kisses me passionately and my blood rushes to my groin.

"Ben, I want to try it. Please."

I take a deep breath, then tip her chin up so I can look into her eyes and make sure she's telling me the truth. "Okay, but if you feel the least bit anxious, you tell me, agreed?"

"Okay." She lies down on her back, her head on the pillow, staring up at me with so much trust it catches the breath in my chest.

She's a gift that I will never take for granted. Tonight I want to show her how much I adore her. I lie on my side next to her, then reach around her back and unfasten her bra, tossing it to the floor after I pull it off. I lower my mouth to her breast, making sure to rest my weight on the hand I have propped next to her. Soon she's squirming and I lift my gaze to check on her. "Are you okay?"

She nods, panting. "Don't stop now."

Grinning, I move my mouth lower, lightly skimming the skin of her abdomen until I stop at the edge of her panties. I quickly pull them off and search out the spot between her legs that drives her insane. Watching her writhe and moan from what I'm doing to her turns me on more than I can stand. I lift my head and brace my hands on either side of her waist, making sure no part of my body is resting on top of her.

"Alexa, do you trust me?"

She watches me for several seconds, fear flickering in her eyes, but I know she's not afraid of me. She's afraid of how she'll react. "Yes," she finally says.

I roll away to put on a condom before returning between her legs, my hands on the mattress. "Wrap your leg around my waist."

Her fear returns when she realizes she's staying on her back, but she lifts her leg and hooks it around my hip.

"If you want to change positions at any time, tell me. Don't feel like you have to do this. Okay? Promise me."

"I promise."

I lower my right arm to my elbow, still making sure not to put pressure on her while I lift her hips with my other hand and enter her. "How are you doing?"

She presses into my pubic bone. "Don't stop."

I move slow, resting my weight on my arm, but I realize I won't last long this way. I rise up to my knees, lifting her other leg to wrap around my waist, so her ass is lifted high off the bed.

She looks up at me, her eyes hooded with lust and need and it's nearly my undoing. But I not only want her to have sex this way without freaking out, I want her to come too. I grab her hips and thrust deep, grinding into her pelvis. She's always responsive to me, even tonight when she has every right to be anxious, but I can tell she's not anxious when I look into her face. Far from it. Her eyes are clenched shut and her fingers are grabbing the comforter in two fists. She totally trusts me and I'll make damn sure never to betray that.

I'm closer to coming that I'd like, but she's close too and I don't want to stop or slow down. I grit my teeth as I hold on, awaiting her release. She arches up, gasping and as I feel her tighten around me, and I can't hold back anymore. I press deep inside of her and come.

When I'm done, it takes all my willpower not to collapse on top of her. Instead, I roll to my side.

"Was that okay?" I ask.

"Okay?" she asks in disbelief. "No."

My heart sinks.

"Euphoric? Life-changing? Yes. But definitely not okay."

I release a deep breath.

"Thank you for being patient with me," she whispers.

"How can you even say that?" I ask. "Patience? We're experimenting with other positions. Do you know how many guys would kill to be in my shoes?"

She rolls to her side so we're chest to chest, staring into each other's eyes. "You're the only one I want."

"That's good to know. Because you're stuck with me, Alexa."

She gives me a soft kiss. "I'm counting on it."

Acknowledgments

Thank you to my assistant Heather Pennington, who helps me somewhat organized. Thank you to my awesome beta readers: Rhonda Cowsert, Anne Childon, Becky Podjenski and Stormy Udell.

BUSINESS AS USUAL wouldn't be what it is now without the invaluable input from my wonderful editor Angela Polidoro. Thanks to Cynthia L. Moyer and Paola Bell for your proofreading expertise.

And always, thank you to my readers. You read my books and like them then tell your friends. Because of you, I'm doing what I love: writing the stories the pop into my head.

About the Author

Denise Grover Swank was born in Kansas City, Missouri and lived in the area until she was nineteen. Then she became a nomadic gypsy, living in five cities, four states and ten houses over the course of ten years before she moved back to her roots. She speaks English and smattering of Spanish and Chinese which she learned through an intensive Nick Jr. immersion period. Her hobbies include witty Facebook comments (in own her mind) and dancing in her kitchen with her children. (Quite badly if you believe her offspring.) Hidden talents include the gift of justification and the ability to drink massive amounts of caffeine and still fall asleep within two minutes. Her lack of the sense of smell allows her to perform many unspeakable tasks. She has six children and hasn't lost her sanity. Or so she leads you to believe.

You can find out more about Denise and her other books at:
www.denisegroverswank.com
or email her at denisegroverswank@gmail.com

32882423R00198

Made in the USA
Middletown, DE
21 June 2016